The Seven Rules of Elvira Carr

1. THE

2. SEVEN

3. RULES

4. of ELVIRA

5. CARR

6. a novel

7. FRANCES MAYNARD

sourcebooks
landmark

Published by Sourcebooks Landmark, an imprint of Sourcebooks, Inc.
P.O. Box 4410, Naperville, Illinois 60567–4410
(630) 961–3900
Fax: (630) 961–2168
www.sourcebooks.com

Published simultaneously as *The Seven Imperfect Rules of Elvira Carr* in 2017 in the United Kingdom by Mantle, an imprint of Pan Macmillan.

Library of Congress Cataloging-in-Publication Data

Names: Maynard, Frances, author.
Title: The seven rules of Elvira Carr : a novel / Frances Maynard.
Description: Naperville, Illinois : Sourcebooks Landmark, 2017.
Identifiers: LCCN 2017001927 | (pbk. : alk. paper)
Subjects: LCSH: Women--Fiction. | Self-realization in women--Fiction. |
    Self-actualization (Psychology) in women--Fiction. | Domestic fiction.
Classification: LCC PR6113.A9837 S48 2017 | DDC 823/.92--dc23 LC record available at https://lccn.loc.gov/2017001927

Printed and bound in the United States of America.
VP 10 9 8 7 6 5 4 3 2 1

To Lorelei

1.

Preparation, Elvira, is the key.

—Mrs. Agnes Carr (Mother)

I was scrubbing potatoes when it happened.

Mother liked them with the skins left on, because of Vitamins, but I had to make sure any little marks or green bits were cut out. My feet were aching, and I was just about to take off my slippers to rub them when there was a crash and a moan from the living room.

My heart thudded. I knew this kind of thing happened because I'd seen it on *Casualty*. Old people often collapsed and fell, but I'd never thought it would happen to Mother. I was surprised she'd allowed it to.

I wished she'd fallen in her Opera Class or on her Bridge Afternoon where there would be people who knew what to do. I went into the living room, my feet throbbing. She was lying on the floor beside her chair, trying to pull herself up.

"Are you all right?" I asked. I'd never been in this situation before, so I didn't know what else to say. I twisted the hem of my apron—it was the one with Dog Breeds of the World on it—and looked at her. Normally, whenever Mother saw me doing this, she'd shout *Apron!* or *Sweater!* depending on what I was wearing, but this time she wasn't looking at me. She wasn't saying anything either, which was unusual. The noises she was making sounded like the monkeys in David Attenborough's Nature Documentary, *The Life of Mammals.* They weren't proper words, but groans with gasps in between.

I tried to pull her up. Mother was quite a thin person, not like me, but I couldn't lift her. Her left hand was white as she hung on to the chair leg.

I was struggling to get *my* words out. "Have you…broken your hip, Mother?" I asked. This was a common accident for old people. Old*er* people. (*No*, just *people*, Mother would say, scowling. She said she was wrinkled before her time because of having to screw her face up into expressions clear enough for me to recognize.) My heart was still thudding, and I couldn't think straight because of the suddenness.

Mother groaned again, and I thought I heard a familiar word: *useless*.

"Shall I call the doctor, Mother? Um…or go next door and fetch Sylvia and Trevor? What should I do?"

Mother's moaning got louder. She lifted her head slightly. Her hair hung over her face like the madwoman in a Classic Horror Film I'd watched with Father when she'd been Away. Her mouth was twisted. People who had strokes on TV fell and were paralyzed down one side, and *their* mouths were lopsided.

"Have you had a stroke, Mother?" I asked, bending down. She snorted. *Call an ambulance*, I thought. That's what people did.

It came very quickly with two men—*paramedics* was the correct word who looked young and strong. They moved around as if they were used to people having strokes, and they told a lot of jokes. I knew they were jokes because the one telling the joke looked at the other one, and then they both laughed. I don't like talking to Strangers, but I liked them coming. It made me feel safe. I think even Mother would have liked them if she'd been feeling better.

They carried her into the back of their ambulance: *Light as a feather you are, love.* She clung to the sides of the stretcher and kept making the monkey noises even though no one could understand them.

"Have you checked out soon, no worries," one said, and then to me, "Are you coming with your mother, love?"

My face went hot when he called me *love*.

Coming with your mother? I hardly ever went anywhere. Father was dead, and Mother had sold his car. When I'd made trips on my own, there had been Incidents. I occasionally went to places, places such as the Dentist, on the bus with Mother, but that was a *palaver* and made her knees hurt.

I would have enjoyed a trip out, but I knew ambulances were only for sick people.

"No thank you." I stared at his ear. "I'm not ill. And I haven't finished getting lunch ready."

They looked at each other. I screwed up a fold of my apron and held it tight. The apron ties cut into my waist. I could do with losing a few pounds. (*More than a few*, Mother used to say, looking at me and sniffing.) We ate a Healthy Diet, because Mother decided what we ate, but I had an interest in cookies. I did the shopping—I was used to our local grocery store Asda and could manage going there on my own—so I bought them then, sometimes without Mother knowing. I liked trying out different brands and varieties and comparing them. It added another dimension to my life.

"We'll be off then." The ambulance man was looking at me. "Queen's College Hospital. Give us an hour or so before you ring."

"Why do you want me to ring you?" I asked, chewing my lip.

"Not *us*, love," he said very slowly. People often talked slowly to me. Mother didn't. She talked fast and loudly and didn't leave room for replying. "Ring the hospital to find out how your mum is. All right?"

"I'm all right, thank you." I wasn't ill, but my feet ached and my heart was still pounding, and there was a new hollowness inside me that was like the feeling I got when I looked down from the top of the escalator in the Shopping Center.

The house felt strange without Mother there. It was very quiet. I like quietness, usually, but this time there was too much of it. I liked Mother going out, but that was because I knew when she was coming back. She taught a U3A Appreciating Opera class on Tuesday mornings, which was *unpaid but rewarding in other ways*. I'd thought U3A was a code, or even a type of glue, but Mother said it stood for the University of the Third Age, which meant older people exercising their brains. She liked Operas. She played CDs of them in the living room, and the noise vibrated through my head.

Mother knew the stories behind Operas. She'd gotten my name, Elvira, from an Opera by a famous composer named Mozart. Mother was the only person who called me Elvira. At school, they'd called me Ellie—at least, the teachers had. And Poppy, the friend I sat next to at lunchtime. Sylvia-next-door called me Ellie too.

Mother belonged to the Civic Society. They met every other Wednesday at three o'clock on the next road. She only went to their meetings when she approved of the building they were trying to protect. I didn't like not knowing if she was going to go. I prefer a routine.

She went to the Bridge Club at the Church Hall too (Bridge is a card game, but *far too complicated for you, Elvira*) and organized the refreshment schedule there. Father had once been chairman *and* treasurer of the Bridge Club, but he'd had to resign suddenly because of *commitments abroad*. Mother had left at the same time, but after three weeks, she'd said, *Why should I hide away?* and gone back.

She enjoyed Bridge, even though there was sometimes *unpleasantness*. Once a man had accused her of hiding a card, and there was often what she called an *inquest* from her partner. When I was younger, she used to get cross when I said *Snap!* at the wrong time, so I supposed it was the same sort of thing. Cards must bring that out in people.

When Mother went out, I could take off my slippers and read a Mills & Boon. I like Mills & Boons because I know what's going to happen in the end. I don't like surprises. Mother collapsing had been a big surprise. Having no idea when she'd be coming back felt like sand shifting away beneath my toes.

Her cane—black with a silver handle in the shape of a lion— was lying on the floor now, next to where she'd been sitting. I picked it up and propped it against the arm of her chair to make it feel as if she was still there. I put my feet up on Mother's red velvet footstool and shut my eyes to try to get used to the situation.

I still wasn't used to it when I opened them again. What I found calming was sameness, and there wasn't any. I cooked my lunch—scrambled eggs and two slices of toast and a cup of tea, which was what I always had—but even that was different because I normally had it at one o'clock. Because of Mother's collapse, it was now after three o'clock.

I ate it at the kitchen table with my Mills & Boon, *Affairs of the Heart*, open beside me. Strangely enough, it was set in a hospital, in the Intensive Care Ward. I usually like reading, but today my brain kept getting stuck on the word *hospital*, and then my heart would start thudding again and I'd have to put the book down.

When I was small, Mother used to read to me at bedtime. They were Mother's choice of books: children's books set in Roman times (*At least you will be learning something, Elvira*) or the stories of Operas, or true-life accounts of famous women explorers. I only liked the children's books, except that Mother read the bits about fighting or slavery in them very fast, and kept stopping at Historical Details to explain things. Things I didn't really want to know.

My eyes would start to close, but I had to stay awake because sometimes, the next day, she'd ask me the name of a country a particular woman had explored, or what the Romans had eaten for breakfast. Sometimes she'd sit down with me while I looked up a word I hadn't known in a dictionary and wrote it down. I'd liked Mother sitting and reading to me, and her saying *Well done* if I remembered the word the next day.

I blinked myself back to the present and closed *Affairs of the Heart*. Mother didn't approve of Mills & Boons. Or any made-up stories. Most of the books in the study had belonged to Father. He'd read a lot. Thrillers he'd liked, and spy stories. (Mother would sniff and say it was because he'd had plenty of time to read, with nothing else to do, which always surprised me because Father had been a busy and energetic person.)

Mother especially didn't like fiction if I read it during meals because *sharing food means sharing conversation.* She read out snippets from the *Daily Telegraph* instead. Bits about violent teenagers or welfare cheats or vegetarians. Or she read out crossword clues. Often she got the answer while she was reading out the clue and wrote it in. I wasn't very good at crosswords, not the cryptic ones.

That's good, Mother, I'd say as she leaned back, smiling and putting the top on her pen with its gold-plated nib.

Not bad for seventy-two. Do you see, Elvira, why the answer was…?

I'd nod because if I said I didn't understand, she'd sigh in a tired sort of way and go through it all again, and it took a long time.

When I'd finished my cup of tea, I phoned the hospital. Mother kept useful numbers, like the Bridge Club and the Library, in the front of an address book by the phone. The numbers for the Hospital and the Doctor and the Dentist were written in extra-large writing.

I held on to my apron while I listened to the ringing at the other end. I hardly ever made phone calls.

"Which department?"

"Um. My mother. They took her away in an ambulance. They…"

"Accident and Emergency. Putting you through."

"Hello. A and E. Sister James speaking."

"My mother. She came to you just before lunch. Mrs. Agnes Carr." The phone was slippery in my hand. My heart began to thump again. I wasn't sure what to say.

"And you are?"

"I am Elvira Carr. I live at 41…" I began to tell Sister James my address, but she stopped me. I knew it by heart, including the post code, and my telephone number and its area code. Mother used to make me repeat them to her.

"You are her daughter?"

"Yes," I said. "I'm an only child. She…"

"Your mother has had some tests."

"Oh. Did she pass?" Mother was clever. She'd be good at tests.

There was a pause. "We don't have the results yet. Do you know if your mother takes any medication?"

"Yes, I do know. One digoxin at breakfast time. A blue one." I remembered the digoxin because it was made from foxgloves and because Tosca, our Airedale, had had it too, when *she* was old. It was good for the heart. An Airedale was a kind of terrier. There were fifty-one different breeds of terrier. Airedales were second, alphabetically, after Aberdeens.

"Thank you. What is your mother's speech like normally?"

I screwed up the hem of my apron. Speech? She'd often made speeches about Operas on cruise ships, but…

"Miss Carr?"

"Yes?"

"Does your mother talk in a normal way?"

This was another difficult question to answer because I didn't know what "normal" was. Only that Mother said *I* wasn't.

"She talks a lot. And she's learning Italian from a CD. So she'll understand all the words in Operas."

There was another pause. "Once we've finished the tests, we'll be sending your mother to Jersey Ward, in our older people's unit." Another pause. "*Jersey Ward*," she repeated.

I knew Mother wouldn't be happy about that because of not being old. Or old*er*.

"How long will she be there for?" I bunched up my apron again.

"I really can't say. If you want to visit, visiting hours are from two to four and from seven to eight. Do you need to write that down?" Before I could answer, though, she said "Thank you" and hung up.

"Thank you," I echoed. I put the phone down and leaned against Father's desk with my eyes shut, waiting for my heartbeat to slow.

Back in the living room (*Not the lounge*, Mother said. *I never lounge.*), Mother's ornaments, crowds of African figures in dark wood, were huddled together on the mantelpiece. She'd bought them in Nairobi, before I was born, when Father was in the Army, the engineering part of it. She'd had staff to help her in the house there, and they'd called her *Madam*. She and Father had had to come back when Kenya had gotten *too hot* for him. Africa is a very hot country, I know, but I don't think it was any less hot when they first lived there.

In the middle of the African ornaments was a large golden clock under a glass dome. It was French and had fat, little winged babies (*cherubs*, Mother said) flying around under the glass. It had been a wedding present from Mother's parents. I'd never met them because they'd died before I was born, but Father said they'd lived in a castle.

Mother had never minded the clock chiming, even when it interrupted an Opera she was listening to, but she said me talking to her during one was an interruption. If I asked her a question, or told her a Fact I'd learned, she'd rustle the *Daily Telegraph* without replying. Sometimes the *Daily Telegraph* went up in front of her face as I came into the room.

Standing there now, looking at the ornaments, I swayed a little on my feet. They were Mother's special things, but she wasn't here to look at them. I wondered if they missed her.

The clock chimed half past four. I'd have to go to the hospital this evening. I sat in Mother's armchair, smoothing out the crease between my eyebrows. I'd never been on my own for longer than a day before. Mother didn't think I could manage. She stood over me when I switched the oven on and went back afterward to check I'd switched it off, and she was always sniffing in case I'd left a gas burner on. It made me nervous. I felt nervous now. How would I know which bus to catch? How would I find the right ward in the hospital? I wouldn't be able to ask anybody because I was no good at conversation.

I went upstairs, pulled the curtains, and got into bed, although it was only my brain that was tired. I lay there for a long time, but in the end, I got up because of the potatoes. We normally had dinner at seven, but I would not be at home then. I'd be visiting Mother who would also not be at home.

Mother used to say she *wasn't at home* when people called and she didn't want to see them. It was me who had to tell them, and I didn't like saying it because it wasn't true. When I was younger, there had been unwelcome visitors, men in suits with clipboards, or men with shaven heads who looked like boxers and who tried to peer around the door. Bailiffs, they'd said they were, something to do with taking unwanted furniture away.

I rubbed my forehead. I was still worried about the potatoes. I heard Mother's voice in my mind—*Preparation, Elvira, is the key*—so I cut the potatoes up and put them in a pan of cold water, ready for when I got back. I brushed my hair and put on my shoes and the navy woolen coat I've had for more than six years, since I was twenty-one. It was still smart, even though I could no longer do up the bottom two buttons.

Mother said my fleece jacket was just for informal occasions such as going to the Library. I chewed my lip as I fastened the top button. I wasn't sure if going to a hospital counted as a formal occasion, but it was probably more formal than the Library. Thinking about going to the hospital scared me. I didn't go to new places very often and, since the Incidents, never on my own. This would be the first time I'd been to a hospital, except for being born. The sand shifted beneath my feet again.

I walked along the main road, turning around when I heard a bus. It had *HOSPITAL* written in capital letters on the front, so it was easier to get there than I'd expected. I was surprised how big and bright and shiny the hospital was. I had to screw up my eyes against the glare. It had corridors everywhere, like an anthill. It took me a long time to find Jersey Ward because I couldn't understand all the arrows and the little maps. It would have been easier if the wards had had proper names like Kidneys, Heart, Skin, or Old People.

In the end, I followed an old man shuffling along with a shopping bag, thinking he might be visiting an old person in Jersey Older People's Ward. He was, which meant I'd been *resourceful*, a word Mother used about herself. She would be surprised when I told her.

Mother was in a room with old ladies in it. Although she'd always said she wasn't old, she *looked* old now. She lay with her eyes shut. Her face was sunken, her body tiny under the sheet. For a moment I thought she was dead, but when I said

"Mother?" her eyes flew open and she made sounds and plucked at the sheet with her left hand.

There was a rustling. A nurse in a pale-blue uniform came up, her shoes squeaking on the shiny floor. She had dark skin and a white smile.

"You're Agnes's daughter, are you?"

Mother's eyes opened again and fixed on her. She didn't like strangers using her Christian name. Her lopsided mouth and glaring eyes made her look like the gargoyle above the door of St. Anne's Church Hall where she used to go for Bridge.

The nurse's smile shrank when I asked if Mother had had a stroke. She lowered her voice. It looked likely, but they wouldn't know until all the tests were back. She didn't know how long Mother would have to stay either. There would be an Assessment. When Mother moaned and tried to heave herself up, the nurse gently pushed her back down again, saying, "No exertion please, Agnes. Rest is vital at this stage."

Mother's eyes closed. I'd never heard anyone speak to her like that before. It was how *she* spoke to other people.

It was after half past eight by the time I got off the bus. I rang Sylvia-next-door's bell to tell her what had happened to Mother and how I'd managed to visit her on my own. As I waited for Sylvia to answer, I looked back at our house. I'd never seen it in the dark, without anyone inside it, before.

Sylvia clapped her hand to her mouth when I told her, and I noticed her red nail polish was chipped on her first two fingers. She reached out to pat my arm, saying, "I'll pop in to see her tomorrow, and then we'll have a proper chat."

Ordinarily, I didn't like people touching me. I felt their imprint for hours afterward, like a burn, but this time it made me feel steadier on my feet as I made my way back to our dark house.

Mother used to say Sylvia was *kind but common*. She had been the manager of a Workingman's Club (*fries, beer, and Skittles*, Mother said, her lip curling), but she didn't work there anymore. Sometimes she would *pop in for a cuppa*, which meant coming over to have a cup of tea. Sylvia gave Mother lifts in her car, and I'd buy flowers at Asda for Mother to give her as a Token of Appreciation. Every week, I took over the *Daily Telegraph*s that Mother had finished reading for Sylvia to line her kitchen bin with. (The *Daily Telegraph* has many uses because of its large size.)

Trevor, Sylvia's husband, never popped over for a cuppa. He only came around to change lightbulbs for Mother, because of being tall and not needing a ladder, and to agree with her about politics. He'd look down at me, hands stretched up to the light socket, beard bristling, without speaking. He was always in a hurry, which was why he never had time for conversation.

Sylvia's usual Facial Expression was easy to recognize because it was the same as the card labeled *Happy* in the display of Facial Expressions on the wall of my old classroom at school.

I wasn't sure how old Sylvia was because she had blond hair and wore brightly colored clothes, but when she was hanging out her laundry last week, the wind blew her hair against her head and the roots were white, not yellow. She might be nearly as old as Mother underneath. Thinking about Sylvia being old gave me the hollow, sand-shifting feeling again. I got into bed with my clothes on and pulled the duvet over my head. I didn't feel like doing anything, not even brushing my teeth, but later I worried about it and got up to clean them.

When Sylvia stopped by after seeing Mother, her eyes filled with tears and she called me *pet* as well as *love*. She hugged me too, which I wasn't expecting. I didn't know if I should hug her back because I hadn't been hugged since Father died and I'd forgotten how to do it, so I just let my arms dangle until she stopped. She wiped her eyes, and I went to put the kettle on.

I didn't get the cookie tin out from behind its barrier of serving dishes at the back of the cupboard, even though I knew it was full of Bourbons, because Mother and I only had cookies at eleven o'clock and at three. Bourbons were introduced by Peek Freans in 1910. They were called Creolas at first, and they're an unusual cookie because they're chocolate *flavored*, rather than chocolate *coated*. (I'm interested in all the different varieties of cookies and their histories and packaging. I know a lot about them.)

Sylvia and I sat on the sofa together, and she held my hand. "A real shock for you, pet." She looked into my eyes, and I dropped my gaze. "How are you feeling?"

"Hot."

"You did well going in to see your mum. On your own!"

I glanced up at Sylvia. Her dark eyebrows formed two perfect semicircles.

"She must have been proud of you." Sylvia squeezed my hand.

"She didn't say. She couldn't speak." I pulled at a fold of my gray sweater with my spare hand, then—*Sweater!* I heard Mother shout—and I stopped.

My hand felt sweaty under Sylvia's. She was quiet for so long this time that I had to look at her again in case it was my turn to speak and I'd missed it.

"Your mum used to worry about leaving you on your own. How you'd manage." Sylvia shifted her position.

I nodded. This was about me leaving the gas on and missing Special Offers on vegetables.

The nail polish on Sylvia's hands, clasping mine, was freshly painted. She said Mother had talked to her about what would happen when she… Sylvia didn't finish the sentence. Then she said, *It comes to all of us in the end, pet.*

The *end* meant something to do with death. I pulled my hands away to grip the seat of the sofa. The world slipped away around me, and the inside of my body felt hollow. I wanted to lie down.

"But Mother's still alive." I stared at the floor. I didn't like looking into people's eyes so I looked at the ground instead. Because of this, I had a wide knowledge of floor coverings. I noticed dust too, and dropped things. Also people's shoes and litter.

"Yes, pet." Sylvia kept patting my hand. "But your mum might always need to be looked after now." When I said that that was my job, she asked me how I could lift her on my own, and how would she get to the toilet? "Her brain's damaged, pet. Nobody can mend that."

I thought about Mother's damaged brain. Her crossword skills and all the things she knew about Operas and Adventurous Cooking and other countries would be leaking out and going to waste.

Sylvia said Mother had made Arrangements for me in case… My heart thudded because Arrangements meant people organizing things without me joining in. Mother had arranged things before, like signing me up to a Table Tennis Club at St. Anne's Church Hall without asking me first. She'd gotten cross when I refused to go and kept talking about my BMI. But,

Sylvia said, shifting on the sofa again, it was the financial, legal kind of things she meant. *Things that'll make it easier for you to live on your own, pet.*

On your own. Mother used to tell people she'd been left on her own when Father died. "Except for Elvira, of course," she'd add. She'd look at me without smiling, but the person she was talking to would smile and mention comfort and company, and then Mother would make a sound like she was blowing her nose without a hanky. I'd never been left on my own before. I didn't *want* to be on my own. Not all the time, not forever.

Then Sylvia said that Mother had thought... She stopped and glanced at me. Mother had thought I might be *safer* in Sheltered Accommodation.

Everything seemed to drain away. "I don't want to be sent Away!"

"Shh, shh, pet. Your mum thought you'd get more support there, that's all."

I was rocking to and fro. "I want to stay at home. I don't want to live with Strangers!" I felt Sylvia's arm around me.

"There, there. Let's see, pet. See how you go."

See what? Go where? Everything was bewildering.

Sylvia leaned close, taking both my hands in hers. "Let's just think about *now*, pet." She talked about me taking Mother some clean nighties and a little travel kit with her toiletries and told me that if I wanted a cup of tea and a chat or advice about anything, I knew where she was. I nodded, taking my hands away and holding tightly to the hem of my sweater. I did know. She lived next door.

2.

One is fun.

—Delia Smith, cook and author

*M*other and I were tidy people. *A place for everything and everything in its place, Elvira,* she'd say, looking at me from over the top of her glasses. She kept the toiletries bag she used on her travels in the top left-hand drawer of her chest of drawers. She hadn't used it since Father died because of not being able to leave me on my own. Before that, she'd taken it with her on cruise liners where she gave talks on Operas and Birthplaces of the Great Composers.

It was made of Liberty print with a waterproof lining. Inside were a folding toothbrush, a sponge, and some miniature soaps. Mother had kept it packed in case a cruise liner needed an Opera teacher in a hurry. She kept her passport in it too, in a plastic bag. I took it out now because I knew she wouldn't need it in the hospital.

Pushed right to the back of the drawer was Father's red paisley washbag. I was surprised to see it, because after he died six years ago—suddenly, while he was Away—Mother had gotten rid of most of his things. His washbag was smaller than Mother's, although he'd gone Away far more often. Inside were his passport and a half-empty bottle of English Leather aftershave. I sniffed, conjuring up Father, smiling, eyes crinkling, saying, *Hello, Vivi darling.* He was the only person who called me that. I screwed the wooden lid back on tightly, so the scent would keep, and looked at his passport.

It was in good condition, considering it had been used so often. Father had built bridges in Kenya, and he'd often worked in Japan. The Japanese trips had meant him being Away for ages, once for more than a year. Each time he came back, he'd brought me a different netsuke, a tiny carved animal that Japanese people wore on their belts.

After the very long trip, he'd brought me back a Japanese note-book, patterned with cherry blossom, with a red silk ribbon to mark the page, and Mother a red silk kimono, embroidered with cranes (*birds,* not *lifting machines!* Father had joked. I'd laughed, understanding the joke for once) to wear as a dressing gown. Actually, Mother had hardly ever worn it because of disliking lounging, and it was still hanging up behind her bedroom door.

I liked the idea of Japan. Everyone would be foreign there, so I wouldn't seem so different.

I opened Father's passport. The pages were blank. I looked twice more because I often got things wrong, but they were definitely empty. How could that be possible?

His old passports were bundled together with a rubber band at the back of the drawer. I leafed through them. There were his photos, a younger and younger Father, with swept-back hair and neat eyebrows. Some African stamps from the 1960s and 1970s. I turned more pages. There were no other stamps. There was no mention of Japan anywhere.

In the passport photos, as in real life, Father's mouth had an upward curl. I wished he were still here for me to ask why there were no Official Records of his Japanese trips. Father had never minded me asking him questions, even ones Mother said were silly. *He* had never laughed at them. He'd pat the sofa and say, *Come and sit down, Vivi, darling, and tell me what you want to know.* I used to ask him things like how could people ever have landed on the moon when it was only the size of a football. If he were here now, alive, I'd ask him when he thought Mother would be coming home.

Of course *Mother* would know why there were no Japanese stamps or dates! She'd know. She knew everything. At least she *had.* I leaned against the chest of drawers, a washbag in each hand. I squeezed Mother's gently and thought about her damaged brain, holed like a sponge, with all its information leaking out.

Mother was in the same bed as yesterday. She clutched the sleeve of my coat with her left hand. "Not that way," she said.

"Not which way?" I asked.

"Not that way." Her hand dropped.

She said it again when I asked about Father's trips to Japan, shouted it in fact, and clung to my sleeve again. Her eyes were round and bulging. I knew, from the Facial Expression cards, this indicated Anger.

I didn't mention Father's passport to Mother again because of the shouting, and when I asked Sylvia, she said, "Before my time, pet," very quickly and then asked me about Mother's laundry.

There was nobody else to ask, so I wrote, *Why are there no Japanese Stamps in Father's Passport?* on the first page of the Japanese notebook that Father had brought me back. Things were easier once I'd written them down. Clearer. There were no distractions in written things.

I chewed the end of my pencil. When Father was in the Army in Kenya, he'd worked for the Government, building bridges. Perhaps he'd worked for the Government in Japan too. Perhaps he'd been there on a Secret Mission with another passport and a false name. There was a Mills & Boon story where the hero worked for the Secret Service—*Diplomat in Danger*, it was called—and used different passports. That would explain why Father never spoke about his trips, except to say, *Just business, darling, terribly dull.*

I noted this idea under the question on page one. On page two I wrote: *When is Mother coming out of the hospital?* Then I sat cross-legged on the bedroom carpet and rolled the notebook's silky ribbon between my fingers for a long time.

———

Mother had therapy for her stroke, but she still couldn't move her legs or her right arm, or say anything beyond the three words: *Not that way.*

There were lots of new things I had to do now: visiting Mother twice a day, using the bus, deciding what to eat, shopping without her list, doing the housework without supervision, being alert to Incidents, trying to show I *was* safe on my own. Managing it all sent me to bed in the daytime. In bed, I listed all the different varieties of cookies I knew, *and* their brands, and said them in alphabetical order, but it didn't always make me feel better.

At night, I thought about burglars and worse. That was when I felt particularly unsafe without Mother. When I woke, I couldn't stop listening for sounds, and several times I had to go down and wedge a chair under the front door handle. I'd hear it topple if anyone burst in. I hadn't felt nervous at night with Mother there because, although she was small and walked with a stick, I knew her waving it, or shouting, or looking at a burglar from over the top of her glasses would frighten him away.

On the bus, I'd huddle into my coat and keep my eyes fixed on the buildings flashing by. This was because on one journey a man—quite an old man, with a mustache—sat next to me and asked if I had a boyfriend. When I shook my head, he offered to be my "fancy man" and to do all sorts of things to me, although I hadn't stopped to hear what.

I put my fingers in my ears—he was sitting too close for me to get to the earplugs I kept in my backpack as part of a Safety Kit for when things got to be Too Much—and squeezed past him, the zipper of my backpack scratching his face. (I'd worried about that afterward.) I stood next to the driver for the rest of the journey. There had been an Incident at Sandhaven Museum, years ago, which had left me with the same sort of feeling.

I'd gone to an exhibition of Historical Baking Methods on my own, because Mother said she couldn't bear the tedium and Father had been Away. There'd been a dried bun from the eighteenth century in a display case, and some rusty baking tins in elaborate shapes, and an early packet of Jacob's Cream Crackers with swirly writing.

I'd spent a long time making notes of new Facts. Near closing time, I was approached by a man—the curator, he said—who asked me to pose for their next display, Fashion through the Ages. He said I was just the right shape for a young Victorian lady, and if I wouldn't mind modeling for some background photos, I would be helping the museum *and* I would get free entry to the exhibition.

I wasn't able to look at him. I wanted to help, because I liked museums, but I knew I always looked rigid and stiff in photos. I hadn't liked the idea of putting on a tight corset that had belonged to someone else either.

The curator had smiled a lot. He asked me if I was interested in baking methods, and I said yes, particularly cookies, and he said that, behind the scenes, they had extra cookie packaging, too much for them to display, and I could keep some of it in return for the photos. I'd looked at my watch because of the time. I'd chewed my lip. There hadn't been anyone else around, and in a bewildering change of subject, he'd said I was like a ripe peach. I'd stared at the floor—polished Victorian tiles—for a long time trying to work out what he meant because the exhibition hadn't featured fruit or canning methods.

He'd said I'd have to pose for the photos as soon as the museum closed, but I had to be home by six to put on the dinner so I couldn't do it then. I said I could check with Mother and come back tomorrow, but he had to dash off.

When I'd told Mother, thinking she'd be pleased someone had needed my help, she'd been angry. I should have had more sense than to engage in such a conversation. The curator had *exploited a position of trust*. (Actually, he'd stood quite still; he'd just leaned rather too close.) She'd rung the museum to complain, and I'd run up to my bedroom and slammed the door, fingers in my ears, face burning at having got something wrong again.

Mother had ordered me downstairs. She'd looked like she did when she filled in a crossword clue right away. "There, I knew it," she'd said. The man hadn't even been a curator, but a security guard on a temporary contract, which had ended that day. He probably hadn't known anything about cookies. Or fashion through the ages.

I knew Mother wouldn't want me to eat Convenience Foods, stripped of Vitamins, or to eat *exactly* the same thing *every* day, because she'd called a stop to it before.

Mother was a fan of Adventurous Cookery, which meant eating strange things from different countries and *having variety in our diet, Elvira*. But, after her knees had lost their flexibility, she'd had to stop making unusual dishes. We'd tried having me do the Adventurous Cookery, but her voice had gotten hoarse from repeating the instructions. I was *perfectly capable* of cooking the recipes from Delia Smith's cookbooks, though, because they were *foolproof*. Mother bought me one, a different one, every Christmas. Delia Smith went through things step-by-step and wore a cardigan in her picture.

I made a list, which was always calming, of seven Delia Smith dishes, such as Vegetarian Shepherd's Pie with Cheese Mash, and wrote them down like a menu on the calendar in the kitchen. The calendar had a picture of a different terrier for each month. Sylvia had bought it for Mother because of our dog, Tosca. This month's was a Jack Russell. I added the activities I was participating in too: the dates and times of *Casualty* and *Coronation Street*, and the days the bins had to go out.

At the start, buying food without Mother's list meant I bought too much or too little or the wrong thing. I panicked once when a cauliflower wouldn't fit in the fridge's vegetable drawer. How was I going to eat it all? I wasn't supposed to

throw away food. In the end, I had to cook it as a bonus vegetable and add it to every Delia Smith meal for the next five
days, even though it wasn't mentioned in her recipes. It made
me feel uncomfortable.

Eventually, though, *because* of eating exactly the same things
every week, I was able to make a master shopping list and take
it with me each time. This was the sort of thing that, if Mother
had thought of it, she would have called *Maximum Efficiency*.

I'd always shopped at Asda, so at least that wasn't new. It
was within walking distance of my house. (There'd been an
Incident—one of a series, none of which Mother had allowed
me to forget—involving another Asda, but I tried to put it to the
back of my mind.) I liked Asda because the layout of its aisles
stayed the same, and because I had friends there.

The man who collected the shopping carts—his name badge
said *Clive*—always said *Hello*, and Dennis behind the cheese
counter wrapped up small quantities of Stilton and mature
cheddar cheeses without me even asking. He said it was because
I was a regular customer. I always went to the checkout where
Janice worked because she said *Hello* too, and sometimes added a
comment about the weather. She asked me once what my name
was, and when I told her, she said, "*Elvira*. Now that *is* unusual."

I used the terriers calendar again—it was proving to be
invaluable—to add a housework schedule and checklist where
I could tick off the tasks as I did them. There was one like it on
the back of the Ladies' Toilet door at Asda. I'd wanted to do this
before, but Mother had said it was ridiculous. *Ridiculous* was one
of her favorite words.

I gave myself Thursdays off from housekeeping, but I still
went to see Mother. I wasn't sure what else to do on a day off. I'd
never had one when Mother was at home because I'd had to buy

her *Daily Telegraph* and take back her Library books and get her prescription and do the food shopping every other day so that things still had Vitamins, and go up and down stairs fetching her glasses.

I didn't have to do any of those chores now. But not having to do them made me feel empty inside.

3.

Never rely on assumptions.

—Mr. Watson, lawyer

The phone rang. I didn't like answering it because of not knowing when it was my turn to speak. It stopped, then rang again. My hand hovered. It might be the hospital. I lifted the receiver.

"Hello, dear. How are you?"

No nurse had ever called me *dear*. I was silent.

"Is Mother there? I haven't heard from her for weeks. I'm your mother's old school friend, dear. Jane. From Dunstable."

"Jane from Dunstable," I echoed. I knew *her*. She'd advised Mother to put me in a home. Mother used to ring her every Sunday evening at six thirty. It was the only time I ever heard Mother laughing. The receiver slipped from my hand, and I felt the world draining away again. *Could* Mother put me in a home now, when she couldn't even *speak* to Social Services? Could Jane, although she lived in Dunstable? I scrabbled for the phone on the floor.

"Hello, dear. Is everything all right?" Jane asked.

"Mother's had a stroke," I babbled. "She's in the hospital. She can't walk."

"Oh! Oh! Poor Agnes! Struck down!"

"I didn't strike her," I said, my heart thudding. "She fell down. I wasn't even in the room."

"No, dear." Jane pronounced each word separately. "I was using the verb *strike* in its passive form. Oh, your *poor* mother. She'll be coming home soon, will she?"

"No." My heart was beating so fast I felt light-headed.

"Won't you be looking after her, dear? I'd come and care for her myself except for the weakness in my spine."

"We...we're waiting for her to be assessed."

"We?"

"Me and Sylvia next door."

There was a sniff and then a long pause from Jane's end.

"I'm not surprised, you know, dear," she said. "About the stroke. If ever there was a woman driven to one, it was your mother."

I was silent again. Mother hadn't driven for years, not since she'd sold the car. The car's name had been Morgan—or that might have been its brand name. It had been Father's pride and joy. Mother had sold it while Father was Away on the very long trip to Japan, *to recompense the Bridge Club members*, she'd said. I'd been puzzled by this because Father had lost interest in Bridge, and it was *his* car, and not having it anymore was the reason he'd shut himself up in his study for days when he got back.

"I shudder at what she had to put up with...the deceit and the lies. And then, of course, there was the *shame*... And yet, at first, she forgave. How such a clever woman could be such a fool! I told her. I told her *many* times. *Make a clean break*, I said. She used to say that because I was a *single* woman, and not a mother, I wouldn't understand, but in the end, of course, she'd had enough." Jane sniffed. "All in the past now, and yet here she is, poor, dear Agnes, still paying for it."

I stood by Father's desk, gazing out at the oak tree in the front garden. What Jane had said—*Deceit, Lies, Forgiveness, Shame*—sounded like the titles of the Foreign Films Mother was so fond of.

I fetched the Japanese notebook to get my thoughts in order and wrote down Jane's words, then a question: *What did she mean?* Underneath, I added that it couldn't have been *me* who'd deceived Mother because I didn't tell lies. They were too complicated. Jane had called Mother a fool *and* a clever woman. How could she be two such different things at once? A fool was what Mother used to call *me*. I'd never heard her say it about herself.

"Of course I'll come with you, pet." Sylvia hung up my coat. "Go and sit down, and I'll make us a nice cup of tea. I've got some cookies from Marks & Spencer. In a tin!"

Earlier at the hospital, a nurse had told me they'd be assessing where Mother should go. Just when I was getting used to her being *there*. Moving *again*. Where would she move *to*?

The gold cookie tin was a Continental Assortment. I kept looking at it, wondering if the cookies inside were different from those in Asda's Extra Special Continental Selection. When Sylvia opened the tin, some of the cookies were wrapped in *gold* foil, rather than silver, and the chocolate fingers were *plain*, not milk. I hugged my knees for a moment.

I took a white chocolate triangle and a praline wafer and tried to make sense of what Sylvia was saying. *Keeping an eye on me*, and *Mother's lawyer*, and *managing the money side of things*, I heard. "She was a wise old bird, your mum," Sylvia went on.

"Thought of everything. Well, she had to, didn't she? What with your dad…"

I looked away, seeing Mother, her gaze stern and all-seeing, perched on top of a tree. It was a disturbing image. My mind strayed to the cranes on her Japanese kimono, then to them flying thousands of miles without using maps. Maps led to passports, and to Father's being empty, and then I thought about the unanswered question of Mother leaving the hospital. Leaving the hospital to move where? *Not that way*, I heard over and over again. I saw Mother at home with me, her face lopsided, waving her lion-headed stick with her one good hand. I couldn't finish the praline wafer, and I found myself rocking to and fro.

Sylvia put her arms around me. "It's difficult, pet. All these changes."

I nodded, my head squashed against her chest. Although it was soft, I didn't like the feeling of being squeezed.

She said how well I was doing and how not everyone could visit their mother in the hospital twice a day. When I looked up, Sylvia's eyes were filled with tears.

I didn't understand why she was crying when she was saying nice things. "Shall I make you another cup of tea?" I asked. We'd been taught at school to make tea whenever someone was upset.

She laughed and blew her nose. "No, you're all right, pet. I'm not sad, love…only sometimes, when I think about your poor mum."

Sylvia gave me some of the cookies to take home, wrapped in a napkin with holly on it. We'd spent nearly all the Christmases Father was Away at Sylvia's. When he was at home, they came to us for drinks on Christmas Eve. That hadn't happened for a while, though, because of Father dying in 2010.

Last year, I'd taken an Asda bottle of champagne, a Best Buy in the *Telegraph*, and Mother had brought them a richly fruited Christmas cake in a special box. Trevor, looming above me on the doorstep, his beard bristling, had taken the champagne and muttered about opening it being the only bit of excitement he'd get all day, and then Sylvia had called out from the kitchen, "Come in, come in. Happy Christmas!"

Father had gotten *lots* of excitement from celebrations. He had a loud voice, and he smiled and laughed and reached out to touch people, especially women, on their arms. He'd say, *How marvelous, darling*, or if they were men, *Well, you're spot on there, old chap*. He'd have a glass in one hand and a cigar in the other, and would be enveloped in a cloud of smoke and brandy fumes. *Larger than life*, Mother called him, but although he was tall, I would not have called him large.

At home, I wrote what Sylvia had said about me doing well, with the date, in the Japanese notebook as evidence against being sent Away. In bed, I unwrapped the Christmas serviette and laid the cookies out in a row on the pillow with the same size gap between them. There was a round white one with a scalloped edge—a Coquille—one I'd never seen in any other Continental Assortment. I saved it till last.

There was a plate of Custard Creams at Mother's Assessment Meeting, on a side table next to a box of tissues. Mother's complex needs and nursing home requirements were discussed, and a doctor said a medical word that Sylvia, pencil poised over her British Legion notebook, asked him how to spell. Mother, in a wheelchair, shook her head—*Not that way*—but whether she meant the doctor had spelled it wrong, or that she was refusing to go into a nursing home, I didn't know. I counted the number of zigzags on the parquet floor. Nobody suggested that Mother should come home.

When they asked me what I felt, all I could feel was my heart thudding. Sylvia said, *Honestly, pet,* she couldn't see any alternative. I swallowed without saying anything, quicksand sucking at my feet, because I was part of arranging things for Mother, who'd always arranged things for me. I'd worried so often about *her* sending *me* Away, and now here *I* was doing the dispatching.

I stared at a spot on a parquet tile where the polish had worn off. A hospital social worker told me, slowly, that I'd be able to see Mother whenever I wanted, and hesitating between me and Sylvia, handed us *A Directory of Nursing Homes in Sandhaven.*

When Sylvia and I said good-bye to Mother, she drew herself up in her wheelchair and turned her head away. There was a bony hollow at the base of her neck when she lifted her chin. Sylvia didn't say anything as we drove home. But she sighed a lot.

———

I got the Spinach Gnocchi ingredients out for later. I was in a sort of daze. I made a cup of tea in the *Coronation Street* mug that has Ena Sharples, Elsie Tanner, Rita Fairclough, Hayley Cropper, and Deirdre Barlow in a garland around the sides. It was a Christmas present from Sylvia three years ago.

Upstairs, I switched on the radio in Mother's room and left her door open to make it seem as if she'd just gone into the bathroom for a minute. I got into bed and lay there, repeating

David Attenborough's words from *The Blue Planet* out loud to
block out Mother's refusal to look at me earlier.

———————

I kept my eyes on the furrows a vacuum cleaner had made
through the plush carpet of the office of Mr. Watson, Mother's
lawyer. His voice bounced from its paneled walls. He'd advised
Mother *many* times over the years. When I glanced up, his
shaggy eyebrows were leaping up and down. Had that been
about sending me Away?

Since Mother had Lost Capacity, he said, we had to decide
things for her. I stared at my shoes, my best ones, thinking about
Mother hating that.

Sylvia looked up from writing in her notebook. "And how to
pay for it all."

Mr. Watson explained that Mother had a Trust Fund set
up for her by *her* parents to protect her interests in marriage.
This was unusual, but there had been concerns about Mr.
Carr's—Father's—finances.

I sat up. What had been wrong with Father's finances? Sylvia
was examining her red fingernails. I took the Japanese notebook
from the pocket of my coat and wrote the question down. I also
added another one: *Where is Mother's Lost Capacity?*

Mother's nursing care would be paid for by her Trust Fund.
"A most reliable source of income," Mr. Watson said, "being
impregnable to the persuasion of others." Mother had arranged
for her Fund to pay me an allowance, should she be incapaci-
tated. This would enable me to stay at home, provided I was
managing, even though Mother would no longer be there.

I felt my toes unclench. The master shopping list could

be evidence for that. And the terriers calendar. And the Japanese notebook. Mr. Watson said Mother had made these Arrangements a long time ago, at the same time he'd helped her to rearrange her finances, *protect her inheritance, close joint accounts, that sort of thing*. I didn't ask him what these words meant in case it was a sign of me not managing.

"I believe there are no other claims?" Mr. Watson looked at Sylvia. She adjusted the strap of her leopard-skin shoe, not answering. "No?" His eyebrows rose, then he turned to me. "Elvira, have you any questions?"

I'd been prepared for this. I looked at his ear, which had a tuft of hair coming from it, and asked why there were no Japanese stamps in Father's passport.

Sylvia and Mr. Watson laughed, and she said Mr. Watson had meant *legal* questions, *pet*. My face grew hot. He had not specified this. I told him Father had brought me back something Japanese each time he'd gone Away and held up the notebook as an example.

"Ah," he said. "How interesting." There was a moment's silence, then he leaned forward: "One word of advice, dear young lady. Never rely on assumptions."

I shut the front door and slumped against it. Everything was going to stay the same. Except for Mother not coming home again. I went upstairs and plumped up the comforter on Mother's bed and checked that the silver-framed black-and-white photos on her chest of drawers were in the right order. One of Father, young and wearing a tropical hat, one of Tosca, lying on her back, paws in the air, on the Persian rug in the study, and one of me when I was a child, standing in front of the British Museum where Father had taken me to see a mummified cat. There was one of Mother and Father's wedding too. They were smiling, standing on a long flight of steps, surrounded by a crowd of guests all wearing hats. I stared at it, wondering why Mother's financial interests had needed protecting.

There had been a postcard recently from Spain that had mentioned the word *finances*. From a Stranger and addressed to Father, even though he was dead.

> *My Dear Gregory,*
>
> *I haven't heard from you in the last five years. You may have moved—did your wife come to her senses?—or been ill, or the other. I've been very patient, but that scheme you recommended came to nothing, old chap. There must be some sort of compensation, surely? Let me know details soonest— finances are running short.*
>
> *Yours, Teddy*

There was no address, so I couldn't let Teddy know Father was dead. His card didn't make any sense, but I put it inside the cover of the Japanese notebook, in case it contained a clue about Father's spying or his own finances.

Sylvia's shiny red fingernail pointed to a nursing home in the directory. "Trev's mum, bless her, was in this one, Everdene. Homey sort of place." She turned a page. "This new one,

Woodside, got a good report. *And* this one, Bay View Lodge. A bit more expensive, but it's small, with sea views. They're all near here, pet. You'll be able to just pop in." She patted my arm. "In a month or so's time, we'll be laughing."

Laughing. *No sense of humor. That's your trouble, Elvira,* Mother used to say. She'd try to explain why something in the *Daily Telegraph* was funny, but then the tone of her voice would change, and she'd roll her eyes and put the paper down with a thud. Sometimes this had led to things getting to be Too Much. Then she'd ring Jane in Dunstable, even though it wasn't her normal time to phone, and keep the study door shut.

I didn't feel like laughing now. "Mother won't like *any* nursing home. She'll want *me* to look after her. She always said she'd cared for me all my life, and one day it would be my turn."

Sylvia pushed her hair back from her face and said it was different now, and nobody could care for Mother on their own. "Better for all of us to get things sorted out."

I heard Trevor slamming the front door, or it might have been Josh.

Sylvia and Trevor's son, Josh, had moved back in with them four months ago when his marriage broke up and his wife, Shelbie, ran off to Spain with their little girl. Sylvia was sad about not seeing Roxanna because she was her favorite granddaughter. Actually, Roxanna was her *only* granddaughter; her other two grandchildren were boys.

Sylvia worried about Josh even though he was forty years old and owned a giant motorbike and had big tattooed arms with words I couldn't make sense of: *Living Dead* and *Thrash Metal*.

There were a lot of things I couldn't make sense of.

4.

You've got to keep up with the modern world.
                    —Mrs. Sylvia Grylls, neighbor

S ylvia drove us to Everdene. She picked up her leopard-skin handbag and slammed shut the car door. "Let's do it then. Get it over with."

I followed Sylvia, my sneakers dragging a path through the gravel. Then I remembered the vision I'd had of Mother—at home, shouting the only three words she had left—and hurried to catch up.

Inside there was a smell of fries and air freshener, and the matron wore a pink crackly uniform. A big TV was blaring in the lounge, with two old ladies asleep in front of it. They woke with a start when we came in because the matron clapped her hands.

The vacant room was small and bare, and the bed had an orange nylon bedspread with a ruffle.

We gave Everdene two stars out of five. Sylvia said it had gone downhill, and she couldn't see Mother playing bingo, even now.

Woodside was a low, modern building with State-of-the-Art Facilities. Its glass doors slid open like they did at Asda. It was white and muffled inside.

"Quiet in here, isn't it?" Sylvia said to the manager. "Like being onboard a spaceship!" I walked close behind her, on tiptoe, wondering how she knew what being onboard a spaceship was like.

The lounge smelled of lemons. The fragrance was piped through, the manager said. Music was also piped in, the same breathy music I'd heard groups of South American musicians play on their panpipes in the town center. When she could still Get Out and About under Her Own Steam, Mother had tutted as we passed them.

The manager showed us a vacant room decorated in white. He ran to the window as something gray and furry flashed across it. "Blasted squirrels!" He banged on the glass.

A bird feeder, half-full of seed, was attached to the outside of the window with a suction cup. The manager surveyed the garden and made a shooing motion at a squirrel sitting in a nearby tree. The squirrel watched him but didn't move.

I gave Woodside three stars because of the squirrel and the bird feeder.

Bay View Lodge was up a steep path, and Sylvia had to stop to get her breath back.

A small, smiling lady with golden skin—Maria—answered the door. Inside, a group of ladies and one gentleman were sitting around a table making Easter cards and eating cookies. (McVitie's, I noticed.)

Maria showed us upstairs. The room we saw belonged to one of the old ladies in the lounge. It didn't look like a nursing-home room. It had flowery wallpaper and a brightly colored bedspread made of little knitted squares. There were paintings of country scenes with horses, and a stuffy smell of lavender.

"Most residents have sea views," Maria said, pointing to the window. Beneath the pine trees was the sea and, in the distance, the cross-channel ferry.

Maria opened a door. "Here is the bathroom."

There were a pink sink with pink soap and a pink toilet with a knitted white poodle sitting on the tank. Sylvia turned the poodle upside down, and inside were two rolls of pink toilet paper.

Downstairs, a fat lady with puffy cheeks—Susan Hulme, the matron—came out of an office. She was sorry, but there weren't any vacancies. "Have to go on the list," she said, wheezing. All her sentences ended in a wheeze.

Back in the car, I gave Bay View Lodge four stars.

A collapsed feeling that Sylvia had explained was grief or sadness swept over me when she said there'd only be a vacancy when someone went into the hospital or died, but she snapped her leopard-skin handbag shut and said it was the way of the world and would come to all of us in the end. She put Mother's name down and said it would *be a relief to get it sorted out.*

We drove off. I watched the blur of buildings while Sylvia talked about Josh. "Says I'm doing too much. Mind you, he's a fine one to talk! We never see him. We see less of him now than when he was living with Shelbie and Roxanna! I do miss them, you know…"

My mind drifted to Mother in her own room at Bay View Lodge, looking out the window at the sea view, the cross-channel

ferry reminding her of Opera Cruises, and Maria, smiling, bringing her a cup of milky coffee and a plate of Extra Special Asda
Assorted Biscuits, and then Mother going into the pink toilet
and using pink paper from the poodle toilet-roll holder.

Sylvia blew air out with an explosive sound. "Let's get telling
your mum over and done with." I trailed behind as she marched
down the hospital corridor.

I'd worn today's clothes in bed last night, ready for telling
Mother I wouldn't be looking after her. I'd woken in the dark,
my heart racing, and stumbled into Mother's room. I'd buried
my face in the Japanese kimono and stroked its silky fabric,
trying not to let tears stain the material. The label had caught
on my fingernail. *John Lewis: Hand Wash Only*. John Lewis was
a reliable upmarket shop, Mother's favorite. I hadn't known they
had branches in Japan.

"Well, here we are, Agnes." Sylvia sat down heavily. She gave
Mother a wide, lipsticked smile.

"Not that way." Mother lifted her head to stare at us. I handed
her half a banana, its skin peeled back.

"I'm not sure how much fresh fruit you get in hospitals," said
Sylvia, "but I expect there'll be plenty at Bay View Lodge." She
raised her eyebrows at me, her voice louder than usual as she
continued. "Ellie...I mean, Elvira...and I have been looking at
nursing homes for you, Agnes."

Mother dropped her banana skin on the floor—or threw it; it
was difficult to say which.

"Whoops-a-daisy! You'll have your own room. Ellie—
Elvira—and I will make it nice for you, and it's got a lovely

view of the sea. *And* it's near your old house. Only ten minutes' walk away…"

Mother shook her head, a thread of dribble whipping from cheek to cheek. "Not that way."

"The thing is, Agnes"—Sylvia shifted in her chair—"you can't stay here because they need the bed. And you can't go home. How would Ellie cope with you in a wheelchair?"

Mother looked down with a little jolt of surprise. She attempted to move her legs. There was a faint tremor in the left one. She tried to lift her arms, but only the left one worked.

"Not that way, not that way!" she screamed.

"Shh, shh." Sylvia patted Mother's right arm, the paralyzed one. "I *know* it's dreadful for you, pet, with you being such a bright lady and always in charge, but there's no other way, Agnes. Believe me. I've kept Trevor awake at nights, going over it all."

I put my fingers in my ears while Mother shouted. She *had* always been in charge. In charge of the students in her Opera Classes, the Bridge Club Refreshment Schedule, the household bills, me, even Father. I pictured him, his arm around her waist, saying, *Your mother's a wonderful organizer, Elvira. Where would we be without her?* and her leaning away from him, her lips thin. *I know where you'd be, Gregory. What we* need *is a settled life, but what you seek is extravagance. And look at the consequences.*

***

In the car, Sylvia said, "It's done, pet. The worst bit's over. No secrets… Well"—there was a moment's silence—"no secrets *there*, anyway." She didn't say anything else until "Good night, pet. Sleep tight" when I got out of the car.

The collapsed feeling swept over me as soon as I was alone. That night, I kept my clothes on again—and the reading lamp, to stop myself from dwelling on the image of Mother, crumpled in her wheelchair, attempting to lift her legs.

In the morning I went to Mother's dressing-table drawer and took out the hundred and twenty pounds' weekly cash allowance—arranged by Mr. Watson—that I stored in Father's wallet. I used this for food and for what Mother had called *sundries*—any item that wasn't food, such as a new Mills & Boon. I had a bus pass because of having a Condition, and Sylvia and Mr. Watson paid all my utility bills by direct debit from Mother's Fund. If I needed a large item—for example, *a new wardrobe*, Mr. Watson had said, leaning toward me, his eyebrows leaping—I would have to apply to him for extra money. I didn't need a new wardrobe. Mother's carved antique one had been handed down through generations of her family, and I wanted to keep it.

Father's wallet had lots of little pockets and zipped-up compartments, all empty now except for the space for bank notes. I turned it over and felt the outline of something small and square. Stamps, I thought, but it was a photograph. A photo of Mother with me as a baby. The house behind her was large, like the house where we used to live, which had had a pony, I remembered, in the paddock behind. When I looked at it closely, though, it wasn't a house but a hotel, and the woman holding me wasn't Mother. I turned the photo over. *Paris, K with C b. July 29, 1994.* Father's looped handwriting.

It looked like a date of birth. Mine was November 7, 1988. I knew lots of birth dates by heart because I was good at remembering Facts. Mother's was August 4, 1943, and Father's was October 23, 1940.

But, since this wasn't my birth date, this baby wasn't me. Why had Father kept it? It wasn't a nephew or a niece because, like Mother and myself, Father was an only child. The woman in the photo had what Mother would have called—with a sniff and a toss of her head—*a lot of shape*. She wore a top with flowers on it and jeans. Her long, blond hair was blowing across her face, and she was laughing. I went downstairs to get Mother's magnifying glass. There was a gap between her teeth, and the baby wore a stretchy orange suit with black stripes and a hood with little rounded ears like a tiger cub's.

I took the photo to the hospital to ask Mother. I didn't have much hope that she would know anything about it, or that she'd be able to tell me, and I was right. She spluttered, "Not that way," spraying the photo with a mouthful of tea and knocking it out of my hand with surprising strength.

I called on Sylvia afterward to show her the photo. She looked at it carefully, taking it over to her living room window and telling Trevor—who, for some reason, was saying, "Uh-oh"—to be quiet. But she couldn't help either. They were people she'd never seen before. She began to polish the window because the sunlight was showing up all the smears. At least I had the Japanese notebook to keep track of things that puzzled me. I'd have to add *Who are the woman and the baby (b. 7–29–1994) in the photo from Father's wallet?* to the other unanswered questions.

As I came out of the bathroom, Trevor was telling Sylvia that getting involved in other people's problems would raise her blood pressure. Blood pressure was a serious thing to do with hearts. In her cooking days, Mother had used a pressure cooker that hissed and rattled. Touching it was Strictly Forbidden. Once, without me touching it, it had exploded, its lid crashing to the floor and jets of lentils and barley and stewing beef spraying across the ceiling. I worried about the same sort of thing happening to Sylvia.

Trevor obviously meant Josh's problems. "Poor lad," Sylvia was always saying. "What kind of life is that for a man, back home with his parents while his wife's off living the dream in Spain?" Shelbie, Josh's wife, was working at a resort where English people went on vacation. "Goodness knows who's looking after that poor little mite." The *mite* was Sylvia's granddaughter, Roxanna. I'd looked up the word. *Parasitic arachnid*, Father's dictionary said, which didn't sound as nice as *pet* or *love*.

Sylvia's eyes filled with tears when she talked about Roxanna, but if I tried to change the subject or offered to make her a cup of tea, she immediately went back to talking about her again. They'd told us at school that it wasn't a good idea to tell someone you were bored with what they were saying, even if you were, so I switched my mind to other things.

I thought about the town of Reading, home of Huntley & Palmer's, and how the factories there would vary the color of their packaging according to the brand. I imagined the constant, soothing hum of the machines and the scent of baking cookies filling the air. I tried to explain all the different ways a cookie could be packaged to Sylvia, but she was talking too fast to interrupt.

Josh had met Shelbie when he was thirty-four and she was eighteen: "a lovely-looking girl, all legs and long hair," according to Sylvia. He'd come to install new pipes in the shower block of her trailer park in the New Forest. "First time he'd ever brought a girl home, although he'd had plenty of girlfriends before, of course. With his looks, he's always had to fight them off."

I wondered if Josh had hurt the unwanted girlfriends when he'd fought them. I thought about his looks. He had shaggy hair that fell over his face, and he wore tight black T-shirts with things like *Cannibal Corpse* written on them.

Then my mind strayed to the differences between Short*cake* cookies and Short*bread*. Short*cake* cookies were always rectangles, but Short*bread* came in fingers and in triangle shapes called petticoat tails. One Christmas, a client, in appreciation of Father's engineering, had given him a hamper of Gourmet Foods that included a large tin of Shortbread. They were in unusual shapes I'd never seen before: clubs, squares, even castles!

Shelbie had lost her mother to breast cancer when she was fifteen. Sylvia had taken to the girl: "Felt sorry for her, poor motherless scrap. Butter wouldn't melt." Shelbie had set her sights on Josh because he was a plumber and she knew which side her bread was buttered on. "Got her claws into him, poor lamb." They'd had a fairy-tale wedding, with Shelbie's dad providing not a white horse, but one that was *all-over brown splotches, like something out of a circus.*

In Sylvia's living room there was a photo of Shelbie at a family celebration. You wouldn't know from looking at her that she came from a forest, or that she had claws. *Or* that she was obsessed with butter. My mind drifted back to Shortbread. Strictly speaking, Short*bread* should be made with butter, but Short*cake* didn't have to be. That was another difference.

Sylvia couldn't forgive Shelbie *for taking Josh's princess away to get her fair skin burned to a crisp in Spain.* Now he could only Skype Roxanna on the computer. "No wonder he smokes and goes to the pub. Trev's heard he leaves early, mind. Now, him getting a lady friend would wipe the smile off Shelbie's face."

Father had smoked cigars. He'd kept them in an initialed case, a gift from Mother when they got engaged, and tapped the ash into a silver ashtray shaped like a woman's hand. He was only allowed to smoke in the study. I'd find him there, not studying but sitting in his battered leather armchair, staring out the window, wreathed in smoke like the picture of the genie coming out of the bottle in *The Thousand and One Nights*. Even now, when I looked up a word in his dictionary or dusted one of his thrillers, I could still smell his tobacco.

Sylvia invited me over for a Sunday roast dinner. I didn't really want to go because of not being able to make conversation. Mother was good at it. She could talk for a long time on many different subjects—politics, Opera, Vitamins, and all the countries she'd visited or lived in, such as Kenya—so I'd always left it to her.

I took a bottle of champagne with me to the roast dinner, the same *Daily Telegraph* Best Buy as at Christmas. I no longer had the *Telegraph* to advise me because I'd stopped buying it. Mother hadn't been able to hold it because of her right side not working, and when I'd folded it up small so she could do the crossword, she'd dropped it on the floor, her eyes bulging behind her glasses. Sylvia had said, "Thanks, pet," but it wasn't worth buying a *posh paper* just for her to line her bin with.

Now she said, "Oh, you shouldn't have, love," but Trevor gave me a thumbs-up sign and Josh flicked the hair out of his eyes to read the bottle's label. Katie, Sylvia's daughter, said, "You've got to watch the pennies." Katie's marriage was not in trouble, but Sylvia often phoned her, even though they lived in the same town and saw each other more than twice a week.

I wanted to explain about my Trust Fund so Katie would know I was well provided for, but Sylvia had told me people didn't discuss finances in conversation. I didn't know why—*I'd* find it interesting—but it was another of those unwritten Rules I didn't understand, but that made people angry or upset when I broke them. I didn't know why I shouldn't have brought Sylvia a present either.

I stared at my plate, not looking at anyone. Everybody talked about different things, and nobody took turns. They kept changing the subject so I couldn't keep track of what was being said. They asked me questions, but by the time I'd thought of the answer, they'd started talking to someone else. It was how I imagined being Abroad would be like. I thought about the silence of my own kitchen and eating Sunday's dinner (Stuffed Baked Potatoes with Leeks) on my own.

Trevor asked me, twice, how much longer Mother would have to wait for a place at Bay View Lodge. This played on my mind too. My heart thudded each time someone with a clipboard walked by Mother's hospital bed in case they'd come to turn her out of it. She'd be angry with me if that happened. She might come home.

Sylvia stood up to pass the gravy. "Leave the girl alone."

"I'd like to see a bit more of you, pet, that's all," Trevor told her. "You're always dashing about, hospital this, nursing home that, lawyer whatever."

"Not good for your blood pressure, Mum." Katie speared half a roast potato.

"Yeah, ride pillion, Ma. Take a backseat. Let other people sort out their own crap." Josh stuck his hands in his jeans pockets and tipped back in his chair. He was probably tired of Sylvia talking about his marriage breakup too.

Katie was flicking through her cell phone. "You ever thought about getting a computer, Ellie? Broadening your horizons? Finding out things?" Katie was the same shape as Sylvia but younger, and her eyebrows weren't perfect half-moons.

I stared at the flowered pattern in Sylvia's dining room carpet, trying to answer accurately. "Mother said computers kept people imprisoned in their bedrooms, not communicating with the outside world." They stared at me from around the table, although what I'd said was true. Mother *had* said that. "And she thought *I'd* find learning to use one a struggle," I added. My face was hot.

There had been another reason too, one neither Father nor Mother had explained. I could be targeted by predators, they'd said. In David Attenborough's Documentaries, these were large animals such as tigers, animals at the top of the food chain. Carnivorous animals. I'd failed to understand what Mother and Father meant and they wouldn't explain, which had led to me going to my room and slamming the door.

Katie tapped on her phone. *She* was always on Facebook. Communicating with the outside world. She didn't know how I survived without a computer or a phone. Mother hadn't approved of cell phones either because they went off in Operas and disturbed the singers. I didn't like loud noises or speaking to people, but Sylvia said I could text. "You've got to keep up with the modern world, pet."

Oh, do keep up, Elvira was something Mother often said

when I asked her what was happening in a Foreign Film, or what someone had meant, exactly, by puzzling phrases like *We must meet up soon* (why must we?) or *A change is as good as a rest* (but it's completely different) or *It's as plain as the nose on your face* (why is my nose plain?).

5.

It's better to have a system.

—Mrs. Sylvia Grylls, neighbor

The phone rang. My heart raced. It was always difficult to answer, whether it was an insurance company, a prerecorded message, or someone from a charity. Part of it was the not knowing who it would be. I fumbled with the receiver. It was Mrs. Hulme, from Bay View Lodge. I could hear her wheezing. "A vacancy has come up, Miss Carr. Would your neighbor…?" I ran next door. Sylvia answered, chewing. When I told her, she did a little dance on the tiled floor of her porch and Trevor shouted out, "Thank God for that!"

We rushed back for Sylvia to answer the phone. Mother could move in the day after tomorrow. All her things to move there! A new place for me to get used to! I sat down and rocked. *For goodness' sake, Elvira! We are not in an asylum!* I heard Mother say. Sylvia put her hands on my shoulders and said *she'd* felt awful when Trev's mum had gone in, but she'd settled in soon enough and it would be the same for Mother.

That afternoon, Sylvia came around in a red gingham apron. She took off her high heels. "We'll have a system, pet. Sort out what your mum needs."

System was reassuring. We ticked things off in Sylvia's British Legion notebook. We took the throw from the study armchair for Mother's bed. Sylvia said Katie could make copies of Mother's photos. She picked up Mother and Father's wedding picture and said how tall and handsome Father had been, like a film star, and then put it down.

"Your mum must have been dazzled," she said, and then, under her breath, I thought I heard her say, "but she saw the light eventually." I suppose she meant that photographers had to use a special flash in those days.

We took two pictures for Mother's walls. Her favorites were by Turner, of sunsets, with sometimes an old-fashioned ship being tossed around by a giant wave. Her last vacation had been a cruise to the Canary Islands. It had been free in return for giving talks on Operas. She hadn't enjoyed it, though, because the sea had been rough and people kept having to leave her talks.

I'd never been Abroad. Mother used to say taking me would be a waste of money and no break for her. She and Father had gone one at a time because I couldn't be left on my own. Mother had stopped going altogether when her knees got stiff, except for an occasional Opera cruise, but Father had still gone Away. She'd shrugged her shoulders.

She was *past caring*, she said, adding: *Your father had* free rein *to do what he liked*. When I'd asked if that meant him going on horseback riding vacations on his own, she'd snapped, *No, it does not!* Perhaps he toured countries that needed improving through engineering, countries that Mother had no interest in. When he'd come back, it had all been too dull to talk about.

After I'd explained all this to Sylvia, she looked at me for a long time but not quite long enough to be a stare, another thing they'd warned us about at school. "Well, you're on your own *now*, pet, and look how well you're doing."

We chose a little carved chair from the study to take for me to sit on when I visited Mother, and a couple of cushions from the sofa in the front room. It was a red brocade sofa with tassels and dark, wooden feet. Trevor said it looked like it came from a harem, and I'd had to look up the word. Trevor was wrong, though, because Mother had bought the sofa at John Lewis.

Decorations. We needed decorations for Mother's room. The animals' horns on the walls of the utility room, personally shot by Mother's grandfather, weren't suitable, Sylvia said, nor were the African warriors from the mantelpiece. I fetched the Japanese netsukes, even though they were really *my* things.

Sylvia picked one up. It was a boar with tusks and bristles. "Look at the detail, pet." She turned it over. I noticed part of a price label underneath. I took it. *Ashmole*...something. It didn't sound Japanese. Another word looked like *shop*. I turned over the others. One, a grasshopper, had a tiny scrap of paper with the word *Museum*. Sylvia took it quickly. "Perhaps your dad bought them somewhere else."

I gazed at the group of animals. They could have been part of Father's cover if he'd worked on a Secret Mission for the Government. He might have been sent to a different country entirely, one we were at war with, with a fake identity. Japan might have been a front for something far more important. Making things up, lying, was wrong, but if you were protect-ing your country, then it was the Right Thing to do. I took the

Japanese notebook out from my apron pocket and made a note about this.

Sylvia made a mark in her own notebook. "Clothes next, and then we'll have a cuppa." She headed for the stairs.

We opened the carved door of Mother's wardrobe with its ornate mirror. There was a nose-prickling smell of mothballs and, underneath, a faint trace of Mother's Je Reviens perfume.

Smelling Je Reviens on the dark-blue velvet dress Mother wore when she went out with Father gave me the collapsing feeling again.

A picture surfaced of Mother in a pearl necklace and matching earrings, handed down through generations, and her best glasses, blue ones with jewels, which went up at the outside corners of her eyes. She hadn't looked like Mother then, but like a queen in a fairy tale.

When Mother and Father went out, I'd had a babysitter, Mrs. Carver, a cleaner at St. Anne's Church. She'd sit in front of the TV all evening without going upstairs to check I'd brushed my teeth. She always brought a box of Cadbury's Milk Tray with her, because babysitting was *an evening out*, and gave me the Orange Creams because she didn't like them.

Mrs. Carver came in the daytime too occasionally, when Father was Away and Mother had to research the cultural background of Operas at the Ashmolean Museum. She'd take Father's leather briefcase with her to carry her notebooks and her Sheaffer pen and some pencils. Once, I'd sharpened two of my own for her, but when I'd put them in, there weren't any notebooks in the briefcase. Or pencils. Instead, there'd been a brand-new book, *A History of the Kenyan Mau-mau Uprising* by Colonel W. R. Leys, two bars of Asda Extra Special After-Dark chocolate with 70 percent cocoa solids, a bottle of

English Leather aftershave, and a box of the same cigars that Father smoked.

I'd run into the kitchen to tell Mother she'd forgotten her writing things, but her lips were a thin line and she'd snapped at me for being nosy. She didn't say thank you, which is what you *should* say when somebody does something kind for you. Taking my pencils out might have been *being nosy* again, so I'd left them in the briefcase. I never saw them again.

Now, we put Mother's clothes in a suitcase and packed a box with everything else. Seeing her possessions lined up in the hall as if she were going on vacation gave me the collapsing feeling. Sylvia fetched the cookie tin and asked Trevor to come and pick up Mother's things.

As I went to put the kettle on, I heard him say, "Let's hope this is an end to it! We've been through it with your mum, with my mum, never mind the bloody neighbor's mum. Anything else, and I'm ringing Social Services. I mean it, Sylv!"

"Shh," Sylvia whispered and then said louder, "Take it all up to Agnes's room at Bay View, could you, Trev? There's a pet."

As soon as she left, I got into bed. My heart was pounding. *I'm phoning Social Services* was something Mother used to say when things got to be Too Much, and she'd had a phone conversation with Jane in Dunstable. *Dear Jane suggested Sheltered Housing might be the best thing for you, Elvira.* She'd talk about *no time off for good behavior* and *a life sentence* and kept taking off her glasses and polishing them. Shelters were for animals no one wanted, and Sheltered Housing was living in a different place on my own, under supervision.

I'd cried every time she'd threatened it. Now that Mother couldn't speak, could Trevor send me to Sheltered Housing? Sometimes, when I saw him staring at me over the top of his glasses, not saying anything or smiling, it reminded me of Mother. I'd hoped I could stay here, safe, at home, without anything changing except for Mother not being there. I didn't want to be sent Away.

I sat up and looked around my bedroom. It was tidy, and I'd dusted it only yesterday. I ran downstairs. There was no decaying food in the fridge to constitute a Health Hazard and lead to me being thought incapable. I scanned the kitchen. A Social Worker would be impressed by my meals and housework schedule, with its ticked-off checklist, and my shopping list, and the Japanese notebook where I was trying to find the answers to things.

Sylvia could give evidence that I put my bins out on the right days. Since Mother had been gone, there'd been no loud music in the house, and since Father, no alcohol or tobacco. I did not take drugs, not even digoxin. I racked my brain. There were all sorts of other possibilities. I went back upstairs, my brain whirring with them.

Had I forgotten to pay a bus fare? Stayed five minutes beyond visiting time at the hospital? Might Social Services think sending an elderly person to a home against her will was abuse? Because Mother was going to hate Bay View Lodge. She was going to hate everything about it, even its view, because she wanted to be at home, in charge.

I threw back the duvet, all the things I might be doing wrong buffeting my brain. My armpits and the soles of my feet prickled. Once, when I'd asked Mother what she was doing—she was sorting a stack of papers to take to Mr. Watson, slapping them down into piles—she'd shouted, "For goodness' sake, stop asking questions! Can't you see I'm out of my depth here?" She'd probably used a Figure of Speech, I thought, one I could identify with now.

I *had* been out of my depth once—literally, I mean; not a Figure of Speech—at Lyme Regis, when I was eight. We used to go there for vacation. Mother would take me to stroke the donkeys on the beach and give them an apple. She'd shown me how to feed Grace the pony in the paddock behind our house so I knew to hold my hand out flat. I remembered her sitting down on the sand to watch a *Punch and Judy* show with me, and telling me afterward about the history of it, about it coming from Italy and being hundreds of years old.

On the out-of-my-depth occasion, I'd gone paddling by myself. A group of children on a yellow float wouldn't let me play with them. I kept walking out to sea, my red bathing suit getting darker and darker. Suddenly, my feet thrashed. I couldn't feel the bottom! My mouth was filling with water. My heart was bursting. Something grabbed and lifted me out of the water. I thought a seal or dolphin had come to save me, but it was Father, wearing his trousers and his shirt and his tie in the sea. He carried me back to the beach in his arms. My heart had hurt, and my throat had been sore from salt water and crying; Mother would be angry with me for making Father's clothes wet.

Mother had sighed a lot. She'd held up a big towel so Father could take off his wet clothes and put on his swimming trunks, and after that bought him a mug of tea, with sugar, from a stand on the sands. A lady bought me an ice cream. Later, when Father was dry, he'd made a sand tower—*Bigger and better than a sand castle, Elvira!*—with a moat and a drawbridge made from a piece of driftwood. It was studded with seashells and was nicer than any sand castle I'd ever seen.

Father had stood by it, laughing. He'd beckoned to the lady who'd bought me the ice cream. "Come and see my masterpiece," he said, and leaned close to her and chatted. I hadn't wanted to go back to the hotel and leave the sand tower on the beach to be washed away, but in the end, Mother said it was just a pile of sand, not the Sistine Chapel—and hadn't I caused enough trouble for one day?—and pulled me away.

6.

Guinea pigs get a bad press.

— Brenda Cunningham,
pet therapist

*M*other arrived at Bay View Lodge in a hospital taxi, sedated for the journey, her glasses slipping down her nose. I clenched my toes inside my shoes. Mrs. Hulme grasped the handles of the wheelchair and pushed her up the ramp.

I'd positioned Mother's photos in the same order as at home. I moved the photo of Tosca a fraction now, avoiding Mother's gaze when she raised her sagging head. The netsukes were in a row on the windowsill, the same size gap between them, looking out to sea. The symmetry of their arrangement gave me a physical thrill.

Mother's head drooped. "Not that way," she said quietly, her eyelids closing.

"Bless her, she's out for the count," said Mrs. Hulme. "I'll get Maria to put her to bed. Later, she might fancy some toast and Ovaltine. All right, ladies?" She turned to us, a smile puffing her fat cheeks into pouches like the giant desert rat's in *The Life of*

Mammals. "Plain sailing so far. No storms yet!" She pointed to one of Mother's ship pictures, and she and Sylvia laughed and then shushed themselves.

———

At home, I made a mug of tea and went upstairs. I lay in bed with my eyes shut for a little while, and then I wrote an answer to a question in the Japanese notebook: *February 12, 2016,* adding, *Now at Bay View Lodge* under question two: *When is Mother coming out of the hospital?* The questions about Father's empty passport and his finances, and who the woman and the baby were in the photo, and what Jane from Dunstable had meant by her comments, and where Mother's Lost Capacity had gone remained unanswered.

———

The next day, Mother was in a high-backed armchair by her window. She stared at me without saying anything. Sylvia was busy, Trevor said, so I was on my own. This was showing I was capable, I kept telling myself.

At the back of my mind were past Incidents when I hadn't been. Mother was no longer able to remind me of them, but they were still there. She'd called one of them the Asda Bus Incident. The shame of it still haunted me, although I'd since caught the right bus to visit Mother in the hospital (seventy-two times) *and* gotten off at the right stop without there being any repetition of the Incident.

I'd wanted to go to the opening of a new Asda on the other side of town. There was going to be ten percent off everything and a free tangerine and Asda paper hat for each customer. Mother had highlighted the bus timetable and the name of the stop. These came up on an illuminated sign inside the bus, but it was possible it could malfunction.

I had caught the right bus. Two stops later, lots of people had gotten on, a whole crowd of foreign students with broad shoulders and big backpacks. When I'd tried to get off, a wall of them had blocked the aisle. They hadn't heard me say *Please* or *Excuse me*. I'd had to stand there, my face on fire, my toes clenching painfully, until they all got off.

I'd ended up in a suburb I'd never been to before, miles away from the new Asda. I'd had no idea where I was. My breath had come in gasps. I couldn't ring Mother because: (a) she would have been angry, (b) she wouldn't have known where I was either, and (c) even if she did, she wouldn't be able to come and get me because she no longer had a car.

There'd been a red telephone box on the corner of the street. I'd opened the door and dialed the emergency number.

I'd traveled home in the back of a police car. I felt like a criminal. They'd tried to talk to me, but I couldn't get the words out to answer them.

Mother's facial expression when she answered the door had been Surprise. She'd never expected *me* to have any dealings with the police. I couldn't get my words out to her either. I'd gone straight upstairs and under the duvet.

Afterward, Mother had tacked a map of Sandhaven onto the wall of the utility room, under the dead impala's horns, with our road marked with a thumbtack. She'd made me go through different routes home with her, but after a while, her throat had gotten too sore for her to carry on and she said she thought it best for me to just stick to the local area.

"Been as good as gold," said a nurse (*caregiver*, Sylvia said) in a hoarse voice, coming in now to spread a crocheted blanket over Mother's knees. The caregiver was a big lady with her hair in a high ponytail. She wore a blue nylon tunic with the name badge *Kim*. "Haven't you?" Kim said to Mother, tucking in the blanket, then to me, "Her name's Agnes, isn't it?"

"Mrs. Agnes Carr." I looked at the pink swirls in Mother's carpet. I noticed patterns in things all the time, but especially in carpets, because of looking down.

There was a pause, then Kim asked, "What does she *like* to be called?"

"My father called her Agnes, but waiters and her students and people at the Bridge Club call her Mrs. Carr. Called. I call her Mother." There was another pause. I chewed my lip.

"Not that way," said Mother.

"Oh hello!" Kim turned to Mother. "You're speaking now, are you? Sedative's wearing off," she added in a whisper. "Takes a long time when they're elderly."

"Mother isn't elderly," I said.

"No?" Kim's ponytail bounced.

"Not that way," Mother said louder than before.

I was tired when I got home. I put my feet up on Mother's footstool and rubbed my face. I didn't know if I was tired because of walking up and down the hill or because of listening to Mother saying "Not that way" over and over again in a small space for a long time.

I visited again after lunch, because *a girl should respect her mother* and *your knees are younger than mine,* and *is it too much to ask for a little assistance?* Maria's eyebrows shot up when she opened the door. Mother was asleep, but Maria took me upstairs to see her.

Mother lay very still with her eyes shut and her mouth open. She looked like the mummies in the British Museum, except that you could see her face and there was no black wig.

In the lounge the next day, the cords of Mother's neck stood out. "Not that way, not that way, not that way!" she shouted.

I tried to explain where she was, but she just kept shouting over the words *stroke* and *nursing home.* My heart jumped around in my chest.

Maria came in with a tray. "What this noise? Why you shouting, Agnes? Have nice coffee for you. And cookies." She patted Mother's shoulder. "I put music on. What sort you like?"

Maria found a CD called *Chilled Classics,* not one that Mother owned. "We give it go," said Maria. "Perhaps it calming."

It wasn't.

I kept my hands behind my back in case people thought I was hurting Mother. Would Bay View Lodge turn her out for shouting like they'd done with a boy at my school who'd screamed and hit walls? Where would she go then? Sand slipped away beneath my feet when I thought of Mother back at home. Then she stopped shouting. A piece of music I'd heard before was playing, by the same man, Mozart, who'd written the Opera with my name in it.

"Magic." Maria patted Mother's shoulder. "You listen to nice calm music, Agnes, and have nice chat to nice daughter come to see you." She held out a plate of cookies. I recognized them as Sainsbury's Belgian Chocolate Biscuit Selection because of the red foil. Mother took a long, curled one, a Cigarillo, and nibbled the end of it until the piece of music ended.

Four days later, just as I was leaving, my head aching, my shoulders stiff from shrinking back in my chair, Mrs. Hulme called me over. My heart began to thump, and I squeaked my sneakers together on the linoleum, sure this would be Mother's final warning. But it was to tell me about Bay View Lodge's leisure activities: Musical Entertainment and Pet Therapy. When I mentioned Mother's shouting, Mrs. Hulme said it would be drowned out one way or another: either by people singing or dogs barking.

Musical Entertainment was led by a young man playing Wartime Classics on an electric organ. Kim came in with a tray of tiny glasses of sherry. She offered one each to Mother and me. "Go on, spoil yourself. Put hairs on your chest." Mother's left hand shook toward a glass. I hesitated, thinking about the hair, but… "Take one," urged Kim. "Help you unwind." I put it down on a side table next to Mother's chair. Mother smacked her lips and finished hers. She picked up my glass and drank that too, so in the end, I didn't have to worry about chest hair, or unwinding.

Mother jumped when the music started. It didn't sound like Operas or Mozart. I could see her mouth opening and closing, but because she was drowned out, I didn't know if she was enjoying herself or not. Shrieks of "Not that way!" filled the lounge when the music stopped.

Kim hurried over with a tin of Walkers Scottish Shortbread Fingers. "What's the matter, Agnes? I thought you liked music."

"Not that way!" Mother glared.

Kim wheeled her to the elevator. "Let's take you back upstairs before *all* our heads explode. Hang on to your shortbread. Going up."

Mother and I sat by the window in her room. I was on the little carved chair from Father's study. She was nibbling her Shortbread Finger and not shouting, and I was checking the number of holes pricked in the top of mine. There were twelve. That was the correct number.

———

The lounge chairs were arranged in a big circle for Pet Therapy. Mother had just taken a Nice cookie from a tin of Tea Time Assortment. There was barking outside the door, and Maria slammed the cookie tin lid back on.

Twenty years ago, Father had bought our dog, Tosca, for my seventh birthday. "You're old enough to appreciate a dog now, darling."

"But not old enough to look after one," Mother had snapped. She'd said that would be her job, she supposed, since Father was never here, and the dog was going to compensate for that, was it?

"It'll turn out wonderfully, darling," Father had said. "Just you wait and see." Mother had made a *hmph* sound through her nose.

Perhaps his only child would prefer to see more of her father than a dog, she'd said, staring at him over the top of her glasses.

Tosca was mine, but had seen Father as pack leader. When he was out or Away, she'd jump on the sofa and stare out the living room window, watching for him to come back. Tosca had spent a lot of time at the window. This was when Mother had started liking her. "I know precisely how you feel, Tosca," she'd said. "Gregory seduces everyone he meets. And more the fool us."

I'd looked up *seduce*: to lead astray. It was incorrect because Father rarely took Tosca for a walk.

The other meaning was not appropriate.

A white-haired lady Pet Therapist in beige trousers brought in a golden retriever. Kim quickly collected the empty cups. "You could clear a table with one sweep of your tail, Buster. I know you." Her words sounded cross, but she was laughing. This was the type of thing that utterly confused me.

Buster wore a red dog jacket with *Caring Canine* embroidered on it. He stopped beside each resident, his tail waving. "Like the Queen opening a community center," commented Kim.

The white-haired lady asked me to hold Buster's leash while she got herself a cup of tea. Her teeth were long and stuck out slightly, like Grace the pony I remembered from my childhood.

I would have loved to lie down beside Buster with my head on his tummy, but I knew this would make Mother cross because of the lounge being a public place.

Mother stroked Buster, her *Not that way* quieting. She didn't notice Brenda, a lady with black hair in a fringe and a brightly colored face, bringing in a large box. The box rustled and squeaked.

The white-haired lady's teeth flashed. "Goldie, Gertie, and Geraldine: *Guinea Pigs Who Give*. Who'd like to hold one?" She surveyed the lounge. A lady attached to an IV spread out a napkin on her lap. "Ah, here's someone keen to have a go."

I remembered a TV Variety Show I'd watched with Father while Mother was teaching Opera on a cruise. As I got older, Mother had begun to go Away as soon as Father came back from an engineering trip. Sometimes it was to teach Opera, and sometimes it was to stay with Jane in Dunstable. Mother and Father had almost seemed to avoid each other! On the TV show, there'd been a magician with a wand and a pack of cards and an assistant who'd encouraged the audience to Join In. That was not something I was good at, Mother said.

Brenda lifted out a black-and-white spotted guinea pig, her tiny feet making bicycling movements, "On duty now, Geraldine," she said, handing her to me. I stroked her stocky little body with one finger, and she snuggled into my sweater.

Mother raised her drooping head and stared. Her voice rose. "Oh dear," said the white-haired lady.

Brenda bent toward Mother. "You might be thinking Geraldine is a rat. Some people do, you know. Guinea pigs get bad press."

Mother screamed, not listening, until Maria rushed over with a Pink Wafer from the cookie tin.

I pinned a pair of navy trousers on the line. The elasticated waist sagged. My clothes were looser because of walking up and down to Bay View Lodge twice a day and not eating so many cookies. Mother and I used to choose our favorites from the Peek Freans Family Assortment tin twice a day, at eleven and three o'clock. *It is our one indulgence*, she used to say.

After her stroke, it wasn't the same. There is no point in choosing a cookie on your own. I hadn't had much time to compare varieties either, so the barrier of dishes hiding the tin had hardly been needed.

Sylvia's French doors opened. She'd had a *brainstorm*. "Your mum going quiet when they played that Mozart made me think…and then it suddenly came to me now. What about an iPod?" Sylvia leaned back, eyebrows arched, mouth open, like people did when they'd won things.

She explained what one was and that Katie could record all Mother's Opera CDs onto it. Sylvia touched my arm. "We'll calm her down *and* bring you into the modern world, pet. Don't you worry."

I turned a clothespin around and around in my pocket. But I did worry. I worried about Mother being excluded and about Trevor phoning Social Services to send me Away. The unanswered questions about Father's empty passport and faulty finances, about Mother's Lost Capacity, and the identity of the woman and baby were niggles at the back of my mind too. *And* I worried about the Modern World. Managing it without upsetting people or getting shouted at, or there being Incidents.

7.

A soft cookie saves dunking.

—Gregory Carr (Father)

It was a Wednesday, my scheduled day for dusting and vacuuming upstairs. I was wiping Mother's dressing table with a damp cloth, replacing the original photos in their exact positions. I looked at Mother and Father's wedding photo again, thinking how young they looked, and happy.

Mother had told me they'd gotten engaged at the Ritz. She'd spoken about it once when Father was Away for a long time, when I was about twelve.

"The night we got engaged, he took me for dinner and dancing at the Ritz," she'd said. "At midnight, the band played 'Volare,' and Gregory got down on one knee and asked me to marry him. Everyone held their breath."

"What did you say?" I'd asked.

"I said *yes*, of course!" There was a snort. "Otherwise you wouldn't be here now, would you? I was head over heels. We both were. He was the most exciting man I'd ever met. Tall, charming, energetic. Like Laurence Olivier. My friends envied me."

"What shoes were you wearing?" I'd wondered if Mother's slippers had been made of glass.

She'd stopped smiling. "They were turquoise blue to go with my dress. Pointed. That was the fashion."

"Did you leave one behind?"

Her frown had returned. "No, of course not. How could I have walked with only one shoe?"

She'd looked down at her antique engagement ring and turned it around and around on her finger, its diamonds glinting. "All a long time ago. And now your Father is away and I am left, again, to pick up the pieces." She'd flashed me a glance that stopped me from asking where the pieces were.

"He's always ignored his past mistakes, and he answers my pleas for caution with a joke or an endearment." She let go of the ring. "*There are none so blind as those who cannot see*, dear Jane has so often told me. But then dear Jane is not a mother." Mother sighed, then snatched up her crossword again. But she could see the clues quite well, even though the print was small.

Yes, I'd understood what Mother meant. Father had once burned a hole in his study chair with his cigar and had never mentioned it to Mother. That was *ignoring past mistakes*. He *did* put his arm around Mother when she was cross, or said in a funny voice: *Trouble at t'mill* or *The native is restless*.

The Great Dictator was another of his names for her. She didn't like it, even though it made her sound important, because she left the room when he said it. Suddenly. With a slam of the door. Sometimes Father marched on the spot as well, as if he was reliving his days in the Army. All these were jokes because Father laughed when he said them.

Mother didn't laugh. She used to widen her eyes at him and tilt her chin toward me in a signal I didn't understand. In the end she'd say *Oh, I give up* and stop mentioning *debts* or *risks* or *schemes*. She'd pick up a book on Ancient History—*there is comfort in revisiting the grandiose folly of others*—and it took her mind off what was *bound to happen, yet again*, to Father.

I'd tried to imagine Mother and Father when they were young, long before I was born. I screwed up my eyes and saw them dancing at the Ritz, saw the people clapping when Mother said yes, saw them turning joyful somersaults together around the ballroom.

Sylvia came over with the iPod. I hadn't imagined something so tiny, something you just rubbed with a finger, like Aladdin's lamp in *The Thousand and One Nights*, to bring it to life. I half expected an Opera Singer, mouth open, arms outflung, to materialize.

When I brought the iPod into Bay View Lodge, Mother wouldn't look at it and swatted the earphones away. Her *Not that way* got louder, and I felt heat rising in my face. It was only when I turned the volume up that she looked around her.

"In here, Mother." I tapped it. "All your Operas are in here now."

She let me put the earphones in her ears, and then she sat, silent, her left hand clutching the side of her chair. A tear trickled from under her glasses. I took a startled breath. Had I hurt her? I dabbed at her cheek with a tissue, but she smacked my hand. I was looking at her, chewing my lip, wondering if I should ask Maria to make her a cup of tea, when she smiled.

I was bouncing up and down on my toes when Trevor opened the door. "Here comes trouble," he said. It was something he often said. I stretched my mouth in case it was a joke and stood up very straight so he would know I was managing on my own.

"Seriously, love, I hope you haven't come here with any more problems for Sylv."

"Let the girl in, Trev," Sylvia called.

Josh pushed past me at the living room door and went upstairs, taking the steps two at a time.

On the table was an opened package of Jaffa Cakes. Jaffa Cakes are made by McVitie's. Their name makes them difficult to categorize. On the one hand, they have a layer of sponge *cake*, but on the other, their orange filling and chocolate coating make them more like cookies. Father had told me they *were* cookies, but were classified as cakes for tax purposes.

Father's favorite cookie had been Shortbread because of his Scottish heritage. He also had what he called a *guilty pleasure* cookie, which was a Jammie Dodger.

"And that is your only one, is it, Gregory?" Mother had asked. She'd called Jammie Dodgers *common* and *synthetic*.

"I know, I know"—Father shook his head, eyes crinkling— "and all the more delicious for it."

Jammie Dodgers, or a cookie very like them, were in Tea Time Assortments. Once, when Father was Away, I'd chosen a Jammie Dodger every Friday at teatime. I'd kept them in a red telephone money box with a slot in the top. I had twelve by the time Father returned. I'd had to dig my nails into my palms to stop myself from telling him until after dinner.

When he was drinking a cup of Lapsang souchong tea with Mother, I'd brought them in, wrapped in a handkerchief, a clean one.

"Vivi! What have you brought me? Oh! Lots of Jammie Dodgers! How yummy!"

"I saved them up for you in the money box." I stood in front of him, my face pink.

"That's for pennies, Elvira, not cookies," Mother said. I knew this. I'd saved them in there because the box was the same size and shape as a cookie package. "They'll be horribly soft," she'd added, sipping her tea.

Father put one in his mouth, whole, and lifted me onto his knee. "I like them when they're soft, darling," he mumbled. Mother would have told me off if I'd spoken with my mouth full. "Saves me dunking them. Thank you, darling. What a thoughtful girl!"

"Well, Elvira"—Mother's eyes had glittered above her teacup—"perhaps *you*, and *your* thoughtfulness, can prevent your father from straying, because I cannot."

I'd chewed my lip. I wasn't old enough or clever enough to keep Father from doing anything.

I focused on Sylvia's packet of Jaffa Cakes again. She patted the space next to her on the cream leather sofa. "Tell us how it went."

"Mother liked—" I began, but then Sylvia carried on talking. I'd have to excuse them for being preoccupied, but Shelbie, that minx, was seeing someone else, a property developer, and Josh was *in bits*, although I'd just seen him climb the stairs two at a time.

Now, when I visited Mother, she'd be leaning back in her chair, eyes shut, not saying anything at all. "We take away iPod to recharge battery at night. Only time mum shout now," Maria said. Mother noticed me visiting because I said "Good morning, Mother" or "Good afternoon, Mother" in a loud voice. She'd look at me for a moment, as if she was waking up from a dream, and then sink back in her chair again, music flooding from the earphones.

There was no risk of Mother being excluded, because she no longer said anything, let alone shouted. Now it was only me who was at risk of being sent Away. "Why not just make the one daily visit?" Mrs. Hulme suggested, since Mother was settled now, and in a World of Her Own. "Not a bad way to spend your life is it, listening to your favorite music, looking at a lovely view, eating cookies? In fact"—she leaned forward to tap my arm—"it sounds like Paradise!"

8.

A computer's your best mate.

—Micky Baines, computer buddy,
Sandhaven Library

I pushed open the swinging doors of the Library. Now that I had more time, I could get a book out again, one on guinea pigs. Sand shifted beneath my feet because this was the first time I'd been back since Mother had her stroke.

Juliet Underwood, the librarian, asked how Mother was. I told her she was at Bay View Lodge and not reading now, not even the *Daily Telegraph*. Juliet took off her glasses. "Oh, I'm sorry. What a shame! Sad for both of you." I had to think about that. I wasn't sure if I felt sad, or if Mother did, because of her being in a World of Her Own, and because I wasn't very good at understanding other people's emotions.

I told Juliet about the volunteer guinea pigs at Bay View Lodge. There was nothing about guinea pigs under *Pets and Domestic Animals* so we had to Google them, which was using a search engine on a computer. "It'll tell you anything you want to know, and lots you *didn't* want to," Juliet said.

I remembered the layout of the screen from school. Website

addresses came up, and I clicked on *The Guild of British Guinea Pigs*. Juliet Underwood said, laughing, that using a mouse was appropriate for researching rodents. I guessed it was a joke because of her laughing, but actually, I thought it *was* appropriate. The screen filled with pictures of different breeds.

"I'll print those out for you." She pushed up her glasses. "We've got a computer buddy here now, you know. Shows people the ropes. Why not come along?" The sessions were informal, and nobody would shout if I made mistakes, she said. She took off her glasses again. "I expect you had quite a lot of that at home. Our nearest and dearest aren't always patient, are they?"

Nearest and dearest must mean Mother. I shook my head. The Library was empty save for a gray-haired couple browsing the Crime section. Juliet Underwood polished her glasses slowly with a little yellow cloth. "She always seemed rather an unhappy person, your mother." She glanced at me, eyebrows raised.

Was Mother unhappy? I was surprised. She'd never said.

"I know her arthritis held her back"—Juliet went on polishing—"*and* she was lonely, after your father passed away. Perhaps before too. Some of the remarks she made—" Juliet Underwood stopped suddenly and examined her glasses. "I wonder," she said, breathing on the lenses, "if there was a hint of bitterness too."

I stood at the Library counter, blinking. I looked at the small pearl stud in Juliet Underwood's ear. "Mother wasn't lonely because I was always there."

"Yes." She held her glasses up to the light. "You were, *are*, very good to your mother." She laughed. "Goodness knows how many books you've gotten out for her over the years."

I nodded. I wished I'd counted them now.

"Anyway..." Juliet Underwood replaced her glasses.

"Moving on… I shall look forward to you coming to grips with computers."

I walked home thinking about Mother's bitterness, remembering the bottles of fizzy bitter lemon I'd been allowed to drink on our vacations in Lyme Regis and the taste of cough medicine at the back of my throat. I couldn't see the connection.

I read the printouts until I knew the different breeds of guinea pig and their color variations and characteristics by heart. Geraldine was an Abyssinian Dalmatian. I tore up *Guinea Pigs as a Food Source* without reading it, but found some interesting Facts elsewhere to tell Brenda at Pet Therapy: Queen Elizabeth the First of England had had a guinea pig as a pet, and *Portrait of a Guinea Pig*, dated 1580, was in the National Portrait Gallery in London.

I lay in bed thinking about the computer sessions. Juliet Underwood said I'd picked it up easily today. I twisted a corner of the sheet. Sylvia and Katie said owning a computer would give me *greater independence* and *keep me up with the modern world*. They'd said computers had the answers to things. Mother had said I'd never manage a computer, but it was possible she'd been wrong. She'd already been wrong about buses.

The computer buddy was called Micky. He had prominent ears and wore a baseball cap. He was doing Community Service. It was kind of him to serve the community without getting paid.

Micky showed us—there were only me and an older gentleman

called Bill—the clever things a computer could do. "See these, like, professional-looking letters, yeah? A computer'll underline your spelling mistakes, correct your grammar, practically wipe your ar...nose for you!" Micky and Bill laughed. I looked carefully at the computer. "Yeah, I've got mates inside who use 'em to write *very* convincing letters, but, hey, let's not go there, eh? Happy?"

I *was* happy. The computer did the same things in the same way each time. I could do everything Micky showed us. I was quicker than Bill. If I owned a computer, I could create tables, spreadsheets even, to organize the different guinea pig breeds and put Geraldine in under Abyssinian Dalmatian. And I could find the answers to the questions in my Japanese note-book: *Why are there no Japanese stamps in Father's passport? What did Jane from Dunstable mean about* Deceit, Lies, Forgiveness, *and* Shame? *Why were there* concerns *about Father's finances? Where is Mother's Lost Capacity? Who are the woman and the baby (b. 7-29-1994) in the photo from Father's wallet?*

I must have said some of this out loud because Micky pushed up his baseball cap. "Yeah! A computer's gonna be your best mate." He finished his hour's service time then and had to dash off, although later I saw him outside, smoking.

I popped around to Sylvia's with a packet of Foxes Favorites to tell her about the computer sessions. I thought I saw Trevor going out the kitchen door when I came in, but I might have been mistaken. Roxanna was Skyping from Spain, bouncing up and down on the chair. When she tucked her hands under her knees, there was a long scratch on one of her bare arms. I wondered if Shelbie had done it with her claws.

Roxanna soon slid off her chair altogether because she didn't want to miss the rest of her CBeebies cartoon. Sylvia ended the call, her half-moon eyebrows sloping downward, expressing Concern, Worry, or Sadness. Shelbie hadn't been in the flat with Roxanna. She'd been brushing up her skills in a hairdressing salon.

"Got it through that property developer she's seeing." Sylvia's lip curled. "Did this hairdressing course at college, you see, when she was sixteen. In the New Forest. Never finished it. All at sixes and sevens then with her mum dying. Always been into hair and makeup. I wonder if I was a bit of an influence there. You know what I'm like about my appearance."

I knew Sylvia spent a lot of *time* on her appearance. On using a hair dryer to make her hair stick out. My toes clenched with the effort of not talking about the computer.

"Now she wants her own salon, wants to be independent," Sylvia was saying, "What married woman wants to be *independent*?" and "Left alone in a flat. It's not right. Shelbie could bring Roxanna over here for *me* to look after while she gets this training done."

Quickly I got in, "*I'm* training on computers at the Library."

"*Are* you, pet?" Sylvia turned from the screen, her eyebrows arched again. "You fixed it up yourself? Well, you *definitely* need one of your own now." Sylvia hunted through a tray of papers to find the phone number of the man who'd got hers wholesale.

I shut my eyes. I might not be able to work it at home and on my own. I might turn into a robot, like Mother said.

"Stuff and nonsense," Sylvia said, and five days later, the new computer sat on Father's desk, covered with a Kenyan tribal throw of Mother's. (Mother hadn't reacted to me telling her about it at all, not even to say, "Not that way," but Juliet

Underwood had punched the air, saying, "Yay! Computer whiz!" and my face and ears had gone pink.)

I sniffed the computer's plasticky fragrance. Father would have been good at computers if he'd had the time to learn. He could have used one to organize the Foreign Investments he'd encouraged the people at the Cricket Club to buy. Even Mother might have approved of computers, eventually. She could have watched people singing on YouTube, like Micky had shown us. He'd shown us gambling websites, where you could play cards for money too, glancing over his shoulder before he clicked on to them. Mother could have played Bridge online, by herself, without any *unpleasantness* being involved.

At the next computer session, Bill offered me a Rich Tea cookie from a package he kept in his briefcase. I took it, checked the number of holes (fourteen), then handed it back because, as Father said, *Where's the fun in a Rich Tea?* The most exciting thing about it was the fourteen holes. Bill started telling me about his grandson who'd been to a Special School. I'd been to one too. When you went to one, you didn't feel special; you felt the opposite. I chewed my lip and poked at a carpet tile with the toe of my shoe.

"A natural with computers is Paul, rather like yourself. Keen on animals too," Bill added. "Very keen. Always rescuing things and bringing them home. Always got something in a cardboard box in his bedroom. Something recovering. Drives his dad mad. My son, Paul's dad, he's a single parent, you know."

I shook my head. I didn't know.

"Paul does voluntary work at Animal Arcadia. Heard of that?"

I shook my head again. It was an animal conservation center out in the country that might suit me too. "They're always glad of another pair of hands." I looked at my hands. "Paul," Bill went on, "works in the café. Moves sacks of food and that. My goodness, those animals get through a lot of cabbage, even the tigers!" He nudged me in the ribs and laughed. I smiled too because *I* liked cabbage, *and* it was full of Vitamins.

I found a lot of comfort in creating spreadsheets. Getting things in order. Spreadsheets helped Micky to keep track of his secondhand cars. "How much I sell 'em on for. And"—he winked—"what I have to pay out for disguising a bit of damage. Know what I mean?" He winked again and screwed his mouth to one side. It wasn't a facial expression I recognized. I didn't always know what Micky meant, although he was always asking us if we did. I did understand spreadsheets, though. In fact, in the end I had to show Bill how to do them because a policeman came to the Library and asked to speak to Micky and he had to leave suddenly to help him with something. Micky was a helpful person.

I showed Sylvia the computer—I wanted to talk about it all the time—and told her about Bill and his grandson.

She looked at me, then said, "Maybe at school break me and you and Katie and the boys could take a trip to Animal Arcadia. Have a look around." I could Google it first and tell her what it was all about.

The computer knew a lot about Animal Arcadia. I'd thought it would be a kind of zoo and that seeing animals in cages would give me the collapsed feeling inside, but they'd all been rescued *from* cages and were now living a Life of Freedom in the Heart of the Countryside.

Animal Arcadia's website displayed each animal's name, species, photo, and background. There was a section on volunteering with people wearing yellow T-shirts, shuffling information sheets, and working behind the scenes. They were smiling, but apart from that, there was nothing special about them. I chewed my lip, picturing myself helping there, mixing with abused animals and telling people Facts. I heard Mother's voice, *You wouldn't be able to cope, Elvira*, and then Sylvia's chiming in, *You're doing so well, pet.* Their voices clashed inside my head, and I had to lie down with the curtains drawn for a while.

I came downstairs with the Japanese notebook. I was finding it hard to stay away from the computer. I typed in my unanswered questions and sat back, waiting for everything to be clarified. Not knowing why Father's passport was empty, and what was wrong with his finances, and where his Secret Government Missions had taken him, and who the people were in the photo from his wallet, and what Jane had meant by her comments, played on my mind.

But Google didn't give me any proper answers. It got bogged down in irrelevant details like "Is vegan breastfeeding enough?" and went off at a complete tangent about the photo. It knew nothing at all about Father's finances. In fact—I banged the mouse down on the desk—it made the same mess of things that Mother said *I* did when I tried to answer something difficult. I shut the notebook with a snap, unable to tick any of my questions off, no nearer to understanding things than when I'd started.

I made a cup of tea and then switched on the computer again, hoping I wasn't wearing out its insides. Since Bill had mentioned Special Schools, I must have had them on the brain. Without thinking what I was doing, I typed: "Are Special Schools Special?" I waited, blinking, but Google's answers were unlikely and useless, just as before. No, wait, here was a link to Learning Difficulties.

I clicked on it, the familiar hot feeling of being different, slow, of having an inactive brain, sweeping over me. And there, on the screen, was *my* Condition. My Condition, mentioned under Mother's breath to strangers, and loudly (*You and your blasted condition!*) to me. Here it was in public, without shame, with its own website! Actually—I scrolled down to check—it had lots of websites! I clicked on one specifically for girls and women. It had news, fact sheets, links to information, and a message board.

I stared. I hadn't known such things existed. I read about other women finding it difficult to fit in and how *their* brains got overloaded. I leaned forward, absorbing information. They'd *all* felt like outsiders at coffee mornings and said the wrong things about people's hairstyles. I couldn't be as odd as I'd thought, because here were lots of other people, women, feeling exactly the same things that I did.

I wasn't alone.

They wrote conversations to one another. Supportive conversations. I read all of them and every message, life story, and piece of advice. When I looked up, it was dark outside. I went to put the kettle on. In the hall mirror, my eyes looked bloodshot from staring at the screen. I hurried back to click on *Fact Sheets*. If I'd had a computer earlier, I could have read these before. I could have shown Mother. She might even have read bits out at mealtimes.

Mother couldn't advise me anymore. I had the *memory* of Mother's instructions, and my school's guidelines of *please* and *sorry* and *thank you*, and Sylvia who explained the *reasons* for things. But now, best of all, I had a website that knew exactly how I felt! I would have run around the room, I was so excited, but I didn't want to leave the screen.

All of us had problems with other people. With NeuroTypical people. Finding, after a lifetime of being labeled, that *they* had one too, made me shiver with delight. None of us understood NeuroTypicals or how they communicated. Several women likened their experiences, as I had done, to being tourists in a foreign country whose language and customs they didn't understand.

I blinked and rubbed my sore eyes. My grip tightened on the mouse. If I *was* a real tourist in, say, Japan, I'd buy a guidebook to help me communicate with the inhabitants and learn their customs.

I scrolled up and down the website. There didn't seem to be such a thing for people with my Condition. Perhaps I could write my own! Research and organize guidelines to normal behavior into a spreadsheet! List those hidden Rules that were never discussed openly! With Sylvia's assistance, I could include the reasons *behind* the Rules, so I'd understand them. I could even add a check-box column for keeping to them! I felt as if I were filled with bubbles.

I spent a blissful hour cutting and pasting observations and experiences women had posted on the website, and narrowing our difficulties down. NeuroTypicals found us too direct: we lectured people rather than chatted, we found tact impossible, and we looked weird. We didn't understand NeuroTypicals' Rules—often we weren't even *aware* of them—but they still got annoyed or upset if we broke them. That was when they laughed or shouted at us, or patronized us, or left us out.

I organized our troublesome areas into seven Rules. Keeping to these would help me to move around the world of NeuroTypicals without getting into trouble, without Incidents, perhaps without them even noticing I wasn't normal underneath. I was so excited I could hardly keep still. I copied the Rules onto a spreadsheet template and titled it: *The Seven Rules*.

As soon as Sylvia drew back her living room curtains the next morning, I would pop over and show it to her. Once I'd added her reasons, my problems would be over. The Seven Rules were going to change my life!

THE SEVEN RULES

Rule 1: Being Polite and Respectful is always a Good Idea.

Rule 2: If you Look or Sound Different, you won't Fit In.

Rule 3: Conversation doesn't just Exchange Facts—it Conveys how you're Feeling.

Rule 4: You learn by making Mistakes.

Rule 5: Not Everyone who is Nice to me is my Friend.

Rule 6: It's better to be too Diplomatic than too Honest.

Rule 7: Rules change depending on the Situation and the Person you are speaking to.

9.

Sometimes listening is a way of being kind.
　　　　　　　　　　　—Mrs. Sylvia Grylls, neighbor

H ello, pet. Let me just finish sorting out the wash and I'll be with you."

My toes bounced in my trainers. "Thank you. How are you?" I asked. That was Rule One:

Being Polite and Respectful is always a Good Idea.

"I'm fine, pet." Sylvia opened the living room door. I held out the spreadsheet, but she was already heading for the kitchen. She came back, looking at her watch. Trevor was washing up the breakfast dishes, she said. He'd just accidentally ripped open a letter addressed to Josh. Mr. *T.* Grylls and Mr. *J.* Grylls looked alike. It was from the credit union about Josh's savings.

I nodded politely. Mother and Father had often talked about savings and unpaid bills and broken promises. At least, Mother had talked about them. It had led to her eyes going round and bulging, I remembered. And Father going Away soon after.

"We didn't even know Josh *had* a savings account. Let alone there was twenty thousand pounds in it!" Sylvia straightened some cushions as she talked. She still hadn't looked at the spreadsheet. "Trev and I can't think where all the money's come from. I hope he's not planning anything stupid."

Was Josh stupid? It was hard to tell because he didn't say much. Sometimes, when I didn't understand a question, *I* didn't say much and I was called stupid. (*Not* stupid, *different*, said the website.) I rustled the spreadsheet.

It turned out that the stupid thing Sylvia was worried about was Josh snatching Roxanna. "Sometimes I wish he *would*. It'd be lovely to have her here. Not for Shelbie, though."

But Shelbie was busy painting her claws and practicing in a hair salon. "She might not mind," I said.

Sylvia laughed without her eyes creasing. "She *would* mind. For all her faults, she does love Roxanna." And Josh could get into trouble because snatching children was illegal. "Anyway, pet," Sylvia called over her shoulder, going into the kitchen again, "how are you getting on with that computer?"

"I want to show you something," I said from the doorway, bouncing on my toes. "I need you to... I would *like* you to..." I corrected, "add some reasons to it. Please."

Sylvia came back with a tray. For the first time since Mother's stroke, there were no cookies. This was a surprise, and disappointing, but not mentioning it was probably polite. Sylvia put on her glasses and took the Seven Rules.

"A lot of sense in these, pet. How clever of you drawing them up yourself! This one, *Being Polite and Respectful is always a Good Idea*. Well, there's lots of people, people who don't have your diffic...differences, who could do with having a *tattoo* of that." She laughed.

This was a good idea and something I hadn't considered. "You can use it for absolutely anything. I used it just now!" I told her, clasping my knees. "When I asked you how you were."

"You can never say too many *pleases* or *thank yous* or *sorrys*," Sylvia went on, "but real good manners are a bit more. It's making other people feel comfortable. Smiling, nodding, listening, saying nice things." I took out my notebook and wrote this down after the pages of unanswered questions, frowning. I never knew what a nice thing to say would be. Sylvia put on her glasses again. "It links with another one, Number Six, I think."

It's better to be too Diplomatic than too Honest.

I knew them by heart! I'd checked *diplomatic* in Father's dictionary. *Skilled in the management of international relations*, it said, which reminded me of his mysterious Government missions.

"Yes." Sylvia took off her glasses and didn't say anything for a minute. "You could add, 'If you can't say anything nice, don't say anything at all' to that one, pet. A little subsection."

I made a note, feeling my jaw setting. "*NeuroTypical* people, *ordinary* people, *don't* always say nice things, though. A man shouted *Frump!* at me yesterday. From a car window."

"Ignorant!" Sylvia shook her head. "Maybe ..." She looked at the list again. "This one—*If you Look or Sound Different, you won't Fit In*—might call for a little shopping trip. Clothes shopping. Don't make that face, pet."

I *hated* clothes shopping. Sylvia was making the Rules more complicated. They'd been so simple when I'd compiled them. I shut my eyes.

Sylvia took a big gulp of tea. "Think about this one as well, pet. *Conversation doesn't just Exchange Facts*. Sometimes you can get carried away when you're talking about your cookies or your animals, if you don't mind me saying. Perhaps have a bit of a mental time limit there."

I *did* mind her saying. This was all about the things *I* was doing wrong! The website said people with my Condition had an *alternative* way of looking at things, not a *wrong* way. An original and more honest way. I considered for a moment, staring at the swirls in Sylvia's living room carpet. *I* got bored when other people went on about things—Sylvia about Josh, for example.

"I could time myself, I suppose," I said, poking at a swirl in the carpet with my foot. "Two minutes." I paused. "I could time other people too, when old ladies on buses go on about their hips or their veins." I'd been going to mention Sylvia herself, but stopped; it wasn't a nice thing to say. "They might not know they're boring, otherwise."

"No, pet." Sylvia shook her head. "Sometimes listening's a way of being kind. They might not talk to anyone else all day." She looked at the spreadsheet. "That's *It is better to be too Diplomatic than too Honest* again. And, it links to this one, Number Seven." She pointed. "*Rules change depending on the Situation and—*"

"*Person you are speaking to*," I jumped in. *I* was the expert on the Rules because *I'd* compiled them. I hadn't expected Sylvia to quote them to me and to tell me how I was breaking them all the time.

Sylvia nodded. "That's adapting the way you behave, being a bit flexible." She tapped the arm of her glasses to her lips. "You know how much Shelbie taking Roxanna away upset me"—I shifted in my chair, expecting Sylvia to start going on about her family again—"but if I *said* that, Shelbie would get in a huff and it'd make the situation worse. Do you see, pet? And those old ladies on the bus… If you look at your watch, they'll think you're bored."

"I *am* bored." I flattened a tuft of carpet with my shoe, aggrieved. "And I don't like pretending things." The idea hadn't been that I should pretend to be someone I wasn't. Someone completely different.

"Yes, pet, I know. But sometimes pretending's kind. That's *adapting to the situation*, you see. *And being diplomatic.*"

"Mmm." All the Rules were overlapping. I wanted them to be separate. Clear. "But how do you *know* what other people will feel?"

"Age and experience, I suppose," Sylvia said, "plus my brain works a bit differently."

Frowning was making my head ache. If there were all these reasons *behind* the Rules, and you had to change them to fit a situation or a person *anyway*, what was the point of them? A Rule should be perfect; it *shouldn't* change. Rules for operating machines didn't! If I disobeyed the microwave by putting something metal in it, it would explode! I had a flashback to the pressure cooker and shot a quick glance at Sylvia. *She* was smiling; it was me who was getting upset.

"We're social animals," she went on. "That's *why* you have to keep to the rules of the group." She pointed to another column I'd created on the spreadsheet, useful phrases to illustrate each Rule, such as, *I would be interested to hear your view.* "You're not going to just come out with these phrases willy-nilly, are you?"

Willy? I was baffled.

"You've got to show some *feelings* as well."

"Feelings?"

"Just be interested in other people. And then it will come

naturally. All this is new, pet." She patted my arm. "You practiced on the computer, and look how good you've gotten. It'll be
the same with your social skills."

———

I put Sylvia's explanations in the *Reason Behind Rule* column
of the *Seven Rules* spreadsheet. Then I lay down. I dragged the
duvet over my head. The website said NeuroTypicals instinc-
tively *knew* how to behave, but people with my Condition had
to *learn*. My jaw clenched. Sylvia was teaching me, I supposed.

I turned over and reread the spreadsheet. Did I really want
to be "fluent" in Rules that were fussy and pointless? *Im*perfect.
What was *wrong* with making direct comments rather than
aimless chitchat? Why *weren't* people allowed to stand out from
the herd? And, why (Rule Five: Not Everyone who is Nice to me
is my Friend) did *we* have to be alert to NeuroTypicals lying to
us, maybe even tricking us? I flung down the spreadsheet. Why
was it just people with my Condition who had to make adjust-
ments? I threw back the duvet, tears prickling. Because people
with my Condition were in the minority: NeuroTypical was the
way of the world.

———

I had another telephone call from Jane in Dunstable. "I do hope
that lawyer is keeping an eye on your mother's trust fund, dear.
She was so particular about having her finances legally protected.
She'd learned the hard way, you see," Jane said.

"The easy way would be better," I said. Disagreeing with Jane
made my heart thud.

"Well, yes, dear, but that's not always possible. Not when someone like your father is involved."

There was a pause while I tried to make sense of what she'd said. The only person like Father *was* Father.

"You don't *disclose* your wealth to anyone, do you, dear?"

"I haven't told anyone," I said, clenching and unclenching my toes. "Sylvia and Mr. Watson already know, and I don't like talking to Strangers."

"No, quite right. Your mother taught you well. Of course, the biggest threat to your inheritance is no longer with us." She sniffed. "So many burdens to bear, dear Agnes. So much to put up with. She saw the light eventually, of course, but even so…all those wasted years. And now laid low by a stroke. In a nursing home! And only in her seventies!"

So much to put up with. Mother had used the same words. "She had me to help her," I said, my heart thudding again.

"Yes, dear. You did your best, in spite of your disabilities."

My disabilities. I hadn't realized I had more than one. The website said *not* a disability, a *difference*. I began to explain this, but Jane talked over me.

"I was really thinking about your father, dear, but there you are… Don't speak ill of the dead."

"I won't. I don't like talking about dead people. Or dead animals. It makes me sad." I screwed up the hem of my apron, willing Jane to stop talking.

There was a heavy sigh. "No, dear, I only meant, well… Give your mother my love. If it wasn't for my spine I'd… Good-bye for now, dear."

She didn't finish her sentence, and she'd spoken in riddles earlier. I waited for a minute, then the phone started buzzing so I put it down. Actually, I banged it down.

Sylvia let me in with the package of Fig Roll cookies I'd bought to say thank you for explaining the reasons behind the Rules, even though they'd made me want to slam doors at the time.

"Back in a sec, pet," she called to the computer screen. She was Skyping Roxanna again. Behind her, I saw Trevor going upstairs.

I put the kettle on for her. As I came back, she was telling Roxanna about the shopping trip she'd planned for me.

I pulled up my trousers. I had to keep pulling them up, and the hems were fraying from where I'd trodden on them. "I don't really need any new clothes."

"Next Tuesday, Ellie, when Trev's bowling."

Roxanna bounced up and down. "I *love* shopping. I want to come!"

"I wish you *could*, pet. I'd like that more than anything." Sylvia's voice was husky. "You could give us fashion advice."

Mother used to put the *Fashion and Style* section from the *Sunday Telegraph* straight into the recycling bin without even opening it. Sometimes she'd thrown it in.

I made the tea while Sylvia said good-bye to Roxanna. When I came back with the tray, she was crying so it was lucky I was already prepared. She talked for much longer than two minutes about Josh and Shelbie, going on about his "nest egg," which was the twenty thousand pounds in his savings account, and worrying that he'd use it to snatch Roxanna. Finally, she drained her cup and put it down. "I meant to say, pet, Animal Arcadia next Saturday with me, Katie, and the boys—how does that sound?"

I paused, wondering what an animal park would sound like. I tilted back my head and was just about to open my mouth, wide, when Sylvia prodded my arm.

"Clothes shopping first, mind. Then you'll be able to wear something new. You'll enjoy that, won't you?"

I pressed my lips together. I would be *able* to wear something new—I'd done it before, quite a few times—but it would never be something I'd *enjoy*.

RULE 1
Being Polite and Respectful is always a Good Idea.

Reason behind rule:
You may, accidentally, cause NeuroTypicals offense when you get their rules wrong; acknowledge this first.

Being polite and respectful shows recognition of other people's humanity and status. If you treat other people with dignity, they will feel better.

Useful phrases:
"It's nice to see you."
"How are you?"
"I'm sorry."
"Well, I'd better be going now."

Hints and tips:
Smiling and nodding make other people feel comfortable.

When someone is angry with you, apologize. Saying *sorry* defuses tension and makes the other person feel better.

Just because you've got a Condition doesn't mean you have to be rude.

Rule followed? ☐

10.

You can be a bit different, but not too much.

—Mrs. Sylvia Grylls, neighbor

When I couldn't find the right size clothes, sixteens, Mother used to call "Yoo-hoo!" until an assistant came. Then I'd have to try them on in the dressing room with her outside waiting. There was never enough room so it took a long time to get everything off, and I kept seeing unexpected bits of myself because of all the mirrors.

When I'd emerge to show Mother, she'd ask if there was enough give in the trousers, or say *That will cover a multitude of sins*. If I'd asked which sins, her voice got louder: *Oh, for goodness' sake, Elvira*. The new clothes would be like the ones I had already, but I'd have to get used to their stiff new fabric, and their different smell, and the colors being a different shade of black or navy or gray.

Sylvia hummed as she browsed the clothes racks in Asda. I watched her from behind a rack of trainers. She picked out very different clothes from what I normally wore. "Isn't this pretty, Ellie?" she said, holding up a floaty blouse, or "Now, *this* would suit you," waving something in leopard skin. She'd checked my size with a clerk's tape measure, found I was now a twelve to fourteen, and bustled toward a rail of sparkly tops. I didn't follow her. Wearing those would make people notice me, and I didn't want to be noticed. People noticed me too much already.

My face grew hot. Sylvia looked over and held up some plain dark jeans with elastic in them. Mother despised jeans. Even I knew they were fashionable, so wearing them would be a big step for me, but Sylvia said Mother would appreciate how hard-wearing denim was, if ever she stopped to think, and to remember Rule Two: *If you Look Different, you won't Fit In.* When I paid for them at the register, Janice said, "*Very* snazzy, Elvira!" which Sylvia said was a compliment.

———

We headed to Marks & Spencer. This was Sylvia's idea. I wasn't used to its layout, and the grim-faced ladies swishing clothes along the rails reminded me of Mother. Sylvia gathered up some brightly colored T-shirts and sweaters, when what I felt comfortable in were *dark* colors, and the looser the better. I'd feel like a set of traffic lights wearing all that stuff. I had to keep shutting my eyes. Shopping with Sylvia was not so different from shopping with Mother, except that she called me "pet" and said how much *she* was enjoying herself.

She looked at me. "Bit of a change for you, pet, isn't it?"

"Not a *bit*! A *big* change!" I held the hem of my sweater tightly with both hands. If I'd been at home, I would have run upstairs and slammed the door, and Mother would have called me rude and challenging. "People will stare *more* if I wear stuff like that." I backed away from her armful of clothes. "They'll *notice* me!"

"Pet," said Sylvia, "look around. Can you see anyone else

wearing baggy navy trousers with ragged hems and a sweater that's so stretched it's practically a dress?"

"No," I admitted, "they're wearing anoraks. Is that a kind of uniform?" I checked with Sylvia. "Do you *have* to wear one here?"

"No!" Sylvia laughed. "No, bless you. You're right, though, pet. They *are* wearing similar things. That's part of fitting in, I suppose. You can be a *bit* different—like me wearing my bright-pink coat or leopard-print heels, or both," she added, glancing at her outfit in a mirror, "but not too much."

I'd have to add another note to the spreadsheet. A complicated one. "That's very strict." I squeaked a trainer against a chrome post. "*And* mean."

"Yes, but that's the way of the world, I'm afraid, pet, and like it or not, we're all part of the world."

We were at the register by then so I paid, then Sylvia took hold of my arm and said how about having lunch in the café upstairs. My stomach lurched; it would be noisy and busy. When I said how tired I was, she said *she* was tired too *and* hungry, and we'd both feel better after a short rest. I knew I wouldn't. It was my brain that was tired, not my feet.

The only place where I felt comfortable eating, besides home, was Ravel, the restaurant where Father used to take Mother for dinner on her birthday and their wedding anniversary. (Spending other people's money was one of his skills, Mother said. His others included bridge building and Joining In at parties, but she didn't mention those.) They'd stopped celebrating their wedding anniversary, I'm not sure exactly when; after their silver one, I think. Mother said it had become a *sham*. I had to look up the word: *a person who pretends to be something other than he is*. The root word it came from was *shame*, which was odd because that was something Mother said Father never felt.

Mother started taking me to Ravel instead. It was quiet, and we could sit in a corner in the back. There were black-and-white photos on the walls of people playing musical instruments, and the soup had cheese on toast floating in it. Jean Christophe, the waiter, called me Mademoiselle Elvira and asked me how I was. Mother told me to say, "I'm fine, thank you. How are you?" and he'd reply: "I'm very well, mademoiselle. Thank you for asking." It was like a rally in the Wimbledon Championships when no one dropped the ball.

Here, in the Marks & Spencer café, it wasn't quiet; there was an echoing clatter of cutlery and too many people talking.

"Isn't this nice, pet?" Sylvia looked around her, smiling.

"Nice to take the weight off your feet," a lady at the next table said.

Sylvia laughed and stuck out her feet in their leopard-print shoes. "Especially when you're silly enough to wear these!"

Sylvia must have known the other lady at the table as well because they all joined in a pointless conversation about shoes. One asked if I was wearing a comfortable pair. It was difficult to give an accurate answer. They weren't as comfortable as my slippers. I could feel them both staring at me.

"You like to get things right, don't you, Ellie? So an answer can take a long time," Sylvia said, smiling, and then all three ladies started talking about tops with low necks and short sleeves and how they didn't like them.

At home, I sat in Mother's armchair for a while with my eyes shut, and then I tried on the new clothes. I looked at my reflection. The jeans were slim-fitting and the T-shirts and sweaters went in at the waist. I'd never had one like that before. I felt exposed, almost naked. I parted my hair like Delia Smith did hers, and pushed it back from my face.

Sand shifted. I hardly recognized myself. I looked neat and tidy...almost efficient. I walked away from the mirror and then back again. Would people think I was like that inside—a bossy, chatty person, who knew which countries were where and what hip-hop music was? People didn't expect much when you wore baggy clothes. No—I moved away from the mirror—they shouted at you instead.

I put my old clothes in the laundry basket, remembering a slow worm in David Attenborough's *Life in the Undergrowth* that had shed its worn-out skin for a better-fitting one. On the way back upstairs, I caught sight of my reflection in the landing mirror and thought, for one heart-stopping moment, there was someone else in the house.

I called for Sylvia on Saturday for our Animal Arcadia trip. I kept my arms glued to my sides to control the flashes of color I was giving off and walked with a shuffle because the jeans seemed to resist my legs moving.

"You look lovely, pet." She blinked. "A real transformation."

I put my hands in my jeans' pockets; there weren't any folds of fabric to hold on to. We waited ten minutes at the bus station for Katie and the boys, but nobody stared or shouted.

The bus set off for Animal Arcadia, tree branches scraping

against the bus windows as we got deeper into the countryside. I imagined being a jungle creature and hiding away, except that the vivid colors I was wearing would give away my location.

The boys scuffed their shoes and pushed each other, and Sylvia and Katie had to take them to the Adventure Playground. I was left alone in a place I didn't know, wearing clothes I'd never worn before. They felt tight, especially the jeans, although Sylvia said they weren't. Catching glimpses of a smaller, brighter-colored version of myself in the glass of the animal enclosure windows made me jump. I kept checking that my old black sweater and the Safety Kit—my earplugs and useful items such as a Tupperware box containing four cookies (McVitie's, because these had accompanied Scott to the Antarctic)—were still inside my backpack.

I concentrated on noting down new Facts about the animals I saw. I had to turn over several pages of the Japanese notebook to get to a fresh page because of the questions that were still unanswered: Where had Father carried out his Secret Government Mission; who were the woman and baby in the photo from his wallet; what had been wrong with his financial situation; who had deceived Mother; where was her Lost Capacity; and what did Jane from Dunstable's comments mean? Having so many gaps in my knowledge was unsettling. When I dwelt on them, it felt, again, like sand shifting beneath my feet.

While I waited for the orangutan talk to begin, I copied down their names from the information board. The orangutan in charge, Rojo (*king* in Indonesian), looked like the bronze Buddha Father had brought back from Japan, except that Rojo had auburn fur. The baby one, whose fur stuck out in untidy wisps, was called Pernama, which means *full moon*.

The orangutans should have been left in the wild, but there wasn't enough wild left, the keeper told us. It was being destroyed to plant Palm Trees whose oil went into Processed Foods. Mother must have known this already because she always said *Processed Foods* with a curl of her lip.

"Proper gingers, aren't they?" A woman cackled. Other people peered through the fence, pointing and laughing. My heart began to beat very fast.

I reached into my backpack. I had letter-sized version of the *Seven Rules* with me for reference. After a moment's thought I pulled it out. Sylvia had said most people could do with reading it and I'd seen Burger Shop people in the town center gave out leaflets all the time. People were *pleased* to get them. As soon as the talk had finished, I screwed up my toes, took a deep breath, and handed the cackling woman a copy of my spreadsheet.

I walked on to the tiger enclosure. It was a strange sensation not having a T-shirt billowing around me or trouser hems flapping around my ankles. The three tigers were sprawled beside an ornamental pond. They had been rescued from circuses, where they'd been whipped to make them perform tricks. One of them—his name was Vikram, the tiger keeper told us—stood up and rubbed his head against the netting, purring in the keeper's ear while he spoke. My eyes stung. I didn't know why.

I met Sylvia, Katie, and the boys at the gate at four o'clock. The cackling woman was there with a shaven-headed man in a sleeveless T-shirt. They were talking to a woman in a yellow Animal Arcadia uniform.

"That's her!" the cackling woman pointed at me. "Bloody cheek!" The man folded his arms and stared at me.

Sylvia put her head in her hands. She drew the uniformed lady aside, said something that involved shaking her head, and then we left very quickly.

On the bus, Sylvia made me write down why I shouldn't have given the woman the spreadsheet. *I* had been rude, apparently, *and* undiplomatic. It was bewildering.

———————————

Afterward, Sylvia came with me to visit Mother. Her face was turned to the window, eyes closed. She wasn't asleep because the fingers of her left hand were tapping the arm of her chair.

Her eyes didn't open when I told her about Animal Arcadia, not even at there being *two* different types of wolf (red and gray) and *two* different types of orangutan (Bornean and Sumatran). She didn't notice I was wearing brightly colored clothes and *jeans*, whereas before her brain was damaged, she'd have told me to *Take those dreadful things off at once*! The only sign she knew we were there was her eyelids flickering when Sylvia patted her shoulder to say good-bye.

"I know we wanted her to stop shouting but..." Sylvia unlocked the car door. She drove home in silence, as if Mother's had been catching. I looked out the back window, watching Bay View Lodge disappear and remembering how Mother had behaved when she first arrived there. Her not speaking at all now was better, but it made me feel hollow inside.

I went to bed for a while, and then I clicked onto the Animal Arcadia website. I studied the page about rescuing animals and the section on volunteering, with the pictures of people smiling as they volunteered, and clicked an Application Form up on-screen. I could at least have a look at it.

RULE 2
If you Look or Sound Different, you won't Fit In.

Reason behind rule:
We are herd animals. Other people are suspicious of those
  who look different.
Even though you might not care how you look, other people do.
People treat you better if you look neat and tidy.

Hints and tips:
Scruffiness and smelliness put people off.
Dress like everyone else if you don't want to stand out. You
  can be a bit different, but not too much.
Stand an arm's length away during conversation so you
  don't invade people's personal space.
Using very long words and formal language can intimidate
  other people.

Rule followed? ☐

11.

Shiny shoes, a clean white shirt, and a good suit will take you far in life.

—Gregory Carr (Father)

I'd never had a job or done voluntary work before. When I left school, at eighteen, Mother had been sixty-three and Father sixty-six, because of having had me late in life. Mother's knees were getting stiff and the lenses in her glasses thicker and thicker, so she'd needed me at home.

We used to have a cleaning lady, but she'd left when Mother went to the bank and found there was nothing left in their joint account. *We'll have to tighten our belts*, she'd snapped. I'd thought she meant me, that I should lose weight, which is something she often mentioned, but she hadn't looked at me. She'd looked at Father. He'd put down his book and taken a deep puff of his cigar, a long, breathed-out sigh of smoke hiding his facial expression. He was the only one of us who wore a belt, so he must have already been feeling the tightening.

One thing I will say for you, Elvira, is that you are a naturally tidy person, Mother had said. Being *naturally tidy* helped me to do the housework. *We will stick to a routine, Elvira. It will make it easier for both of us.* It was Mother's routine, though, meant to fit around her. Mine would have involved more David Attenborough DVDs. (*You must know them by heart now, surely?* Yes, I *did* know them by heart. That was why I liked them.)

It would have meant visiting museums and places with animals, and not going shopping every other day, or up and down stairs every half hour. It would have involved learning how to use a computer and going to the cinema with Poppy, who I used to sit next to at school and who'd shared my interests in cookies and *Coronation Street*.

Mother had said there wasn't enough time for all *that*; she needed me. I was ungrateful after all she'd done, and I needed to be kept safe at home *for my own protection*. I was *far too trusting*, she'd said, and *a target for predators*, and she reminded me of the various Incidents that had happened when I'd ventured out and done things on my own.

Staying at home meant I'd gotten a Caregiver's Allowance because of Mother's Limited Mobility. Mother had spat out the *c* in *caregiver* as if she was saying *cut* or *kill*. *And who exactly is caring for whom, might I ask?* she'd asked, but I wasn't sure of the answer. Father had told me, when we were on our own, that caregiving was a proper job. "Goodness knows," he'd said, "you earn the money." I didn't have to care for Father because he was often Away and his knees were flexible. We didn't know that, inside, his arteries were furring up. On the twelfth of November 2010, when he was seventy, one of them got blocked. His blood couldn't reach his heart and it had an attack and then he died.

Father had been Away when he died, on an engineering trip to Kenya, which I remembered Mother saying now had been a *cover story*—practically evidence for spying! After the police had told us, and she'd made me a cup of tea, Mother's face had gotten red and swollen, and she'd taken off her glasses.

Well, it was Crawley, not Kenya—reality is far more prosaic—and it didn't have much to do with engineering. I told him this would happen! She'd slammed a document file shut. *He was too old to be leading a young man's life, but there's no fool like an old fool. I should know.* Her face had crumpled, and she'd put her head in her hands.

I'd stood next to her. When I'd asked her if *I* should make *her* a cup of tea now, she'd said no. I'd asked her if she wanted a cookie, but there'd been no reply. So I'd told her, to cheer her up, that McVitie's had been making Jaffa Cakes for ninety years and that each one traveled more than a mile down the production line in the factory, but she didn't respond. She just limped upstairs and banged the bedroom door shut.

―――――――

Because Father's death had been sudden and while he was Away, it didn't seem as if he *was* dead, at first, but only Abroad on a long trip. That's what I was thinking when I'd asked Mother if Father would be coming to the funeral.

Of course he'll be coming to it! she'd snapped. *It's his funeral, you stupid girl.* She'd shouted about it meaning she'd never be able to get Away again, and went upstairs, stumbling because of her stiff knees. From the landing, she'd asked if I realized I'd never be able to watch *those dreadful films* with him again, and then, before I *could* realize, there'd been a creak as she lay down on the bed.

The next day, Mother and I had gone to the Funeral Parlor in a taxi. We were shown into a room with white flowers in it, and there, in a coffin, was Father. He'd looked shrunken and old, and when Mother told me to kiss his cheek, he was as cold as the shoulder of lamb I'd bought the week before in the Frozen Meat Aisle in Asda. That was when I'd realized he was dead.

Mother had packed up his clothes and given them to a charity shop. Apart from his dinner suit that hung in her wardrobe with the blue evening dress. Father had worn it when he proposed to her at the Ritz and for Special Occasions afterward because he'd always been the same weight and height he'd been at twenty-one. Father had taken pride in looking smart: *Shiny shoes, a clean white shirt, and a good suit will take you far in life*, he used to say. Mother had stared at him and raised her eyebrows. *Sometimes to places where you have no choice but to stay.* They'd often spoken to each other in this sort of code.

I'd kept the special things Father had given me in a shoe box lined with one of his silk ties: an ammonite from Lyme Regis; some colorful stamps with animals he'd brought back from Japan and Kenya, and his old *Observer's Book of Dogs* with the Airedale page marked with a cigar wrapper. Later, Mother had bought me a boxed set of Classic Horror Films, which I also kept in the box; I never watched them. I would have been frightened without Father being there. I kept the box under my bed and got it out when I couldn't sleep.

I kept going back to the Animal Arcadia website. I wanted to help the animals there so badly that it felt like being squeezed. I fetched my notebook. To be a Volunteer, I'd have to do the bus journey on my own. I chewed the end of the pencil. I knew which bus to catch now because of going there already, and I had bus experience because of visiting Mother in the hospital. The Asda Bus Incident was unlikely to happen again.

An image of Mother appeared now, her eyes like round pebbles behind her glasses, her voice loud and scornful: *Volunteering? What are you thinking of, Elvira? Of course you couldn't manage.*

I held on to the ribbed hem of my sweater. I'd have to smile at people. Interact Socially and work alongside others. The image of Mother was still hovering, waiting to bang her lion-headed walking stick on the floor and snort *Ridiculous idea!* I *did* have the website now, I told myself. And the *Seven Rules.* Sylvia said I'd understand them all in the end. I gazed out of the window, the pencil to my lips. I could try going to Animal Arcadia, on my own, as a trial run. *Trial*, I'd heard Trevor say the last time I was at their house. *That girl is a trial.* He'd obviously meant Shelbie.

If I managed the trial run, I could do it again, and this time have lunch in the café as well, no matter how anxious I felt, *and* say something to at least one person. If I could cope with all that, without Incidents, or getting lost, or crying, I'd come home and fill in the Volunteering Form. I shut my eyes against Mother and wrote all this down, underlining the last sentence twice.

I got out the *Seven Rules* spreadsheet. Rule Three:

Conversation doesn't just Exchange Facts—it Conveys
how you're Feeling

I circled the explanatory notes: *Nod, ask questions, and only say nice things* and *Eye contact is part of conversation.* The website recommended glancing at people in the triangle between their eyebrows and their nose tip. So far, I could only get as far as people's ears. Sylvia said this could make me look as if I wasn't interested in what people were saying, which was a pity because sometimes I *was* interested.

Sylvia said Rule Four (You learn by making Mistakes) was true for everybody, whether they had my Condition or not. Volunteering was important; I would hate to get things wrong. I used to cry and run upstairs whenever I made a mistake, and Mother would say, *You're a perfectionist, Elvira,* shaking her head so I knew it was a bad thing, *A heavy burden for someone with your condition.* I looked out of the window again so that I couldn't see Mother shaking her head now.

I stood in line for the bus to Animal Arcadia behind a large woman with a stroller. She was smoking. Her hair was striped dark brown at the roots and blond at the ends. I found it hard to stop looking at it. When the bus arrived, she flung her cigarette down and it smoldered on the ground, creating a Fire Risk. I tapped her on the shoulder to tell her.

She snapped her head around from maneuvering the stroller, her face red, and asked me who I thought I was. She didn't wait for me to tell her, which was rude (Rule One); instead, *she* told *me* I was *a fat cow.* This was incorrect because, now that

I'd lost weight, I was a size twelve and my BMI was normal. I told her this, scrunching up my toes because of her red face, but she started shouting and the bus driver told me to go and sit upstairs. When I said, *my* face scarlet now, there were still seats downstairs, and I usually sat in the fourth one on the right, if it was vacant, he asked why he only got aggravation from women.

I paused, trying to think why, but he flung his arm out and pointed to the stairs, so I gave up. I sat in the fourth seat on the right-hand side, *upstairs*, shaking. I fumbled in the backpack for the *Seven Rules* spreadsheet and scanned it, my heart thumping. It seemed I'd done *something* wrong, but I couldn't work out which Rule, or Rules, I'd broken. I'd been polite. I'd tried to be helpful. I hadn't said *anything* that wasn't nice, although I'd wanted to tell her *she* was fat and should be worrying about her blood pressure as the mother of a small child. I huddled next to the window, close to tears. I'd made a mistake, and I hadn't even gotten to Animal Arcadia yet.

Once there, I managed to buy my ticket but I couldn't look up from the floor, which was beige linoleum with a flecked pattern like stone. The woman slammed the ticket down with my change and turned her back with a flounce of her nylon tunic. I couldn't see any of the animals very well because of the blurring in my eyes, so I just walked around the park as fast as I could, to get it over with, and caught an earlier bus home.

I made a cup of tea and went upstairs. I clutched the *Seven Rules*, folded small, to my chest and pulled the duvet over myself. After a bit, I punched the pillow and banged my head on it until I felt dizzy. Sylvia said you only learn by making mistakes. But you had to be able to recognize the mistake—*mistakes*—first.

12.

Keep busy when you've got something on your mind.
—Mrs. Sylvia Grylls, neighbor

I n the bus line, an old lady in front of me dropped a tissue. I froze. I'd had to force myself back to the bus station. The failed trial run had been more than a week ago. I was only here again now because I'd underlined my sentence about applying to be a volunteer at Animal Arcadia. I picked the tissue up and gave it to the old lady, my palms sweating.

Nah, I was chucking it away, love. She had two hairs on her chin, dark ones. *'Ere*—and she threw it in the bin.

I didn't tell her it was wrong to drop litter, although I wanted to, and she didn't shout. In fact, she started to tell me about an operation she'd had on her left hip. On the bus, I sat downstairs in my usual seat.

At Animal Arcadia, there was a different woman in the kiosk. I looked at her ear—she was wearing stud earrings shaped like roses—and glanced once between her eyebrows. I said please and thank you loudly, and although she didn't smile, she did say thank you back.

A plump young man with glasses and red lips that glistened

with saliva served me Scrambled Eggs on Toast and a Cup of Tea in the café. His yellow polo shirt said *Animal Arcadia* on the back. On the front was a round blue badge that said *Volunteer*. I stared at it.

He said "There you go" and "Enjoy your meal" when he put my food on the table. With training and more practice with the Rules, *I* might be able to say both those things to the public. I wouldn't have to look at anybody because I'd be looking at the food, in case I spilled it.

"Thank you," I said and stretched my mouth up into a smile. I wondered if Bill, from the computer sessions, was his grandfather, but I couldn't find the right words to ask him.

I went to Wolf Wilderness and found a place at the back of the crowd for the talk. The wolves jumped about and licked one another's faces. The keeper told us they were affectionate animals who sometimes sacrificed themselves to protect their family unit. I hoisted my backpack and folded my arms so the collapsing feeling did not take hold. Father's Government Missions might have involved sacrifice; they might have contributed to his heart trouble. Wolves lived in social groups and were *monogamous*, the keeper said, which meant they mated for life. I wrote down the word. Mother would be pleased I was extending my vocabulary. I thought about Mother and Father mating for life.

Mother said it was love at first sight when she first met Father, and he agreed. He had been in his Army uniform, because he was doing military service and had given up his seat for her on a train. Mother had been coming down from Cambridge University where she'd studied Ancient Civilizations. Father had studied at the University of Life. Business Methods and Flexible Accounting, he'd said. Father had *charmed everyone he met—and charmed money out of them*, Mother said.

They'd struck up a conversation and then written to each

other. Mother still had his letters, in date order, in a leather box on the top shelf of her wardrobe. Once, when I was small, I'd seen her reading them. When I'd asked her why, when she already knew what they said, she'd snapped, *To remind myself that he loved me.* Then her voice had momentarily lost its snap. *I was loved once.*

When I got home, my muscles were stiff with bracing myself, and my brain felt overloaded with noise and detail and color. I took the Japanese notebook, with the notes on Animal Arcadia, upstairs. I lay in bed with my eyes shut and then began to leaf through it. I'd neglected the unanswered questions I'd written down a few weeks ago. Sometimes I thought I'd never discover what Jane meant by her comments, who the woman and the baby in Father's photo were, what had been wrong with his finances, or where his Secret Government Missions had taken him.

I turned to the new Facts I'd learned today and numbered the animals I'd seen, matching them to their enclosures around the park. I began to hum. But when I stopped humming, I could hear Mother, as clearly as if she was in the room, saying, *Visiting an establishment is one thing. Working there, Elvira, is quite another.*

I took some deep breaths and printed out the Volunteering Form anyway. I looked at it, then I made a cup of tea and looked at it again. The pen kept slipping in my hand. Mother or Father had always helped me with forms before. None of the questions were about animals, and I didn't know what to put under *Previous Experience.* After a while I wrote: *Caring for Mother,* and underneath that, *Helping with Guinea Pigs in Nursing Home.* Brenda had let me hand them out last week, and she'd said I was *a natural.* I'd had to press my feet flat to the floor when she said it to stop them bouncing.

Give the name and address of a person, not a relative, who has known you for at least three years. Jane from Dunstable? Apart from our phone conversations, I'd only met her once. Mother and I had stayed with her one Christmas, and when I'd been unsure how to answer a question, she'd said, "Cat got your tongue?" and I'd run across the road, crying, thinking the ginger cat opposite was eating it, and Mother and Jane had been angry. I knew now it was a Figure of Speech, but it wasn't a polite or a nice thing to say. Jane had broken Rule One, I thought with a glow of satisfaction. I wrote down Sylvia's name and address instead.

I checked and rechecked the form and stuck three First Class stamps on the envelope. I hesitated at the front door. There was a noise like an alarm clock in my head. I kept hold of the door handle for a while, my eyes shut. Then I saw a crowd of abused animals: Pernama, Vikram, the purring tiger, and the wolves, sacrificing themselves. I saw myself helping them in an Official Capacity. I repeated *official capacity* under my breath and walked to the mailbox.

There was an email from Animal Arcadia! I hesitated; they might be turning me down. I shut my eyes and clicked. They wanted me to come for an interview! I got up and jumped up and down in front of the computer until I was out of breath. Sylvia said it was all right to behave like this in private. The whole house was private now that Mother wasn't here. *Pride comes before a fall*, she would have said (after first shouting, *Stop it!*).

I sat down, holding the hem of my sweater. I might not pass the interview. They might think I wouldn't be able to manage, that I wasn't normal enough.

I still didn't know how to behave in new situations. Last week,

the man who did the gardening for the house across the road had
rung the bell and offered to mow my front and back lawn, I was
relieved, because they both looked untidy, and then I realized he
wasn't being helpful; he wanted to be paid. This was because he'd
said he charged £15 per hour, cash in hand. He'd also winked and
made a sign of rubbing his first finger and thumb together.

I didn't want to employ *anybody*. I'd have to be in charge and tell
them what to do. He'd had dark eyes like little beads and needed a
shave. He'd peered around the front door, and mentioned antiques,
and said he had a mate in the trade who could give me a valua-
tion. Why would I want things valued? *To sell, miss*, he'd said. Why
would I want to sell them? He'd talked about clutter and spring
cleaning and given me his business card—it had had a dirty finger-
print on it—and I'd only gotten away from him because the phone
rang. When I'd answered it, it was from a call center Abroad, and I
couldn't understand what they were saying either.

It had reminded me of people banging at the door, wanting
things, when we'd first moved to Sandhaven. The bailiffs who
wanted to take our furniture, and other people demanding money
and scaring me. Mother hadn't answered the door, and she'd kept
the curtains drawn. I didn't *have* to answer the door, Sylvia said, or
the phone, but *not* doing it made me feel uneasy too.

I'd stuck the *Seven Rules* spreadsheet to the fridge door with an
Airedale terrier fridge magnet. Sylvia said the important thing
was to *apply* the Rules. Then they'd start to make sense. I ran my
finger down the list, revising for the interview.

Being Polite.

I'd added columns for *Hello*, *How are you*, and *Good-bye* in the checklist section.

I tapped my finger on Fitting In, Rule Two. Sylvia had been right about this one. I didn't really like my new clothes, except for the jeans, but they had stopped people from staring. I brushed my hair twice a day now, whether it needed it or not, and used a lemon-scented deodorant under my arms as well. Sylvia had bought it for me. I knew not to rock to and fro, or lie down and rest my head on a dog's stomach, or jump up and down when other people might be watching, even though I *wanted* to do these things and they weren't doing anyone else any harm.

I rested my head against the fridge door. I didn't see anyone *else* doing them; that was the thing. *I* wouldn't have minded if they did, but *normal* people did mind. NeuroTypical people hated other people behaving differently, and that was what made *our* lives difficult.

Conversation doesn't just Exchange Facts...

I'd cut down talking about animals or cookies to two minutes or less by looking at my watch. Last week, I'd asked Clive, the shopping cart collector at Asda, what *his* favorite cookie was, instead of telling him about the new packaging for Malted Milks. He'd stopped and scratched his head and eventually said, Kit Kats. I'd nodded politely, but actually Kit Kats weren't really *cookies*. They were bars of chocolate. I'd clenched my toes to stop myself from explaining the difference and had given myself two ticks on the checklist afterward. Whenever I saw Clive now, he said, *Have a break, have a Kit Kat.*

... it Conveys how you're Feeling.

This was the difficult part of the Rule; I often didn't *know* what I was feeling, let alone what other people felt.

My finger hovered over:

It's better to be too Diplomatic than too Honest.

Sylvia had told me I'd been honest rather than diplomatic with the woman with the stroller. *And* to the lady who'd cackled at the orangutans. People didn't want to hear strangers' opinions of their behavior. I shouldn't have said *anything*, she said.

So that was diplomacy. Thinking things rather than saying them. Another not-straightforward thing that NeuroTypicals did. I shut my eyes. I saw the woman's red face and heard the angry rattle of the plastic rings on the stroller handle, and the cackling woman's swear word. Diplomacy stopped people from getting angry, Sylvia said.

Rule Four:

You learn by making Mistakes.

I understood this one. I just had to practice not *minding* making them. Sylvia said when she first made a Lemon Drizzle Cake, she'd left out the sugar and it had been too sour to eat. I was surprised at her laughing when she told me this. "But you see, pet, it wasn't really an *important* mistake, was it?" she said. But it was *still* a mistake.

Rule Five:

Not Everyone who is Nice to me is my Friend.

Normal people sometimes told lies, Sylvia said, *so just be a little bit wary with any new friends.* "Ask someone you know well if you're not sure about a person, pet." But did that mean you couldn't rely on what normal people said? Ever? And yet I was trying my hardest to be like them. I leaned against the fridge door, suddenly tired.

I straightened up, sighing, to consider the most difficult Rule. Rule Seven:

> Rules change depending on the Situation and the Person you are speaking to.

I tried to puzzle it out. Sylvia said we would work our way up to it.

I wrote the interview time and the bus time on the terriers calendar, under this month's picture of a fox terrier, and circled them in red felt-tip pen. I put on an apron, the one with British Garden Birds on it, and began to clean, dusting high places and sorting out drawers, to take my mind off the Interview. *Keep busy when you've got something on your mind*, Sylvia said. I wasn't sure if it was a Rule or a guideline or just conversation.

I bumped into Sylvia and Trevor in Asda's cleaning products aisle. I'd used up nearly all of mine because of keeping busy. Trevor pretended to run away with the shopping cart, then he stood behind Sylvia looking at me with his eyebrows drawn close together.

Sylvia clapped her hands when I told her about the interview.

"Mind they don't keep you there." Trevor's beard seemed to point at me.

"It's for an interview," I explained. "I'm coming back on the bus."

Sylvia looked at Trevor. She'd put down that I was

conscientious on my Application Form and, lowering her voice, that I'd led a sheltered life looking after Mother.

Sheltered. That word again. Like Sheltered Accommodation. Where Mother said I'd end up. I glanced at Trevor, but it was difficult to work out his facial expression. With his beard and his glasses, there wasn't much face left to interpret. Passing a volunteer's interview might be evidence that I was too capable for Sheltered Accommodation.

Sylvia said, with a little choking sound, that it was nice to hear some good news for a change. "Here we go." Trevor leaned on his shopping cart, arms folded. "This'd be a good buy for you, Sylv." He pointed to some boxes of tissues. "*Buy one, get one free! We should stock up.*" He reached four boxes down and put them in their shopping cart. "If you don't use them, I will." He leaned over Sylvia and put his arms over her shoulders.

Josh had had *Shelbie* tattooed over the top of his *Venom* tattoo, Sylvia said.

"They reused the *e* from *Venom*," Trevor added, "which was appropriate."

Sylvia got out a tissue and showed me a picture of Roxanna on her phone. She was lying on an inflatable crocodile in a swimming pool and laughing.

"Bless her," said Sylvia. "Doesn't she look like our Katie there, Trev?"

Trevor squinted. "Good of Shelbie too. Nice teeth."

Shelbie wasn't in the photo.

"He means the crocodile." Sylvia shook her head. I didn't know what they were talking about. People often exchanged jokes or smiles or catchphrases I didn't understand. I would have liked to write a Rule for spotting them, but it wouldn't have fit on a spreadsheet.

Sylvia waved a hand in front of her face, sniffing. "Sometimes I feel as if I won't see Roxanna again till she's grown up."

"Cheer up," I said, using a phrase from the spreadsheet. "You'd probably still recognize her then," I added to comfort her.

Sylvia blinked. Walking home, I tried to think of what else I could do to help.

RULE 3

Conversation doesn't just Exchange Facts—it Conveys how you're Feeling.

Reason behind rule:

We are social animals. People bond through talking to each other, even if it's just small talk. It's a way of getting to know someone and finding out if you've got things in common.

Useful phrases:

"Would you like to talk about something else?"

"Sorry, my mind was elsewhere."

"Oh, that's wonderful!"

"I would be interested to hear your view."

"Would you like to tell me more about...?"

"How does that make you feel?"

Hints and tips:

Ask some general questions first, rather than just jumping in.

Ask people questions about their lives. Nod to show you're listening.

Don't talk about money or sex or religion because they are private topics.

Smile when you see people.

Turn toward people when they talk to you. Look at them but don't stare.

Don't go on and on about your favorite topic—have a mental time limit.

Other people may have different points of view from you.

Don't outstay your welcome.

Rule kept? ☐

13.

Animals need to be with their own species.
—Rosemary McAlpine,
HR manager, Animal Arcadia

I found it hard to swallow my porridge on the morning of the interview, and I was more than half an hour early for the bus. An interview was a Formal Occasion so I wore my smart coat. It was looser on me now. Underneath I wore a new T-shirt from Asda, purple with short sleeves, because it was hot. On the bus I held on to the hem of my coat without actually twisting it.

A long-haired dachshund was asleep in a basket under *Rosemary McAlpine—HR Manager*'s desk. I recognized it from my Dog Breeds of the World apron and *Observer's Book of Dogs*. She said it was Animal Arcadia's assistant security officer. I took my eyes from the blue carpet tiles. *I* might be taken on if even dogs were given jobs here.

I kept to at least three Rules during the Interview, possibly more, as some of them overlapped. I used a new phrase—"Thank you. I must be going now"—instead of just saying good-bye and walking off. Keeping to the Rules must have helped me pass the interview, because the last question Rosemary McAlpine asked me was if I was free next Friday for training!

———————

When I got home, I rushed next door to tell Sylvia. Trevor answered the door with the chain on. When Sylvia came, peering from behind him, I listed the Rules I'd kept to and began to go through the details of what Rosemary McAlpine had said, but Sylvia couldn't stop. "Ta-ra, chuck," she said, using an expression from *Coronation Street*. She took off the door chain to give me a hug. "Out in the real world now!"

I didn't like the chain, and *out in the real world* sounded like being an orphan in a thunderstorm. I *was* a kind of orphan, living in a social group of one, but it was something I tried not to think about.

I don't want my little girl facing trouble out in the big, wide world, Father used to say. He'd carried on saying it even after I was no longer a little girl. A picture came of Mother putting down her book (*Ancient Civilizations: A User's Guide*), that I'd just collected from the Library, and saying *For goodness' sake, stop twisting that sweater*. Then she'd drawn her own cardigan around her—an Aran one, chunky, with leather buttons, which had belonged to *her* father—and added *Your father's right, Elvira. And he is an expert on trouble. It has taken him years of practice, and me years of practice to recognize it*. Sometimes the things Mother said were as baffling as her cryptic crossword clues.

I went into the kitchen now and filled the kettle far too full. The *trouble* that Father had been an expert on could be things he'd encountered on Secret Government Missions Abroad. He must have known all about spying or terrorism; people planting bombs like I saw on the *News* before I turned it off. I tipped some water out and switched on the kettle. Bombs were unexpected things, not the sort of trouble you *could* protect yourself against, although I could add a bandage and an antiseptic wipe to the Safety Kit, I supposed. I'd never heard of an Animal Sanctuary being blown up.

I got the milk out. Mother and Father had been experts on lots of things: Japan, Operas, engineering, bridges (card games *and* crossing structures), Adventurous Cookery, Financial Schemes, history, and travel. I stirred the mug of tea, my feet prickling. Experts whose advice I was now going against.

I leaned against the worktop for a moment, then I lined up the ingredients for Monday's Spinach Gnocchi and began to chop an onion. I was only going out into the world *one* day a week. The earlier Incidents hadn't taken place in an Animal Sanctuary. I scraped the onion into a saucepan. A place I'd been to three times now. I grated a small piece of mature cheddar. What was more likely would be me forgetting to smile, or saying the wrong thing, or taking too long to answer a question from the public.

———

Two other people were being trained as volunteers: Margot, an ex-teacher with a shriveled brown face, and Mark, balding, with round cheeks, who said *Fantastic!* after everything Rosemary McAlpine said.

When she asked us what we knew about Animal Arcadia, I unclenched my hand and put it up. I began to list the Facts I knew, but there wasn't enough time to say them all, because Rosemary McAlpine held up *her* hand, palm out, in a gesture I recognized. It meant *Stop*. Margot had been coming to the park since it opened, so Vikram, the tiger, knew her voice and came to the netting when she called him.

Mark was more of a practical person, he said, and had a certification in Carpentry. *Just give me a piece of wood, and I'll make you anything you want.* I looked around the meeting room for some loose wood because I needed another shelf for the Mills & Boons, but there wasn't any. I wondered afterward if it had been a Figure of Speech. Mark sat with his legs wide apart and yawned when Margot told us about Vikram.

Rosemary McAlpine took us outside and pointed out where the bathrooms were because that was the question the public asked most often. I rehearsed the answer under my breath. She showed us where Mark would be building animal enrichment equipment—wooden structures to climb and hide in—and the zebra-striped cart that Margot, once trained, would use to take groups of people around Animal Arcadia, educating them.

The Adoptions House, where I'd be working, was a kind of barn decorated in the style of a tropical hut, with palm tree fronds hanging from the rafters and branches of dried leaves above the door. Rosemary told me adoption didn't mean taking an orphan monkey or wolf cub into your own home. This wouldn't be practical because of their size and strength, or kind, because they needed to be with their own species. It was choosing an animal, paying some money, and then getting its photo and a newsletter. Mark asked if the photo was signed, and everybody, except me, laughed.

One of the things I'd be doing was sorting these photos into alphabetical order. I looked up from the ground; I'd already done this with my Mills & Boons. I'd done it quite often. I enjoyed doing it.

Afterward, I remembered to say good-bye to everyone, and Margot said, "Well done, Ellie!" although I hadn't done anything yet, and Mark said, "Cheers," then stared at me in the same way that some of the public had stared at the orangutans.

My head ached from stretching my mouth and trying to understand people's conversations. Once I was at home, I closed the curtains and got the box file of cookie packaging out from under the bed. I sorted through its familiar contents: the smoothed-out foils from unusual Continental Assortments, the labels I'd cut out from new or unfamiliar brands, and the flattened boxes of regional, rare, and Christmas Special cookies.

I put it all back neatly and leaned out of bed to retrieve the shoe box of special things that reminded me of Father. The *Observer's Book of Dogs* fell open at Airedale, because of Tosca. I knew the description by heart. I looked up dachshund, because of Rosemary McAlpine's dog, and read that too.

I tried on the yellow Animal Arcadia T-shirt with its blue badge, and narrowed my eyes at my reflection. I didn't really look like me anymore. No wonder Mother didn't seem to know who I was nowadays.

I hung the T-shirt up on the back of the bedroom door where I could look at it. I fetched the Japanese notebook, sat down on the bed, and wrote down everything I could remember Rosemary McAlpine saying, then tested myself to check I'd gotten it right.

14.

Manners grease the wheels of social interaction.
— Mrs. Agnes Carr (Mother)

I waited outside the Adoptions House, counting. When I got to a hundred, I was going to walk through the door. There wasn't anywhere you could knock because of the palm fronds.

Inside, the walls were covered with animal photos. I was just going to check that all two hundred and sixty-three animals were there, when a female voice spoke. "You the new volunteer then? Rosemary said you'd be starting today."

I hadn't seen the girl sitting behind the Information Counter. I nodded, glancing around quickly. She was thin with short, black hair that stuck up at the front, and something that glinted at the side of her nose. When I looked again, it wasn't that she had a cold; it was a nose stud, a sparkly one.

"I'm Karen," she said. Her sticking-up hair and round eyes made her look like the facial expression recognition card for Surprise.

"I'm Elvira…Ellie," I stammered. I should have smiled, but there was so much to take in that by the time I'd remembered to stretch my mouth, Karen was looking at her computer again.

"You've come at the right time, *Ellie*. Backlog of newsletters waiting to go out."

I had to put these in envelopes and stick on address labels. My hand shook as Karen watched me. She went back to her desk and took down people's details on the phone. The public wandered around, looking at the pictures. I was concentrating so hard on folding the newsletters exactly in half that I forgot to say hello until it was too late. This meant the Rules checklist would not be perfectly ticked. I let a deep breath out slowly.

***

At eleven o'clock, the same time I had a break at home—only then I would be sitting down with a Mills & Boon, rather than a person—I had to fetch coffees for myself and Karen. Behind the café counter was the young man with glasses who'd brought over my lunch when I came to Animal Arcadia on my own. His polo shirt was tight over his stomach, and it had a small red stain down the front. He started talking as soon as he saw me, telling me he worked at Animal Arcadia on Tuesdays and Thursdays, had worked here for thirteen and a half months, and had done loads of different volunteer duties.

"What's your favorite species?" he went on. "Mine's wolves. They're endangered. We've got…"

"Paul!" came a voice from the kitchen. "Are you getting that poor girl her drink?"

"Oh. Yes. What would you like? What's your name, by the way?"

"Ellie," I said without stammering.

I didn't usually like giving my name, in case people shouted it out afterward. Once, I'd had to pick up a parcel from the Post Office, a book on African cookery, which Mother had not been able to get to the door quickly enough to sign for. I'd had to give my surname. The assistant said, "Carr? Now why does that ring a bell?" I didn't know why, but she went on. "Oh yes, my sister was on the jury for… Oh. Well, let's get this sorted out, shall we?" I nodded. She seemed a bit distracted—Mother would have said inefficient—and what her sister had done was irrelevant.

Karen drank her coffee while looking at her screen and grumbling about *other people's exciting social lives*. She didn't look at me much when she spoke, but her upright crest of hair quivered, which made it hard to concentrate on what she was saying.

After coffee, she dragged over a box of sheets, towels, and duvet covers. I had to shake these out and refold them, to check they were clean and there were no loose threads to catch on an animal's claws. These were also Enrichment Items: the apes made "nests" from them to sleep in, or draped them around themselves, and the wolves ripped them to shreds in tugs of war.

I sat outside the orangutans' enclosure at lunchtime. It was a relief to be with quiet creatures who didn't speak. Rojo lay in a rope hammock, scratching the fur on his chest. Pernama's mother, Cinta, was playing with a pink-and-purple bedsheet, like the ones I'd been checking. She dragged it along the ground, scaled their climbing tower, and stood at the top, the sheet streaming out behind her, rippling in the wind like a cloak, its vivid colors bright against her auburn fur. She looked like a fairy princess, or—because she had mated and had a child—a fairy queen.

———

At four, Karen called out, "Quitting time now. See you next week then, Ellie, same time, same place, same mission." Her voice deepened, and she made a pointing, flung-out gesture with her arm.

I headed for the staff exit, passing the orangutan enclosure. Pernama was skittering across the netting like a spider. She stopped and clung to the fence, her small toes as pink and flexible as fingers. Her pale-lidded eyes blinked. She scampered again, then swung upside down to look back at me. It was like chatting, only easier. There were no Rules to remember in a conversation with an orangutan, except for being polite and respectful.

———

I walked to Bay View Lodge from the bus station. Mother didn't take any notice of my uniform, even when I showed her *Animal Arcadia* written on the back. She yawned and put her left hand to her mouth. She hadn't forgotten her manners. She would have approved of the *Seven Rules*. Some of them. *Manners grease the wheels of social interaction*, she used to say—then snap *Oh, for goodness' sake, Elvira!* when I asked her what that meant. Now, she stared out to sea, or kept her eyes shut, hardly interacting at all.

Maria noticed my uniform. "You got job!" She stroked my yellow sleeve.

I explained I was a volunteer.

"You good girl. You help Mum, you help animals. What this place, Animal Arcadia?"

When I told her it was a Rescue Center for Endangered and Abused Animals she laughed. "In England, you have refuge for beaten wives, you have refuge for asylum seekers, and even you have refuge for animals!" I might have spent too long pondering if the beaten wives and asylum seekers' refuges had Adoptions Centers, because Maria smiled and tapped her watch and put her hand to her ear.

I shut the front door and stood in the silence of the hallway for a moment. I took some slow breaths and stretched my arms wide to loosen my shoulders. On the doormat was another postcard addressed to Father. It had a British stamp. My skin prickled as I picked it up because of him being dead but still getting mail. Only yesterday, a Fine Wines catalog had arrived.

The message was very short. The date, last Thursday, was underlined and then there was just:

Still remembering Brighton. Today especially. X, D.

The picture on the back was of Lake Windermere in the Lake District, not somewhere Father had ever mentioned. As he had no family, it couldn't have been from a relation. It might have been from one of his secretaries, perhaps someone who'd retired now but wanted to keep in touch. Mother had said they never stayed long. *I wonder why*, she'd said, staring at Father, who was pulling at his shirt cuffs and looking in a different direction. I'd wondered why as well but hadn't ever come up with an answer.

I fetched the Japanese notebook where I'd kept the first postcard—from Teddy, whose finances were running short—made a note of both of them on a fresh page with a question mark after each, and tucked them inside the back cover. Along with Father's empty passport and *his* lack of finances, Jane from Dunstable's comments, the mysterious woman and baby in the photo, and where Mother's Lost Capacity was, they created yet more unanswered questions. I didn't like uncertain things. I liked answers. Information. I liked things to be organized and definite.

I put on the kettle, sprinkled some cheese over the Cauliflower and Broccoli Gratin I'd prepared earlier, and put it in the oven. I added the Facts I'd learned today to the pages of my notes on Animal Arcadia. Orangutans weren't always quiet. They made lots of sounds, including a loud cry, one Karen had never heard, a fast, long call that males made when rivals tried to muscle in on their territory.

The information neatly organized, I watched *Holby City* with my feet up and the Cauliflower and Broccoli Gratin on a tray, something I would never have done with Mother. Eating in front of the TV was the *death of conversation*, she'd always said. I wouldn't mind if it did die out. Not knowing what someone was going to say next made it exhausting.

I put the tray down on Father's carved wooden chest, my eyes already closing. I'd seen and interacted with more people in one day than I would have in a whole month at home, looking after Mother.

———

"Hello, hello, hello." Karen looked up.

"Hello. Hello. Hello," I replied.

"You've gotten here in the nick of time, Ellie. If it wasn't for you, they'd find my mummified corpse six months down the line, buried under a heap of clean but threadbare sheets." She closed her eyes and held her arms stiffly by her sides. I think she was pretending to be a mummy, but I couldn't be sure because of there not being any bandages. I stretched my mouth and went to my table. There were the same piles of envelopes, address labels, and newsletters ready for me to organize, exactly the same as last week. I began to tidy them into neat stacks of identical height.

Paul sat next to me at lunch, drinking a Coca-Cola. He told me about a wood mouse he'd rescued from his next-door neighbor's cat, and how he was nursing it back to health in a shoe box in his bedroom, and what it had eaten yesterday, and what its natural habitat was, and how many droppings it had done.

"Have you got a granddad called Bill?" I asked, spreading the scrambled egg evenly over the toast.

Paul stopped talking. "Yes, I have. How did you know?"

"I did some computer sessions with him at the Library." I cut my toast neatly into squares. I didn't mind eating in front of Paul. "It was him who told me about Animal Arcadia in the first place. He said he had a grandson who worked here."

"That was me!" Paul laughed. "I've worked here for thirteen and a half months. I'm really good at computers." He put his glass down and burped. "We could email each other. I'll give you my address. I don't do Facebook 'cause of bullying." He got up. "Let's go and see the wolves before you go back. I'll tell you about their breeding program."

The wolves were loping around their enclosure or skulking behind the pine trees, their gray-brown fur blending with the foliage. Paul knew interesting Facts about them—such as that they roamed up to twelve miles a day in the wild—as well as the names of the foreign zoo each wolf had come from *and* the date it had arrived on. He knew each wolf's date of birth too. I had to leave him there talking about them because it was the end of my lunch break. I knew—because of Rule One (Being Polite and Respectful is always a Good Idea)—that this wasn't polite, but there was no other way to stop him.

15.

Plan each charted course, each careful step.
> —Frank Sinatra, singer

*a*ll going OK, pet?" Sylvia called.

I made sure the wheelie bin was exactly parallel to the front wall and hurried over. I started to tell her about Pernama "talking" to me, and how wolves almost never attacked humans, but she couldn't stop because she was on her way to the Club to meet Trevor for a drink.

She squeezed into the driver's seat. "It'll take my mind off poor little Roxanna and my poor boy."

"Oh, that's wonderful," I said, remembering a conversational comment, and then looked at my watch to check I hadn't spoken for longer than two minutes. It was *exactly* two, which meant another tick on the checklist.

I brought in the laundry and set up the ironing board in the living room. Before, I'd always had to do it in the kitchen. I'd spent a lot of time in the kitchen when Mother was at home. The living room was Mother's room, really. Her Opera would be blaring, or there'd be a black-and-white film, with subtitles, on TV. In the kitchen, I'd look through my collection of Delia

Smith cookbooks, or tidy the cupboards. I'd look out of the window too, because it was opposite Sylvia's kitchen window, and sometimes she'd be there and wave.

I sang as I ironed, something I'd heard Trevor sing, loudly and with flung-out arm gestures. I liked the song because it was about planning things and doing them in the right order, one step at a time, which was the only way I could function. I folded an apron—it was the one Mother had bought aboard the *Pacific Princess*, which featured Great Ports of the World—ready to go back in the drawer. I did what I had to do, I told myself, as I ran the iron over my new black trousers. Visited Mother every single day, whether she noticed or not. Contributed to animal welfare through volunteering. Maria (I bounced a little at the memory) had said I was *a good girl* do those things.

Although I didn't get the Caregiver's Allowance anymore, because of Mother being in a nursing home, I was still—I counted on my fingers—helping endangered species, guinea pigs, older people (who held the guinea pigs) and now, Sylvia. Four helpful things! I hummed Trevor's song again, the bit about standing up straight and tackling things, and got up on my toes to stretch.

I put the iron down. I was helping Mother and animals, but not Sylvia. Sylvia was a friendly and cheerful person who had helped me. She always had to rush off to places to take her mind off Josh's marriage situation. Always had her blood pressure checked because of *other people's problems*, Trevor said. The hospital nurse said high blood pressure was bad for your health and might have contributed to Mother's stroke. I didn't want the same thing happening to Sylvia.

I draped one of my long white nighties—far too big now, but Sylvia had never seen it to comment, and nobody else was likely to—over the ironing board. There must be something I could do to contribute to Sylvia's welfare. I smoothed out a billowing fold of the nightie. Something that was *me* helping *her*, rather than always the other way around. I knew that this was what friends did, because Poppy, at school, had put my bags of cookies into alphabetical order for me, ready for a Show-and-Tell, and I'd sorted all the red paper clips from a packet I'd been given, to give *her*, because that was her favorite color. I blinked, returning to the present, then folded the nightie and put it on the pile of ironing to take upstairs.

Sylvia was desperate to see Roxanna, who Shelbie sometimes left on her own. "Locked up as if she was a little prisoner," Sylvia said. I chewed my lip. Mother had kept Social Workers at the back of her mind for when things got to be Too Much. Sylvia's blood pressure shooting up and down might mean things already had for her. So far, I'd only emailed the Guild of British Guinea Pigs and Animal Arcadia, but I *could* email Social Services and tell them about Sylvia and Roxanna. I still worried that people—Jane, Trevor, Josh—might phone Social Services about *me*. Now would be my chance to take the initiative.

I turned to a pile of T-shirts. Sylvia would get what she wanted. Roxanna would be released from prison to live with her and Trevor. She'd have more company because they didn't go out to work. They could take her shopping and buy her pink clothes. And Sylvia's blood pressure would come down. The iron flashed over the rest of the T-shirts.

Google found Sandhaven Social Services's email address. I hesitated, my fingers hovering over the keyboard, as I thought how best to outline Sylvia's situation. Then I typed all the things I'd been thinking about, including the blood pressure and Roxanna's prison. I pressed Send and sat back, smiling. Although I didn't get the Caregiver's Allowance anymore, because of Mother being in a nursing home, I was still—I counted on my fingers—helping: endangered species, guinea pigs, older people (who held the guinea pigs), and now Sylvia. Four helpful things! I hummed Trevor's song, *I faced it all, and I stood tall*, and got up on my toes to stretch.

Social Services emailed me back the next day. They would call on me at five p.m. this Friday, and could I please confirm this would be convenient. I confirmed at once. Mother had always said *computers* and *Social Workers* with a snort and flare of her nostrils. But, now, both these things were helping Sylvia to see Roxanna. It was puzzling because Mother had told me she was never wrong.

Gail Dawson, the Social Worker, smiled a lot and talked about Mother and Father's possessions, so conversation wasn't as difficult as I'd expected.

"Nice to meet you, Miss Carr," she said and sat down on the red tasseled sofa. "This room has such a lot of atmosphere. It's like an explorer's living room! Did your family live abroad?"

I put my foot over a crumb I'd just noticed on the carpet and explained about Father engineering in Kenya and Japan.

Gail Dawson took notes in a plain, official-looking notebook. "I believe you've got some concerns about the little girl next door? I couldn't quite make it out from your email. About her being left alone?"

I twisted a fold of my old gray sweater. I was wearing it for comfort because of never having had a visit from Social Services before. She might notice I wasn't normal and think I wasn't managing on my own. I'd spent all day tidying, cleaning, and polishing, and I'd rested the terriers calendar on the living room mantelpiece, with all my schedules clearly marked, so that she could see I was coping. "Her name's Roxanna. She's Sylvia next door's granddaughter. She *is* left alone. But it's in Spain."

Gail Dawson looked up from her notebook. "And how do you know this?"

"Sylvia says it's a pity Roxanna's left alone when, if she lived over here, *she* could look after her. And she's always talking about Roxanna getting sunburned and not seeing her father—that's Josh, Sylvia's son. And Sylvia says Roxanna is poor."

There was a long gap in the conversation while Gail Dawson wrote my words down. My chest swelled. I'd managed a quick glance at her eyebrows, which were bushy, when I spoke. She twiddled her black pen between her fingers. "There doesn't seem to be any *evidence* of actual abuse." I noticed her dark-navy skirt was made of denim; Mother had always criticized Social Workers for wearing jeans. "I'm grateful for your concern," she was saying. "We always take child neglect or cruelty reports *very* seriously." She closed her notebook. "I think perhaps I should have a chat with your neighbor." She looked at her watch. "Five thirty. Would she be in now?"

"Oh!" I blinked. "I don't want you to talk to *Sylvia* about Roxanna. I want you to bring Roxanna back home without Sylvia knowing. I want it to be a surprise, a nice one. Then she'll stop crying and getting sick with worry. *And* her blood pressure will come down."

"How do you think Roxanna's mum would feel if her little girl was suddenly taken away?"

It took me a long time to answer this. "Shelbie's brushing up her hairdressing skills. She'd be pleased because she'd have more time to practice in the salon."

"I see." Gail Dawson's eyebrows rose slightly. "How do you think Roxanna would feel?"

I looked out of the window at the neat, straight lines of Trevor and Sylvia's hedge and thought about Roxanna. "Excited, because Sylvia would buy her pretty clothes and take her to Animal Arcadia. That's where I'm a volunteer," I added, glancing at the bushy eyebrows again. I wondered if she had to comb them.

Gail Dawson nodded, tapping her pen against her lips. "Would she miss her mum, do you think?"

I considered. "Well…Shelbie scratches her, but it might be by accident." I explained about the claws that were hidden in photos.

"Have you heard of the phrase *Figure of Speech*?" Gail Dawson asked, her voice soft.

I gripped a fold of my sweater. *Stupid! Stupid! Stupid!* I'd been stupid to believe the claws were literally true. But how did people know? I hated Figures of Speech. I'd thought about creating a spreadsheet for them, organized into topics, so I could spot them more easily, but there were so many that even a spreadsheet couldn't keep track. Why did people hide and twist what they were saying instead of just stating the Facts in a straightforward way? I squeezed my eyes shut.

Her voice was even softer now. "What do you think her dad—Josh, is it—feels?"

I thought for a minute, my eyes still shut. "I don't know. He doesn't say much." Sylvia said people having things on their minds sometimes accounted for them being quiet. "He's got a picture of Roxanna on his phone, and his heart is broken and he's in bits," I remembered.

"Does he have any contact with his little girl, Roxanna?"

"Not since Shelbie ran off to live the dream. He *sees* her when they Skype on Sunday evenings."

"Well, let's see how Roxanna's granny feels about the situation." Miss Dawson put her notebook away in a briefcase and stood up.

I got up too. I didn't know what to do with my hands. "Shall I come with you?" I asked. "To explain? Sylvia doesn't know I've emailed you."

"No, no, that won't be necessary, thanks." She smiled and headed for the door. "I always find people open up more when they talk in private, one to one."

This was true. I hated speaking in groups of people. They didn't take turns, and at least one of them would end up staring at me. I wouldn't open up in a group either. I guessed that *open up* was a Figure of Speech.

She shook my hand and thanked me. I remembered to say *Sorry, I must be off* and mentally ticked my checklist. I saw her ring next door's bell and Sylvia answer. Although Gail Dawson had spoiled my surprise by telling Sylvia about it, at least she could still help to bring Roxanna home.

I wondered why Sylvia hadn't thought of contacting Social Services herself. I had gotten something started on my own, something that could cheer Sylvia up permanently and, more importantly, save her life! At the door, I saw Sylvia put her hand to her mouth and look over at me, unsmiling although I gave her a little wave, and Gail Dawson reach out to touch her arm and then both of them go inside.

16.

It's always nice to be appreciated. And apologized to.
—Janice Drapkin,
checkout operative, Asda

a crash outside made me drop the wooden spoon into my Chili Sans Carne. The porch door slammed. I froze. The front door bell rang and kept on ringing. I heard a man's voice shouting. Josh! This might be an emergency! Sylvia might have collapsed with high blood pressure. He might want me to phone the ambulance like I had for Mother. I hurried to the door, my heart racing.

I opened it, and Josh burst through. He slammed it shut behind him. He came toward me, his finger jabbing and pointing as if it were a gun. His face was red, and all his teeth, even the lower ones, were showing. He looked exactly like the facial expression recognition card at school called *Rage*. He spat out his words, a bead of saliva running down his chin. I shrank back and back. He closed in on me until I was flat against the wall.

"You fucking retard!" he shouted, his finger an inch from my face.

My legs were shaking, and I reached out to cling to the living room door. Why was he in a rage? Had he gone mad? Was this a breakdown like the one Mother had had early in her marriage and that she wanted to avoid me driving her to again—although I could not drive?

"Sticking your nose into my business, you spiteful cow!" Spit hung from his chin. "After all Mum's done for you! This is the thanks she gets. *You* snitching on *my* family to Social Services! Well, two can play at that game. You wait till *I* have a chat with Social Services. Report *you* as a nuisance neighbor, you weirdo. None of *my* family has been inside. None of *us* have conned people or pranced around like Lord Muck. If it wasn't for my mum, they'd have taken you away long ago *and* that crazy old bat, your mother. You wait! I'll get *you* moved into a home where you can't cause *me* or *my* family any more trouble! Do you hear?"

My legs folded underneath me, and I fell to the floor.

"Fucking drama queen!" Josh shouted. He stormed to the front door and slammed it behind him.

When my heart had stopped hammering and jumping about, I crawled to the door and pulled myself up. I put the lock down and the bolt across. The Chili Sans Carne was burning. I went to switch it off. My knees buckled again, and I had to crawl upstairs on my hands and knees. I climbed into Mother's wardrobe, gasping at its smell of mothballs and Je Reviens. I sat there, knees to my chest, hidden by my parents' clothes.

The doorbell rang again. I stiffened. I pulled the wardrobe door tightly shut. Josh wouldn't be able to find me in here. A voice called through the letterbox. "Ellie, Ellie!" It was Sylvia. I stuck my fingers in my ears because I didn't want to hear any more shouting.

I stayed in the wardrobe all night with Mother's blue evening dress draped around my shoulders for warmth. I couldn't sleep because there was so little room and because of the blood rushing through my ears.

Rocking to and fro made the coat hangers swing and rattle against the sides of the wardrobe. Which home would Josh get me sent to? Somewhere I couldn't cause *any more trouble*, he'd shouted. I stopped. Did he mean prison? Was it against the law for me to contact Social Services? I didn't think so, but I didn't always get things right. Would the police come around to interview me like they had done once with Father?

That had happened—I shifted my numb legs—when I was about ten or eleven. Two policemen, one in uniform, the other not, had sat with Father in the study for hours. They'd come around for advice about an engineering firm using substandard material for its bridges. While they were there, Mother had turned off her Opera and made me sit quietly and read my animal book from the Library, although I'd read it twice before. It wasn't even so she could concentrate on the crossword or on reading *The Emperors of Rome*, because I remembered her hunching forward the whole time they were there, hands on her knees, staring into space, not reading anything.

I rested my head on my knees. The residents of Bay View Lodge couldn't get out of the building to cause trouble. Is that where Josh meant? There was a taste of blood in my mouth where I'd bitten my lip. They might move another bed into Mother's room and I might have to live there, with her, forever!

I didn't understand what Josh had said about his family staying outside, or who Lord Muck was. Why was life so baffling? I wiped my face with the sleeve of Mother's dress, hoping the wet marks wouldn't show. I held Father's evening shoes against my hot face. I remembered the smell of leather. Part of Father's smell. The shoes were sleek and elegant. Like him.

Like Laurence Olivier. I slipped my hand inside one. My hand stopped. Something inside didn't feel right.

When dawn broke, I examined the shoe in more detail. The outside looked normal but the inside was shallow. The other shoe was exactly the same, except that it was for the left foot. Both shoes had a hidden space that didn't show outside. I clapped my hand to my mouth. These could be Government Mission shoes with secret compartments! I shook one. There was no sound. Neither could I see any opening. But, of course, the compartment would be so well designed that a casual observer would never spot it. *Observer's Book of Dogs* flashed through my mind because of the word *observer*. That had been a present from Father.

I liked observing things. Noticing detail. Sometimes, when people weren't looking, like on the bus or in the line at Asda, I watched them behaving and listened to their conversations. Copying what they did might make me more normal. Sylvia said it could be useful as long as I didn't invade their personal space or make it too obvious.

I rubbed my eyes. I'd never improve further if Sylvia was angry with me too. But what did that matter now, anyway? I put down the shoes and sobbed. When I was moved into a home, I'd be shut away from normal life. I wouldn't have any social relationships. I'd be the one *receiving* a guinea pig, not giving them out! I'd have all my dinners cooked for me without knowing what they were beforehand. I'd be cared *for*!

———

Josh's motorbike roared off to work at quarter to eight. I crawled out of the wardrobe. My legs were stiff, and I desperately wanted to go to the bathroom. I went downstairs and checked that the door was still locked and bolted. I scraped the cold Chili Sans Carne from the saucepan and put it in the fridge. I didn't think I'd ever feel hungry again. I made a mug of tea and went to bed. The curtains were still drawn from last night. It was just a matter of waiting for someone to come and take me Away.

Later, the doorbell rang and Sylvia shouted through the letter box again. I didn't get up. I wanted to stay *here*, in my *own* home. *My* sanctuary. I didn't go to Asda, and I didn't visit Mother. The phone rang twice, but I didn't answer it. It might be the police, or a Social Worker, or Josh, shouting. I couldn't sleep. I lay there with the duvet over my head. I tried to soften my muscles by breathing out slowly, but they got rigid again as soon as I breathed in. I lay there all day.

Late that evening, I heard something being pushed through the letterbox. After a few minutes, I got up to see what it was. It was a note from Sylvia, without an envelope:

Dear Ellie,

I'm writing this down because I might fly off the handle if I say it to your face. I know it's not in your nature to be spiteful. You must have thought you were doing the right thing contacting Social Services, but you've got things very wrong. I have never accused Shelbie of neglecting or abusing Roxanna. I'd love to see them all reunited as a family. It was wrong of Josh to come around and give you a good talking-to, but he was angry and you have to see his point of view.

Shelbie taking Roxanna off to Spain has been very difficult for him.

Best if I don't see you until I get my head around all this upset.

Sylvia

I knelt on the floor and read it again. The space where Sylvia would normally have put "love from," like she did on her Christmas card, was empty. I tracked each line with my finger. But there was no mention of me being sent Away! No mention of a home! I flopped onto my stomach, arms and legs spread-eagled, face squashed into the carpet. I sat up after a while.

Should I reply? What would be the right thing to do? It was Sylvia who usually explained these things. If I went to see her, she might have to duck out of sight. Should I buy her flowers? Flowers were to say sorry as well as being Tokens of Appreciation. I knew this because when Father came back from trips Away, he always brought Mother a huge bunch of flowers.

Once I'd heard her ask him if they were to say sorry, and what had he bought them with? She'd said they were *an empty gesture* and *too late. The best present*, she'd added, *apart from you acquiring a moral compass, would be you spending time with Elvira.*

I got up. Thinking about Father reminded me to make a note about his shoes and their secret compartments. Another question I didn't know the answer to. Another question there was nobody to ask about. I added it to the Japanese notebook after the others about Father's finances and his empty passport, and who the woman and baby in the photo were, and where Mother's Lost Capacity was, and what Jane from Dunstable had meant by her comments.

The next morning, I went to Asda as soon as it opened. I'd woken at four anyway. It was a Friday, not my normal shopping day. Nothing seemed normal anymore. I'd thought I was fitting in, becoming more NeuroTypical myself, but now here I was, right back where I started, a *weirdo*, someone who got everything wrong.

"You're an early bird." Janice at the checkout counter wrapped the stems of a £4.99 Mixed Bouquet in an Asda shopping bag. "Nice flowers. They'll cheer someone up! Someone's birthday?"

I nodded, then shook my head. "They're a token of my appreciation *and* to say sorry."

"Always nice to be appreciated." Janice taped the Asda shopping bag into position. "*And* apologized to, come to that," she added.

My eyes prickled. When I got home, I put the flowers in the sink and went upstairs and cried.

As soon as I heard Josh's bike leave, I wrote: *Dear Sylvia, I'm sorry for your troubles. Love from Ellie* neatly on a piece of airmail paper that I found in Father's desk. I *was* sorry people were angry with me, and that the upset might send up Sylvia's blood pressure. I didn't know what else to say. I put the note in the shopping bag with the flowers and, dodging under her living room window, left them on Sylvia's doorstep.

I went upstairs to lie down for a while, and then I visited Mother. "You not come yesterday." Maria opened the front door to me, smiling. "First time! Don't worry. Mum not notice."

17.

There's nothing that can't be sorted out.
　　　　　　　—Brenda Cunningham, pet therapist

ylvia didn't reply to my note or say thank you for the flowers. This wasn't *Polite* (Rule One). My next-door neighbors weren't sending me Away to a home, but neither were they speaking to me.

I did an extra load of laundry. *Keep busy when you've got something on your mind.* Sylvia's advice echoed in my brain. While I was hanging out the sheets, I heard her voice in real life. Her French doors were open. She was Skyping someone. Shelbie. I froze, my hand reaching up with a clothespin.

"You don't *believe* what that nutcase next door told Social Services, do you? They won't take Roxie away, will they?" Shelbie's voice cracked.

I stretched up to peer over a sheet. I could see Sylvia's head shaking. "I put the social worker right on that one. Ellie got hold of completely the wrong end of the stick. The social worker realized that from chatting with her. No, pet, you and me have had our differences—I can't say I liked the way you walked out on our Josh—but I've *always* thought you were a good mum."

"Have you? Really?" I could just see a blurred Shelbie. She seemed to be twisting a strand of her dark hair, her eyes lowered.

I turned a pillowcase the right way out, swallowing. *Pet* was what Sylvia used to call me. I heard sobbing. Why was Shelbie crying when Sylvia was saying nice things to her? *I* was the one who'd been shouted at and called horrible names. I clicked a peg open and shut, imagining clamping it on Shelbie's mouth. *I* was the outcast now. And there was still the risk, if I put a foot wrong, that *I* might end up, not in Spain, but in Sheltered Accommodation. Then I heard Sylvia crying too.

"Oh, pet, all I ever wanted was you to be a happy family. You know Josh hasn't looked at another woman, since…since you left. But you… That property developer?"

Shelbie sighed. "Richie. I don't know. He's losing his hair, for a start." She was fiddling with a strand of *her* hair again. "It means a lot to me, you know, you saying I'm a good mum. Not having mine around. You've always been, like, the next best thing."

"I know, pet, and you've been like a daughter to me," said Sylvia. "Oh no, here we go again. I'll have to get another tissue. I tell you what, pet." She wiped her eyes. "At least *something* good's come out of all this."

I tiptoed back into the kitchen with the empty laundry basket. I started to clear the larder cupboard. All the labels on the jars and cans kept swirling together. I stood on a chair and wiped down each shelf with a soapy sponge. *Something good's come out of all this.* Not for me it hadn't. I wrung out the sponge, feeling the relief of twisting something. All I'd wanted to do was help Sylvia. I'd thought it would be simple. I'd made a mistake. Again.

I still didn't understand exactly what. I banged my head against the cupboard door. Everything I did, I got wrong!

Sylvia had told Shelbie she wanted them to get back together and be a happy family. But—I scrubbed at a smear of dried-on Marmite—Sylvia had often said unpleasant things about Shelbie. *Minx* and *That Girl*, I remembered. That was why I'd thought Sylvia would be pleased at having Roxanna taken away from her. I got down to make a cup of tea, staring at the clouds of steam from the kettle.

I went over to the *Seven Rules* spreadsheet, but all the Rules seemed to blur into one. They weren't the absolute, unchanging, perfect guidelines I'd hoped for, anyway. I still had to constantly flex my brain to try to work out what was happening and why. I shut my eyes, the mug of tea untouched in my hand. The Rules hadn't explained that NeuroTypical people could believe two completely different things at once.

I opened the kitchen window to release a small fly. Voices came from next door again. This time, it was Trevor and Sylvia and Josh, shouting.

"You *told* Shelbie that Social Services came around to check up on her! I can't fucking believe it!"

"Watch your language when you speak to your mother."

"I'll use whatever fucking language I fucking well like!" shouted Josh.

"Not in my house you won't." Trevor emphasized the ends of the words. They were in the garden. That was why Josh had been able to use a swear word three times.

"Pet." Sylvia's voice was low.

"Don't pet me! This is all your fault! If you hadn't mollycoddled that weird retard next door, none of this would have happened."

I shrank back into the shadows of the kitchen and huddled in the corner by the fridge. I couldn't seem to be any other way *but* weird, no matter how hard I tried. *Retard…* My eyes prickled. I tried to console myself. I knew more long words than most people. And Facts about animals, and about cookies and their packaging. I'd never met anyone else who knew so much about cookies, not when they were first made and who'd manufactured them, and that kind of thing. I swallowed. I would have exchanged all my cookie knowledge for Sylvia being my friend again.

"She's *my* wife. It's *my* marriage. It's up to me to fucking sort it out. Nobody else."

The roar from Josh's motorbike drowned out everything else.

"Whatever's the matter?" Brenda sat next to me, holding Goldie, her brightly colored face showing either *Concern* or *Sadness*. I hadn't felt like going to Pet Therapy, but I didn't want the guinea pigs to think I'd abandoned them.

I tried to explain. I had to clasp my hands together to stop myself from twisting my sweater.

"Dearie me. Well, there's nothing that can't be sorted out, is what I always say." Brenda got a little brush out of her pocket and began to brush Goldie. "Did you *mean* to upset your neighbor?"

"No!" I didn't even need to think about the question. "No, I thought I was *helping*."

"And have you said sorry?" Brenda turned Goldie around to brush her other side.

"I wrote *Sorry for your Troubles*." I told Brenda about the Asda Mixed Bouquet.

"Mmm." Brenda stopped brushing. "Let's have a think." Goldie began making a bubbling sound, which I knew—from the Library printouts and my online research and Brenda herself—meant contentment. Geraldine joined in. It was a soothing sound.

Brenda tapped my arm with the guinea pig brush. "Write something a bit more personal. Say you were trying to help. And you're upset yourself. That would sound more...caring."

Would it? How did she know? I'd thought flowers and a note would be enough. I considered. What Brenda said was true; I *did* feel those things. I reached out to stroke Goldie. It was a long time since I'd given Brenda a new guinea pig Fact. Not since I'd started at Animal Arcadia, working with larger, rarer animals. I told her one now: the world's oldest guinea pig had lived to be fourteen years, ten months, and two weeks old.

"Josh! Josh! Are you there, son?" Trevor called.

The cherub clock chimed nine. I pressed Save. I was trying to write something *more caring* to Sylvia.

"Joshie!" I heard Sylvia's voice.

I went into the kitchen without putting the light on and opened the window a crack. I hadn't heard Josh's bike today. I opened the window wider.

"He's gone off to Spain, Trev. Gone to snatch Roxanna!" Sylvia's voice rose higher. "Or he's taken that twenty thousand pounds he saved and headed somewhere like Australia. Or he's had an accident! He was that upset. I can't bear to think about it, Trev."

I closed the kitchen window. Had Josh gone to Spain because I'd contacted Social Services? I'd thought Josh and Shelbie's marriage was over, not that he'd go off to find her. Why didn't people say what they meant? Why didn't they just say *I'm cross because...*

and then give the reason? If they did that, I wouldn't get so many things wrong. I got out a bowl and measuring cup for tomorrow's porridge. I let the water run, watching it overflow the cup and trickle down the sides. I added the water to the oats and put it in the fridge. Presoaking oats saved cooking time. It was Maximum Efficiency. It was about the only thing I *was* doing right.

The white space of the *Seven Rules* checklist column caught my eye as I closed the fridge door. It was a long time since I'd ticked it. I knew, somehow, that not following Rule Seven (Rules change depending on the Situation and the Person you are speaking to) was why I'd gotten things wrong. Nor had I kept to Rule Four (You learn by making Mistakes), because I hadn't learned anything! Only that mistakes were painful, and I knew that already.

"You OK, then?" Paul asked, dragging a chair out with a scrape that set my teeth on edge.

The warmth of the café was making my eyes close. I hadn't slept well since the night Josh stormed over to my house. "Tired."

"Does Karen make you work really hard?" Paul took a gulp of Coca-Cola and wiped his mouth with the back of his hand.

I looked at the looping white letters on the can. Mother hadn't approved of Coca-Cola—*full of sugar and chemicals*—and had once put a penny in a glass of it, bought for educational purposes, and left it there overnight. In the morning she'd fished it out with a teaspoon. The penny had been bright and shiny. *There you are. That's what it will do to your teeth.* When I'd said it looked better, Mother had thrown the glass's contents, a brown arc, into the sink and demanded to know if I wanted *my* teeth stripped of enamel.

"No," I answered Paul's question. "It's because I've upset my neighbor. I worry about it when I'm going to sleep."

"When I'm worried, I can't sleep either." Paul blinked. I could see smudged fingerprints on his glasses. "I worry about wolves dying out and whether my wood mouse will survive and if I'll ever have a girlfriend. I like Kate Humble from *Springwatch*. I wrote to her asking if she'd like to go out with me because we're both interested in wildlife, but she wrote back—actually, the BBC Press Office wrote back—and said she already had a partner. I only like blonds," he added.

My hair was brown. Although I liked David Attenborough, he was old, like a grandfather, and I'd never thought of going out with him. I hadn't thought of going out with anybody. A boyfriend would mean extra housework and cooking and not being able to watch the TV programs I liked, although he might mow the lawn. The gardener from across the road hadn't come back, but there was always the risk that some other man might want me to pay him to do it.

Mother had said a boyfriend would not be sensible because of my Condition (*You can barely look after yourself, Elvira, let alone someone else*), and Father had said *Young men are only after one thing*, leaving it to Mother to hiss *Sex*. (Then she'd added, looking at Father, that *he* should know. But, I wondered, if he *had* known, why hadn't he answered?)

I finished my cup of tea. Paul didn't mind gaps in conversations. Usually, people filled up the silence or stared or said *Did you hear what I said?* in a loud voice. Paul just swallowed his Coke and waited. He didn't stare at me while *I* was talking, and I didn't look at him while *he* was talking. He didn't laugh at me when I made a mistake. If everyone was like Paul, it would be easy to fit in.

I looked at my watch and got up, partway through Paul's account of wolves being reintroduced to the National Parks of America. Once he started to tell you something, he only stopped if you actually got up and walked away. As soon as I left the café, Sylvia returned to my mind, a collapsed hollowness at the back of it.

At home, I printed out the note I'd written to her:

Dear Sylvia,

I wanted to help you because you have helped me a lot. I wanted your blood pressure to stop bubbling. I asked Social Services to get Roxanna to live with you because you missed her, but Miss Gail Dawson said there were other people's feelings involved and they would feel hurt. I do not like hurting people. I am sorry that I have got things wrong and that I have not helped you. I would like to be your friend again.

Love from Ellie

I put the note in an airmail envelope and crept next door, where I weighted it down with a stone. I felt sorry for it lying there, alone and vulnerable, on Sylvia and Trevor's doorstep. I tiptoed home, my fingers crossed that I hadn't written something that would make Sylvia angrier.

In bed, I crossed my first toe over my big toe as well. I could only do that with the left foot because, as Sylvia said, I wasn't very flexible.

18.

It's never a good idea to get involved in other people's private business without checking first.
—Mrs. Sylvia Grylls, neighbor

I was lifting Mother's African figurines by the slender legs to dust beneath each one when I heard a sound. Looking up, I saw Sylvia and Trevor coming out their front door. She bent down. There was a snail crawling over my envelope. Trevor made as if to throw the snail into my garden, but Sylvia stopped him. He swung his arm round and round and hurled it over their rear fence like a cricketer.

Father had watched cricket on TV when he was At Home. When I was young, Mother had watched it with him, the *Daily Telegraph* crossword on her lap, shaking her head and saying, *They just make up the rules as they go along.* I felt that too, and not just with cricket.

Father used to play cricket for the Sandhaven Second Eleven. He'd organized the Cricket Club Dances. Mother had worn her midnight-blue evening dress to them with her Je Reviens perfume. She'd had to go, even though, as she said to Father, the diamonds on her blue evening glasses flashing, the other people were *boors and charlatans, like all your acolytes.* I'd looked up all three words. I often had to use a dictionary to find out what Mother meant. None of the words had been nice things to say about Father's friends, I thought now, thinking of Rule Six (It's better to be too Diplomatic than too Honest).

"They won't want to speak to me," Mother had continued, "and those who do will ask awkward questions. Especially if their checks have bounced." I'd known checks were a safer alternative to cash, but I'd been surprised they had a rubbery quality, and that Mother was not looking forward to conversations. I hadn't realized *she* found them difficult.

Mother had sighed and rolled her eyes as she put on her dress, and talked of *ostracism*, which I also had to look up, and it all being Father's fault, even though Father always looked forward to conversation. He'd been good at talking to people. *Gift of the gab*, someone said he had. *A born salesman.* Someone else—a woman—had called him a *sweet-talker.*

Sylvia put the letter in her leopard-skin handbag, and they drove off. I shook out the duster, wanting to run outside and shout to her to open it.

Welcome, Ellie, the computer flashed up. I was Googling Father's birth date and name to keep myself busy. I needed to look for clues about his secret Government Missions and the other unanswered questions in my Japanese notebook. His lack of finances, and who the people were in his photo, and why his shoes had secret compartments, and what Jane from Dunstable had meant, and where Mother's Lost Capacity was, were still mysteries.

I found *a* Gregory Carr straightaway, an Irish professional soccer player, born in 1991, and another who was a Senior Attorney in America. When I added Father's place of birth, Edinburgh, to narrow down the search, it brought up the footballer again with Edinburgh and Father's birthday crossed out. *No match found*. No clues at all. But then Father had never used a computer, to my knowledge.

I typed in Father's birth date on its own and discovered it had been a Wednesday and a Mr. Roosevelt had been president of the United States. I did learn something about Father, though, because the film *Rebecca* had come out in the year he was born. It had starred Laurence Olivier and Father had looked just like him, except for having a thinner nose.

There was an email from Paul about a TV program, *Whale Watching*, that was on this Friday. Paul kept in touch with lots of people, school friends, and went to the cinema with them. I hadn't kept in touch with anybody because of picking up *more eccentric habits*, and being *safer at home*. I would have liked to have met up with Poppy, who used to wait for me at break times. Sometimes we'd see who could make their cookie last the longest. She always wore a bracelet with little, round, wooden beads threaded on elastic, red ones because of her name.

I covered up the computer and began to cook dinner. I was watching *Coronation Street* when the doorbell rang. I gripped the sides of Mother's chair, a prickle of sweat in my armpits. It couldn't be Josh. He'd gone off to Spain. I crept to the door and opened it, the chain on, holding it ready to slam shut.

A voice whispered, "Only me, pet. I don't want Trev to know I'm over here."

Sylvia! I flung open the door.

"Put the kettle on, pet, I've got lots to tell you."

We sat on the sofa together like we'd done when Mother first had her stroke. Sylvia had brought some cookies I'd never heard of before: Wessex Wafers. They were in a cream-colored package with dark-brown lettering and a picture of a country scene with horses on the front.

A royal connection. Sylvia tapped the side of her nose, a gesture I couldn't interpret, one I'd seen Trevor make when I'd asked him who his favorite politician was. "All the profits go to horse welfare. I bought them at that giant Marks & Spencer in Southampton. Trev took me there today to cheer me up. *Retail therapy*, he said. *Go wild with my credit card.* Only I didn't feel like it. I only bought a couple of bits. Anyway"—she reached out and touched my arm—"I had some much better therapy when I got home. You wait till I tell you." She sipped her tea.

I waited, examining the Wessex Wafer closely. I unwrapped its purple foil and took a bite. Dark chocolate covered a thin hazelnut cookie studded with—I checked the package— sun-dried blackberries from Wessex Hedgerows. It was the nicest and most attractively packaged cookie I'd ever seen. I smoothed out the foil and asked Sylvia for the empty box for my collection.

She promised to keep it for me, then sat back, eyes sparkling.

"My news! So there was Roxanna, waiting to Skype. She had something very exciting to say, I can tell you."

It was a relief that Sylvia could tell me. And that she hadn't brought up me contacting Social Services. Or mentioned Sheltered Accommodation. "How does that make you feel?" I asked.

Sylvia paused. "I'm just going to give you all the details. So Roxanna comes on. I could hardly see her because she's got this huge sombrero over her face and a great big Spanish donkey on her lap. A toy one." Sylvia put down her tea. "I rang Josh's work, after he left. Soon as I found out he'd booked two weeks' vacation, I felt much better." She patted her plump chest. "It wasn't your fault, pet, not really"—she reached out to touch my hand—"and you wrote a lovely note. I know you had the best of intentions, pet, but it's never a good idea to get involved in other people's private business. Not without checking first."

Me telling Social Services about Roxanna being imprisoned *had* broken Rule Seven (Rules change depending on the Situation), Sylvia told me. It wasn't my place to be a policewoman. I should have talked it over with her first, but *now we've put an end to it, pet, and you have to get things wrong before you can get them right.*

Josh had gone all the way to Spain on the bike. He'd brought Shelbie a gold pendant and showed her her name tattooed over *Venom*. "Swept her off her feet all over again," Sylvia said.

I pictured Shelbie, tottering on high heels, then falling over, as Josh whisked around her, a broom in his tattooed arms. "It sounds like a Mills & Boon story I read last year, *Spanish Sunset*."

Sylvia nodded, smiling. "A proper happy ending. Josh is taking Shelbie to the poshest restaurant in Marbella tonight. Spending those savings of his! Remember when he was off out every evening and we thought he was drowning his sorrows?"

I nodded, seeing Father wade toward me in the sea at Lyme Regis. "You thought he might have got himself a Lady Friend," I remembered, "who'd Wipe the Smile off Shelbie's Face."

Sylvia frowned. "Yes, I did think that, briefly. Of course," she went on, "he's only ever had eyes for Shelbie. Anyway, he was moonlighting. Had *two* jobs, would you believe. Did all the plumbing for that block of posh new flats on the seafront. And do you know, pet"—she put down her mug—"he saved every single penny of it. Remember Trev opening a letter for Josh by mistake? About savings?"

I nodded. Josh plumbing by moonlight to the sound of waves, and being paid in sacks of pennies, sounded like another fairy tale.

Sylvia said Josh had saved thousands while he was living with them. Enough, she clapped her hands together, to put down a deposit on a hair salon for Shelbie in the New Forest. *Nearly thirty miles away*, I thought. I leaned back against the sofa.

Sylvia held her mug without drinking from it. "I had a very nice chat with Shelbie last week. In a funny way, it was *because* of you, because of you contacting that social worker."

I hesitated. "So, I did help you, in a way then?"

Sylvia wagged her finger. "Yes. But don't do it again!" She offered me another Wessex Wafer. At that moment, I knew what Mrs. Hulme had meant when she said Mother listening to an Opera while looking at a view and eating a cookie was the closest most people got to Paradise. For me it was here, now: eating a Wessex Wafer, enriching my collection with its rare wrapper, and with Sylvia, my friend again, next to me on the sofa. All it needed to be truly perfect was her to be listening to me relating the history of McVitie's, and not talking about Josh, Shelbie, or Roxanna.

Sylvia put down her mug. "Better get back. Trev thinks I'm looking for bin bags in the garage. He'd have a few words to say if…"

I flinched. If what…? I didn't think his *few words* would be
nice ones. His beard would jut at me as he said them. One more
mistake, and Trevor would be on the phone to someone official
about me. Trevor or Josh.

Sylvia hugged me, and I put my arms a little way around
her middle. "Josh and Shelbie, eh?" She blinked, her eyes moist,
even though making someone a cup of tea was supposed to stop
them from crying. Sylvia had had two cups. "I'm praying they'll
come back here together, and I can hug my Roxanna till her pips
squeak!" I was going to ask where Roxanna's pips were and what
their squeak would sound like, but then I guessed it was another
Figure of Speech. Sylvia said they took too long to explain, and
it was better to just accept them and move on.

Come back here together. Gang up on me, I thought. My stomach tightened. Josh might shout, Shelbie could swish her hair
and point a clawed fingernail, scratch me, even. A girl at school
had scratched me once. Her name was Ruth Pengelly, and she'd
launched herself at me, snarling, teeth bared, hands clawed,
because I'd knocked a waterpot over onto her painting, and
green had run into her sky. She'd drawn blood before the teacher
took her outside. I'd cried, but Mother had been cross at having
to pick me up from school for *a storm in a teacup*, and she'd got
even crosser when I'd cried that it was a *waterpot*, not a teacup.

I stretched up to dust the top of the bookcase, my eyes meeting
the beady gaze of the stuffed bird whose glass case rested on top of
the encyclopedias. He looked down his long bill at me, the stripes

around his eyes like war paint. He was called Jack Snipe. Mother's grandfather had shot him in the Highlands, but I tried not to think about this. We stared at each other, unblinking. "Mother isn't coming back," I whispered to myself. "She would never know."

I climbed onto a chair and lifted the glass case down, avoiding the bird's glittering eyes. I let down the folding staircase to the attic and climbed up, squeezing through the narrow hatch. I faced Jack Snipe's case to a chink of light coming through the roof tiles so he still had a sense of outside.

I turned around, dusting off my hands. The attic was nearly empty. I'd thought it would be full of boxes and trunks handed down through generations of Mother's family.

There were some large, dreary-looking pictures of children with ponies, a set of golf clubs, a pair of tennis rackets, the wicker hamper that had contained the shortbread, our old picnic basket, and two cardboard boxes. I had no idea what these contained. I hesitated, then: "Mother isn't coming back," I said again. I crouched on the wooden floor and peeled off the parcel tape.

Inside one box were some objects wrapped in tattered sheets of the *Daily Telegraph*. I thought of the mummies in the British Museum. I stopped. I was alone in the attic; nobody knew I was here. I got up to check that the ladder was still in place, then knelt down and unwrapped one of the parcels. I let out a long, disappointed breath.

Underneath the wrapping was a crystal decanter. It looked as if it had never been used. Next to it were some crystal wineglasses, and underneath them, in flat, velvet-lined boxes, sets of tarnished silver cutlery, with swirling letters I couldn't read on their handles. There were more glasses, of different sizes, all with stems, and boxes of cocktail sticks and napkins. I rewrapped it all, sighing.

Inside the second cardboard box was a smaller wooden one. I

took it out, weighing it in my hands. But suddenly I knew what it was, and it was like the security light outside switching itself on, illuminating a sudden bright memory of a Christmas more than twenty years ago. I remembered Father taking the wrapped box from under the Christmas tree and handing it to me.

Now I slid open the lid, holding my breath, and gently removed the contents, arranging them on top of the cardboard box. Perfect little items of furniture.

"Made for fairies," he'd said, smiling down at me. A little kitchen table with matching chairs and a cupboard with drawers that opened. A bed with a carved headboard and a little blanket box with a hinged lid. A rocking chair that really rocked and two miniature armchairs. There were no people, or fairies, but that didn't matter. I gazed at them, my toes tingling in my slippers, and then a hollowness came over me when I remembered what had happened next.

Where did you get these, Gregory? Mother had asked, frowning. *Or can I guess?*

I called in a favor, darling. Someone made them in the workshop. Especially for Elvira. Father had put his arm around her. *Isn't that enough?*

Knowing where they've come from, I can't bear to look at them. Mother had pulled away and bent down.

For a moment I'd thought she was going to play with me, something she'd never done, not that I could remember, but instead, she'd piled the little pieces back into their box.

No! I'd wailed.

Now see what you've done, Gregory, she'd said, but it was *her* making me cry, not Father. She'd snatched up the box, stowed it away in the attic, and told me to forget about it. But I couldn't, not for a long time.

Why had she taken them away? What had been wrong with them? Afterward, she'd read to me from *The Thousand and One Nights*, *her* present, and let me eat as much chocolate as I wanted. She'd even let me choose three chocolates from a pink-and-gold velvet box from Harrods, her present from Father. She'd turned the chocolate box upside down before opening it and peered at the label, even asked Father where he'd gotten it, although *Harrods* had been written in big gold lettering!

Now, more than twenty years later, I could examine each individual piece of furniture properly for the first time. I stroked the smooth, pale wood, imagining what it would have been like to play with them as a child before replacing them in their box. On the side was written the name of the man who'd made them. His surname was Gloucester and his initials were *H* and then two others that had faded too much for me to read.

I held on to the box, hesitating, then "Mother isn't coming back," I said—out loud this time—and carried it down the ladder. I put it on top of the bookcase where the stuffed Jack Snipe had been. One day, I might get the little pieces out and display them. I might even put them on the mantel. I might push back the crowd of Mother's African figures, with their spears and animal skins, and put the tiny fairy furniture in front.

RULE 4
You learn by making Mistakes.

Reason behind rule:
A mistake is just a step in the learning process. Everyone makes them sometimes.

Useful phrases:

"I'm sorry."

Hints and tips:

If you're not sure what you've done, or what you should do, ask. You are allowed to ask people to explain and to repeat things.

People are more accepting of your shortcomings if you're honest about them.

Don't be a perfectionist—settle for good enough. Nobody can get things right all the time.

Rule followed? ☐

19.

Feel free.

        —Karen Hutchinson, adoptions administrator,
                                  Animal Arcadia

*H*ello-o-o." Karen drew out the *o* sound, winking. Karen made a lot of jokes. I knew they were jokes because she said, "That's a joke, by the way." I wished everyone signposted their jokes.

I placed the newsletters in a neat pile with the envelopes alongside and the address labels next to *them*, ready to stick.

"You look organized," said Karen.

I straightened the piles. "I like organizing things."

"Wish *I* did. You should see my flat." Karen yawned again. "It's a mess. Too much socializing, that's my problem. Never at home to clean."

"I'm always at home to clean," I said, "except when I'm here or visiting Mother."

Karen looked up from her computer screen. She swiveled her chair toward me. "Did you know there's a music gig here next month?"

I shook my head. I'd have to look up the word *gig*.

"Yeah, *Songs for Species* it's called. On a Friday evening. I might give it a go. See if my fella can tear himself away from his surfboard. If you want to tag along, feel free."

I nodded, a hot rush of bafflement rising. Was Karen's boyfriend really stuck to a surfboard? Was the gig *for* animals? I couldn't imagine orangutans liking anything loud, but other animals might howl along with the music, or bang something with a stick. *Feel free!* Karen had said. Sometimes I *did* feel free. I chose my own dinners. I didn't *have* to stick to any of my schedules. I looked at Karen, wanting to ask her what she meant, but it was like sticking a big sign above my head, one that said *I'm stupid*, and, anyway, Karen was staring at her screen again.

———

Paul kept talking about the *Songs for Species* gig. "Are *you* going, Ellie?" He tapped out a rhythm on the café table with his empty can of Coke. "It's going to be great."

Our table was spotlit by a shaft of sunshine, and Paul's hair shone dark auburn. It was a similar shade to the fur of an orangutan.

I paused. I didn't go out in the evenings, except for visiting Mother when she'd been in the hospital. Paul smoothed out a crumpled poster:

SONGS FOR SPECIES

Benefit Concert to aid the
Wolves Breeding Program

Local Performers Play All Your Favorite
Animal-Themed Music: Folk, Jazz, and Rock
Tickets £10. Bring a rug or folding chair.
7:30–10 p.m. Friday, July 14
Light Refreshments and Licensed Bar

"How would I get here in the evening? How would I get back home?"

"I'm going to get the bus." Paul's glasses glinted in the sunlight. "My dad checked the timetable. There's one every half hour, and my dad can give you a lift from the bus station. Do you want to come with me? As friends," he added.

I blinked. "You can let me know next week," said Paul. "Here…" He got out his phone and showed me a photo of a male wolf that had just been reintroduced to the Alps. It was Paul's dream that wolves were brought back to Scotland and that he'd go up there to look after them. He showed me an Internet site where he could order a kilt.

I sat near the orangutans, at the furthest end of the bench in case they felt uncomfortable with me looking at them, or they wanted the pear I was eating. I'd be with Paul at the concert, I told myself, pear juice trickling down my chin, not wandering the streets at night, which was what Mother had feared me doing if I was left on my own. It had been the reason Mother and Father took separate vacations, she'd said, and then, later, why Mother stopped going Away altogether. Paul would be the first friend I'd ever gone anywhere with because Mother hadn't wanted me to mix with people from school, not even Poppy.

Poppy and I had wanted to go to the cinema together to see a film, a Nature Documentary featuring penguins. Mother hadn't let me go, and I'd run upstairs and slammed my bedroom door twice. Later, she'd said I could go and see it on my own, in the afternoon, as long as I was careful. I *was* careful, but the trip had still developed into an Incident, another one that Mother often referred to.

The film was showing in a Multiplex. It was at the end of the bus route, so there'd been no worries about me missing the stop, and I could see the flashing lights of the cinema as I got off the bus.

What *was* difficult was walking through groups of young people shouting and laughing and eating hot dogs. It had been like the bus station, only worse. I'd walked as quickly as I could, my hands in my pockets, eyes on the ground. There was a lot of litter, mostly Fast Food items. I'd been relieved to get inside the cinema foyer with its twinkling lights and smell of popcorn. I'd found the right line and gotten a ten-pound note out from my wallet, ready.

There'd been two girls about my own age, but even larger, with scraped-back hair and loud voices, behind me. They'd pushed and shoved each other, but because they were also smiling, I'd known this was rough-and-tumble, not fighting. It was sometimes difficult to tell the difference.

One had spoken to me. "You here for the penguins then?" and I'd frozen, which was appropriate, given that the film was set in the Antarctic. It should have been obvious from the line I was in! I'd just nodded.

She'd said they were too, which was also obvious, and that they both loved penguins, but their favorite animals were cats, especially kittens, and what was mine? She'd had a rough voice and stood practically touching me, while her friend hung back and ate a bag of Tesco Salt and Vinegar Chips. It had been nice of her to chat to a stranger in a line and to be interested in my favorite animal. (Dogs.)

I'd stuttered when I bought my ticket and heard someone say, "P-p-p-p-pick up a penguin," and someone else say, "No thanks, mate."

A young man in a maroon uniform, with a badge that said *Cinema Staff,* arrived to direct the line. For some reason, the girls had run off, although they were at the front of it by then. The chip bag had fallen to the floor and become litter.

I'd found my seat. I'd enjoyed the film and laughed along with the rest of the audience. I don't normally understand jokes.

It was still light when I got home. I'd rung the doorbell—I wasn't allowed my own key until I *could be trusted to look after it*—and begun to tell Mother new Facts about penguins.

It was only when I took off my jacket that I realized my wallet was missing. I hadn't dared tell Mother but she guessed at once because I'd stopped talking. I sometimes thought Mother should have been a detective.

She'd thrown down her crossword and rung the cinema and the bus company. My wallet hadn't been handed in. I'd had to *go through* my steps with Mother, and when I mentioned the two girls behind me, she'd said, *Well, there're your culprits.* I'd thought

they wanted to be my friends. I had been *naive and careless* not
to have noticed them stealing from me.

I'd run upstairs and thrown myself on the bed and sobbed
because I'd made a stupid mistake, and I hadn't been so interested in penguins after that. The next day, Mother had bought
me a new backpack, a red one, with a zipped pocket on the inside
to keep my wallet in.

Now I was watching *real* animals, and going to a concert with
a *real* friend. That was Paul.

BBC2 warned that Wimbledon Tennis Fortnight was coming
and advised stocking up on strawberries. I took a large basket to
Mother so we could watch the matches together. There was a knot
in my stomach. She might not realize I was there. She often didn't.

I switched on the TV. The familiar tennis theme song burst
out, and the screen was filled with the commentator Sue Barker,
standing with a microphone against a bright-green tennis court.

Mother opened her eyes and turned her head. Two muscular
young men in dazzling white shorts leaped about the court, hit-
ting the ball with loud thwacks. She sat upright, her eyes tracking left to right. Should I switch off her iPod so she could hear
Sue Barker? I reached toward her cardigan pocket. "Not that
way," she said before I got there. My hand shot back. It was the
first time she'd spoken in months.

Mother took a strawberry and put it in her mouth, whole.
She picked up another one, her eyes still following the tennis
ball. I looked at her, remembering how, at home, she used to
explain the scoring system, and how to pronounce all the players'
names, and who'd won the Championships and in what year.

I took some strawberries in for the guinea pigs too. Fruit was good for them because of the Vitamin C. Mother would have been interested in this, or may have known it already, of course.

I thanked Brenda for her advice about Sylvia, and her pink cheeks got pinker, which I interpreted as embarrassment rather than overheating. NeuroTypicals had a strange reaction to getting compliments and presents. My toes would have bounced or, if I was at home, I would have run around the room.

Brenda stood up. "Now, Ellie, if you can collect Goldie from Florence… Time to go home, girls!" In the corner, a group of old ladies stirred and tried to get up. Brenda lowered her voice. "It's been a long day. St. Michael's Preschool this morning, then the Hospice, and now here. You need your own tax code numbers, girls," she told the guinea pigs, closing the door of their traveling box.

I guessed this was a joke because they would not be able to remember numbers.

20.

Laugh at yourself before someone else does.
                    —Mrs. Sylvia Grylls, neighbor

*Y*oo-hoo, Ellie!" Sylvia waved. She did a few jiggling dance
steps on the pavement. The rolls of fat around her waist
carried on jiggling after she'd stopped. "I'll put the kettle on,"
she called. "Trev's playing bowls. I've got a bit more news for
you, pet. And it's still good!"

She'd left the front door open, and I went in and sat down.
I guessed Sylvia's news would be about Josh and Shelbie. It
would not make *me* happy, but when Sylvia came in with the
tea, I tried to listen and make eye contact and nod, because I
knew *she* would be. She leaned forward. Some of her eyelashes
were caked together with mascara. "Josh and Shelbie are going
to give their marriage another go!" Her hands and mouth flew
open as if she was producing a rabbit from a hat.

Give their marriage another go. I'd heard those words before,
years ago, when I'd gone to Sylvia's to pick up the richly fruited
Christmas cake tin. Sylvia had said it, and then *Shh!* to Trevor
as I'd come in. Josh and Shelbie hadn't met then. Father had
been Away for a long time, I remembered. He'd left some

kind of paper trail behind him: *bounced checks, unpaid bills, and broken promises,* Mother had said, Possibly it was some kind of treasure hunt.

———

Paul nodded when I told him I'd come to the gig. There was a silence. He sipped his Coke. He took off his glasses and wiped them. "My wood mouse died on Sunday," he said.

I looked at him, remembering Tosca dying, and how seeing the loose threads on the back of the sofa where she'd stood, watching for Father, and the worn bit of carpet outside his study where she'd scratched to get in, had given me a stab of pain for months afterward. "Sorry," I said. If Paul had drunk tea, I would have brought him a cup.

"Everyone else laughed when I told them. Well, not my dad, but here." Paul looked around him. "Someone said, *It was just something the cat dragged in,* and a friend from my old school emailed to say, *It was only a mouse—get over it.*"

My face grew hot. Those people had broken Rules One and Six, *Politeness* and *Diplomacy.*

Paul wiped his glasses. "I tried to save it but it didn't survive, even though Dad bought it a jar of peanut butter specially. Organic. It's good for mice. I've buried it in the back garden. Wrapped in a tissue, in an empty Earl Grey tea box, a small one."

I nodded.

"I've marked the grave with an ice-cream stick. Magnum White Chocolate. It's my favorite."

"Did you write on the stick?" I asked.

"No." Paul put his glasses back on. "I could, though. What could I write?"

I looked out the window. I'd only seen Father's gravestone once. It had a quote from an Opera on it, in Italian. Paul wouldn't be able to fit anything like that on an ice-cream stick.

"At the cemetery, my gran's stone says *In Loving Memory of Beryl*," said Paul.

"So, *In Loving Memory of a Wood Mouse?*"

"Yes, that sounds good." Paul blinked toward me. "I'll do it tonight. I'll write it in black ink. In capital letters." He pushed up his glasses. "It's good that you can come to the concert, Ellie. As friends. Because of me liking blonds," he added.

"You're a dark horse," Karen said when I told her.

I pushed my hair back from my face. It was brown, rather than dark. "Paul only likes blonds," I said.

"Does he now? And do they like him?"

"I don't know." I didn't know any blonds to ask, except for Sylvia, whose hair was dyed.

"I'm going and all." Karen leaned back in her chair. "Matt said he'll come. I had to twist his arm, though."

I looked at her arms. They were thin but muscular.

Karen talked about my "date" for the rest of the day.

"We're just going as friends," I told her. "I don't want a boyfriend because of the extra work."

Karen laughed. She often laughed when I hadn't made a joke. Sylvia said to laugh at yourself before somebody else did, so I stretched my mouth open and made a faint braying sound.

At a quarter past six on Friday, the bus station was full of teenagers clattering on skateboards and leaning against walls, shouting and laughing. I kept as far away from them as I could. The shops were shut, and there were three empty fried chicken boxes on the ground. I noticed details like that. Things like a missing capital letter on a shop sign, or a speck of food at the corner of someone's mouth. I noticed things other people didn't. NeuroTypicals ignored detail. Sylvia did too. She thought that was a *good* thing. She said *I* got bogged down in it.

"Hi, Ellie." Paul was wearing a green-and-yellow-striped T-shirt with a picture of a Womble—Uncle Bulgaria—on the back. I was wearing jeans and my Animal Arcadia polo shirt. They were the clothes I felt most comfortable in. People didn't look at me when I wore them, or if they did, it was only to ask for directions.

The concert was in a field next to Animal Arcadia. There was a stage made of hay bales and a smell of freshly mown grass. We sat on a tartan rug I'd brought in my backpack, and Paul said hello to everyone who passed. "I've got loads of friends," he told me.

The music was loud, louder than Mother's Operas. It made the ground vibrate. Paul kept slapping his leg and saying, "I know this one." I didn't recognize any of the songs, even when Paul showed me the program. There was one from a Monkees tribute band—it was a pity about the spelling mistake—and one about a gorilla, in French, from an unshaven man with a guitar. A band called The Animalz (I worried, again, about the spelling) played another. I *did* recognize a piece played by a group of girls with long blond hair. *Peter and the Wolf.* When I was a child, Father used to prowl about to it, making his hands into pointed ears and throwing back his head and howling to make me laugh.

Paul went to buy a Coke in the intermission.

"Hey, Ellie!" There was a thud as someone dropped down beside me. I shrank back. "Didn't mean to make you jump. Remember me? Mark from the volunteers' training?" He stuck out his hand.

I shook it, which was the correct thing to do, but Mark kept hold of my hand, which wasn't. Now it felt slippery with sweat. He laughed as he released it and held out a bottle of beer.

"Fancy a swig, Ellie?"

I shook my head. Him being completely bald at the front, with short hair around the sides, didn't match his smooth, young-looking face.

"You're not here on your own, are you?"

"No." I kept my eyes on the rug. It had a threadbare patch in the middle from past picnics.

He laughed. "Who *are* you with then?"

"I've come with Paul. It's not a date." I glanced at his ear. The lobe had a hole where a stud had once been.

"Yeah? So, how are you getting on then?" Mark tipped back his head and drank from the bottle.

Did he mean now, at the concert, or at Animal Arcadia, or At Home without Mother? Did he mean *getting on* with the job or *getting on* with people? I had no idea.

"All right, thank you," I said, twisting a fold of the rug.

"Making tunnels and lookout stations for the wolves is a good laugh. I'll be able to give more time to it next week." He took another gulp of beer. "Yeah, work's a bit thin on the ground at the moment so I'll be doing extra hours here. I might see a bit more of you. Which day do you work?"

"Tuesdays."

"Me too. Oh, is this Paul?"

"Hi." Paul's face was red and shiny, and there were dark stains under the arms of his Womble T-shirt. He held a can of Coke in each hand. "I didn't get you anything, Ellie," he said. "I know you don't like Coke."

"Hi, Paul. That was good of you," said Mark, laughing. He turned to me. "How are you getting home, Ellie?"

"I'm getting the bus with Paul," I said.

"My dad's giving her a lift from the bus station." Paul sat down with a thud, dropping one of the cans.

Mark laughed again. I didn't know why he kept laughing.

"See you around then, Ellie. Don't do anything I wouldn't do." He wagged his finger at me and walked off, waving the beer bottle.

"What does he mean?" I asked Paul, but he didn't know either, except that he'd often heard people say it.

⎯⎯

The clapping at the end of the concert hurt my ears. I started to get up, but a woman in a short dress and Wellington boots came on to introduce a Grand Finale: all the performers singing "I Wanna Be Like You." Paul said the song came from a Disney cartoon featuring jungle animals. He knew all the words. *Everybody* knew all the words. *And* the gestures. Paul nearly knocked me over with one. People were all joining in together, whooping and laughing. I sat there, not knowing how to. Noise enveloped me. Even the earplugs from my backpack couldn't stop it battering at my brain.

I stood up. I wanted to tell Paul I'd meet him at the bus stop, but I couldn't get the words out and he wouldn't have heard me anyway. He was waving his arms to the music, his mouth wide open. I walked off as fast as I could, weaving around the chairs and the spread-out rugs and the audience all singing and making the same movements together. Once there was some clear space, I began to run.

21.

Doing something new is a learning experience.
　　　　　　　　—Mrs. Sylvia Grylls, neighbor

*I*t was dark, and I stumbled on the uneven ground. Above the fading music, I heard my footsteps thudding on the grass and, as I got farther away, my heart pounding. Stopping to catch my breath, I could see people still swaying to the music and hear shouts and cheers and laughter. Being in the middle of it had been like being inside a switched-on washing machine. What I would *imagine* one would feel like.

I headed for the blacker darkness of the trees that bordered Animal Arcadia. I walked alongside them, breathing in the lovely, familiar park smell of hay and manure. I slowed down as the noise grew fainter. I was wandering alone at night, but I didn't *feel* alone because of all the animals sleeping a few feet away.

The music stopped before I got to the bus stop, but I could still hear clapping and make out the muffled words *thank you* and *wolves*. I looked at my watch. Ten minutes for Paul to get here before the bus arrived. I yawned. I put my hands in my jeans pockets and walked up and down the grass verge. There was the sound of an approaching car. It drew up, and a man with almost no hair put his head out of the window.

"Hey, Ellie," Mark said.

It was the second time that evening he'd made me jump. "Hello," I stammered.

"Your boyfriend's gone and left you, has he?"

"No," I said, avoiding his gaze. "And he's not my boyfriend."

"Gone behind a bush to take a leak, has he? Two cans of Coke, I ask you! That was going it some." Mark laughed.

I didn't understand what he meant. "Paul's still at the concert." I looked at my watch again. "He'll be here in the next eight minutes because of the bus."

"Wouldn't you rather *I* gave you a lift home?" Mark asked, his face and bald head gleaming white in the darkness. "Save you waiting around."

"No, thank you. I've got a bus pass." I hunched myself into my jacket.

Mark laughed again. "Let me at least give you…" He switched off the car engine and got out. He came very close. He was a lot taller than me. He smelled of beer. What was he going to give me?

"Let me…give you"—his words were slurred—"a little good-night kiss." He bent over me. I shrank back against the cold plexiglass of the bus shelter. Was this because we both worked at Animal Arcadia? But Paul didn't kiss me. Was *this* what happened after gigs? Or when people met at night? Was this the *trouble* Mother and Father had been afraid of—because I felt afraid now.

Mark grasped my face with one hand and pulled my shoulders to him with the other. It hurt. "Relax," he said. "I'm not going to hurt you." He kissed my cheek. His skin felt like sandpaper. "Ever had a proper kiss?" he asked.

Father had kissed me, but he'd never pulled me to him or held my face. Mother had kissed my cheek before and after going on vacation. Tosca licking my face had felt like kissing. I couldn't answer Mark's question without a lot of thought, and he didn't give me any time to think because he fastened his mouth to mine like the suckers of the octopuses (*octopi*, Mother would have said, frowning) David Attenborough featured in *The Blue Planet*.

There was a taste of beer and salt, and then Mark forced something into my mouth. Something strong and muscular. A tentacle, I thought, but no, it was his tongue! I tried not to gag because of *Being Polite and Respectful*. Was *this* a proper kiss? A mouth sucking on mine and a tongue pushing in? There would be germs. Is this what boyfriends and girlfriends did? What you did when you were married? Did you *have* to do it?

The proper kiss lasted a long time. I could hardly breathe, and my jaw ached. Mark removed his tongue but instead of him saying good night, his hands slithered downward and he began to feel my body. What was he looking for? He wasn't a doctor. He was a *carpenter*. I tried not to squirm because he was being friendly. I froze instead, my body rigid. Someone, who was not *me*, was touching *my* body.

"Ellie, Ellie," Mark panted.

Above his heavy breathing I could hear the sound, growing louder, of someone singing.

Mark dropped his hands.

Ooh-bi-doo, I wanna be like you…

Paul!

I scrubbed my mouth on the bus and spat into a tissue from the Safety Kit. My legs were shaking. I felt the same sick feeling as when I lost things.

Paul didn't stop talking about the concert. "You missed the best bit, Ellie. We got to the end of "I Wanna Be Like You," and then we sang it all over again—from the beginning! It was magic! You needn't have worried about missing the bus, you know. There was plenty of time."

"It wasn't that," I said. "It was the noise and the crowd. I didn't know a gig would be like that." I twisted a fold of my sweater... *Sweater!* I heard faintly, and I took my hand away. I rubbed at my mouth again.

"Yeah. I'd forgotten it was all new for you. I've been to a lot of gigs. Watched loads of bands." Paul leaned back in the bus seat and listed their names and the dates and places where he'd seen them. His stream of words and the way he thumped about on the bus seat, reenacting the best bits of shows, drilled into my brain.

I looked at my watch. Paul had been talking for much, much longer than two minutes. In thirty-seven more, I'd be home. Alone. Quiet.

Paul's dad looked like Paul, only fatter and with gray hair.

"All right, kids?" he asked as we got into the car. "Hello, Ellie. Had a good time?"

"Yeah!" Paul smacked his hand against his dad's outstretched one. "Ace! Loads of people. Eleven songs *and* an encore! We sang 'I Wanna Be Like You' twice."

"What about you, Ellie?" Paul's dad asked.

I clenched my hands. I'd rehearsed a conversational phrase about cookie packaging (*I would be interested to hear your views on cellophane*) to use on Paul's dad, but I didn't feel like talking now. "What about me?" I asked. My face grew hot. I sounded *rude and challenging*.

"Did *you* enjoy it?"

"No, thank you. No, I didn't."

"*Didn't you*, Ellie?" Paul turned to me, his eyebrows raised, his open mouth glistening in the light from the streetlamps.

I shook my head, tears prickling.

"Had you been to anything like it before?" Paul's dad asked.

I didn't have to make eye contact; his back was to me because he was driving. "No," I said. "I've led a sheltered life." Sylvia had explained that had nothing to do with Animal Rescue Centers or Sheltered Accommodation, but meant I hadn't left my own home much without Mother supervising, and I'd never worked or had friends.

My life was getting less sheltered now I had the computer and the website and Animal Arcadia and I could watch *Casualty* without Mother criticizing it. But sometimes, like tonight, I would have liked the sheltering back.

Paul's dad nodded. He didn't laugh. "It takes time to get used to new experiences. To take it all in."

"Yes, it does," I said. "How did you know that?"

"I suppose because I've lived with Paul for a long time. Because I'm his dad."

"Yo, Dad, high five." High five meant smacking the open palm of your hand against another person's outstretched hand. It was a friendly gesture, Paul's dad said. Paul's dad couldn't reach Paul's stuck-out hand because he was driving, and I didn't feel like touching anybody.

I had a shower, the second of the day, and put my clothes in the laundry basket even though the jeans had been clean that morning. I brushed my teeth for four minutes by the electric toothbrush timer instead of two. I bolted the front door and left a light on downstairs.

I lay in bed in a clean nightie, shuddering at Mark's mouth clamping on mine and his hands exploring my body. He might want to kiss me again. He might want to be my boyfriend, even though I didn't want one. I didn't want one even more now. Telling him would be *honest*, rather than *diplomatic*, though. And how *could* I tell him anyway, when I couldn't even get out the words for a simple conversational phrase?

"Pet!" Sylvia called from her lounge chair. She was fanning herself. "Hello, pet. Shelbie and Roxanna are coming back, day after next. We're having a welcome home barbecue. I'd like you to come, pet." She squinted up, shading her eyes. "I know we've all had our moments, but I want us all to get on. We're neighbors, aren't we? And friends."

My stomach lurched. I hesitated, remembering Josh's shouting, and Sylvia calling Shelbie *pet* instead of me. Then I nodded, remembering politeness. "Thank you."

She flopped back onto the lounge chair and asked me how my night out had gone. I grimaced, feeling the suffocation of Mark's tongue. Not Everyone who is Nice to me is my Friend (Rule Five) leaped out at me. Had Mark been nice? I wasn't sure. I wanted to tell Sylvia about him, to ask her if he could just *make* himself my boyfriend, but I couldn't find the right words. I didn't know *what* I felt. I muttered, "It was too loud." Which was true.

"Never mind, you went." Sylvia looked at me and wiped a bead of sweat from her upper lip. "You did something you hadn't tried before. It was a learning experience."

I wasn't sure what I *had* learned, except that I didn't like gigs or kissing.

22.

Anything might happen.

—Gregory Carr (Father)

There was another postcard for Father. His *Harrods* magazine and Fine Wines catalog had stopped coming but here was someone else, or perhaps Teddy, or "D" again, still writing to him.

It was from Spain, with a picture of a bright-blue sea and white high-rise buildings. *Greetings from the Costa Brava* it said. The other side was written in a mixture of capital letters and small ones. There were two spelling mistakes and a blotch of something yellow and greasy just under our address:

Greggy, mate, long time no Sea. Lads are having a Get toGether. sep 9th. My place. try and mak It if you can.

your old mate Tel

I felt sad for Father missing a party Abroad because of being dead. He'd liked parties, although we hadn't had one in our house since I was small. Father had been the life and soul of them. I put the postcard with the others in the Japanese notebook.

———

Kim put a feeding cup of coffee beside Mother. "Oh, Elvira"—I could smell cigarette smoke on her breath—"Mrs. Hulme wants a word with you." My feet prickled. *I want a word with you* was what Mother used to say when I'd done something wrong, like not screwing the lid of the toothpaste tube back on tightly enough. Sometimes Father had whispered, *Sorry, darling, your mother wants a word*, and it would be the same kind of thing. It had been always more than *one* word.

At school once, a teacher had *wanted a word* with me. My stomach had knotted and I couldn't eat my lunch, but it had only been to ask if I could go on a school trip to the Science Museum in London. I'd wanted to go, and Poppy and I had been going to sit next to each other on the bus, but Mother had feared me learning *further unusual habits*, and Father had worried I'd get lost: *Anything might happen, darling.* I'd run upstairs to my room, and that had been one of the occasions when Mother had said I was *rude and challenging*.

———

Mrs. Hulme pulled the fabric of her uniform away from her body. "Too hot for me. Especially in a nylon uniform." She looked stuffed into it like a sofa. Her *word* was about Mother's birthday. She'd noticed it was soon. Bay View Lodge's residents were allowed a birthday wish, something they'd really look forward to, and what did I think Mother would enjoy? Bay View Lodge's idea was a bit like the enrichment items at Animal Arcadia.

I stared at a coffee stain on the carpet, thinking. Mother already listened to Operas all day, and she couldn't play Bridge anymore because of her brain being damaged. She couldn't read about Ancient History for the same reason. I wondered about bringing it to life, perhaps hiring a man dressed in a toga with an olive wreath and a scroll, and then I remembered Ravel, Mother's favorite restaurant.

Mrs. Hulme tapped a note into a small computer, an iPad. "Your mother couldn't get there now, but perhaps the restaurant could come to her?"

"They'd have to dig up the whole building," I pointed out. "It wouldn't be practical."

I shriveled at Mrs. Hulme's laugh. The restaurant *experience* could come to Mother. I wished she'd made that clear. Bay View Lodge would set a table up in Mother's room with a proper linen cloth and flowers, and cook her something French. I told her about Jean Christophe and the classical music playing in the background.

Mrs. Hulme clapped her hands together. "There you go!"

I looked at my watch. She laughed again, heaved herself up from the chair, and headed back to ring Ravel to hire Jean Christophe for a Monday night, when the real restaurant would probably be closed. I recognized the rasping sound her thighs made, rubbing together, because mine used to do the same.

Mrs. Hulme thought surprises were treats, but I didn't. Once, Father had come home from Away when Mother hadn't been expecting him, and it had been a surprise. He'd been Away a long time. It must have been to Japan because his skin was pale. If he'd been to Kenya, it would have been tanned. Mother had cried, I remembered, and talked about Father not putting her through *it* again, and Father had spoken about *trumped-up charges* in a husky voice.

I'd put the kettle on, to make them both feel better, but Mother had taken over because of scalding. I'd gone to my bedroom and drawn the curtains and lay down with my eyes shut to get used to Father being there when I hadn't known he was coming.

Now I went to say good-bye to Mother. She looked tiny in the wingback chair, and her cardigan was crumpled. She was staring into the distance, her left hand tapping her half-empty cup, incapable now of taking over anything.

My stomach had felt tight for days. I might say the wrong thing at the barbecue. I might not keep track of conversations, which were always so quick. People might stare at me or whisper behind my back. Josh and Shelbie, and perhaps even Roxanna, might work as a team to take me to the bottom of Sylvia and Trevor's garden and shout and scratch—and Sylvia wouldn't notice because she'd be busy with salads.

I spent hours under the duvet thinking of all the things that might go wrong. Then I made a decision. I'd write what I was feeling on the website for women with my Condition. Someone might have experienced the same kind of thing. It took me a long time to find the right words, but, in the end, there it was on-screen. My first message!

I got up to stretch my shoulders and to put the kettle on. By the time I got back, somebody had replied! A woman called Amy, from America, who'd been to a church social only the week before where people had stared at *her*. One had walked away while she was still talking, and she didn't know why. *Her* stomach had knotted too.

———————

I stood by the landing window looking into Sylvia's garden. People were swarming about the lawn: hugging, chatting, kicking a ball about, playing on the swing. I took a couple of deep breaths, picked up the bottle of champagne I'd bought for Sylvia, and went down.

Once I'd given the bottle to Sylvia, I stood at the edge of the lawn, clasping my hands and looking from one person to another for clues as to what I should be doing. Sylvia brought Shelbie over to say hello. She said it without looking at me. Then there was a silence. Sylvia talked about putting things behind us. I nodded, but Shelbie tossed back her dark hair and started talking about the towels she was buying for the salon. Her voice was high, almost a squeak, and when she did look at me, she seemed to give off flashes of electricity.

I was glad when she went to help Sylvia in the kitchen. I drifted about and looked at my watch. Trevor was prodding something on the barbecue, and Josh was dragging over a propane tank, the muscles on his arms making his tattoos stand out, as if they were in 3-D. I said hello, but they didn't hear me.

Roxanna was on the swing, wearing a dress with a large bow, poking her tongue out at Katie's boys, and calling for someone to push her. I went over; it gave me something to do, plus I didn't have to look at her because I was pushing her from behind. I asked her what she knew about monkeys because Sylvia had told me they were her favorite animals. Roxanna didn't know much about the different species so I told her, listing them geographically. When she asked if I played with them, I explained about the enrichment items, using the sheet Cinta had draped around herself as an example.

She jumped off the swing and ran to Josh. For an awful minute I thought she was going to tell him I'd pushed her too high, but it was to ask him to take her to Animal Arcadia.

"Please, Daddy. Ellie knows a lot about monkeys."

"Takes one to know one." Trevor looked at me over the top of his glasses. He turned a sausage over, and it rolled off the rack into the grass. He looked around quickly and put it back. "That didn't happen," he said, but I'd seen him do it. The sausage lay next to a group of burgers, pink and glistening with grease. I wrinkled my nose. Trevor clapped a hand to his brow. "You're not going to tell me you're a vegetarian now, are you? Not after I've gone to all this trouble."

"I've been a vegetarian since I was sixteen," I said, my voice louder than I'd meant it to be. "I don't eat turkey at Christmas. You've *seen* me not eating it."

"What's a vegetarian, Daddy?" asked Roxanna, tracing the tattoo of her name on Josh's arm. He'd had it done over *Possessed*.

"Somebody who doesn't enjoy a good steak, darling," he growled, undoing a clip on the gas bottle.

"Somebody not in their right mind, if you ask me." Trevor pounced at the burgers with his spatula as if they were still alive.

"*I* don't enjoy a good steak." Roxanna frowned. "I don't *like* steak. I like fish cakes."

"Here we go," said Trevor.

"Do you like fish cakes, Ellie?" Roxanna asked, leaning close.

"No," I said. I stood stiffly, my arms hanging by my sides, my face hot. "I don't eat meat or fish."

"Just grass," put in Trevor. He stared at me. There was a

mooing noise from Josh and they both laughed, although I didn't think either had made a joke.

Roxanna clung to Josh's arm, "*Will* you take me, Daddy, please, please, please?"

Josh scooped her high in the air, her blond ponytail brushing his face. "So, shall we go now, eh? Eh? Eh?"

"Don't be silly, Daddy. We're at a party *now*. *My* party."

"Shall we find a nice cage to lock you up in?" He blew into her neck, making a Rude Noise, and she giggled and squealed. "With just a banana for your tea?"

"Actually," I corrected, "there *aren't* any cages at Animal Arcadia, and the monkeys are only allowed one banana a week because…"

"Hey, hey, shall we chain you up instead, you little monkey?"

Roxanna shrieked with laughter. I wanted to put my fingers in my ears, but Sylvia had said it wasn't polite.

———

"Isn't this nice?" Sylvia beamed, as we all sat around the patio table. "One big happy family." I sat between Katie and Shelbie, watching as Sylvia passed around bread and salads to see how much you were supposed to take. I wasn't really part of Sylvia's family or social group. I had a different surname and lived in a different house.

"When does the salon open for business?" Katie heaped potato salad onto her plate.

Shelbie pulled her hand out from under Josh's. She tapped her nails together, long nails—*not* claws; I felt a flush of shame—with sunsets painted on them. "Got to get the paperwork sorted out first. Sign the mortgage agreement and…"

"You can leave all that to me, Shell." Josh tore off a hunk of bread.

"Well, no." Shelbie looked at him, a frown pulling her dark

eyebrows together. "I've got to know what's going on, babe. It's me that will be *running* the business."

"Yeah"—Josh lowered his knife—"but I'll be doing the finances. Taking the responsibility."

"Look how clever Josh was, saving all that cash on the sly for you and Roxanna," said Sylvia. There was a pause. Sylvia passed around the lettuce, but nobody wanted any. I'd just clenched my toes to ask Katie's husband, who was a quiet person, the Queen's favorite conversational topic, *Have you come far?* when Trevor brought over the tray of meat.

"I don't want those black things. I want what Ellie's having," Roxanna said.

"No," said Shelbie. "Granny got you fish cakes specially."

"Ohh!" Roxanna drew out the sound into a moan.

"I don't want you eating any of that cranky stuff," Josh said.

"Now, Ellie"—Trevor pointed with his fish slice—"vegetarian sausage? Or, let me see, a little specialty of the house?" He winked at Josh. "Grassburger!" He held out a round object, heavily speckled with green.

"Do you really eat grass?" asked Roxanna.

"No, I don't." I shifted in my seat. "No, thank you."

"Well, now you *do*." Josh grunted from beneath his hair.

"Stop playing around Trev, and give the poor girl her burger," Sylvia intervened. "It's Welsh, Ellie. From Waitrose. The green bits are leeks. Don't listen to him."

I copied Katie's clearing of the table and headed toward the kitchen with a half-empty bowl of tomatoes, but before I could get there, Shelbie stopped me.

"It wasn't right what you did to me," she hissed, her black-rimmed eyes narrow.

I looked at her quickly. In the fading light, I could see smudges of eyeliner under her eyes. Her breath smelled sour, like the champagne, *my* champagne, we'd toasted her salon with earlier. We were alone in the garden. My heart jumped around in my chest.

"Sylvia might want us all to be one big happy family, but I don't! If I hadn't had Roxie and a career to think about, I'd have sorted you out—or gotten someone to do it for me!" Shelbie spat out the words, chin jutting. "Count yourself lucky Josh and I are making a second go of things."

I could see she was angry. Saying sorry helped people not to be. I knew this from school and from a note under Rule One (Being Polite and Respectful) even though Shelbie was neither. "I'm sorry," I said, staring down at the tomatoes. It was hard to speak. And why was I *lucky*?

"How dare you say I was a bad mother!"

"I didn't," I mumbled. "I wanted to make Sylvia feel better." I couldn't take my gaze from the tomatoes. I tried to explain Rule Four (You learn by making Mistakes), but she jabbed her finger, with its sunset nail polish, in my face.

"What do *you* know about anything in life? Tell me that."

I put down the bowl of tomatoes to obey her. "I know about orangutans and guinea pigs and David Attenborough and cookie packaging and Delia Smith…"

"Yeah! The sad thing is you probably *do* know about all that rubbish. But that's *all* you know. You don't know anything about *life*. So don't interfere with what you don't understand. Do you hear?"

I nodded vigorously. "I can hear you really well." My fingers explored a tiny hole in my T-shirt. I tried to explain there were actually *seven* Rules, which were all helping me to be normal, but Shelbie interrupted.

"Good," she said. "Now, we'd better get back inside, or Sylvia will think I've been having a go at you." She snatched up the bread basket.

"But," I said, "you have…"

Shelbie had already marched ahead, staggering slightly in her high heels.

23.

We don't always get what we deserve.

                    —Mrs. Agnes Carr (Mother)

*T*hat'll be over and done with now then," Paul said when I
told him about Shelbie. He swilled a gulp of Coca-Cola
around in his mouth.

"I hope so." I chewed a toast crust, then changed the subject.
"It's my mother's birthday next week. She'll be seventy-three."

"That *is* old. *My* mum's fifty-four. Your mum's nearly as old
as my grandparents!"

I frowned, aligning my knife and fork neatly together on the
plate. "They had me late in life. Mother said they'd given up
hope, and then I came along and took them by surprise." I didn't
think Mother liked surprises any more than I did, because of her
being cross when Father had come back unexpectedly.

"What are you going to get her?"

I shrugged my shoulders, sighing. "All she does now is listen
to her iPod and look out of the window."

"Cool," said Paul, tilting the can upright to get the last drops.
"What does she listen to?"

"Operas," I said.

"Oh." Paul stopped smiling. "All day?"

"Yes. All the time except when they recharge it at night."

"You could get her a nighttime iPod then." Paul put down the empty can and belched.

I thought for a minute. "That's a good idea."

"Yo…" Paul raised his hand to meet mine in a high-five gesture. "Sorted out! Hey, have you seen what they've done to the new wolf enclosure? The lookout post?"

I put down my teacup with a clatter. Mark was starting work here on Tuesdays. He was probably in Wolf Wilderness now. Would he come to the Adoption House? Wait for me after work? Did he still want to be my boyfriend? My stomach lurched, and some scrambled egg came up in my throat. He might have another girlfriend now. Him liking someone else made my stomach turn over again with a mixture of fear and what might be jealousy. Whenever I thought about Mark, I felt bad in one way or another.

I wrote out a script of what to say in the shop and bought Mother's nighttime iPod on my own. I'd walked up and down outside the shop for a bit, first, before squeezing my hands tight and going in. I emailed Katie and asked her how to download Mother's Operas. I bought Mother a card with a picture of a retriever that looked like Buster—the *Caring Canine*—on it, some strawberries, and a box of Extra Special Chocolate Biscuits from Asda. They didn't sell Wessex Wafers.

Jean Christophe was in Mother's room laying the Ravel table, while Bay View Lodge's cook was in the kitchen making Onion Soup.

"It's a lovely idea," Sylvia said to Mrs. Hulme. "You're a proper fairy godmother."

I'd seen a proper Fairy Godmother once, in a Pantomime at Christmas. She'd had a wand and a sparkly dress, and although she'd been old, she hadn't been the same shape as Mrs. Hulme.

"Oh, I wish." She made a waving movement with her hand, and they both laughed.

Mrs. Hulme said they'd had a belly dancer in last week and, no, it *hadn't* been for a gentleman resident, but for a frail lady who'd always wanted to go to Turkey.

Sylvia said "Aah!" in the way people did when they heard other people's bad news and asked Mrs. Hulme to put her name on Bay View Lodge's waiting list *now*, even though she wasn't old enough *or* sick enough, in spite of her high blood pressure, to go into a nursing home.

We went into the lounge. "Happy Birthday, Agnes, love." Sylvia held out a bunch of flowers from her garden—roses, and something with berries, and some feathery leaves. "Happy Birthday, Agnes, love." Mother glanced at the blooms, then bent her head, eyes shut, and sniffed.

"Lovely, aren't they, Agnes? I picked them this morning. Now if it's all right with Matron, *Ooh-er*," Sylvia added incomprehensibly, "I'll take them up to your room and put them in water." She winked. "That way I get a peek at Jean Christophe and his table arrangement."

Mother pushed her card away. I put it with the others on the table. One was from Mr. Watson; one, with a picture of a cathedral on it, was from Jane in Dunstable. *Courage, mon brave*, it said inside. Another, three ginger kittens in a basket, was from the Staff and Residents at Bay View Lodge. Mother hated cats. She said they were ungrateful. Sylvia's card had a picture of Venice on it. The last card, of a Scottish glen, said *Best Wishes from Charlie* and underneath, in brackets, *Charles Hargreaves (Carr)*. Someone I'd never heard of, although our surnames were the same. A coincidence, since I didn't have any cousins because of Mother and Father being only children.

I unwrapped Mother's present for her. She hadn't always liked the presents I'd bought. She'd said an unusual cookie tin, in the shape of a steam engine, with Royal Scot cookies inside, was tacky, and when I'd bought her a pink bottle of Extra Special Fragrance from Asda because her Je Reviens was nearly finished, I'd found it, only a week later, not yet opened, in the recycling bin.

I dangled the white headphones of the new iPod. Mother's gaze wandered toward me, her eyes widening behind her slipping glasses. She touched the iPod's smooth aluminum surface and then slowly reached into her cardigan pocket and felt for the other one.

Sylvia popped back to say we were in for a real treat. I showed her the Scottish birthday card. "Do you know who Charles Carr is? Is he a distant relation of Father's?"

Sylvia put on her glasses and peered. She dropped the card, and then put it behind the others. "Not anyone I've ever met, pet." She had to dash off because Mrs. Hulme came in to take Mother upstairs in the lift.

I could hear classical music as I went upstairs. Jean Christophe, smiling, in white jacket and black bow tie, stood in Mother's doorway. Behind him, two large black-and-white photos of musicians had replaced Mother's shipwreck paintings. He bowed and ushered me inside.

"How are you, Mademoiselle Elvira?" he asked.

"I'm fine, thank you. How are you?" I replied.

"I'm very well. Thank you for asking."

I felt a little rush of joy at the words being exactly the same as before.

"Here we are, Agnes. Surprise!" Mrs. Hulme leaned over Mother. "Ravel has come to you!"

"Happy birthday! How are you, Madame Carr?" Jean Christophe asked, pushing Mother's wheelchair close to the table.

Mother fixed him with her watery blue eyes, then turned her stare to the table's white cloth and gleaming wineglasses. Sylvia's flowers were in a silver vase in the middle. There were the shining cutlery and the starched serviettes (*napkins*, Mother would have said) that she used to comment on at the real Ravel. People had polished and ironed to get things right for her, and she'd had no hand in cooking, or instructing how to cook, the meal herself.

It took her back to when she'd had servants to wait on her hand and foot. (*Only what you deserve, darling*, Father had whispered. *We don't always get what we deserve, though, do we, Gregory?* she'd replied with a flash of her glasses. Although she'd had to wear thicker lenses as she'd gotten older, she'd still had good sight. This was because *the scales have fallen from my eyes*, she'd said. The absence of scales had enabled her to always notice what I was doing.)

"Not that way," she muttered now, sagging to one side of her wheelchair.

Mrs. Hulme smiled from the doorway. "That's a good sign. We haven't heard you speak for weeks, Agnes."

A good sign of what? I didn't want Mother to start shouting again. Or, I thought with a guilty stab, to recover enough to come back home and be in charge. Mrs. Hulme could just be making conversation. People spoke for the sake of it, I was finding, without there being much point in what they said. They wasted a lot of time.

Jean Christophe handed Mother a piece of paper, neatly handwritten, but not quite like a proper menu, with the things we always ordered. "Might I recommend the cutlet, Madame? It is very tender-r-r." Jean Christophe *r*'s were soft and purring, like a guinea pig's contentment noise.

Mother gazed at him, her mouth slack, but... "Ver-ry good, Madame." He took the menu from her as if she'd spoken. In the real Ravel, Mother used to order for me because I'd get it wrong, and she'd said the French words.

Jean Christophe had chosen *a little white wine* for us. Mother stared at the wine bottle, its green glass, and the white cloth behind it, reflecting in her spectacles. I reached out to scratch off the Tesco price label. I didn't like pretending things, but this was for Mother's birthday.

The Onion Soup came with its little floating island of Cheese on Toast, although it was square, from a sliced loaf, rather than a baguette. Mother's spoon trembled in her hand, but she ignored Jean Christophe's offer of help. He returned with Kim, who stood very close to him. If it had been me, Sylvia would have said I was *invading his personal space*, another thing NeuroTypicals were sensitive about. Kim tried to move Mother's soup bowl but she shouted, soup dribbling from her mouth. Kim told her to keep her hair on.

"*Oui, non de cette facon*, Madame. You prefer-r to be independent, I think," Jean Christophe said.

Kim said *that* was a tactful way of putting it, in her sore-throat-sounding voice. She raised her eyebrows at Jean Christophe and winked at me as she left. I didn't know why.

Mother took twenty-three minutes to finish her soup. I timed her under the tablecloth. Jean Christophe sliced her cutlet—it looked more like a pork chop—and she ate it one morsel at a time. "*Merci*, Madame." Jean Christophe smiled when he took her empty plate, as if she'd paid him a compliment. She picked up the tiny, dolls' tea-set sized wineglass with shaking fingers, drained it in one gulp, and smacked her lips together. Then she sat, head drooping, glasses slipping to the end of her nose, the white headphones of her iPod just visible, as if she was examining the shiny surface of her dessert spoon. She only took fourteen minutes to eat her *Little Fruit Tart*, with its whole strawberry, but without the usual glistening slices of pineapple and kiwi fruit, because she ate it with her fingers.

Afterward, Mother and I sat by her window, drinking coffee and eating Chocolate Truffles. Again I had to scratch off a price label.

"All is clear-red away now." Jean Christophe bowed. "*Au revoir*, Madame, *au revoir*, Mademoiselle. I hope to see you again next year."

"Good-bye," I said then, clenching my toes. "It was marvelous." That was what Mother had always said.

24.

Not seeing much of someone helps you stay together.
—Karen Hutchinson, adoptions administrator,
Animal Arcadia

"I hardly see Matt in the summer," Karen said, gulping down a coffee. "He's always out on that bloody board. He *is* ever so brown, though," she added, folding her arms behind her head, "and his hair's got lovely blond streaks."

"Mmm." I folded a donated towel.

"In the winter, he spends hours practicing maneuvers on a *skate*board. I *still* don't see much of him. Perhaps that's why we're still together." She laughed, and I stretched my mouth upward. It was almost a reflex action now. I'd overheard Mother say a similar thing about Father to Jane from Dunstable in one of their Sunday night conversations. It was only seeing so little of Father that kept *their* relationship civil. That and giving him the small spare bedroom. When I'd asked her why they no longer shared her room, she'd said that she needed more space, almost as if she was still growing, and I'd had to look closely at her to check. She'd also mentioned living her own life, but who else's *could* she live?

Karen sat upright. "Hiya." It was Mark, his Animal Arcadia polo shirt unbuttoned at the top, his nearly bald head at odds with his round face. I refolded the towel, my heart beating uncomfortably. "I've seen you before, haven't I?" she said, "Building enrichment stuff for the wolves? Hammering away."

"Yep. That's me. Always hammering away." He laughed. Sunlight exposed a jagged tooth. He turned to me. If I had been nearer the door, I would have run out. "Hello, Ellie," he said.

"Oh!" Karen tipped forward in her chair. "You two know each other?"

"Yeah." Mark laughed again, although Karen hadn't made a joke as far as I could understand. "We're old friends. Aren't we, Ellie?"

Were we? I'd only met him twice, and neither of us was old. My armpits prickled. I dropped the towel altogether.

"Here, let me." Mark stepped forward to pick it up, his hand brushing mine.

"Quite the gentleman, aren't you?" commented Karen.

"Yeah, that's me," Mark said, laughing. "What are you doing at lunchtime, Ellie?" he asked, his voice low, his gaze intent on me.

"I always go to the café to see Paul, and on the way back, I visit the orangutans."

"Paul? That guy with the glasses you were with at the concert?"

"Yes." I held the towel tightly.

Mark laughed. "So"—his hand touched mine again—"I might see you there then."

"You will see me," I said, looking at the floor, at a whorl of darker color in a floorboard, "because I always go there."

"You crack me up, Ellie. You really do," he said, laughing, showing his broken tooth again. "Better get back now and help out the guys. See ya, ladies."

After he'd gone, Karen turned to me. "Yuck. Creepy or what? I *hate* being called a *lady*." She pouted, her hand on her hip. "Ooh, I'm a *lady*."

But Mark had picked up the towel for me and asked what I was doing at lunchtime. He was interested in me. He laughed a lot, which meant he was a happy person. He'd remembered my name and said we were *old friends*. Those were nice things. If he'd said, "See ya, *females*," it would have sounded rude. I didn't like the way he laughed at *everything* I said, though, or the way he stared at me as if he was hungry. Or the jagged tooth.

———

I sat, hunched forward on the café chair, waiting for Paul. And Mark. I could ask him what his favorite animal was, and Paul and I could tell him ours. But Mark came in with a group of other carpenters and sat with them and only waved at me. I felt uncomfortable, knowing he was there, and disappointed.

———

Sylvia lowered her voice as Roxanna pirouetted around the lawn. "The salon refit's not finished. And there's still the upstairs flat to sort out. It'll be a strain on their relationship. That's what worries me. What with them only just getting back together."

"Why are you whispering?" Roxanna looked from me to Sylvia.

"I was just saying, pet, that Mummy and Daddy have got a lot to think about, with the new salon."

"Mummy's *always* thinking about the new salon. She's always reading magazines about hair and looking up hair things on the

Internet, and staring in the windows of hair salons to see what *they* charge and what color *their* chairs are."

"Chair color *is* important, I've always found," Trevor called out. He was just off to the Club. Sylvia's lips pursed when he told her.

Was chair color important? I'd never thought so before. My head ached. One person's remarks led to another person saying something that didn't quite fit, and then the conversation changed to a different subject, and then somebody laughed, for no apparent reason, and then another person, usually Trevor, started singing. It was bewildering, and yet even Roxanna, who was only four, managed to keep up.

"Of course"—Sylvia lowered her voice again—"Shelbie can be a little bit *too* independent with her having lived out in Spain on her own." She looked at me. "Remember not to repeat that to anyone else, pet. Or Shelbie. That's one of your rules, isn't it?" I nodded, my face reddening. Rule Seven. The difficult one.

Rules change depending on the Situation and Person you are speaking to.

It meant you could say something behind someone's back that you wouldn't say to their face. You could say something unpleasant to let off steam, without really meaning it. In fact, you could be indirect and devious, and nobody would think you were a bad person.

"Ellie!" someone called out. "Don't walk so fast!"

There were running footsteps behind me. It was Mark, racing

to catch up with me. He'd been in the far corner of the café again earlier and had given me the same slight wave as before, this time accompanied by laughter from his friends.

"I've only got seven minutes of my lunch break left, and I always see the orangutans before I go back," I said, turning, but not slowing down. He couldn't kiss me if I was walking. I pressed my fingertips into my palms. I didn't know how to say, *diplomatically*, that I didn't want a boyfriend. "No, thank you" wouldn't be enough.

Mark laughed. His face and the top of his bald head were pink from running. He had made an effort to see me. He came very close, looking me up and down as if he was searching for something.

"You are a strange little thing, aren't you?" he said, panting.

My nails dug into my palms. I remembered his muscular tongue and the ache in my jaw after his proper kiss. "I'm not little," I corrected, staring straight ahead. "I'm five foot six." I didn't say I wasn't strange because I knew I was. I had a feeling someone had said the words *You are a strange little thing* to me before, which was impossible, as I'd never had a boyfriend. Then I remembered I'd read them in a Mills & Boon, *As Tears Subside*. Adam, the hero, a global-warming activist, had said them.

"We were just getting to know each other before, weren't we? At the concert? And then your boyfriend and the bus interrupted us." Mark was walking close beside me. Too close. His elbow jostled my shoulder. "So what we need now is a bit of privacy."

I walked faster, but I didn't have time to think of a reply or about anything at all, because he pulled my arm, roughly, and dragged me behind the bushes next to the orangutan enclosure.

Immediately, we were hidden from view, although I could

still hear the public talking and laughing and, behind us, soft thuds and thumps as the orangutans moved about. Mark pinned me against the wire fence of their enclosure. I couldn't escape. I could barely move. I squirmed and wriggled but he was too strong. The netting sagged behind me, and my body bowed back with it.

"You're enjoying this, aren't you?" Mark grunted in my ear. "I bet nobody's ever paid you this much attention before, have they?" He rammed his tongue into my mouth again. It felt huge. I couldn't breathe. I was choking. My heart felt like it would explode with fear. His hands were underneath my Animal Arcadia T-shirt, in my bra, squeezing and pinching. On the other side of the bushes, I heard a member of the public shout, "Come here! I *told* you to hold on to the stroller!" It was the sort of thing I heard all the time at Animal Arcadia. It made what was happening to me here in the bushes seem more unreal.

I wanted desperately to run, but I couldn't move. I wanted to push Mark away, but he was too strong. I wanted to scream, but my throat was blocked by his tongue. I struggled not to retch.

Behind me, I heard the heavy thudding of an orangutan as it ran across the enclosure. I hoped it wasn't Cinta with Pernama clinging to her. I didn't want them to see me like this and be afraid. Mark pulled up my Animal Arcadia T-shirt, and the wire of the fence dug into my naked back. He yanked at the waistband of my jeans, struggling with the metal button, grunting and pushing me, hard, against the netting. He tugged but couldn't undo them. This was when I was most glad Sylvia had steered me away from elasticated waists.

"Fuck you! Fuck you! Fuck you!" he said over and over again. I heard the noise of a zipper being pulled down. The zipper of *his* jeans. I shut my eyes. Blood pulsed and roared in my ears. I could no longer hear the angry swear words. A grumbling noise from the background rose, then intensified. A huge sequence of bark-like pulses and roars was all around me, so loud and so close it seemed to be coming from inside my head. This was it. I was going to die, explode, disintegrate.

25.

Animals are more reliable.

—Keith Curthoise, Paul's dad

I staggered. I was loose, free! Mark ran, crashing through the bushes, holding on to his jeans. The noise was still there, a long barking roar, close to my head, but not in my head. It surrounded me, fast and whooping, pulsing like a burglar alarm. I heard a small child wailing and a woman saying, "It's just the silly old monkey. He must be in a bad mood." Behind me, loud thuds shook the ground. Rojo, the orangutan, was making the noise!

Karen had told me dominant males made an enormous roar—a fast, long call—when they sensed threat or danger. Mark had thrown me against the netting of the enclosure, and Rojo had been defending his territory. My heart seemed to burst in my chest. Rojo had saved me. I clung to the fence, my legs shaking. I wanted to sit down, but I was frightened Mark would come back. I had to get out.

I stumbled from the bushes, the sunlight dazzling. Members of the public stared. I pulled down my T-shirt. A woman tutted, "So that's what the keepers get up to, is it? I've just seen her boyfriend running off. Disgusting when there are kiddies around. Worse than monkeys."

"You're only young once," a man replied. His bare shoulders were scarlet with sunburn. I wanted to run, but my legs were still shaking. I walked back to the Adoption Center, praying they wouldn't collapse under me.

Karen was filling in Adoption Application Forms for a group of white-haired ladies. They were laughing at a photo of Rojo, taken from the front.

"Ooh, I say!" yelped one.

I went to the box of donated sheets and towels and tried to unfold one, but my hands were trembling too much for me to hold it. I felt like the can of Coca-Cola Paul had dropped on the café floor last Tuesday: an uncontrollable stream of fizzing emotion, bubbles of fear, and shame hissing and splashing everywhere. I felt the old ladies staring at me as if they knew what I'd done, but when I shot them a glance, they were still laughing at the photo and clinging to each other for support.

I looked at my watch. The bus to Sandhaven left in twelve minutes. I was desperate to catch it, although it would mean leaving Animal Arcadia hours before my finishing time. I ached to be at home with the curtains and the duvet blocking out the world. I sat down, something I never did, and waited. I couldn't even stack the envelopes.

Karen was shaking her head, saying, "I don't know, the older generation. What *is* the world coming to?" The white-haired ladies didn't answer her question but shrieked with laughter and gave each other little pushes.

As soon as they'd gone, I asked Karen if I could go home. She looked up from the computer, eyebrows disappearing into her crest of hair. "You mean to say you're deserting your post?"

I nodded. I had to lean on her desk because of my trembling legs.

"Is this medical leave?" Karen asked.

I heard the word *medical*. It was true that I didn't feel well. I nodded.

Karen looked up at me, her nose stud glinting. "You look really pale. Are you going to be OK getting the bus home?"

I nodded again. "It goes in nine minutes," I said.

"Off you go then. I'll email you later, check you're OK. See you back on the front line next Tuesday." She saluted and went back to her screen.

I hurried through the park as fast as my shaking legs would carry me. For once, I was glad there were crowds of people around. They would stop Mark from dragging me away again. I headed for the exit, avoiding Wolf Wilderness. Two keepers were standing, arms folded, looking at the orangutans. Rojo was swinging from rope to rope, the climbing frame creaking under his weight. Above him, Cinta and Pernama peered out from the top of their tower. "Unsettled," I heard one of the keepers say as I hurried past.

At home, I drew all the curtains, although it was the middle of the afternoon and the sun was blazing outside. Was it only two hours since Mark had pulled me behind the bushes? I took off my clothes and put them straight in the washing machine. I'd gone through the same procedure after Mark's proper kiss at the bus stop. But this time had been much worse.

I showered again, standing under the hot water for a long time, wishing I could wash myself away. I put on a clean

nightdress, checked the front door was bolted, and got into bed.
I lay under the duvet,

I got up in the evening and made a pot of tea. I couldn't face
cooking or eating dinner, so I just microwaved the broccoli and
ate it standing up in the kitchen, because the Vitamins would do
me good. Then I went back to bed.

I woke in complete darkness, my heart pounding. I sat up, struggling to breathe, feeling Mark's tongue blocking my throat. I
retched. I ran to the bathroom and got to the toilet just in time. I
vomited up the broccoli. I wished Father was there to stroke my
back and say *There, there, get it all up, darling*, or even Mother.
It was lonely being sick with no one else in the world knowing
about it. I watched the green swirls of broccoli vanish down the
U-bend, then sat on the toilet seat until I stopped feeling sick.
When I washed my hands, my face looked white and clammy in
the mirror, my normally pink cheeks bloodless.

I made another pot of tea and walked around the house in
the darkness. I didn't want to go back to bed. Whenever I lay on
my back, I thought of Mark pinning me against the fence and
retched again.

Mother's eyes flickered briefly when I went to see her. I stayed for
an extra quarter of an hour. I felt no one could hurt me if I could

just sit there, next to her, forever. I wished she'd open her eyes and speak to me, even though it would only be to say, "Not that way."

Mind you, *Not that way* would be appropriate. She would be right. I had behaved in a stupid way. Stupid to believe Mark wanted to be my boyfriend, stupid for not pushing him away after the concert, stupid for not realizing he was a creep. I'd been stupid for not understanding Rule Five—Not Everyone who is Nice to me is my Friend—even though I'd drawn up the Rule myself, and the spreadsheet containing it had been stuck on my fridge door for weeks. *Stupid, stupid, stupid.*

Too stupid to go back to Animal Arcadia *and* too frightened. Mark would be on the loose. He could pounce on me at any time. I shivered and retched again, the noise making Mother's eyelids quiver. I massaged my forehead, wishing I could rub out the whole episode. Except for Rojo saving me. If Rojo hadn't frightened Mark away, he would have carried on hurting me. I'd *never* feel safe at Animal Arcadia, so I'd never see Rojo or Vikram or Pernama or any of the animals again.

I wiped my face with the sleeve of my T-shirt. I'd never wear the yellow Animal Arcadia uniform again either and have the public look at me as if I was important. Karen would lie in a rubble of backlogs. I'd never have Scrambled Eggs on Toast in the café with Paul, or talk about animal programs on TV. All that had gone.

———

At home, I emailed Paul and Karen to say I was OK but I wasn't coming back. Then I emailed Rosemary McAlpine to say sorry and to thank her for her trouble and to say I couldn't be a volunteer anymore.

———

After lunch, I went back to bed. I took a Mills & Boon, *Irish Idyll*, upstairs but couldn't concentrate on the story. The ache in my spine brought back Mark trapping me against the fence. I wanted to tell the heroine, Shannon, not to believe *anything* the hero, Patrick, said, *not* to get into his car and to push him away when he kissed her. In the end, I shut the book without even marking the page and mopped my face with a tissue.

Karen replied:

What's up, Doc?

Have you gone AWOL? The sheets and towels have reached my knees! Surely you weren't that fed up with me moaning about Matt? Is there anything I can do to lure you back?

Toodle pip, Karen x

I didn't understand much of what Karen had written. I emailed her to say I wouldn't be returning, and I didn't want to say why. I put *Love from Ellie* at the bottom because Karen was a friendly person.

Paul wrote:

Wassup Ellie?

Why are you leaving Animal Arcadia? I thought you liked it there. I will miss you even though you are not my girlfriend. Do you want to come to the cinema with me some time?

High Five, Paul

p.s. My dad said we are going for a country walk and

picnic on Saturday. Do you want to come with us? It is not a date because of me liking blonds and waiting to see if Kate Humble comes back on the market. P.

We'd had picnics when I was a child. Mother had cooked unusual things in pastry from recipes in the *Daily Telegraph* and there'd been a lot of hard-boiled eggs. Our wicker picnic basket was still in the attic. I'd seen it when I put the Jack Snipe up there. I could get it down and take it on the picnic with Paul and his dad. I might as well go, since I would not be seeing Paul anymore at Animal Arcadia.

The picnic basket had been an anniversary present from Father to Mother. It had come from Harrods, because Father had an account there. The account came with a special card, a gold one, with *Harrods* written on it in green writing. Mother had cut it up with the kitchen scissors when Father was Away, muttering something I didn't understand about giving brandy to an alcoholic. She hadn't seen me watching from the doorway, and I'd tiptoed back upstairs because of her angry facial expression. I'd seen Father drink brandy at parties when I was young, and at Christmas. I hadn't realized that that could make him an alcoholic.

The picnic basket had neat compartments for everything and a dark-green insulated pocket for keeping a wine bottle cool. The pocket had a gold Royal Coat of Arms because the Queen shopped at Harrods. She'd been there on the day Father bought it, he'd said, but he'd only caught a glimpse of her, wearing a jeweled crown and a red cloak trimmed with ermine, because of all the security guards around her.

We'd used it on our Lyme Regis vacations when I was young, and taken it to Stately Homes. Mother and Father had wandered around these, hands clasped behind their backs, examining paintings and antiques. I'd only liked the picnic food and the peacocks and the lawn-grazing sheep.

The picnic basket hadn't been used for years because we'd stopped going out as a family and Mother and Father's vacations had become separate ones. When I'd asked her where the picnic basket was, she'd snapped, *In the attic with my ruined dreams.* Her face had looked too cross for me to ask what the ruined dreams looked like, and if they were in a bag, although I'd wanted to. Whatever they were, they'd gone from the attic now, because apart from the Jack Snipe and the box of tiny furniture, there was very little left.

"High five!" said Paul, as I got into the car. "Cool basket! What's inside?"

"Scrambled Egg Sandwiches and some peaches. Nearly the same as what I always have for lunch."

"Hi, Ellie." Paul's dad turned around. "Nice basket."

"Yes." I looked at his ear. It was large with a fleshy lobe. "I've brought some cookies. McVitie's Chocolate Digestives. They're the most popular cookie in Britain. And in the space where the chilled wine goes, I've got Sparkling Apple Juice." I showed Paul the insulated compartment. "It counts as a fruit portion."

Paul opened his rucksack. "I've got Coca-Cola, ham sandwiches, chips, and a Mars bar. A big one."

"No fruit?" I asked.

"We're two men living on our own, Ellie," Paul's dad said as we drove off. "We don't do fruit."

"What about Vitamins?" I chewed my lip. Paul and his dad could become diseased.

"You're right, Ellie. Add some fruit to the shopping list, son."

Paul crossed his hands in front of him, like I'd seen heroines do in Classic Horror Films to ward off evil.

There were people walking along the beach, and dogs running in and out of the water, barking. The sand was white and stretched as far as I could see in front of me.

"It's like being on vacation." Paul threw his arms wide.

Paul's dad locked the car. "Are you OK carrying that basket, Ellie?"

"Yes, thank you. I'm quite strong." Not strong enough to escape Mark pinning me against the fence, though. My flesh chilled in spite of the sunshine.

Paul took a ball from his backpack and bounced it along the sand at the shoreline. Two Irish setter dogs ran over, wagging their tails.

"All right then." His voice carried to us on the wind. "Fetch!"

"He'll be happy now," said Paul's dad, shading his eyes from the sun. "He does love his animals."

We strolled along the beach. I felt the sun warming my body. "*I* love animals too," I said. Paul's dad was easy to talk to because he was like Paul. He didn't seem to mind pauses in conversations.

"Yes," he said, gazing over the sea, "animals are reliable, aren't they? Straightforward. Much easier than us humans."

I nodded. "They're always pleased to see you, and they don't criticize. They don't treat you like you're nothing. And they don't *PRETEND*." *Pretend* came out of my mouth fiercely as if it were in capital letters and lit with neon lights. There was a pause.

"That's why I was surprised when Paul said you'd left Animal Arcadia," Paul's dad said, his eyes on the horizon.

There were lots of seashells on the beach, half-buried in the white sand. I bent to pick one up, brushed it off, and kept it in my hand.

"Is that something you want to talk about?" Paul's dad looked at me.

"No." I shook my head.

"All right." He gazed at the sea again. "I won't ask you any more questions." There was another pause. "Just remember, Ellie. People like you and Paul are very trusting." He glanced down at me. "And, well, there are some cruel people about who don't care about anybody else, just as long as they get what *they* want. And sometimes they pretend to be something they're not, in *order* to get it."

I turned the shell over and over in my hand. "You know that, and you haven't even *read* the Rules." I told him I'd gotten Rules Five (Not Everyone who is Nice to me is my Friend) and Seven (Rules change according to the Situation and the Person you're speaking to) wrong.

"It's great you've drawn up some guidelines, Ellie." A breeze fluttered the hem of his shirt and outlined the rounded bulk of his tummy. It was big because he didn't eat fruit. "You see, my brain works a bit differently from yours, *and* I've seen a bit more of life. And, more importantly, I've learned things from being Paul's dad." He stopped. "What *is* he doing with those dogs?"

A collie was chasing after the Irish setters. There was frenzied barking as each dog tried to get the ball. Paul held on to it, dodging in different directions. He stretched up, laughing, and hurled it across the water, the dogs plunging in after it.

"Bella! Beatrice!" A woman ran up, holding a leash in each

hand. "I *told* you not to go in the sea. You *know* salt water mats your coats. Come here!"

"Whoops," said Paul's dad.

The Irish setters approached their owner, thin and apologetic in their wet fur. They shook themselves vigorously.

"Now *I'm* soaked," said the lady.

"Double whoops," said Paul's dad.

The collie raced away down the beach, the ball between its teeth.

"That's another one gone, son."

"I don't mind." Paul's cheeks were blotched pink and white from running, and the hems of his jeans were wet. His eyes were sparkling behind his glasses. Paul's dad put his arms around our shoulders.

"Come on. Time for lunch. There's a stretch of beach over there that's sheltered from the sun. I'm looking forward to one of Ellie's plain chocolate cookies."

"They were invented in 1925," I told him. "Quite a long time ago for a chocolate cookie."

Next morning, I put on clean clothes from top to bottom. For the first time in days, I added a Fact to the animal notes in my Japanese notebook. It was about baby orangutans being dependent on their mothers for longer than any other species, except humans. I had to flick through the unanswered questions first, though, which was always unsettling. It was frustrating still not knowing where Father had been and what had happened to his money and why his shoes had secret compartments and who the woman with the baby in his photo were and what Jane from Dunstable's comments had meant.

I closed the notebook and made a mug of tea, humming. Paul's dad said I knew more about cookies and their history and packaging than anyone he'd ever met. I hugged myself at the memory. Mother had never thought I could be an expert at anything.

When I'd got back from the picnic, I could hardly squeeze in the ticks on the spreadsheet's checklist, there were so many: "Would you like to talk about something else?" I'd asked Paul's dad, realizing I'd spoken for a lot longer than two minutes. (He didn't.) On the way home I'd apologized—"Sorry, my mind was elsewhere"—when he had to repeat a question about *Coronation Street*. Then I'd asked him what *his* favorite TV program was, and, when he said *Newsnight*, remembered to say *That's wonderful*, although it wasn't my cup of tea. I blinked. I had thought in a Figure of Speech. Without even trying.

I took some gulps of tea. Mark must be one of those cruel people Paul's dad had talked about because he'd tried to get what he wanted from me by force, without asking, as if I didn't exist. Karen was right too; he *was* a creep. It *hadn't* been my fault. I'd only been stupid in believing he was nice. No, not stupid. The website said it was part of my Condition to believe people were what they pretended to be. If NeuroTypicals were more like us, there wouldn't be these sorts of Incidents. Or any of the others that still made me screw up my face when I remembered them.

I wrapped my fingers around the mug and thought about Animal Arcadia. I loved Pernama and Vikram, with his engine-like purr and whiskers like broom bristles. But I *couldn't* go back there. Mark had dragged me away without anybody noticing. In broad daylight. I put down the mug of tea. I hadn't realized Mark was dangerous. The same thing could happen to me again. How would I feel safe anywhere?

RULE 5

Not Everyone who is Nice to me is my Friend.

Reason behind rule:

Be wary of strangers in case they lie and take advantage of you.

They may get pleasure from hurting people more vulnerable than themselves because they feel inadequate inside.

Hints and tips:

Don't be too trusting and eager to please.

Relationships take time to develop.

When you meet someone new, ask someone you already know and trust if they think that new person is trustworthy.

If the situation or person makes you feel uneasy or afraid, then it is best to avoid being friends with that person.

Rule followed? ☐

26.

A trouble shared is a trouble halved.

—Mrs. Sylvia Grylls, neighbor

*E*llie! My little leaflet stuffer! How are you doing?"

Karen! I blinked. I'd never seen her away from Animal Arcadia before. I'd almost thought she lived there, except for her mentioning her boyfriend and his surfboard. I swallowed a feeling of shame and nausea. "I'm all right." I kept my eyes on the concrete floor of the bus station, at the marked white lines that kept the buses in their allotted spaces.

"I miss you helping me out, you know." Karen's round eyes searched my face. "And don't talk to me about backlogs."

"I won't," I promised. I shifted the backpack, full of Asda shopping, from one shoulder to the other. Around us, people jostled, steering mobility scooters and dragging toddlers.

"Ellie." Karen spoke softly. "That Tuesday. I think I missed something. You were very quiet when you came back from lunch, quieter than usual. And"—her eyebrows sloped—"you seemed a bit rumpled." She paused. "You had leaves in your hair."

"It wasn't my fault. I didn't want it to happen." I held up

my hands ready to clap them to my ears when she told me I'd been stupid.

But her voice was still soft. "Hey, I'm sure it wasn't. Come on." She lowered my hands. Then her eyes got even wider. "Oh! You hadn't just fallen over, had you? I think I know what happened to you."

How could she know? I hadn't told her anything. I hadn't told *anyone*. I felt a *thump, thump, thump* from my heart.

Karen looked around. "Let's go and sit on one of those benches."

I trailed after her to a little grassed area beyond the bus station where a group of seagulls and pigeons had surrounded a woman eating a sandwich. We sat on a vacant bench. Close up, in the bright daylight, Karen's eyes were very green, like seaweed. Her voice was breathy.

"It was that creepy guy, wasn't it? That what's-his-name, Mark, the one that was doing the carpentry in Wolf Wilderness? Fancied himself as a bit of a smooth operator, didn't he?" Karen put two fingers in her mouth and mimed being sick. I remembered the green swirls of broccoli vanishing down the toilet. "Did he…did he…" Her nose wrinkled, its stud shifting upward. "Did he attack you?"

I stared at a crushed cigarette packet in front of the bench. *Smoking Kills*, it said. I couldn't answer her question. Not without looking up the meaning of the word *attack* to get it absolutely right. I knew Father's heart had been attacked when he died and that some animals attacked smaller animals to eat them, but neither of those sounded like what Mark had done to me. I was still alive.

"I bet he *did*. If I ever see him again…" She touched my arm. "Hey, you know he's in trouble, don't you?"

"No." I stiffened. "I didn't tell anyone."

Karen's eyebrows shot into her hair. "No, *not* for what he

did to you. *Should* have been, but no, this is something *else*. Two things, actually." She lowered her voice, like Sylvia did when she was about to tell me something Private. "I don't know if you know her, but there's a biggish girl, brown curly hair, Gemma, works in the café...?"

I nodded. Paul knew her.

"Well, she complained about Mark to Rosemary. Said he attacked her, groped her in the storeroom... Well, tried to. She kneed him in the balls. Like I said, she's a biggish girl."

I felt a rush of hatred. So Mark had forced himself on *another* girl. Tried to. Why couldn't *I* have kneed him in the...? *I* should have made a complaint, but I hadn't known what I was supposed to do. I felt a stupid, stupid pang of disappointment at there being another girl. I'd thought I was the only one. Special. Especially stupid, more like.

Karen leaned forward. "And there's something else. One of the keepers saw him shouting at the wolf cubs 'cause they were chewing the wood of that lookout post he'd built. Yeah, shouted *and* swore, apparently. Looked like he was going to *throw* something at them. Bastard!"

I felt another rush of hatred toward Mark.

"Yeah, poor little things were cowering."

A seagull flew past us with a piece of tomato in its beak. I bent forward, my head in my hands, trying to process what Karen had said.

"So," she said after a moment, "Mark's gone. Sacked. Good riddance."

An avalanche of information. "They don't want him to volunteer anymore? Not even with his carpentry?"

"Bugger the carpentry. They don't want nasty, bullying perverts like him working for them, do they?"

I shook my head. *Nasty, bullying pervert*, I repeated silently. Mark had behaved badly to Gemma, a NeuroTypical, *and* to baby animals. He'd probably behave badly to anyone if he could get away with it. It wasn't because I'd gotten things wrong. It *really* wasn't my fault. I sat up and took some deep breaths.

"So, will that affect you coming back?" Karen looked at me, her head on one side. "Those towels have reached my eyeballs, you know, without you there to sort them out."

"Have they?" That would affect Karen's breathing. If her airways were blocked, it could lead to suffocation. I glanced up and saw her smile. Figure of Speech. "I don't know." I thought of Animal Arcadia without Mark there, just with animals. Inside me was a tiny flicker of joy.

———

At home, I checked the meaning of *attack*. It meant: *to injure or affect adversely, to corrode or corrupt. Adversely* meant *hostile, unfavorable to one's interests*. My heart pounded. Mark had definitely affected me in a way that had been *unfavorable to my interests*. I'd felt sick for days afterward *and* shaky, *and* I'd cried *and* I'd had to leave a volunteer's job I loved. Gemma from the café, the wolf cubs, and I had *all* suffered at Mark's hands. He'd attacked *all* of us. My fingers suddenly itched to claw and scratch him.

I tore a piece of paper from the printer and wrote Mark's name all over it in block capitals, pressing so hard the pencil broke. I threw the paper on the kitchen floor and stamped on it, my feet scuffing and smudging his name. Then I ripped the paper into tiny pieces. I'd once seen Mother do the same with a letter on pink notepaper with a picture of a kitten in one corner, and then stomp out, not to the recycling bin, which she *should* have used, but to the ordinary black waste bin. She'd thrown the pieces in, and they'd gotten mixed up with some used tea bags.

I tried to burn my torn paper on the stove, but there was a lot of smoke and ash, and the kitchen tongs got too hot for me to hold. I flushed the bits down the toilet instead and stabbed at the ones still floating with the toilet brush. I looked around. I took the half-used toilet roll, unrolled it, scrawled *Mark* on every sheet, rolled it up again, and put it back by the toilet, ready.

I took a huge breath in, stretched my arms above my head, and released the air slowly. Then I went downstairs to switch the computer on.

Sylvia invited me over for a cuppa. Josh and Shelbie were out, being interviewed by a Bank Manager. She asked why I hadn't been doing my volunteering. I held on to a fold of my sweater behind my back. I'd have to say about Mark. I didn't want to go into details. It might make Trevor think I wasn't coping. It might make him think about Social Services. For my own protection.

"Someone was nasty to me there," I told Sylvia.

Her face softened. "You should have come and told me, pet. A trouble shared is a trouble halved."

"I felt too stupid," I said, letting go of my sweater. "I got Rule Five wrong: *Not Everyone who is Nice to me is my Friend.*"

"Ah, pet." She gave me a hug. "That's a hard one to learn. Painful. We've all been there." She nodded at my surprised face. "Oh yes, even me."

She handed me my tea. "That's the real world, pet, I'm afraid. You've just got to pick yourself up and learn from the experience.

Ask me, ask someone you trust, if you're not sure about someone, pet," she was saying when Trevor came in from the garden. He looked at us over the top of his glasses without saying anything, and then I heard him on the phone. It reminded me of Mother's Sunday night chats to Jane. I racked my brain for anything that might make him phone Social Services. I wasn't always aware of what I'd done wrong. The way Trevor's beard had bristled at me gave me an uneasy feeling. Thank goodness he didn't know about Mark.

Sylvia gave me a very wide smile, and then Roxanna came over and demanded we played Snap. I liked Snap. I liked games with Rules. I'd played Snap when I was young, with Father. It wasn't challenging enough for Mother, and she didn't like it when I made mistakes. We'd played it at school, though, with the facial expression cards.

Roxanna shouted *Snap* much too often, without really looking at the cards. It was easy for me to win. Each time Roxanna said, "Oh!" in her long, drawn-out way.

"Let *her* have a go at winning," whispered Sylvia. "It'll make her happy."

I had to press my lips together to stop myself from saying *Snap* first. It was hard, not keeping to the Rules. It was cheating, really. I let Roxanna win the next two games and then she climbed onto my lap, saying she was bored again.

Before that, I'd only held a guinea pig, and Tosca when she was a puppy. My whole body stiffened, and I didn't know where to put my hands. Roxanna put her arms around my neck and said to tell her a monkey story, *now*. Then *Hello, sweetheart* came from the hall, and Shelbie came in, her long, dark hair piled up on top of her head, her bare legs orange.

"Oh," she said. Her shiny mouth stayed in an O shape as

she looked at me. "I didn't know you had company," she said to
Sylvia. "You never said."

Sylvia got up from the sofa. "How did you get on?"

Shelbie called the Bank Manager a *prat* and bent down, staggering, to take off her high heels. She darted about the living
room picking up Roxanna's coloring book and felt-tip pens. She
went into the kitchen to get the tea ready, staring back at me
from the doorway. Her expression was Anger.

———

Paul came with me to see the orangutans. He'd scratched his
head when I'd asked him to walk with me around the whole
enclosure. "I want to get used to it again," I tried to explain,
without telling him about Mark. When we got to the actual
spot, it didn't look any different from the other bushes. I winced
when I saw the netting, but there was no mark or reminder of
what had happened. I almost felt there should be. But it meant
I could be with the orangutans again without thinking about
creeps like Mark.

It was a hot day, and they were sitting quietly on the grass,
their deep-set eyes dark against their auburn fur. Rojo was eating
a Popsicle. "Thank you," I whispered, smiling at him, but he was
concentrating on breaking the frozen fruit juice apart to get to
the peanut, in its shell, in the middle. The keepers hid them
there for enrichment purposes.

"Why are you thanking Rojo?" Paul scratched his head again.

It was hard to think quickly. "Because he's very, very, um…
protective."

"He's got loads of girlfriends, well, *wives*, to protect," said
Paul. "It's all right for some, eh, Rojo?" Then to me, his face

red and glistening in the heat, "Are you used to the orangutans now? Only I've got to get back to the café in case they want me to lift anything. Yeah? I'm glad you're back on Tuesdays, Ellie. High five!"

—

"I don't want you filling my Roxie's head with nonsense about monkeys wearing clothes. Josh said she was really disappointed at Animal Arcadia when they were just lounging about, being animals!" Shelbie stood by Sylvia's fence, hands on hips, sunglasses pushed to the top of her head, dark eyebrows pulled together.

"I didn't," I said. "Sometimes they *do* drape towels and sheets around themsel—"

"Oh, yeah, and they've got duvets and electric blankets at night, I suppose."

"No." I stopped to think, twisting the hem of my apron. "Just the towels and sheets but…"

"I don't want her getting any more weird ideas from *you*. I want you to stay away from her." Shelbie's jabbing finger seemed to give off a bolt of electricity.

"Sometimes she comes to the fence to…"

"Well, you don't have to have a conversation, do you?" Shelbie's mouth closed like a trap, then opened again. "Just tell her you're busy."

"But I'm *not* busy, not all the time," I said.

"Well, you'll just have to tell a lie then, won't you, like everyone else. Like you did to Social Services," she added, over her shoulder. She walked into the house very fast, arms swinging, flicking her hair back over her shoulders.

27.

Operas enrich the soul.

—Mrs. Agnes Carr (Mother)

From my bedroom, I could hear the ropes of next door's swing creaking and the swish of leaves as Roxanna's feet reached the lower branches.

I never told lies. It was wrong. It was a Rule I found easy to follow. (*The only advantage to your condition, Elvira, is that you always tell the truth.*) It would be too complicated to make something up and then to keep having to pretend. I knew I wouldn't be able to lie to Roxanna.

───

"Ellie! Ellie! I went to the Animal ark…"

"Animal Arcadia," I corrected, taking a clothes peg from between my teeth. A rush of heat swept over me. I wasn't supposed to talk to Roxanna. I didn't look at her again. "Good-bye, Roxanna," I called out as I went inside.

"Where are you going?" Roxanna wailed, her voice rising on the *O*.

———

"Fancy bumping into you, pet," said Sylvia.

She was with Trevor and Roxanna outside Marks & Spencer.

"What *are* the chances, eh?" Trevor stuck his hands in his trouser pockets, his beard jutting. "We live in the same town, shop in the same shops, and live next door to each other." Trevor may have found eye contact difficult too, because he had a habit of looking above my head, rather than at me, or staring at me from over his glasses in a way that reminded me of Mother. They *had* always agreed about politics. I shifted my feet on the pavement, wondering if not talking to Roxanna was child abuse.

"Ellie, Granny and Granddad are taking me to Marks & Spencer to have a salad." Roxanna beamed. She was wearing a bright-pink T-shirt with *Princess* written on it. "And if I eat it all, I can have ice cream afterward. Any ice cream I want!"

I nodded, feeling hot and uncomfortable. It was difficult *not* to have a conversation with Roxanna.

"Let's just concentrate on the salad first, shall we, pet?" said Sylvia.

"Takes a lot of concentration, does a salad," said Trevor, frowning at his watch.

"You OK, pet? On your way to Asda, are you? How's your mum?"

I nodded. I was just about to say Mother was *About the same, thank you*, because that's what I always said when people asked, but actually, Mother hadn't been the same. She'd had a cold. "They're keeping her in bed today," I said, "to rest."

"Still plugged in, is she?" asked Trevor, yawning without putting his hand to his mouth.

"Not to the wall outlet. iPods have *rechargeable* batteries," I explained.

"Are you going to buy clothes in Asda?" asked Roxanna.

I shook my head.

"Is it a secret what you're going to buy?" Roxanna swung her hand in Sylvia's.

I shook my head again.

"Tell me then," commanded Roxanna.

"Ever considered a career in special services?" Trevor asked her, beginning to move away.

"Don't be so nosy, pet." Sylvia tugged at Roxanna's hand. "Ellie doesn't have to answer all your questions."

"She does usually," said Roxanna. "Ellie, why aren't you—"

"Come on, pet. We'll look at the clothes in Marks while we're there."

Trevor rolled his eyes. "Clothes shopping followed by a salad. Sometimes I think the excitement will kill me."

Neither Sylvia nor Roxanna seemed worried about Trevor dying from excitement. In fact, Roxanna smacked him on the arm as they moved off.

"Ellie," Sylvia called over the fence a few days later, "Mum any better?"

I propped the leaf rake against the wall. "She's still in bed," I said, "resting. They're giving her antibiotics for her cough."

"Poor Agnes," Sylvia shook her head, her dangly earrings swinging. "Still, she's in the best place." She leaned over the fence, looking at me. "Try to have a little chat with Roxanna sometimes, pet. She likes you, you know. She loves hearing about Animal Arcadia."

"I can't," I said. I looked at the ground and moved some leaves

I hadn't swept up yet with the toe of my shoe. "I'm not allowed to talk to her."

There were many, many things I hadn't been allowed to do when Mother was at home. I hadn't been allowed to mix with people from my school, nor, after various Incidents, was I allowed to go anywhere unfamiliar on my own.

Mother hadn't allowed me to use, let alone buy, a computer, or to do the ironing in the living room, although there was more space, nor watch *lowbrow* television programs in there either. This meant *Casualty* and *Coronation Street*. I hadn't been allowed to be rude or challenging because slamming doors made Mother's head ache. I hadn't been allowed to talk about cookie packaging because Mother said it was dull, or to beg her for another dog because I'd been *far too attached to the last one* (Tosca). I hadn't been allowed to use slang or to disagree with what the *Daily Telegraph* said. I hadn't been allowed to complain about the noise of Operas because *they enriched the soul*. And I'd been forbidden to discuss Father's business trips.

When I'd asked Mother why, she'd been silent for a moment, and then she'd said, *What you don't know can't hurt you.* Her face had puckered up as if she was eating something very sour, or perhaps bitter, and I remembered what Juliet Underwood had said in the Library about Mother being bitter. She must have seen the same facial expression. Mother had been wrong, though, because *not* knowing things—answers to the questions I'd written in my Japanese notebook about Father's empty passport, his lack of finances, the secret compartments in his shoes, who the woman and the baby were in the photo, where Mother's Lost Capacity had gone, and what Jane from Dunstable's comments meant—made me feel unsettled and confused.

"What do you mean, not allowed to talk to Roxanna?" Sylvia had stopped smiling. "Who said?"

I didn't like telling on people. At school, people had pinched me when I'd done it.

"Shelbie," I said very, very quietly, hoping it wouldn't count. "In case I give Roxanna weird ideas and fill her head with nonsense," I whispered. "But I don't make things up and I don't tell lies." I wanted to bang the rake, hard, on the path.

"I know you don't, pet." Sylvia patted my arm. "I don't think you'd know how to. You're not that type of girl."

I looked at Sylvia's dyed-blond hair, which didn't move around much, her dangly earrings, her purple top with its design of black flowers, her small jeans and red-painted toenails, and thought she was very different from Mother.

She sighed. "Shelbie's got a lot on her mind with the salon. But telling you not to speak to Roxanna was being a bit overprotective. I'll have to have a word." She leaned closer. "Do you know I sometimes wish Josh didn't worship the ground Shelbie walks on." She stood up straight. "But that's Josh for you. Loyal and loving." "And blind," I thought I heard her add as she went back inside, but I couldn't be sure, and in any case, Josh didn't even wear glasses.

———

"Susan Hulme here. Bay View Lodge." We were both panting. Mrs. Hulme's size made her short of breath, and I'd run in from sweeping up the leaves.

I asked her how she was first, before she'd even had a chance to ask me. If I'd been in the kitchen, I would have ticked the Rules checklist column.

She lowered her voice. "Elvira, I'm phoning about your mother."

I clutched the phone. Something clamped around my heart.

"What has she done?" I asked. My mind flashed back to Mother's first weeks at Bay View Lodge and the shouting.

"No, no, she's been fine, a different lady altogether. No, Elvira, I'm phoning to say she's rather poorly, I'm afraid."

"But she's had antibiotics and she's been resting." Mother hadn't been in the lounge for weeks. She'd been tucked up in bed, quietly listening to her iPods.

"Yes, three courses of antibiotics. They haven't touched the chest infection, I'm afraid."

"What medicines *would* touch it?" I asked. Small pieces of leaf were stuck to my sweater sleeve from where I'd been sweeping. I brushed them off, swapping the phone to my other ear.

"There *isn't* anything else, I'm afraid," said Mrs. Hulme. There was a pause and a wheeze from her end. "We'll just make her as comfortable as we can."

It was my turn to pause. I wasn't sure why Mrs. Hulme was ringing me. "She will get better in the end, though, won't she?" I asked her. "When she's rested enough?"

"No, dear, I'm afraid she won't." Mrs. Hulme had never called me *dear* before. "She's got pneumonia. Had a very bad night with her breathing." Mrs. Hulme wheezed on the word *breathing*. Her voice softened. "She could go at any time."

There was a landslide of sand beneath my feet. I gripped the phone. "Go? Go back to the hospital?" I asked.

"No, dear. They won't be able to do anything more for her there than we can here. No, dear. I'm afraid your mother could pass away at any time. That's why I'm ringing."

"Pass away. That means 'die,' doesn't it?" The sand shifted so much my legs gave way, and I sank to the carpet. Tosca had

Passed Away. So had Father, but I'd never thought Mother would. She'd always been there. And where exactly *was* Away? My brain buzzed so much that I had to put the phone down and cover my ears. After a moment, I picked it up again to ask Mrs. Hulme how long it would take for Mother to Pass Away, but she couldn't say.

28.

It very sad when your mum dies.

—Maria Esposito, caregiver,
Bay View Lodge Nursing Home

I washed my hands and face and brushed my hair and put on a clean T-shirt, the red one for First Aid, and rushed out of the house. I walked as fast as I could up the hill, but every few minutes I had to shut my eyes and put my hands over my ears because of the words *Pass Away* and *Die* jangling through my brain.

———

Maria came upstairs with me to Mother's room. At first I thought Mother looked the same as usual. Her gray hair was neat and tidy. Her eyes were shut. I could see the white earphones of the iPod leading under the bedclothes. But, when I leaned over her, her breathing sounded scratchy and painful. Her face was white and her nose blue at the tip.

Maria stroked Mother's hand. "Mum very poorly now. Poor Mum. We keep iPod switched on. Still playing music but turned down low." She looked at me. "You want cup of tea?"

"Yes, please," I said automatically.

I didn't like it when Maria went to get the tea. I didn't like being alone with Mother who was Passing Away. I could see her thin chest, under her nightie, moving up and down with the effort of breathing. I put my hand to my own chest to feel it not struggling.

"Mother," I whispered. "Are you all right?" I thought I saw a faint flicker from her eyelids, but it might have been a moving shadow from the half-drawn curtains. I thought about stroking her hand, like Maria had done, but I wasn't sure if Mother would like it. I'd never done it before. If she hadn't been weak from Passing Away, she might have brushed my hand off as if it were a mosquito.

"Here we are," Maria said as she came in with the tray. There was a plate of Rich Tea cookies but only one cup and saucer. There'd always been two cups before, although for the last few months, Mother's had been replaced by a feeding cup with a spout. Now there was just a plastic container with some little sponges on sticks. Maria leaned over Mother, her uniform rustling. "I wet your lips, Agnes"—she moistened them with one of the little sponges—"so you not get thirsty."

"Why can't she have a cup of tea?"

"She too poorly. She choke." She patted Mother's hand. "No more tea for you, Agnes, poor lady."

Mother would never have a cup of tea again, nor, I thought, looking at the Rich Teas with their pattern of fourteen holes, any kind of cookie. My eyes prickled.

Maria put her arm around my waist. She couldn't reach any higher because she was short. "It very sad when your mum dies." She gave me a tissue and pushed the little chair from Father's study next to Mother's bed. "You sit down and drink tea," she said. "I come back in few minutes."

I sat there drinking the tea almost as if it was a normal visit, except that my face was wet and every few minutes I had to put the cup of tea down to put my hands over my ears and shut my eyes to keep Mother's Passing Away from overwhelming me.

At lunchtime, Mrs. Hulme came upstairs. I heard the clatter of the lift and her wheezing as she walked down the corridor. She made some notes on a chart and moistened Mother's lips again. She tucked Mother in, although the bedclothes were still tidy because Mother hadn't moved at all, except for her chest heaving and an occasional twitch of her hand and her eyelids.

"I don't think it will be long now," Mrs. Hulme whispered.

I wiped my face with the back of my hand.

"It might be a good idea if I phone your neighbor, dear. What do you think?"

"I think it's a good idea," I said.

I heard Sylvia's clickety footsteps on the stairs and the jingle of her car keys.

"Hello, pet," she whispered. "This is a shock, isn't it? You said the cold had gone to her chest, but even so, you don't expect…"

There was a smudge of red lipstick on one of her front teeth. She drew up Mother's armchair, and we sat by her bed together. It was very quiet, apart from the rasp of Mother's breathing and a faint soar of Opera music from the iPod. The light was dim because of the half-drawn curtains. Sylvia reached out and took Mother's hand.

"Hello, Agnes, love. It's Sylvia, come to see you. You look very snug in that bed, I must say."

Sylvia was wearing a different pair of earrings from when I'd last seen her. Small gold hoops that didn't move when she shook her head. "I don't like the sound of that breathing," she whispered.

I didn't like the sound either. For a moment I thought of Mark's panting when he'd attacked me. I remembered what he'd whispered, and the pain in my back when he'd forced me against the fence, and shuddered.

"You cold, pet?" asked Sylvia.

"No, I'm all right, thank you."

I don't know why she did it, but she leaned forward and wrapped her arms around me, and we rocked together for several seconds.

————

Mother Passed Away at four minutes past three. Just before that, her breathing got worse, and Sylvia went to fetch Maria. I did hold Mother's hand then because Sylvia said it might be a comfort. Mother took four more breaths, with long pauses in between, and then she stopped. I held her hand even tighter, but she had already Passed Away. A few seconds ago, she was with me, here, the noise of her breathing the center of everything, and now she was gone.

Mother had attended St. Anne's Church's Bridge afternoons for years, but that was in the Church *Hall*. Neither she nor Father had believed in God, although they'd both liked looking around Churches. The older style of Church. So Mother couldn't have gone to Heaven. She wouldn't have been allowed in. My face grew wet thinking about Mother's Spirit, homeless and wandering. It didn't seem fair; Mother said listening to Operas *enriched your soul*, and as she'd done little else *but* that over the past year, her soul must be bursting with goodness.

Sylvia and Mrs. Hulme were at the door.

"She's gone, pet, hasn't she?" Sylvia whispered. "I can't hear her breathing."

Mrs. Hulme leaned over the bed. When she'd gotten her own breath back, she listened to Mother's chest with a stethoscope. She looked at her watch, wrote something down, and turned to me. "It was very peaceful, wasn't it, dear? What we'd all want at the end." Then she called the doctor although it was Too Late.

Afterward, Sylvia took me home and helped me make the dinner. It was Spinach Gnocchi because it was Monday. When she'd gone, I went upstairs and sat on Mother's bed, on her slippery eiderdown. Mother would have been very cross if she'd known she'd died. Cross not to be in charge anymore or able to check anything. How could such a *definite* person no longer be here? Sand slid away beneath me, and my whole body shook.

29.

The mind plays funny tricks.

—Mrs. Sylvia Grylls, neighbor

Sylvia said there was always a lot to do when someone dies. There was a large blue file in Father's study, labeled *What to Do in the Event of My Death*. It was behind Mother's file of Opera Lecture Notes in the big bookcase. Inside were important documents about the house and Mother's money and a sealed brown envelope with *COPY OF MY WILL* written on it in Mother's capital letters.

Sylvia's lips pursed as she looked at it. "That's important, pet. That'll be another trip to Mr. Watson. Let's just get the funeral over with first, though, eh?"

One of the documents was headed *My Funeral* and another, *Death Notice for Daily Telegraph and Sandhaven Courier*. "Thought of everything," said Sylvia, shaking her head. Mother used to read the death notices in the *Telegraph*. She'd read them out loud. She'd always hoped there'd be one about someone she knew, but that had only happened once, a lady who'd taught her math at school. *Shriveled old prune*, Mother had commented, *seemed old even then*. Now it was Mother's turn.

Sylvia put on the lilac-framed glasses she kept on a gold chain hidden inside her top because her eyes were aging. She read out the death notice Mother wanted put in:

> **Carr—*Agnes Margaret Montague*.** Beloved wife of Gregory James Carr, deceased, and dearly beloved mother of Elvira Jane.

"Ah, pet." Sylvia lowered the document. "Makes it very final, doesn't it?"

> Suddenly at home/peacefully after a short illness/peacefully after a long illness—DELETE AS APPROPRIATE.

Sylvia's eyebrows shot up. "Ooh, that's given me goose bumps, reading that. But of course she *wouldn't* have known how she was going to die." She looked at me over the top of her glasses.

"She had a top-quality brain," I said. "She thought of everything."

"Certainly did," said Sylvia.

> Greatly missed by family and friends. Funeral at St. Anne's Church, Sandhaven, on.......................... at....................................

"She's left blanks for the date," said Sylvia, shaking her head.

All friends welcome at the church.

One family wreath only, but donations in lieu to Opera for All would be appreciated.

Sylvia looked up again. "I'll come with you to order that wreath." She turned to the last page, wincing as if she'd hurt herself. "Oh, pet, this last bit's about her ashes." She moved her finger along the line of writing, not speaking for a minute. "She says she doesn't want them put in with your dad's. That's unusual, pet." Sylvia blinked. "But I expect she had her reasons."

She continued, "My ashes are to be scattered from a cruise ship, to the sound of 'Remember Me' from Purcell's *Dido and Annie…Aeneas*." She took off her glasses. "My goodness, she certainly knew what she wanted, your mum. A real stickler for detail." She tapped the paper. "That's going to be difficult for you, pet, isn't it? The scattering might have to wait till me and Trev go on our dream vacation. We've been promising ourselves a cruise around the Norwegian fjords for our golden wedding anniversary."

She put the pages back into the file. "Your mum's notes will make things easier. Always knew what she wanted." Sylvia closed the file with a sigh. "Didn't always get it, though."

I chose a wreath with blue flowers, because of the midnight-blue velvet dress in Mother's wardrobe. There was a card that came with the wreath for the relative or friend to write a message. I wanted to put *Not that way*, because they'd been Mother's last words, but Sylvia said they had to be *my* words. It was very difficult to make a decision so, in the end, I just wrote *MOTHER* in capital letters.

———

Mother's friend Jane telephoned from Dunstable. It was a difficult conversation with lots of pauses. She wouldn't be able to come to the funeral because of her spine.

"Nobody else has contacted you, have they, Elvira dear?"

I told her about the *With Deepest Sympathy* and *Precious Memories* cards I'd received from people at Mother's Bridge Club and Opera Classes and Cruise Talks, and that I'd had a telephone call from the Vicar to discuss the talk he was going to give on Mother. It had been a short telephone call.

"Nobody else, Elvira dear? Nobody you didn't know? Nobody claiming to be a relative?"

I shook my head. "No. I haven't got any relatives." I swallowed. "Not now."

"That's good, dear, because you never know."

I remembered Mother's words from long ago: *What you don't know can't hurt you.* I wanted to ask, *Never know what?* but Jane had to go and lie down.

———

In between registering the death and arranging the funeral, I stayed in bed. On Saturday, I got up at quarter to ten. It was nearly time to visit Mother, and I was late. I went to the drawer to find a clean T-shirt, and then I remembered Mother had Passed Away. The realization hit me like a great wave at the beach. Surf roared in my ears, and the hairs on my arms stood on end. I got back into bed, pulled the duvet over my head, and cried.

The next day I was in Sylvia's car—we'd gone to book the café next to St. Anne's Church for the funeral refreshments—when I saw Mother coming down the High Street. She was walking in her upright way, wearing one of her tweed skirts and carrying her black stick with the silver lion handle.

"It's Mother!" I banged my hand on the dashboard. "Stop! Stop!"

Sylvia darted me a look and drew in to the side of the road. I unfastened my seat belt.

"It's Mother!" I pointed. "Come back from Away!"

"Oh, pet," said Sylvia, peering through the windscreen. "That's not possible. We saw her body."

Mother went into Barclays Bank, even though her bank was the Royal Bank of Scotland. I chewed my lip.

"We'll wait here until she comes out." Sylvia gave my arm a little squeeze. "So you can have a good look."

Mother came out, fastening her handbag. On each of her fingers, on both hands, was a chunky, silver ring. Mother hated wearing rings. "Why should I have to tell the world my marital status when men don't have to?" she'd said and refused to fill in the right box on forms. This lady wasn't Mother. A shock ran through my body.

"There, there, pet," said Sylvia. She tried to hug me, but the hand brake was in the way. "The mind plays funny tricks. When Trev's mum died—Vera, you know—I was *convinced* it was her at bingo, same cauliflower perm, same pink glasses. I couldn't stop staring. It was only when she shouted "House!" in a Scottish accent that I realized it wasn't her. And that was *after* her funeral."

"You could get seasick in here," Trevor said, swaying from side to side and jerking his bristly chin at Mother's shipwreck pictures. He put the little chair by the door, ready to carry downstairs, then reached down to her suitcase because he was tall. I think the chair slipped from his hand because he put it down with quite a bang.

I had to sit down, not because I was seasick, but because Mother's things were here, waiting for her, not knowing she was never coming back.

"Faced the final curtain here, didn't she, old Agnes?" Trevor adjusted his glasses.

I looked at the curtains. They'd been partly drawn, like they were in my bedroom, when Mother Passed Away.

"She was happy here, your mum, with her opera music and this lovely view and the nice staff," said Sylvia, taking a pair of Mother's shoes from the wardrobe.

"Life of Riley," said Trevor. He stretched up to the *Storm at Sea* painting.

I nodded, even though I didn't know who Riley was. "She didn't like the guinea pigs, though," I added, "or the entertainment."

"Especially when the two were combined." Trevor tipped Mother's photos into a box.

Sylvia frowned at him.

"Often she didn't know I was there," I said.

I got up to pack Mother's clothes, as if I was helping her to go on a cruise, when, really, she was already Away. I folded the blue, defeated-looking cardigan with the leather buttons that she'd worn in the hospital. I had to wipe under my eyes with my sleeve.

30.

Humans contain dust from distant planets.
—David Attenborough, wildlife expert

*M*other's death notices appeared in the Friday editions of the *Daily Telegraph* and the *Sandhaven Courier*. I bought copies, cut the death notices out, and put them in Mother's Documents File. Seeing them in print meant there could be no mistake now. Mother had Passed Away and would not be coming back.

I sat on the floor of Father's study with the file open in front of me, sunshine lighting up the dust particles swirling in the air. David Attenborough said humans contained dust from distant planets. In a few days, after her funeral, Mother would be dust. Part of the Cosmic Swirl. Her dust might float off to a distant planet. That might be where Away was.

The only funeral I'd been to before had been Father's. There had been lots of people I didn't know there: men in suits with shaven heads or very short hair who'd engineered with Father (one had a tattoo of a snake on his neck), smartly dressed women with lots of jewelry, who were the wives or secretaries of the men in suits, and a long-haired man in tracksuit bottoms who'd smelled of alcohol.

Mother hadn't cried. She'd been angry, I remembered. Angry with Father for dying while he was Away and because of something he'd left behind him. She wouldn't say what it was. But, when you die, you can't take *anything* with you. The short-haired strangers had also enraged her. She'd glared at them during the service and hadn't spoken to them afterward. When I'd asked why, it was because she hadn't invited them. "I didn't expect *them* to read the *Telegraph*," she'd said.

She'd been cross with the two men who'd sat at the back of the church without joining in the hymns or the prayers. They'd scanned the congregation and taken notes. They hadn't stopped for refreshments; they'd climbed into a Police car and driven off. Mother said the funeral had *turned into a circus*. She'd been angry with me too, for not being able to do up the zipper on my trousers.

Now I was mourning the death of another parent, Mother herself. Instead of a *With Deepest Sympathy* card, Roxanna gave me a drawing of an orangutan, bright orange with a red mouth and wearing a purple skirt. I blue-tacked it to the fridge. Shelbie had suggested that Roxanna do me a drawing, apparently. "She's moved on," said Sylvia, nodding. I thought she meant gone to live above the salon, but Sylvia said, no, it meant stopped being angry.

I told Janice at the checkout in Asda that Mother had died, and the next time I went in, she gave me a *Thinking of You* card. It was nice of her to think of me. I also had an *Our Thoughts Are with You at This Difficult Time* card from Brenda at Pet Therapy, signed *With Love from Brenda and the Girls*. I wasn't sure if *the girls* meant the ladies from *Canines Who Care*, or the guinea pigs.

Sylvia and I had had trouble deciding what I was going to wear for Mother's funeral. We'd agreed on a pair of smart black trousers from Marks & Spencer, and I'd wanted to wear a black T-shirt and a black V-necked sweater with them, because that was the color of mourning, but Sylvia said, "Too death metal, pet. You're not exactly going to fit in wearing those!" (Rule Two.) I wore navy and gray instead, with my smart navy coat on top. I hadn't worn it for months because of there not being any other Special Occasions. Now it hung about me like a tent, and I could do up all the buttons easily. Mother would have been pleased about that.

Sylvia and I sat in the front pew of St. Anne's Church. My eyes were gritty and bloodshot because I hadn't slept, in spite of Sylvia telling me I didn't have to *do* anything, just *be* there.

"You've been bereaved, pet. Nobody'll expect you to make conversation."

This wouldn't mean breaking Rule One, *Politeness*, and actually, *pet*, it was a good example of Rule Seven, the difficult one, about *Rules changing to fit the Situation*.

Sylvia looked around her and clasped and unclasped her hands as if she was waiting for someone, although she said she wasn't. A funeral was a bit like a party, except for not knowing who was coming and it being a sad occasion. A tiny part of me still expected Mother to arrive and take charge, to peer at me over her glasses, tug my coat straight, and disagree with what the Vicar said about her.

The funeral pallbearers carried Mother's coffin in as if it weighed nothing at all and put it on an altar, covered with a red throw. I felt people looking at me. Apart from Mother, in her coffin, I was the center of attention. I clenched my toes and kept my eyes on some graffiti that was carved into the side of the pew: *EW 1938.* When I glanced around, I saw Maria and Kim from Bay View Lodge sitting near the back of the church, not wearing their uniforms. Maria gave me a big smile.

Across the aisle, Paul, with his dad, put his hand out to me in a high-five gesture. The other mourners were older people with faded hair—students from Mother's Opera Classes or members of the Bridge Club. There were seventeen mourners altogether, counting Sylvia, Trevor, and myself. Josh and Shelbie couldn't come because of Roxanna and the salon, and Katie couldn't come because of the boys.

I lay in bed now, my head throbbing, my brain overflowing with detail: the smell of mold and candles; the egg and cress sandwiches in the Church Hall being made with white bread, not brown; the dark clothes people had been wearing, and how they'd all looked at me, especially when Mother's body was brought in and out. I couldn't remember exactly what people had said afterward, but it had involved shaking my hand, and them saying Mother had had *a formidable intelligence* and had been *a force to be reckoned with.*

Sylvia said Mother's will needed to be dealt with by an expert: Mr. Watson. In Mills & Boons, family members gathered in a lawyer's office and the will revealed an exciting inheritance for one of them and nothing but trouble for the rest. As I was the only member of my family left, there couldn't be any trouble, but just the sight of the will's stiff cream paper, with its black italic writing and red seal, made my hands clammy.

"I was sorry to hear of your mother's death, Miss Carr... Elvira," Mr. Watson said, his shaggy eyebrows low. "Always a sad and difficult time."

"Thank you." Mr. Watson's office, with its high windows and walls lined with shelves of documents and portraits of well-known lawyers and their clients, turned my voice into a whisper, like it had done after Mother's stroke.

"Now." Mr. Watson tapped his fingertips together. "I have reacquainted myself with the contents of your mother's will. It is an unusual will in some respects."

"That was what I was afraid of," said Sylvia. She grasped the strap of her leopard-skin handbag with both hands and looked over her shoulder as if she expected someone pretending to be a family member to burst in.

"And in other ways," Mr. Watson continued, "it is very simple. You are the main beneficiary, Elvira, and your mother's trust continues in your name." He drew a document toward him. "Financially, the provisions are exactly the same."

I nodded, relieved at the words *continues* and *same*.

Sylvia leaned back in her chair. "Well, that's straightforward, anyway, pet."

"There are several smaller bequests." Mr. Watson turned to Sylvia. "One to yourself, Mrs. Grylls."

"Is there?" Sylvia blinked and held the leopard-print handbag closer to her chest.

Mr. Watson read out: "To my true and faithful friend, Mrs. Sylvia Grylls, I leave the sum of £10,000."

"Oh!" Sylvia opened her handbag and got out a tissue. "Bless her."

Mr. Watson leaned forward, his voice the boom I remembered from before. "Your husband gets a mention too."

Sylvia dabbed her eyes. "Does he? That'll please him."

"To a marvelous friend, Mr. Trevor Grylls, I leave the sum of £1,000."

Less than Sylvia. I chewed my lip, thinking of the Mills & Boons.

"Oh, bless her," said Sylvia again. "He'll be thrilled."

"She left £10,000 to a Miss Jane Fisher of Dunstable, who she describes as being"—Mr. Watson looked down at the will—"'a haven in a storm.'"

"Aah." Sylvia used her tissue again.

"And some smaller bequests." Mr. Watson traced down a list. "Her music collection."

"Oh dear," said Sylvia. "All those opera CDs."

"A hundred and two," I said.

"Your mother has left them to the local U3A 'to promote the civilizing power of opera.' And she has left £100 to Sandhaven Bridge Club, with the specification it was to… Yes, here we are"—he found Mother's words—"'to be spent on a silver cup, awarded annually for good sportsmanship.'"

Mr. Watson's finger moved downward. "She has left a year's subscription to *Money Management—A Guide to Increasing Your Personal Wealth* and a copy of *How to Marry a Rich Man: Find, Attract and Marry a Wealthy Husband in 10 Easy Steps* by Marybeth Kline, to Ms. Katharine Hargreaves of Crawley." Mr. Watson looked up, his eyebrows raised. "An unusual bequest."

"I've never heard of Katharine Hargreaves," I said. "Or Crawley."

Sylvia shifted in her chair and put away her tissue. She glanced behind her again.

"There is another bequest in a similar vein. 'To Mr. Charles Hargreaves of Crawley, I leave one year's membership in the Great Bustard Club and a copy of John Major's *Autobiography*.'" Mr. Watson shook his head. "Most unusual. I thought the Great Bustard was extinct."

"I don't know who Charles Hargreaves is either," I said.

Sylvia fastened her handbag with a click. She looked at her watch. "We mustn't take up any more of your time. That *is* it, isn't it?" she asked.

"Yes, indeed," Mr. Watson put Mother's will back into a large file. "We await probate, and then funds are released." He drew out the word *probate*.

"But that's it, no more bequests?" Sylvia asked, standing up.

Mr. Watson's fingertips tapped together again. "No."

"That's a relief," she said. We shook Mr. Watson's hand, and I followed Sylvia out. She was walking so quickly, in spite of her high heels and large waist, that I could hardly keep up.

In the lift, she clicked her handbag clasp open and shut, her scarlet fingernails vivid against the gold metal. Her voice was louder than usual. "I'm really touched your mum left me and Trev all that money. And those lovely words too."

I nodded at this large token of Mother's appreciation. "I'm glad the Arrangements have stayed the same." I frowned. "I don't know who those Hargreaves people are, though. I never heard Mother mention them." I stopped. "They could be something to do with teaching Operas on cruises. People she met onboard ship." Sylvia did not reply, except to say how smooth the lift was, which was changing the subject. I thought again. It was also possible they were part of Father's secret Government Missions, even fellow spies! But Father would have had to keep things like that secret, even from Mother.

In the foyer, I took the Japanese notebook out from my coat pocket and squeezed in another question—Who are Katharine and Charles Hargreaves?—beneath question one (Why are there no Japanese Stamps in Father's Passport?). I added *Spies?* in tiny letters, so that Sylvia could not see, after their names.

"Hey up!" Karen's crest of hair bounced as she got up from her chair. "You've returned in the nick of time. I'm surrounded by boxes of newsletters. I've been trapped at my desk for days!"

I wondered how she'd gone to the bathroom and was about to ask when I realized it was a Figure of Speech. Karen used more of them than anyone else I knew. She got up from behind her desk and came over.

"Can I give you a hug?" She patted my back. "There, there," she said. "You've really been through the mill, haven't you?"

I nodded, wondering about the mill. I gave Karen's back a tentative pat.

"Back from the wars, you are," Karen said, returning to her computer. "Confined to desk duties. Of which there are plenty," she added, pointing to the boxes of newsletters. "Seriously, though…" She leaned forward, her nose stud—a diamond like the one Micky, the computer buddy, had worn in his ear—twinkling. "Are you going to be OK? Not going to be too much?"

I shook my head, beginning to arrange the envelopes into symmetrical piles. "I need structure and purpose in my life now that Mother's Passed Away." Sylvia and I had had a little chat about this yesterday.

"You're right there." Karen looked back at the screen. "Give that girl a medal."

Paul sat down with a plate of fries. "Where did your mum's coffin go after those men carried it out of the church?"

"It was cremated—well, burned—at the Crematorium. I've got to collect the dust next week."

Paul's eyes were round behind his glasses. "Why? Why do you want to keep the dust?"

"It's got to be scattered from a ship. That's what Mother wanted. She wrote it all down." I'd reread the last page of Mother's *What to Do in the Event of My Death* file, my eyes screwed nearly shut. Once her dust had gone, there would be nothing of Mother left.

"Sounds messy." Paul squeezed ketchup over his fries. "*My* mum doesn't live with us now, she lives with Brian, but I see her loads. It would be weird if she wasn't there anymore to tell me when my T-shirt needs washing and to eat salad."

I pushed my half-eaten scrambled egg away. In the next enclosure, I could see a group of wolf cubs, the ones Mark had bullied, tugging at a floral pillowcase. "Every morning, I feel I should still be going to visit Mother. And I am completely on my own now. I try *not* to think about it, actually." I massaged my forehead, the snarling from the wolf cubs boring into my brain.

"You're not on your own really, because I'm your friend," Paul sucked some tomato sauce from his fingers. "I care about you *as a friend*. Dad said he'd give us a lift if you wanted to go on a trip out somewhere. Somewhere with animals."

"That would be nice," I said.

I watched the orangutans from behind a tree while I finished my banana. They were only allowed one each a week because of weight issues. The weather was cooler. Cinta sat, long arms wrapped around herself, her auburn hair like a shaggy coat. Pernama swung, upside down, above her. She stretched out a tiny arm and leg, like a ballet dancer, and twined herself around her mother's neck. I had to wipe my face, and I got a bit of banana in my hair.

31.

Once you've found out something, you can't unlearn it.
                    —Mrs. Sylvia Grylls, neighbor

O n Friday, there was a handwritten envelope on my doormat. *To the Estate of Mrs. Agnes Carr*, it said, with my address underneath. *Estate* was a legal term which, when I checked, meant *property or possessions*, so since I owned all of Mother's, I opened the envelope.

Inside was a card with a picture of an owl on it and an address in Crawley:

The estate of the late Mrs. Agnes Carr to whom it may concern:

I've been told I have inherited something from the above lady's will, and I am writing to thank you for the bequest. Species preservation is a special interest of mine (I'm doing an MA in ecology at Bath University), so I was thrilled about the Great Bustard Club membership. They're doing great work in trying to reintroduce the species to the UK, I know. I don't know much about John Major, but as I like biographies, I'm sure I'll enjoy it.

260   FRANCES MAYNARD

I was pleased but surprised to be left a bequest by someone
I've never met. My father's name was Carr, Gregory Carr.
There might be other members of his family still around? If
any of them would like to get in touch, my email address is:
charliehargreaves24@hotmail.com.

Kind regards,
Charles Hargreaves (Charlie)

My father's name was Carr, Gregory Carr. I remembered
Mother's birthday card. A picture of a Scottish glen from
someone called *Charlie Hargreaves (Carr)*. I sat down, suddenly, at the kitchen table. My hands trembled as I reread the
card, tracking each word with my finger, checking I'd understood it. Carr was an unusual name. When people needed to
write it down, I often had to spell it. Gregory wasn't a common
name either. It was odd that Charles Hargreaves's father had
exactly the same Christian name as well. Perhaps Gregory
was a family name handed down through generations, like
Mother's possessions.

I'd never met any other members of my family. I was an only
child, as was Mother, and all my grandparents had died before I
was born. I'd never heard Father talk about his family except to
say they came from Scotland. He told me he had no brothers or
sisters, or any family at all, because he'd been found and raised by
wildcats in a Scottish Pine Forest, which always seemed unlikely
to me as Scottish wildcats are solitary animals who do not have
a family life.

Charlie Hargreaves must be a family member on *Father's*
side, yet didn't use his surname. *Mother* must have known he was
a distant relation to have left him a bequest in the first place. I

turned the card over, chewing my lip. There was no mention of Ms. Katharine Hargreaves who'd also been left a bequest.

I looked out the kitchen window. A light was on in Sylvia and Trevor's living room. Should I show her the card and ask what to do? There was still the worry of Trevor phoning Social Services. If there were any signs of me not managing, he might go ahead and do it. Anyway, Sylvia didn't know who Charlie and Katharine Hargreaves were either. She'd never met them. Nor had she recognized the people in the photo from Father's wallet. I smoothed my forehead with my fingers. Did I actually want any more family? A dizzying line of unknown relations stretched away into the distance, strangers who might make me go up and down stairs for them all day, and tell me to *keep up*.

I went upstairs. I didn't have to meet Charlie Hargreaves. I didn't even have to email him if I didn't want to. He was a *distant* member of my family. But I hesitated, sitting on the bed. I didn't have any family left now, and his card had an owl on it, and ecology was something to do with nature. If Charlie Hargreaves liked animals, he was unlikely to be a bad person. Although, I thought, jerking the bedspread straight, that had not been true of Mark.

I fetched the Japanese notebook. I'd found an answer to one of the questions, and, now that Mother had Passed Away, where her Lost Capacity had ended up was no longer relevant. But Father's finances, and the lack of Japanese stamps in his passport, the secret compartments in his shoes, and the identity of the woman and baby in his photo were still mysteries. And I still didn't understand what Jane's comments about Deceit, Lies, Forgiveness, and Shame had meant.

I tapped my pencil on the question I'd written down after Mr. Watson had read out the Will: Who are Katharine and Charlie

Hargreaves? Writing something down made it seem like there might be an answer, somewhere. I went downstairs and switched on the computer. I only typed Charlie Hargreaves into Google because Katharine Hargreaves hadn't been mentioned on the card.

Google discovered a Charlie Hargreaves who'd been an American baseball player and who'd died in 1979 and nine other Charlie Hargreaves. Three of these were also dead and, of the six others, none lived in Crawley. I only looked at Google's first page because Micky had said you could waste hours trawling through rubbish otherwise. He hadn't used the word *rubbish*.

I settled Geraldine on the new lady resident's lap. It was the first time I'd been to Pet Therapy since Mother Passed Away. Brenda had said she relied on me with the guinea pigs. When she opened the door of their traveling box, their greeting whistles made my eyes prickle.

"There, you see? They've missed you." Brenda reached inside. "Now, who's ready to provide a bit of TLC? Here you are, love." She put Goldie into an old gentleman's outstretched arms. "Give her a cuddle." She bustled around the residents, handing out towels for the guinea pigs to sit on. "Social animals, you see, make friends with all sorts. Hate being on their own, do guinea pigs."

I gave the residents turns in holding Geraldine and demonstrated how to smooth down her black-and-white fur. *I* didn't hate being on my own. I'd gotten used to the quiet of the empty house and liked it now, especially after a day out in the real world. I liked there being nobody to tell me what to do, or to keep up a conversation with, or to work out if they were joking or not.

There was a hollow feeling when I returned Geraldine to her

box and her sisters, though. Coming back to Bay View Lodge made me feel lonely. The new resident, a frail, bent-over lady called Beatrice, was sitting in Mother's chair. After Pet Therapy, she went upstairs, and I imagined her sitting in Mother's room and looking at Mother's view.

I bent to fasten the catch of the guinea pigs' traveling box and noticed a faint gray line of dust on the baseboard. Ashes to ashes, dust to dust. Mother's ashes were on the living room mantel now, in a plastic urn next to the cherub clock, waiting to be scattered. Dust to dust. Mother had sat here in the lounge every day for the past seven and a half months. She must be part of this dust. And, if she was part of it, part of the Cosmic Swirl, she was still here.

I thought about Charlie Hargreaves's card. I'd put it in a plastic pocket, filed it in Mother's *What to Do in the Event of My Death* file and pushed the whole thing back on the shelf, out of sight. Although I couldn't see it, I knew it was there. Somewhere, in Crawley, there was a complete stranger who was part of my family. I went upstairs to lie down for a while. The only family I'd ever known were Father and Mother. Would Charlie Hargreaves be like Father because he came from his side of the family? Did *distant* mean he'd be aloof?

"Did you see *Dog Rescue* last night, Ellie?" Paul asked as we walked to the Adoption Center after lunch.

I *had* seen it. I'd rushed in from dishwashing when I'd heard barking. "I liked how they matched the people who wanted to be dog owners with the dogs who needed homes." Dogs searching for families reminded me of Charlie Hargreaves's card.

"Yeah! Magic." Paul was quiet. Then he said, "I don't want to be a lone wolf."

One of the wolves at Animal Arcadia was being kept temporarily apart from the others because he'd had an operation on his tail. His howling sent shivers down my spine. I didn't want Paul to end up like that. Or me.

"I worry what will happen when Dad dies. And Mum." Paul kicked a stone along the path. "*I* might need a home then. Otherwise there wouldn't be anyone to give me lifts, and I might wear the same T-shirt for weeks without noticing. I've got an older sister in New Zealand," he added, kicking the stone between two fence posts and flinging up his arms. "I might go and live with her."

"I could tell you about your T-shirt," I offered, "because I notice that sort of thing." I considered, then added, "If I still know you, of course."

"Thanks, Ellie. There's a possibility I might be married to Kate Humble by then, but it's unlikely. It's hard when you only like a certain type of woman." Paul kicked another stone with each foot in turn, like a footballer.

Ahead of us, some orangutans were ambling across the grass. Rojo, twice as big as the others, was squatting on a higher patch of ground, his deep-set dark eyes scanning the horizon.

"Hey." Paul gripped my arm, his eyes sparkling. "Did you know Utari was pregnant?"

"Is she?" I breathed. Utari often sat close to Cinta. "Is the father Rojo?"

"Yeah, he's the *only* male. Lucky primate." Paul lined up his stone for a penalty kick, a football term he'd often explained. I wasn't interested in football really, but I sometimes listened to how Norwich City was doing because it was Delia Smith's team. They were called the Canaries.

I went close to the netting, the memory of Mark's attack flitting briefly through my mind. Another baby orangutan would mean that Pernama wasn't an only child anymore. I paused, tapping a finger against my lip. Pernama would still be *Cinta's* only child, though.

———

I turned on the bedside lamp and took out the bookmark from page forty-seven of *Long-Lost Love*. Distant relations, lost family members, and people and animals searching for homes were everywhere, even in Mills & Boons. Robbie, the hero of *Long-Lost Love*, discovers he's been adopted as a baby. He finds his long-lost birth sister in Nuneaton on Facebook, and she introduces him to her best friend, Zoe. Robbie was now taking Zoe out to country pubs and country horse centers.

I closed the book without reinserting the bookmark. For some reason, I remembered Sylvia's words, *You're out in the real world now, pet*, and how I'd felt like an orphan in a thunderstorm. Sand shifted beneath my feet even though I was lying down. But, sometimes, I *was* quite happy being in a social group of one, I told myself.

I got out of bed and listed the *disadvantages* of contacting my distant relation Charlie Hargreaves:

1. I didn't know him.
2. I didn't know how to behave with relations. I might have to cook Christmas dinner for him and visit him on Sundays.

3. He might try to make Arrangements for me.
4. He might want to come and live with me.
5. He might want me to come and live with him.
6. He might take away some of Mother and Father's pos-
    sessions because he was family.
7. He might be a cruel person, like Mark.
8. He might want me to move near where *he* lived, and I
    didn't want to move.

On the other side, I listed the *advantages*:

1. I would no longer be in a social group of one.
2. I would be a member of a family again.
3. I could add him to my contacts list on email.
4. I would enjoy talking about owls and ecology.
5. He might take me to shire horse centers.
6. Mother had left him a bequest, so she must have
    approved of him.

Next morning, I sat at the kitchen table eating my porridge, the lists in front of me, no clearer as to what to do. I had to do *something* because the picture of the owl swooped into my brain every time I went into Father's study. The spoon clattered as I pushed the bowl away. The light was on in Sylvia's kitchen. She would know what to do. I was only asking for *advice*; it wasn't evidence I wasn't coping.

Sylvia slowly chewed a raspberry, her face puckering. I'd gone to Asda before popping in. A blood pressure website had recommended fruit rather than cookies. Shelbie had refused a raspberry. She'd popped in at the same time to run some salon design ideas past Sylvia and to tell her Josh had rejoined the Hells Angels, the New Forest Chapter. Neither of them had thought this was a good idea. Shelbie had turned her wedding ring around and around and told Sylvia she had an accountant now, and Sylvia had put her teacup down with a bang.

When Shelbie left, I showed Sylvia Charlie Hargreaves's card. She looked at me for a long time without saying anything. Then she said, "That's a difficult one, pet." Her lips and front teeth were stained a reddish-purple. After the long look, she seemed to find it difficult to maintain eye contact. "I just don't know, pet." She held her cup in both hands and looked out at the garden.

"I don't know how to advise you. On the one hand, this Charlie might be a lovely fellow who'd enrich your life. On the other hand..." She paused, shifting her weight from one buttock to another. "Well, you might find out something you wished you hadn't." She put the cup down and smiled without her eyes crinkling. "Now, did I tell you about Roxanna's sc—?"

"But I *like* finding out things," I put in. "With Google, it's easy. I don't like not knowing the answer."

"I know, pet, but those are *facts*. People are more complicated."

I began to rub my forehead.

After another silence, Sylvia leaned forward. "The thing is, pet, once you've found out something, you can't *unlearn* it, can you? It might make you look at"—she hesitated—"well, *things*, in a different way. Maybe not in a good way either."

I nodded. I remembered the shocked, sinking feeling I'd experienced when I'd learned that orangutans weren't completely vegetarian and sometimes ate small animals.

"But then, you see"—Sylvia shifted in her chair again—"you *are* on your own. And this *is*"—she tapped the owl card—"a relation."

It was my turn to be silent. During the silence, Sylvia got up to put the kettle on again. "If I don't contact him," I said, when she sat down, "I'll just keep thinking about his card and…wondering. When I go into the study, Mother's documents file is sort of lit up and…*signaling* to me."

"Maybe you should go with your gut instinct then, pet, and do it. Hang on to your hat, though. It's going to be a roller coaster of a ride."

I put my hand to my head and then put it down again.

Sylvia hadn't explained what I should do like she had done when she'd given me the reasons behind the Rules. She'd just said about going with my gut instinct. While I was sitting in front of the computer, my stomach gave a loud rumble. I took this as a sign, breathed in deeply, and typed Charlie Hargreaves's address into the email box.

Dear Mr. Charles Hargreaves (Charlie),

My name is Elvira Carr, and I live in Sandhaven. My father's name was Gregory Carr, and my mother's name was Agnes Carr. Who are you? Are you the same person who sent Mother a birthday card? Since Mother died, I am the only member of my family left because I am an only child. It is possible you are a distant relation, but I don't want to move or to cook a Christmas dinner for anyone.

I liked your owl card although I have never seen a real one. I have never seen a Great Bustard either, except for a stuffed one in Sandhaven Museum. I like all animals. I volunteer at an animal sanctuary, Animal Arcadia, every Tuesday. I am a vegetarian. I looked up "ecology" so I know it is about living organisms. How does studying it make you feel?

Yours sincerely,

Elvira Carr (Miss)

There was a reply the next morning. Heart thumping, I opened it.

Hi, Elvira.

It was great to get your email and find there's a fellow animal-lover in the family! It must be in our genes. Animal Arcadia sounds fascinating. And, yes, I really enjoy studying ecology.

Strange that your dad's name was exactly the same as mine—they could be quite closely related!

Sadly, Dad died in 2010. The twelfth of November. He was only 70. We were gutted. Mum put it down to all the cigars he smoked and the stress he was under.

You said you were an only child—me too!

Looking forward to hearing from you. This family history thing is really interesting, isn't it?

Charlie

P.S. Yes, your mum's birthday card was from me. Guilty as charged!

I pushed my chair back from the screen. My brain felt suddenly full. I shut my eyes to think, and then my fingers flashed over the keys.

> Dear Charlie,
>
> Thank you for your email. I am glad that you are an only child and that you love animals.
>
> Family history is quite interesting, but also puzzling. Father died the same year as yours did, and at the same age, and he smoked cigars. It almost sounds like they were the same person, except that Father couldn't have been in two places at once. Do you think he could have had an identical twin brother who lived in Crawley? That would mean you were my first cousin. Although Father never mentioned a brother. He never mentioned any family. Mother said they were all dead. Well, she actually said, "Dead to him, anyway." I don't know the difference. I don't know why Father would have kept an identical twin brother secret. I wondered if it could be connected with Government Missions, with spying? A spy with a natural double would be invaluable. I would be interested to hear your view.
>
> There is another puzzling thing… Why did you feel guilty about sending Mother a birthday card?
>
>   Yours sincerely, Elvira Carr (Miss)

Charlie replied thirty-six minutes later:

> No, Dad never mentioned an identical twin brother. He never mentioned any family either, except I knew he'd been married before. Mum said he was still in touch

with his wife. It used to upset her, so I didn't press her about it.

Dad was away a lot for work. Engineering. I don't think he was anything to do with spying. Liked reading about spies, yes, and he got through a lot of thrillers. He read the paper and did the crossword as well. Never finished one, though!

His birthday was on October 23, 1940. How about your dad's?

This is all a bit of a mystery—exciting, though!

Yours, Charlie

P.S. "Guilty as charged" was just an expression—sorry, didn't mean to confuse you!

32.

Don't build houses on shifting sand.
            —Reverend Basil Tipper, vicar,
St. Anne's Church (and, before him, the Bible)

There was a small cold spot in my stomach. *Father's* birthday was on October 23. *Father* was an engineer. *Could* they be the same person? But Father was Father, and Charlie's father was Dad. I read the email aloud again, trying to make sense of it, and then I went upstairs to lie down. When I'd gotten up this morning, I'd been Father's only child, but now…a whole sand dune slithered away beneath my feet. *Could* Father have been Charlie Hargreaves's parent too? But how?

I got up at twelve. The owl card was still on the kitchen table from when I'd shown it to Sylvia. Until I saw it again, a tiny part of me believed that I'd dreamed up the whole thing: distant relations, bequests, Crawley, dads, owls. I picked the card up between finger and thumb and, holding it as far away from me as my arm could reach, put it back into Mother's Documents File. I pushed the file to the very back of the shelf with Mother's Opera Notes and another file, *Legal Matters*, jammed in front of it. Then I went on the computer and deleted Charlie Hargreaves's emails.

I closed the front door behind me.

"Hello, pet," Sylvia called out, a Marks & Spencer shopping bag dangling from each hand. "How are you getting on? Did you, you know, make that contact in the end?"

I turned away. "Yes, but I'm not going to carry on with it." My head ached.

Sylvia put the shopping bags down. "Why's that, pet? He wasn't rude, was he?"

"No." I squeezed my hands tight to stop myself from twisting my sweater, something I'd been doing less frequently. Until Charlie Hargreaves, that is. I'd had to put on my old black sweater and roll its hem between my fingers only last night, while I was watching *Coronation Street*. "Not rude. Friendly. But what he said can't be true." I shook my head vigorously. "It's not possible."

Sylvia looked at me, pressing her lips together. Her lipstick was a reddish-purple, or it might still have been the stain from the raspberries. "Come in for a bit, pet. You can do your shopping after."

Sylvia took her shopping bags upstairs so Trevor wouldn't see how much she'd been spending. I'd bought something that wasn't on my shopping list only last week. An Extra Special Exotic Fruit Platter. And a new Asda sweater. A red one. Would that be something Trevor would criticize me for? Beard bristling, eyes staring over his glasses, would he phone Social Services to report me? I had enough on my plate at the moment.

I'd just thought in another Figure of Speech, I realized, but it failed to cheer me up. I stared at the picture of thatched cottages around a duck pond that hung above the fireplace in Sylvia's living room. There was a large tree behind the cottages, and I peered into its branches, imagining an owl swooping down from them at night. I saw owls everywhere now.

Sylvia's voice disturbed the owl. "So, what is it he's been saying, pet?"

Words rushed out. "He said—well, he *wrote*—that his dad had the same name as Father *and* the same birthday. *His* dad smoked cigars too, *and* he was an engineer. *And*"—I held the sweater's hem tightly—"they both died on the same day! He made it sound like they were the same person!"

My throat was suddenly tight. My eyelids prickled. "I've tried to stop thinking about it, because each time I do, my brain gets tangled and I feel like crying." I was crying now, I realized. "I've spent hours lying down with the curtains drawn trying not to think about it. But it doesn't work." I heard the word *work* rise to a wail.

"Pet." Sylvia put both arms around me. "Come on, come and sit down. Let's get you a tissue. That's it. Now, sit there and don't move while I put the kettle on."

It was impossible to mop my eyes without moving; I had to wait until I heard the kettle switch itself off. When Sylvia returned with the tray, there was a plate of cookies on it. "Viennese Whirls," I noticed dully, probably McVitie's, because of the cherry halves on their tops.

"I'm not supposed to be eating these but I weakened," Sylvia admitted. "They're from a tin Trevor keeps in his shed. Under lock and key. But, I told myself, in a situation like this, cookies are medicinal." She offered me the plate and took one herself. "I'm afraid what I've got to tell you *needs* a bit of sweetening, pet."

After she'd told me, Sylvia squeezed my hand, "I'm sorry, pet."

"Why, what have *you* done?" I looked up, my eyes blurred.

"No, pet." Sylvia took hold of my other hand. "I mean I'm sorry you've had to find this out. I know how much you looked up to your dad. He was a charmer." She smiled and looked away for a moment. "I'm only telling you because it's better you find out from me rather than a stranger, even though he *is* family."

I released one of my hands to wipe my eyes and nose. "How could Father have been two different people at the same time? How could he have been this Charlie's *dad*? Why did he do it?"

Sylvia smiled sadly. "He did it because he could, I suppose. That's men for you. Some men." She sighed.

"Mother must have known. She must have known to tell *you*."

"Oh yes, pet. She was a clever woman. Your dad couldn't get much past her. Well, perhaps at the beginning. When she was young." Sylvia reached for her tea, sighing. "She had a lot to put up with, your mum."

Jane had used the same words. Words I'd thought referred to me. "Why did she then?" A wave of heat rose in my face. I put my hands over my face to keep the suddenness out and sobbed. Sylvia heaved herself up from the sofa and brought over the whole box of tissues.

"Here, good thing Trevor made me stock up, eh? Let it all out, pet. It's an awful shock, I know, especially for someone like you." I looked up sharply, tears running down my face, but Sylvia went on. "Someone who's never told a lie in her life."

I listened, blowing my nose. Sylvia was telling me the truth. At least, I think she was. Now that I knew both my parents were liars, it was hard to believe that NeuroTypicals ever *did* tell the truth. I was trying my hardest to keep to my seven Rules, but Father had broken Rules all over the place. He'd lied, been unfaithful, been selfish. How could I trust anything he'd said now? He might even have lied to me about the Moon Landings.

Sylvia shook her head, sighing. "You idolized him, didn't you?" she said. "Bless him. *Yes*, pet, bless him, in spite of what he put your mum through. *And* you, now. Because your dad wasn't a monster, was he, pet?" She sighed again, a small smile appearing, "He had that… What do you call it? Carry…*charisma*, that's it. Had a lot of that. Always a smile on his face, and well…he could get away with murder." She leaned toward me with the box of tissues. "In a way, it was good of your mum not to tell you. It would have spoiled the image you had of him."

I shook my head, tears wetting my hair. "I've got lots of photos of him. They're in good condition."

"I meant if you'd known about your dad's other life, you might have had a different idea about him."

I nodded. But at least it would have been *true*. My eyes filled again. When he was with us, was he thinking about his other "wife" and child? His *NeuroTypical* child, his *university student* child. Why did he want *another* set when he had one of each already? Why weren't Mother and I enough? He'd called us *my darlings*. He'd tried to put his arm around Mother's waist; he'd hugged me, and not just when he came back from Away. He'd called me *Vivi*. He'd never been cross with me, even when I didn't know things. Tears spilled over and ran down my face. It was *because* I didn't know things. He'd really wanted a *normal* child. A clever one.

———

When I got home, I picked up things that had belonged to Father: the ashtray in the shape of a woman's hand and his special mug, with the text of the Rosetta Stone from the British

Museum on it, and put them down again. I banged them down actually, but not hard enough to break them.

Father had sometimes read the Rosetta Stone text aloud, translating as he went, because he could read Ancient Languages. It was the story of Noah's Ark, and each time he read it, the words were slightly different. Father said this was because translation was an art that involved free license. Now I wondered if even that was true.

I lay in bed staring at the ceiling. My eyes were swollen and sore. In the corner of the room lay the photo of Father in his tropical hat, the glass cracked in two places from where I'd hurled it. A collapsed feeling, grief, washed over me in waves. I was the daughter of a liar. Father had lied to me all his life.

I cleaned the bathroom, although it was Thursday, and not my usual day for cleaning, because lying down in the dark only worked for a little while and then the jumble of thoughts came back and all the questions I would have asked Mother—had I known about Father—rattled around in my brain. I scrubbed the toilet bowl, my sore eyes smarting from the bleach fumes. Mother wouldn't have given me the answers anyway. She'd have said, *Mind your own business* or *Don't be ridiculous, Elvira* or *Never you mind*. I stood up and pulled the chain, the toilet bowl gleaming a brilliant white. She'd have said, she often *did* say, *Your father is away, and don't ask me where*, in a cross, frowning voice that made me not want to ask anything else.

I used an old toothbrush and some Ajax on the bathroom taps, concentrating on removing every speck of lime scale. Mother had thought I was stupid, with my questions and my not understanding, when what she and Father had been doing was lying. My family, my childhood, everything they'd ever told me had been lies! I was drowning in them, all the breath knocked out of me by waves of them, and I had to crouch on the floor, my head between my knees.

The Vicar at St. Anne's, who came to my school for special occasions such as Harvest Festival, had told us not to build our houses on shifting sand. I stood up and leaned against the sink, still holding the toothbrush. Since Mother's stroke, I'd some-times felt sand shifting under my feet, but, actually, it had *always* been shifting. I just hadn't known about it before.

How had Father found the *time* for another family, with all his engineering and his business trips Abroad? I visualized his passport, his *empty* passport, and sat down, suddenly, on the side of the bathtub. He'd never been to Japan! I'd believed he'd gone there because that's what he'd told me, and because he'd brought me back Japanese presents: a doll, the notebook, the netsuke animals. It *hadn't* been a disguise for secret engineering work or spying missions for the Government. He *didn't* have another secret passport somewhere else.

I shifted my behind on the cold enamel, the movement reflected in the bathroom mirror, clear and sparkling now that I'd polished it. I looked pale and hunched, with a deep groove between my eyebrows. When Father had said Japan, he'd really meant *Crawley*. He'd been not a spy, but an old man having an affair with another woman, Ms. Katharine Hargreaves, and father (dad!) of a child, Charlie Hargreaves, by her. He wasn't a hero, a Laurence Olivier, a tortured, clever soul who did the right thing. He'd been like a character from a Mills & Boon, the man with the flashing teeth and sports car who the heroine rejects for someone more reliable.

I knelt beside the bath, shook scouring powder inside, and scrubbed at the barely visible ring. I hadn't had a bath for years—I preferred showers—but Mother had had lots of them. I'd had to run them for her. I stopped. The ring I'd just erased had been another part of her dust. I wished I hadn't scrubbed it away.

I sat on the white cotton bath mat, hugging my knees. I felt sorry for Mother. Mother, who'd had *a lot to put up with* and who had been *good* not to tell me about Father's other life. I rested my chin on my knees. I didn't want a boyfriend, but if I *did* have one, I certainly wouldn't want to share him. Mother had had to share Father. Charlie Hargreaves must be at least twenty-one years old, so she'd had to share Father for all that time, even longer. And yet she'd been kind enough to leave them something in her will. I rocked to and fro. A cold dread seized me. The photo from Father's wallet that I'd blue tacked to the fridge!

I ran downstairs. The woman in jeans with her hair blowing over her face, holding a baby, must be Ms. Katharine Hargreaves of Crawley, and the baby must be Charlie Hargreaves! I stared at them. Now that I knew who they were, they looked different. Katharine Hargreaves's hair was untidy and her gaze to the camera bold and triumphant, while Charlie Hargreaves's face was pudgy and his tiger onesie garish and cheap looking.

I stuck the photo back on the fridge, facedown, and fetched the Japanese notebook. I sat down at the kitchen table—I couldn't bear to sit at Father's desk—chewing my pencil. I had lots of answers now to the questions I'd noted over the last months. They were all unpleasant. They needed to be written down, though, because they were *true*. With all my memories turning out to be lies, it was important to have a record of what *had* happened.

Wiping my eyes with the back of my hand, I began. There were no Japanese stamps in Father's passport (question one) because he'd never been there. He'd led a double life with another family instead. Katharine and Charlie Hargreaves were that family; they were the people in the photo from Father's wallet, and Father had been the source of the Deceit, Lies, and Shame that Jane from Dunstable had shuddered about. I hadn't yet found the answers to what was wrong with Father's finances, or why his evening shoes had secret compartments, and I'd already crossed out the question about where Mother's Lost Capacity had gone because of her Passing Away.

I pushed Roxanna on her swing, my mind still on Charlie Hargreaves. I hadn't replied to his last email, and I'd deleted two further ones without reading them. Perhaps it wasn't *Polite* or *Respectful*, Rule One, to keep him in the dark.

"That's enough pushing," shouted Roxanna from the depths of the apple tree. "My legs are getting scratched!"

I could hear her words, but it was if I was behind glass listening, in a world of my own.

"Stop!"

My hands dropped. The arc of Roxanna's swing slowed. She jumped off. "When we don't listen, our teacher tells us off," she said severely. She used my arm to steady herself. "What are the monkeys doing now, Ellie? Tell me a story. About them dressing up and dancing."

I shook my head so firmly I felt dizzy. "They don't wear clothes. They just drape sheets around themselves to play with or to keep warm." Roxanna's mouth formed an O shape when I added quickly, "And they *definitely* don't dance."

"Roxanna, sweetheart, Daddy's back," Sylvia called.

"Daddy!" Roxanna took her hand from mine and ran inside. "Have you brought me something?"

Sylvia waved to me. "We must have a catch-up soon, pet."

I went back to my house and switched on the computer. It couldn't help being on Father's desk, but it was still irritating. I was trying to block him from my thoughts. If I didn't, I knew I'd throw things, or bang them on the table like I'd seen Josh do, or slam doors over and over again. Or I'd stay in bed forever, with the outside world—where people lied—muffled by the duvet and the drawn curtains. I rested my head in my hands. There was still the problem of Charlie Hargreaves.

I let all my breath out in a long sigh and clicked on to the Internet.

Dear Charlie,

I think you should sit down, although you are probably sitting down already because of being at the computer, because I may be writing something that will be a shock to you.

Your "Dad" had another child. It is me. He was my father.

I am telling you because otherwise it would be like

lying, and I don't tell lies (unlike Father). I know I am not being diplomatic by telling you. That is another reason why I wanted you to sit down.

Yours sincerely,

Elvira

33.

No one is a hundred percent good or a hundred percent bad.
—Karen Hutchinson, adoptions administrator,
Animal Arcadia

I woke, before the alarm, to the cold misery of realizing, again, that Father's other life hadn't been a bad dream. I went downstairs to make a cup of tea, pushing his photo farther under the dressing table with my slippered foot.

I switched on the computer. There was a reply from Charlie! I sat up, muscles tensed. I put a hand to my chest, ready. Everything Charlie Hargreaves had written to me so far had been a shock.

Hello, Ellie,

I was really pleased to hear from you again. Finding out about me must have been a complete shock. I'm sorry, perhaps I didn't take that into account. Anyway, it's great we're in contact again.

It was kind of you to explain things about your father and mother, but I have a confession to make. You didn't know I existed, but I knew you did. I already knew about

Dad, your father, having a wife and child (you!) who lived in Sandhaven. Because I thought you might not know about Mum and me, I've tried to take things slowly. Perhaps not slowly enough!

Do you realize we're half brother and sister!! That's so cool! I never liked being an only child, and now I've got a big sister. You must be a few years older than me?

When you've gotten over the shock, it would be great to have a chat on the phone. Perhaps, when you feel ready, we could even meet up?

Love from your brother,

Charlie

I printed out the email. I read it over and over again. Sylvia had told me things about Father, and I'd thought about them, thought about them all the time, pieced them together, but seeing them written down made them real. My *brother*, Charlie.

I sat there for a long time, blood throbbing in my ears, staring at Charlie's email. He'd known about me when I'd had no idea about him. I looked out the study window. Sunlight was breaking through the leaves of the oak tree. One magpie chased another away with a harsh, rattling cry. Across the road, the postman ran from house to house in loping strides. A small, blue car drove past with a bicycle on its roof rack. It seemed impossible that normal things were continuing like this when my world had completely changed.

I folded the email, pressing it into a neat and perfect rectangle, the collapsed feeling sweeping over me even though I had nothing to grieve about. I had my volunteering, my friends at Asda and the Library, Paul, Karen too, Sylvia next door, and Roxanna, and in the evenings I had *Coronation Street, Casualty,* my David Attenborough DVDs, and all my Mills & Boons. I had a full life. But, at this moment, I felt empty rather than full. Not just empty but…naked. Charlie knowing about me, when I'd known nothing about him, made me feel like I was in an enclosure at Animal Arcadia, with the public staring at me through the fencing, knowing where I'd come from, knowing my name, watching my private moments, and laughing at them. Now I knew exactly how an orangutan felt.

Later, at Animal Arcadia, I shook out a sheet and folded it carefully, placing it on top of a pile of bed linen. I got into a rhythm of shaking, folding, placing. I wished the rest of my life was so simple. Charlie's email was still on Father's desk at home, waiting for me to know what to do with it. It was unsettling, not knowing.

"You OK over there in the ranks?" Karen's chair swiveled toward me. "Did I hear a sigh of insubordination?"

I looked up, baffled, as usual, by Karen's conversation. "Mmm."

"Are you all present and correct? No more skirmishes with neighbors or creepy keepers?"

I shook my head, unsure what a *skirmish* was. I kept my eyes fixed on a striped towel I was folding. "I've been traced by a distant relation," I mumbled to the towel.

"Sounds painful! What sort of distant relation?"

Karen was right. It *was* painful. I put the towel on the pile and picked up a pink sheet, shaking it out to check it was clean. "The half brother sort of distant relation." My heart raced as I said the words aloud for the first time.

"Oh!" Karen's crest of hair quivered, and she said a swear word. "That must have been a shock."

"It still is a shock," I said, my face hidden behind the sheet.

"Give me a full report then." Karen folded her arms. "Start at the beginning."

I put the sheet on the pile and tried to work out where the beginning was. "I don't know *when* Father's other life began, but I've found out he had one, one that nobody told me about." I grabbed a gingham duvet cover and shook it open.

Karen nodded as I told her the rest of the story. The pile of folded linen grew higher. "Crikey! You must be seeing your dad in a whole new light." She spun around and around in her chair, silent for a moment. "It doesn't take away what he felt about *you*, though."

"He told me a lot of lies." I threw a folded sheet onto the pile.

"Not good." Karen paused mid-swivel. "But nobody *is* a hundred percent good or a hundred percent bad, are they?"

Aren't they? I wished they were. My life would be a lot easier. I recognized Rule Seven: *Rules change depending on the Situation and the Person you are speaking to*—the one I struggled most to understand.

Karen waved her hand, palm up, fingers spread, which people did, I'd noticed (noticed *and* written down), when they gave explanations. "You might be very kind to animals, but cheat on your wife," she explained. "Or, you might never look at another woman, but on the other hand, never do anything nice for anyone else."

My eyes prickled. "Father looked at another woman," I told her. "He cheated on Mother with one. If I'd known about it, I would have been nicer to her." I thought of all the times I'd rolled my eyes behind Mother's back, when she'd sent me upstairs, yet again, to fetch something, and the way I'd dug my nails into my palms when she'd told me things were *Beyond your capabilities,*

Elvira, and recently, how I'd wanted to press my hand over her mouth every time she'd shouted *Not that way!*

"But, your mum and dad *didn't* tell you, so you *didn't* know. Don't beat yourself up." Karen swiveled back to face her screen.

I hadn't. I'd only banged my head on pillows and cupboards. I paused. It may have been a Figure of Speech.

The more I talked about Charlie, the more real he seemed. I didn't know if he was a good thing or a bad thing yet, because of not having had a half brother before.

Paul slapped his hand against mine—"High five, big sis!"— when I told him. He tapped his empty Coke bottle on the table. "You'll be able to boss him around like my sister does me, even though she lives in New Zealand."

I put my cup down, heart sinking. Would I? Is that what big sisters were supposed to do? I crumpled the napkin in my hand. "I haven't even spoken to him yet. I'm trying to get used to the idea first."

"When are you going to? Can I meet him?" Paul's eyes gleamed.

I shut my eyes. "One step at a time," I repeated under my breath so as not to look eccentric, even though I was only with Paul, who wouldn't mind, or even notice. Mother's words. Mother's comforting words. Mother, who'd had to share Father with Ms. Katharine Hargreaves. What would she have felt about me emailing, perhaps speaking to, even meeting, the *other woman's* son? It was a situation I'd never read about in a Mills & Boon.

Mother's jar of dust, waiting to be scattered, had taken center stage on the mantel, crowding out the African figures and looming over the cherub clock. The jar's bronze plastic surface gave off a dull glow, as if the dust inside had a kind of life. A life that still watched over me and was aware of what I was doing.

I'd stood in front of it last week, hands clasped, to ask for advice. I'd bought a four-pack of raspberry yogurts without noticing there were only two days to go before their sell-by date. By the time I'd eaten the third yogurt it would be out of date, and the fourth one would be even older. But throwing them away would be Wasting Money and Wasting Food.

Her jar hadn't spoken, of course. It had no blood supply or vocal cords, but as I'd watched it closely, waiting for some sort of sign, a pulsating gleam of light had seemed to reflect from its bronze surface. I'd watched it, hypnotized, almost forgetting what I needed advice about. A bubble of raspberry yogurt came up in my throat. The gleam was like a spark of life. It must mean I should help save the planet. I didn't throw away the third and fourth yogurts; I ate them. I didn't get food poisoning. Mother— well, her jar—had been right.

I stood in front of her jar again now and asked her if meeting Charlie was the right thing to do. I stood there for several minutes, but this time there was no sign of a reply.

34.

Write down some ideas about what to talk about first.
        —Amy from America, website member

While I was still waiting to know what to do about Charlie, my birthday came and went.

It was my first birthday without Mother, without a trip to Ravel, and without her giving me the money for a new Nature Documentary DVD, two new Mills & Boons, and some new stationery.

I'd gotten used to not having a present from Father and I didn't want to think about him anyway.

Karen gave me a small, cuddly orangutan from the Animal Arcadia shop. I hung it from a nail on my Mills & Boon shelf under *O* beneath *Ocean Odyssey*, a story set aboard a marine conservation ship. Paul gave me a giant chocolate-chip cookie from the café, slightly squashed from having been trapped under a tray of sliced white loaves. Sylvia gave me a *Coronation Street* plate to match my mug and an Asda Fresh Lemon Toiletries Set with shampoo, shower gel, and body lotion.

In the evening, I got out one of my old David Attenborough

DVDs, *The Life of Mammals*, and watched it while I ate the cookie from my new plate.

Later in bed, I lay in the dark with my eyes wide open to get used to being twenty-eight.

Shelbie spread out some glossy black-and-white photos on Sylvia's dining table. The ladies in the photos looked similar and slightly out of focus, as if they'd been photographed through a misted-up window.

"This is before…and this is after."

In the after photos, their eyes drooped under something spidery on their eyelids. "Real-hair false eyelashes. All the way from China," Shelbie said. Their teeth were bared and dazzlingly white against their tanned skin, and their hair was pulled into complicated patterns on top of their heads, or fluttered behind them like horses' manes.

"They're very glamorous, pet." Sylvia bent over the pictures, a dishcloth in her hand, her face pink from getting roast things out of the oven. Her blond hair was curlier than usual. "I feel a proper Cinderella, looking at these, my hair all frizzy with steam." She pulled her leopard-skin top down to cover her bottom, but it wasn't long enough. "I can't shift this weight either. I haven't touched a cookie in over a month, but it hasn't made a blind bit of difference."

I opened my mouth to remind her about the tin that Trevor kept, under lock and key in his shed, but she went on, picking a photo up. "Oh, this is you, pet! I didn't recognize you at first. You look as if you're going to a film premiere!"

"Yeah, Lewis brings out the best in his subjects. Specializes in soft-focus lighting." Shelbie took out a packet of sugar-free chewing gum from her bag. "I've been doing up the storeroom in the salon as a studio. Got different backdrops, velvet curtains, gilt chairs, a wind machine, and all in there now. We've got a makeup artist that comes in *and* a fashion stylist."

"Oh, I say," Sylvia murmured.

Shelbie looked around at us, chewing. There was a strong smell of peppermint. "Yeah! We're offering a complete makeover package that includes the photo session with Lewis. We're calling it *Look Lovely with Lewis*." She tilted her head to one side. "Is that something *you'd* fancy, Sylv?"

Sylvia clasped the dishcloth to her chest. "Oh, I would, pet! That'd be a real treat."

Shelbie pointed a silver-tipped finger at her. "You're on then, Sylv. You can be a guinea pig."

This was a remark so bewildering that it *must* be a Figure of Speech. *I* would have loved to be *made over* as a guinea pig, but, they weren't glamorous animals, so it couldn't have been what Shelbie meant.

"Right, ladies." Trevor put his arm around Sylvia's middle. "Me and Josh have earned a little drink, I think." I stood up straight. I tried to look confident and capable when Trevor was around (and Josh too, because I was frightened of him), in case I made him think about Social Services.

"What's Josh been doing then, while you've been washing the dishes?" Shelbie put the photos back into a padded silver album with tissue paper between the pages.

Trevor picked up the serving spoon Sylvia had dished up the apple pie with and pretended it was a microphone. "*I've loved, I've laughed and cried,*" he sang, throwing his head back, his beard vibrating. He stopped. "Josh took the rubbish out. I haven't seen him since. He's tinkering with the bike, probably. Thirsty work, bike tinkering."

Shelbie looked at him without saying anything, her jaw working.

Trevor tried to hide his face behind the serving spoon. "I'll make him stop and come out for a pint. There's an open mike session on at the pub."

"Wish *I* could stop him," Shelbie said, eyebrows raised.

———

I lay in bed, my brain whirring, going over, like I always did, the wrong things I'd nearly said. Or had said. Charlie Hargreaves also made my brain whir. I'd had days of looking at the advantages and disadvantages list without being able to make a decision. I threw back the duvet, fed up with it all. Contacting him might at least switch off part of the whirring. I ran downstairs and replied to his email. I gave him my phone number but told him I wasn't good on the phone.

As I replaced the tribal throw over the computer, I saw Trevor and Josh coming back from the pub. Trevor, staggering, had his arm around Josh's shoulder, and both of them were laughing. Whatever Mike had opened must have been fun, whoever he was. Or were they laughing at *me*?

———

"What shall we play?" Roxanna hung onto my arm.

"Play? I don't really *play*." I chewed my lip. "We could watch a nature documentary."

"I want to play a *game*."

I suggested Snap, but Roxanna said I'd win all the time. "I know!" She gave a little bounce. "Hide-and-seek!"

I was looking after her while Shelbie and Josh were at work, Sylvia was being *made over*, and Trevor, at the last minute, was helping out behind the bar of the Club. "Granddad or I will pick you up later," Sylvia had told Roxanna.

"But how will I *know* it's you if you've had a makeover?" Roxanna had gazed unblinkingly at her grandmother.

Sylvia had laughed although Roxanna had not made a joke. It was a perfectly logical question. "We'll have a code word then, shall we, pet? Fish cakes."

Hide-and-seek went on for a long time with Roxanna winning more often, in spite of not knowing my house, because she was smaller and could squeeze into places.

My best place for hiding was in Mother's wardrobe. I climbed in, smelling cigar smoke and the sweetness of her Je Reviens. I closed the door quietly and sat down, the swallowtails from Father's evening jacket brushing against my face. The last time I'd hidden here was when Josh shouted at me, when I'd gotten things wrong. Thanks to the Rules and greater exposure to social situations, that was happening less often.

In the darkness, my thoughts turned to Charlie. I'd posted another message on the website for women with my Condition: What did you say when a long-lost distant relation phoned? Again, Amy from America replied. We'd already discovered we had lots of things in common, such as caring for an elderly mother and being shouted at in bus stations (although, because of the jeans, that didn't really happen to me anymore). Amy couldn't wear jeans because of weight issues and was confined to her house for the same reason. She watched a lot of TV—*Oprah Winfrey* and *Judge Judy*—so she knew about life.

Amy advised me to tell Charlie about my Condition straight-away and to explain how it made social situations difficult. Then, if he didn't even *try* to understand, I'd know it would be pointless meeting up. Anybody, she wrote, even a NeuroTypical, would find a telephone chat with an unknown half brother dif-ficult. She suggested writing down some ideas about what to talk about first. I'd printed out her message.

I heard Roxanna downstairs, counting up to fifty. She hesitated over thirty-seven and said thirty-five twice. I nearly shouted she'd made two mistakes, but that would have led to her finding me.

"Where are you, Ellie?" she called, running up the stairs.

I put my hand over my mouth to stop myself from saying, "I'm here. I've won!" I heard her open the door of the shower cubicle. My foot touched a shoe. It was one of the evening shoes I'd once thought Father spied in. I wanted to knock my head against the wardrobe door for thinking Father was spying when he was actually with Katharine and Charlie Hargreaves, but Roxanna would have heard me. I tapped the shoe's hollow inside. Why would you have needed secret compartments in Crawley anyway? How had *they* helped Father with his other life and *other woman*? *And* other child. My fingers recoiled, and the shoe fell.

"I heard something, Ellie. I know you're up here!" Roxanna's voice traveled from bedroom to bedroom.

The wardrobe door was yanked open, and I heard her rapid breathing. I kept completely still. She ran off again, her shout becoming a wail. "Where *are* you, Ellie? I've looked in every single *place*!" The wail disappeared downstairs.

I hugged my knees, smiling. I'd won. Roxanna had spent ages looking but hadn't found me. Then there was a thud from down-stairs and sobbing. "I want my mummy. Mummy!"

I stepped out of the wardrobe. "Roxanna!" I called. "It doesn't matter that I won. You won nearly all the other times."

Roxanna, lying on the hall carpet, sobbed louder.

"You haven't fallen over, have you?" I ran downstairs and bent over her. I knew she was too young to have had a stroke.

"No!" She sat up, her face red and puffy, her blond eyebrows drawn together. She looked like Josh. "Where *were* you? Your house is creepy. I couldn't find you!"

"Behind the clothes in the big wardrobe in Mother's bedroom. I've hidden there before."

"That's cheating then! You *practiced*!" Roxanna drew her eyebrows together again. She got up, wiping her eyes with the sleeve of her pink cardigan. She pushed a blond wisp of hair away from her face and smoothed down her dress. Apart from her face being red and her mouth turning down at the corners, she looked as if she was going to a party, like she always did. "Can I have my fish cakes now?" she asked.

Trevor smelled of beer and cigarettes. He was in a hurry. Whenever I saw him, he was in a hurry. I had just successfully (well, nearly successfully) looked after his granddaughter for two hours and fifty-three minutes. Looking after a small child *must* count as managing. I nearly pointed this out, but his spiky beard, thin legs, and sharp comments always made me feel nervous. I could record it in my Japanese notebook as evidence against being sent Away, though.

"Got everything you came with, love?" he asked Roxanna.

"No." She smiled up at him.

"Run and fetch whatever it is then. Quick! Quick!"

"I can't 'cause it's my fish cakes, and I've eaten them!" Her body shook with laughter. For once I understood the joke and laughed loudly too.

"Oh no!" Trevor clapped his hand to his forehead. "Not another comedian in the family." I wondered how many other comedians there were. "You should be at the open mike night. Die laughing? I thought I'd never start! Come on then, love. I've got a steak pie to put in the oven. Save your gran cooking. Mind you, she might be too posh for pies now."

———

I heard Sylvia's car pull in as I was draining the pasta. I left it in the colander and rushed into the living room to peer from the window. A lady—it must have been Sylvia, because it was her car—got out and teetered toward the front door. Her hair cascaded over her bare shoulders. The evening sunlight reflected from earrings that hung like bunches of grapes. Even from this distance, I could see black fringing around her eyes. *Sylvia* fumbled in her bag, but the front door was flung open. I leaned close to the window.

"No callers, please." Trevor held up his hand in the *Stop!* gesture we'd learned at school. Behind him Roxanna was bent over, giggling.

"Get on with you." Sylvia gave him a push.

"A strange woman has assaulted me on my own doorstep," Trevor shouted. "Officer!"

"Don't make me laugh, Trev. I don't want to smudge anything." She bent down to Roxanna. "Boo! Fish cakes!"

"I *almost* knew it was you, Granny," said Roxanna.

I went back to the kitchen and began arranging slices of

peppers and eggplant in a line of red, green, black, red, green, black on the pasta. I was grating some cheese when the phone rang. I dashed to pick it up and was just about to say *No, thank you very much*, because of it being insurance or double glazing, when the person at the other end said my name.

"Elvira? Are you there? It's Charlie. Charlie Hargreaves. How are you? Is this a good time to talk?"

35.

*It's disappointing when someone you look up to lets you
down.*

—Charlie Hargreaves (Carr),
half brother

O h!" I gasped.

"I'm sorry. I didn't mean to startle you."

"I'm not good on the phone," I managed to get out. I sat
down, the walls of the study closing in. "And I don't like sudden
things." I scrabbled around on Father's desk for Amy's advice
message. I'd added useful phrases at the bottom, including *Tell
me more about*…because apparently everybody liked talking
about themselves. *Tell me more about ecology*, I'd written, and
*If you were stranded on a desert island, which ten cookie varieties
would you take?* I hadn't included any questions about Father
because whenever I'd talked about him, I'd learned something
unpleasant. Something I hadn't wanted to know. His photo still
lay facedown on the bedroom floor. When I vacuumed around
it, I jabbed at it with the hose.

"Easily startled…" Charlie laughed. "Like a wild animal."

I paused and took a deep breath. Charlie didn't fill the pause.

"Father said he was raised by Scottish wildcats," I told him, "so it might be in my genes." Then I remembered this had been a story.

Charlie laughed. "Yeah, right!"

"No, it wasn't right. Father made it up."

"OK. I don't think that was the only thing he made up, was it?"

I shook my head. "He kept a lot of things secret. You, you were a secret."

"And now here I am, making you talk to me. You're doing fine on the phone, Elvira."

I was silent for a moment. "You can call me Ellie, if you like." I breathed out a long breath. "It's difficult when there aren't any set rules for this sort of thing."

"Well, we'll make our own," Charlie said, his voice sounded as if he was smiling.

I took another deep breath. "Charlie," I began, "I've got a condition." I spread out the fingers of my hand, palm up, although he couldn't see me.

"Is it serious?" he asked.

"It means I don't always understand things. Jokes. Figures of speech. How people signal with their eyes. And I can go on about things without noticing I'm being boring. And sometimes things get to be too much."

"I see," he said. There was a silence, and I waited for him to sneer or lose interest. "So, should I explain things, like *why* I'm saying something?"

"Yes, please," I said.

"Cool! An original way of looking at things!"

He was phoning from home without his mother knowing. It was *a sore point* between them, he said, which I think was a Figure of Speech.

I didn't say anything. I didn't even want to think about

Ms. Katharine Hargreaves, who'd made Mother share and whose blond hair blew untidily over her face. Because of her, I didn't really want to talk about Father.

Charlie seemed to pick up on this. "I need time to get my head around Dad. I expect you do too. There'll be plenty of time for that in the future."

There was a pause, which neither of us filled. Charlie asked how I felt about meeting up. He gave me a little time to think about it. I smoothed out the crease between my eyebrows, and when he asked me again, I took a deep breath and said I'd give it a go. My heart was hammering because of him being a Stranger but also a half brother, and because of there not being any rules.

He suggested us meeting somewhere before Christmas— universities broke up early, he said—and I said the Shire Horse Center in the New Forest, because of *Long-Lost Love*, the Mills & Boon story about the long-lost adopted brother. It was the only guidance I had.

I lay down after the phone call, my dinner untouched on the kitchen table. I hadn't thought I'd be able to talk to Charlie at all. Suddenly, like that, with him being two different and difficult things—someone I didn't know, but also a relation—at once.

The doorbell rang the next morning. It was Sylvia, come to thank me for looking after Roxanna. There were smudges at the outside corners of her eyes where the wings of eyeliner had been.

"Any chance of a cuppa, pet?" she asked, coming in.

When I returned with the tray, Sylvia patted her rigid hair. "So what do you think of these extensions then? Shelbie's idea. Ever so expensive, apparently." She took a sip of tea, her fingernails longer and a brighter shade of scarlet than usual. "Yes, I couldn't fault her there. Proper pampered, I was. Manicure, facial, makeup, hair, the stylist. The photo session with Lewis." She pursed her lips. "Bit of a ladies' man is Lewis. Old school friend of Shelbie's. Got in touch on Facebook, apparently. All teeth and tight trousers."

I wondered if Charlie would be like that. I wasn't sure what a ladies' man was, except that Sylvia and the lady who'd done our cleaning had both said the same thing about Father. I squeezed my knees together. I wanted to tell Sylvia about Charlie's phone call, but it was hard to change the subject.

She leaned forward. "Shelbie and Josh had a bit of a row. Josh tripped over Lewis's tripod. He's never been keen on the makeovers. Says there's no profit in them. Then Shelbie started hissing it was *her* salon and *her* ideas, and Josh went straight out the door." Sylvia drained the last of her tea. "I'm worried about their marriage. I really am." She heaved herself up. "Well, Trevor's waiting for his lunch. I promised him I'd only stay five minutes."

"Sylvia, I had a..." I began.

Sylvia moving toward the door. She turned, not hearing, "Did I tell you, pet, Josh has joined something to do with Vikings? Where they act out battles. Not really the way to a woman's heart, is it, though?"

I closed the door, considering. No man in any Mills & Boon I'd read had ever tried it. I washed and dried up the tea things. Sylvia hadn't kept to Rule Three (Conversation doesn't just

Exchange Facts—it Conveys how you're Feeling) because she'd gone on and on about her family and hadn't noticed *I* had one now too. And she'd broken her promise to Trevor. He might think that was my fault. I slammed the cutlery drawer shut.

36.

A half brother might be a lovely thing.
　　　　　　　　　　—Mrs. Sylvia Grylls, neighbor

*C*harlie phoned me again. He said he'd keep the call short. He needed to keep it short anyway because of his mother not knowing.

He'd pick me up next Friday. I put the date down on the calendar, under this month's picture of a Bedlington terrier, and added another conversational topic to Amy's advice message: *What is your favorite breed of horse?*

I knew we could talk about dogs because Charlie had one, Akira, not a definite breed but *a bit of an assortment.* He'd mentioned him on the phone, and my mind had flown to Peek Freans Family Assortment with its pink-and-gold packaging. He'd told me that *Dad* had named him after a Japanese film director he was keen on.

My heart had lurched at Charlie calling Father *Dad*—and at the mention of Japan. Just saying the word *Japan* made me feel stupid, now that I knew it stood for Crawley. Upstairs, I'd turned around all the little netsuke animals—back on our landing after months of looking out to sea at Bay View

Lodge—so I didn't have to see their faces and feel stupid all over again.

What would I *do* with Charlie when we met? I wouldn't be good at any of the things I'd seen other people do with their brothers: bossing them about, making them do up their shoelaces, playing football with them, wrestling.

Preparation, Elvira, is the key, I heard Mother say, although it was doubtful she would have approved of me meeting Charlie. I packed my backpack, because there were only five days to go, and checked that the Safety Kit, with its earplugs and sunglasses and cookies, was inside. I put my Japanese notebook in too and a copy of the spreadsheet in case I needed to refer to it.

"Off to Asda, pet?" Sylvia called. "Want a lift?"

She was too busy driving to talk about Josh, Shelbie, or Roxanna, so I was able to tell her about Charlie. She turned to me, her eyes wide, freshly painted wings at their outside corners. The car swerved. Sylvia jerked the steering wheel.

"You're actually meeting him, pet! I knew you'd been emailing each other, but…" She shook her head. "My goodness, you *have* come a long way! What would your mum say?"

"I've only come…" I stopped myself. Mother would probably have said, *Ridiculous idea!* I could only *assume* that though, because of there being no flash from her jar when I'd asked it what I should do about Charlie.

"She might not have been too keen, but she's not here now, is she, pet? It's wonderful you're moving on." Sylvia was smiling. "So, what's he like?"

"He likes animals, and he doesn't mind pauses in conversations."

"Well, that sounds good, pet. Have you spoken to him about..." She stopped while she negotiated a mini roundabout. "About your dad?"

"A bit." I folded my arms. "But I don't want to find out any more." I thought of Father's photo. "It'll make me rude and challenging."

"Ah, pet." Sylvia clicked her tongue. "You've had a lot to contend with. One surprise after another. Hard for you to see a different side to your dad." There was a moment's silence. "This Charlie," Sylvia went on, "your half brother...*half brother*, pet, fancy! If he's nice, that might be a lovely thing, pet. It could open up a whole new life for you." She swallowed. "You're in it together now, aren't you? He knew you *existed*, yes, but I expect there's a lot he *didn't* know about your dad." A truck labored up the hill, its engine giving a high-pitched squeal of protest, and in the distance, there was the faint, insistent sound of an ambulance. "You'll be able to support each other now, won't you?"

Charlie's car was older than Sylvia's. It had a *Save the Badger!* sticker in the rear window and a familiar, comforting smell of dog. On the backseat was a mud-stained tartan rug and a crumpled copy of the *Guardian*.

"This is really weird, isn't it?" Charlie said, shaking his head and laughing.

"Mmm." I nodded, holding tight to the hem of my purple sweater. Sitting next to a relation I'd never met before was overwhelming. I wished I could sit in the backseat or, even better, lie down there to get used to the situation, but I was too afraid to ask. I didn't find anything funny in our meeting, but Sylvia had said people sometimes laughed in new or strained social situations to show they wanted to get on with each other. I hadn't thought about Charlie finding the situation difficult.

He wore jeans and a red-and-white sweater with a complicated pattern of deer on it. His mother had knit it, he said. I shifted in the car seat. I didn't want to hear about his mother, Ms. Katharine Hargreaves, who'd made Mother share Father, especially now I knew she saw me as *a sore point*.

————

It was easier at the Shire Horse Center because we talked about the horses. I didn't have to use any of the conversational topics I'd written down. We watched a girl demonstrate grooming a Percheron, and then walked around looking at horses gamboling or grazing in the fields. My arms swung stiffly, and I glanced up at Charlie to see what I should be doing. He was tall, like Father, I thought with an uncomfortable jolt.

He walked bent slightly forward, in long strides, his striped scarf flying out behind him. He had light-brown curly hair, and he smiled a lot—like Father, I thought again, but then not completely like Father, because Charlie only smiled at *me*, not at the lady who took our money, or at the girl groom whose jodhpurs were so tight.

We stood gazing at a group of three retired Shire Horses standing close together.

"They could be chatting," said Charlie, "talking about the old days." He wound his scarf around his neck. "Having a heart-to-heart. It's hard for *us* to talk about our backgrounds, isn't it?" He put his hands in his jeans pockets. "It's such a weird situation."

I put my hands in my jeans pockets too and kicked at a clump of grass.

Charlie turned, looking at me. "You must be really angry about Dad, Ellie. It's worse for you because it was a complete shock."

I looked up into the branches of the tree next to us, trying to put my feelings into words, but then I got sidetracked and wondered if there was an owl asleep there or even a Great Bustard. In the end I just gave up and kicked the grass again, muttering, "I keep cleaning the house, I'm so angry."

"At least there's a payoff then." Charlie smiled.

"No." I shook my head. "I don't get any pay." My hands clenched. "Father told me a lot of lies."

"Yes." Charlie rocked backward and forward on his heels. "It's really disappointing when someone you look up to lets you down."

I nodded, my eyes prickling. "He already had a family. He had Mother and me. Why did he want another one?"

Charlie sighed. He didn't know either. "He got into the habit of lying, I suppose. And he could charm the birds from the trees, Mum always said."

I looked up at the tree again, imagining a line of owls, Great Bustards, even cranes, shuffling their clawed feet along a branch, eager to fly down at the mention of Father's name.

Charlie bent to pick up a piece of dry wood. "I suppose if Dad *hadn't* been like that, hadn't won Mum over, *I* wouldn't be here." He broke the wood in half with a snap that made me jump. "Mum's never talked about him much. Her lips go sort of tight when I mention him. I think she always felt second best, not good enough. She used to watch loads of documentaries on BBC4 to try to keep up with Dad."

I glanced at him, surprised. I tried to decipher what he said. *I* had trouble keeping up, Mother said. I hadn't thought NeuroTypicals did too. But, if Ms. Katharine Hargreaves had found keeping up with Father a struggle, she should have found her own husband, a less clever one, not shared someone else's. Besides, Father had only watched documentaries when Mother was around. With me he watched Classic Horror Films and Variety Shows.

Ms. Katharine Hargreaves feeling *second best* had caused friction, Charlie said, fights. *Good*, I thought. There had been a row the night before Father died. A bitter feeling came to the back of my throat because of it being with them.

"Wasted the best years of my life on you," Charlie's mum had shouted. The next day *Dad* had treated her to a new sofa from IKEA, and dragging it in from the car had given him a heart attack.

Father had had a heart attack because of a sofa. *We* didn't shift furniture about at home, and we used Tofu to stave off heart attacks. There was a pause so long it was a silence. "What color was the sofa?" I asked.

"Pale green. A two-seater. Why?"

"Father—" I stopped. We were talking about the same man, but it was difficult to see Father as this...other dad. "*Our* father. He and Mother bought *our* sofa from John Lewis. It's big, dark red, with mahogany legs. It sounds completely different from your sofa." It sounded much *better*, but I didn't say this (Rule Six: Diplomacy).

I thought about how I'd found out Father had died. I'd come back from the Library, with a book for Mother about the *Treasures of the British Museum*. Mother had just said, "Your father's dead." A policeman and policewoman had come to tell her, apparently. I'd dropped the Library book, I remembered, and Mother had thrown up her hands. Then she'd made me sit down, and *she'd* made *me* a cup of tea, with *sugar*, in spite of my BMI. We'd just sat there in the kitchen for ages, and we both forgot our eleven o'clock cookie choice. And then Mother's face had crumpled and she'd gone upstairs.

"Neither of us could believe he'd died," I said to Charlie now. "He'd gone Away so often, for months sometimes, that it just seemed like he was Abroad on a business trip."

I bit my lip, feeling stupid. Father being Away had meant Father spending time with—no, not just *spending* time, *living* with—Charlie and the brazen, not-good-enough Ms. Katharine Hargreaves. There *were* no foreign business trips. It was hard to get used to this.

"Yeah, he *was* always away, wasn't he? Those business trips took ages."

I darted him a glance. The *business trips* Father told *Charlie* he went on were when he was living with *us*. I didn't point this out, feeling a faint twinge of nausea. Not pointing things out was *Diplomacy*. At least it would be a tick for the checklist.

Charlie had found out *Dad* was really *Father* when they couldn't go to the funeral. It was only then his mum had told him that Father had a wife already, one that he would never leave because of there being a disabled child involved.

Charlie stopped, clapping his hand to his forehead. "Sorry! Sorry! I don't see you as disabled. That's why I said it."

Other people had said I was disabled. Mother's friend Jane, for one. I crunched my feet through some drifts of leaves, my chin rising. "It's more that I'm *different*."

Charlie smacked his forehead again. "I can't believe I just

said that!" He looked at me. "Yeah, you *are* different. In a good way. Unique."

I blinked and my toes gave a little bounce, then my jaw set again as Charlie continued, telling me how he'd felt sorry for his mum because of Father not wanting to marry her.

"But later, I thought, well, some of my friends' dads walked *out* on them when they were kids, and others had dads who *did* stay around but were really, like, controlling. I always got on well with Dad, when I saw him. The Gregster." Charlie laughed. "That's what I called him. He was a lot of fun, wasn't he? OK, *older* than some dads but with more…style. Except for being, like I said, a flirt. With waitresses and people. That was embarrassing."

That must be what a *ladies' man* meant. Someone who liked ladies and paid them a lot of attention. Someone who ended up telling them lies.

———

After my meeting with Charlie, I thought about Father every time I passed a Greggs bakery. Greg. Greggie, the Gregster, Dad. Not just *Father.* I went into one for the first time, the branch in the bus station, and bought two wholemeal rolls. *Greggs* was on the paper bag. After I'd eaten the rolls, I smoothed it out. I hesitated between the two boxes under my bed, then put the bag, not into Cookie Packaging, but with the other things to do with Father, the ammonite from Lyme Regis and *The Observer's Book of Dogs.*

37.

A ladies' man leads to trouble.

—Mrs. Sylvia Grylls, neighbor

He's left her," Sylvia announced, flopping down with a long sighing breath. "He's come back home. I *knew* their marriage was in trouble. That blasted salon. It's all Shelbie thinks about. My poor boy…" She scrabbled in her bag for her cell phone and a tissue. I darted into the kitchen to put the kettle on.

"Tell me more about…where Josh left her," I asked from the doorway.

"In the blood…blasted salon! In *his* salon! The one *he* provided the money for! Now *he's* had to leave, and *she* gets to keep it all! All his hard work…" Sylvia put the tissue to her eyes.

I arranged the tea things on a tray, listening while she spoke to Katie on her cell phone. "He's down at the club with Trev now. Having his mind took off Madam." I bent down to get out the cookie tin. Sylvia wasn't supposed to eat cookies, but in this situation—her son leaving his wife—she might really need one, or possibly several. I might need at least one too, because of Josh moving back next door. I tore open a new packet of

Hobnobs and put the whole lot on a plate. They'd been invented by McVitie's, in Scotland in 1985.

"Tah-rah, Katie, chuck." Sylvia snapped shut her phone and turned to me. "It's this makeover business. Shelbie's obsessed with it," she said, smoothing back her longer, blonder hair. "That Lewis who takes the before-and-after shots…"

"A ladies' man, you said," I remembered, adding, "like Father."

Sylvia reached out to pat my knee. "Yes, pet, I did, and charming though they are, they lead to trouble."

They lead to Crawley, I thought, to Katharine Hargreaves. To Mother having to share, to her being angry, to Father going Away, to shocks and suddenness. To Charlie.

"Yes, all around the women Lewis is, adjusting their hair, leaning in for close-ups. I wouldn't trust him as far as I could throw him."

"You couldn't throw him at all, probably," I pointed out. When I saw her shoulders shake, I offered to make her more tea, but she carried on talking about Josh and Shelbie. The last straw had been Shelbie taking out a loan, without asking Josh, to open a whole chain of hair salons throughout the New Forest. Sylvia talked for a lot longer than two minutes, but it *was* a type of special occasion.

Charlie had emailed me two days after our Shire Horse Center outing. He said it would be nice to meet up again before Christmas and suggested going to Animal Arcadia! I'd been so excited—I'd be able to show him how the animals knew me and tell him lots of Facts he might not have known before—that I'd had to get up from the computer and run around the study, my arms wide, before I could reply.

Now we were on our way there and I could feel my heart beating because I was excited again and also not very used to Charlie.

"Did Dad…Father talk to *you* about Japan much?" Charlie took his eyes from the road for a moment. "He used to go there regularly for engineering work, didn't he?"

"Yes." I looked out the car window and took a deep breath. "Yes, he talked about Japan a lot. But…" I let the breath out slowly. "There weren't any Japanese stamps in his passport." I stole a quick look at Charlie's face. "Japan meant Crawley. Or Sandhaven."

Charlie burst out laughing. "No! What a nerve! He never went there at all?"

I shook my head. I listed all the "Japanese" things Father had brought me back, supposedly from his "business trips."

"Do you know, thinking about it," Charlie said slowly, "it *was* a bit weird, 'cause when I was younger, I was really into manga, but Dad had never heard of it. And it's *massive* in Japan. And when we went to Wagamamas in Crawley, Dad just toyed with the food. He didn't seem to know what any of it was. Couldn't handle chopsticks. Just kept laughing when he dropped his food. Said it was because he'd stayed in posh hotels over there where all the food was European." Charlie shook his head, grinning. "And all the time Japan was a cover-up for *you*! You almost have to admire him, don't you?"

Did I? I looked out of the window again, noticing a dog trotting past, wearing a black coat with a reflective strip that made it look official. I *used* to admire Father: his important job, his foreign travel, his height and good looks, his lovely smell of English Leather, his classical education. He'd gone to a Private Boarding School, which was a school for especially clever children, he'd said. He'd learned Latin and Greek there, which is why he'd found Japanese easy. I put my head in my hands. Father had probably never learned Japanese, since he'd never been to Japan! A wave of heat rose in me. That was why I didn't admire Father anymore: because he was a liar!

"You all right there?" Charlie bent toward me without taking his eyes off the road. "Like I said, it's worse for you."

"Mmm," I mumbled. I tried to slow my breathing. I sat up straight, staring at Charlie's navy sleeve. He was wearing another sweater his mother had made; knitting was her hobby, apparently. Charlie told me she worked as a secretary for a construction company that put up ticky-tacky new homes everywhere.

"That's why I'm studying ecology. Doing my bit to redress the balance of nature."

I didn't know if that was a joke or just information. It was always hard to spot the difference. I looked out of the window at the empty fields, so far unspoiled by ticky-tacky houses. Mother had hated new houses. She'd thought our 1930s house was too modern. She would have preferred something with a moat and drawbridge, Father said.

I asked Charlie if Ms. Katharine Hargreaves knew he was meeting me. I couldn't bring myself to say the word Mum. *Your mother*, I said. He rubbed his chin. "Yes," he said, "and she wasn't happy. She was always miffed about Dad not marrying her, and your mum's bequest got her so riled up, she tore up the letter from the lawyer."

I whipped around to stare at him, then sat stiff and silent for a moment. Sharing another woman's husband was bound to lead to trouble. But instead, *my* mother had left her a present, *and* one to her son, in her will. I mentioned this.

"They weren't nice things to leave, though, were they?"

"Weren't they?" I glanced at Charlie, surprised. "Yours was to do with animals, well, birds."

"They were a bit mean. Think about the wording, Ellie."

I thought about the wording. I shook my head. "I don't understand."

"Great *bustard* sounds like *bastard*, someone whose parents weren't married, and John Major, who used to be prime minister, was famous for calling his colleagues bastards."

I clapped a hand to my mouth.

"Not your fault, Ellie. Your mum had every right to be angry with us…well, with Mum. But you can see why Mum wasn't keen on me getting in touch. I asked her if she wasn't even a little bit curious, but she said she was too busy earning a crust. She said no relative of your mum's would ever welcome me, and that I should let sleeping dogs lie."

"You said she looks after him," I remembered. I knew it was a Figure of Speech. It just reminded me of Charlie's dog.

"Yeah. Akira. My buddy. Part Jack Russell, that's his short legs, part Labrador, and part Airedale—that's the teddy bear fur." Charlie turned down the narrow country road that led to Animal Arcadia. "You had an Airedale, didn't you?"

"Yes." I looked out of the window at the familiar countryside flashing by. "Tosca. Mother named her. I miss her."

"Yes." Charlie inhaled deeply. "That's the penalty for loving anything, isn't it?"

I told Charlie Facts about every single animal at Animal Arcadia, all two hundred and sixty-three of them. He was really taken with Vikram, the ex-circus tiger, and we spent ages watching him batting a rubber ball about with his enormous paws.

We reached the orangutans. Only part of Rojo's great bulk

was visible, dozing in a hammock, but Cinta was sitting near the fence, with Pernama, auburn fur sticking out untidily, round eyes blinking, swinging around her as if she were a tree.

Charlie stood watching them, smiling. "They look wise."

"They *are* wise." I'd tried modeling myself on an orangutan, because I'd felt like one, but it hadn't worked. I wasn't much good at conversation, but I *could* talk, and, anyway, there hadn't been any other humans modeling themselves on orangutans for me to communicate with. The nearest thing was the website for women with my Condition. I looked at Charlie. "*They* don't tell each other lies so…so there's no disappointment."

"No." Charlie stuck his hands in his jeans pockets. "I expect you know where you are with an orangutan."

"You're at Animal Arcadia, at the orangutan enclosure," I reminded him.

Charlie knocked his forehead against the fence. "So I am. Come on then, show me where you work."

———

Karen was on the phone, sorting out an adoption certificate. I showed Charlie the table where I put the newsletters into envelopes, the pile of donated linen waiting for me to check, and the photos of the two hundred and sixty-three animals on the walls. She put the phone down with a click and a swear word.

"Hello, Karen." I pointed to Charlie. "This is my long-lost distant relation."

Charlie's eyes crinkled. "We're getting less distant, though." He smiled over at her. "Hi, Karen. I'm Charlie, Ellie's half brother."

Karen smoothed back her crest of sticking-up hair. "Hi, Charlie. It's great my little NCO's found some family."

Charlie was *family*, she'd said. I blinked at someone else saying it, out loud, just like that. As if it was normal.

She got up from behind her desk, something she rarely did, to chat with Charlie about ecology and species preservation, while I tested myself against the animal photos, matching all but two to their names.

Karen was livelier than usual, and she and Charlie found a lot of things to talk about before the phone rang again and she had to go back to her desk.

I said the same things about Charlie to Paul.

Paul slapped his open palm against Charlie's. "High five, bro!"

Charlie and Paul had a conversation too, one I could join in, because it was about Wildlife Documentaries.

Josh and Shelbie's car was parked outside Sylvia's house when Charlie dropped me back home. Shelbie was unfastening Roxanna from her car seat.

"Hello, Ellie," Roxanna shouted. "I've drawn a picture of Per...Pern...."

"Pernama," I said loudly, but not shouting.

Shelbie turned around to stare at me through black-lined eyes, then flashed her brilliant white teeth into a smile.

"I've drawn a picture of Pernama wearing a dress." Roxanna struggled free of her straps. "It's in my case. I'll show you."

I closed my eyes, shaking my head. When I opened them, Shelbie was staring not at me, but at Charlie. She tossed back her long, dark hair.

"Hello, Ellie." She shifted her chewing gum to her other cheek and stuck out her hand, still looking at Charlie. "And hello…?"

"Charlie. Ellie's half brother."

Shelbie clasped her hands to her chest. It stuck out in two large pointed peaks, and her hands just fit in the gap between. "Oh! It's like something out of the soaps!" She flapped a hand in front of her face, although it was a cold day. "Sorry! It's just that I *feel* things, you know."

Roxanna clung to Shelbie's leg, encased in pale-blue denim like a sausage in its skin, and stared up at Charlie.

"Hello, Roxanna." Charlie crouched down to shake her hand. "It's great you've drawn a picture of a monkey." He got up. "You must be an animal lover like me and Ellie."

"Pernama's an *ape*, actually, because she's an orangutan," I corrected. A lot of people got that wrong.

Sylvia came straight up to Charlie, her high heels clicking on the pavement, and introduced herself. Her smile was nearly as big as Shelbie's.

Trevor loomed behind Sylvia, his arms folded. "Hello, mate. So, you're Ellie's brother." He examined us both from over his horn-rimmed glasses. "I hope you know what you're letting yourself in for."

Sylvia laughed loudly and gave Trevor a little push, and Shelbie's white teeth flashed again. I stretched my mouth upward.

"I never wanted to be an only child"—Charlie smiled, looking around at everyone—"so I was thrilled to find a sister." He looked down at me. "And such a nice one."

"That's lovely, pet." Sylvia pulled out a tissue from her leopard-skin sleeve.

I bounced up and down on my toes I couldn't stop myself—until Roxanna frowned and said that it was only her that did dancing.

———

Hello, Charlie.

I hope you are well.

I enjoyed going to Animal Arcadia with you.

I'm glad you met Sylvia and quite glad you met Roxanna.

Karen in the Adoption Center asked me for your email address. She wants to send you a link to a Tiger Project in India where they rescue Circus Big Cats and give them a proper retirement Abroad where they should be living. She told me to say that she will Facebook you as well.

I look forward to seeing you again and I hope you have a good Christmas.

Yours sincerely, Ellie

Charlie's email had an e-Christmas card of Father Christmas and some reindeer that really moved. The music to "Rudolph the Red-Nosed Reindeer" played when I clicked on it.

Hi, Ells.

Nice to hear from you so quickly. It was great to meet the clan next door.

Animal Arcadia and your mates there are ace. It'd be

cool if you could give Karen my email address—that Tiger Sanctuary in India sounds really interesting. I've always wanted to travel, especially to that part of the world.

Perhaps we could meet up in January, before I go back to uni, if that's OK with you? When we do, could I go inside your house? Would you mind? I can't quite get my head around Dad living there, leading another life there with you. I hope that doesn't sound crazy. It's just that seeing it might make it seem more real.

Till then, Keep Dancing (as they say on *Strictly Come Dancing*—Mum's favorite TV program, not mine!) and have a happy, happy Christmas!

Love from Charlie

38.

You just never know with Dad, do you?
                    —Charlie Hargreaves (Carr),
                                    half brother

 hristmas 2016 was my first as an orphan, half sister, and
C volunteer. My sessions at Animal Arcadia carried on
throughout the holiday because it was open every day except
Christmas Day, and I helped out at a special festive Pet Therapy
session at Bay View Lodge on December 21. Buster, the *Caring
Canine*, had worn a pointed elf hat and a green coat, and, as
Santa's Little Helper, had delivered small gifts—soap and han-
kies—to the residents. The guinea pigs hadn't been in costume,
but they'd been given presents of seed sticks wrapped in red
tissue paper, which Brenda had opened for them there.

On Christmas Day itself, I'd lit a candle next to Mother's jar
to keep it company and gone over to Sylvia's for lunch. I'd only
gone to be *Polite* (Rule One). Roxanna and Shelbie were spending Christmas Day with Shelbie's father in his caravan in the
New Forest, and Josh was taking part in a pretend Viking inva-
sion down at Sandhaven Harbor. I practiced my conversational
skills on Katie and her husband and found out that his favorite

program was *Top Gear*. The two little boys were not very good at conversation.

I'd been glad to come home and watch a *Coronation Street* festive special in the quiet of the living room. I blew out the candle first so that Mother would not "see" me watching Lowbrow Television.

January 1 passed like any other day except that Asda was shut.

A week later, it was the anniversary of Mother's stroke. I lit the candle again and stood in front of her jar. Until this day a year ago, Mother had still been in charge. A year ago, I'd still looked up to Father although he was dead. A year ago, I had not even heard of Charlie Hargreaves.

"Hi, Ells!"

"Hello." I opened the front door wide.

"Bear hug," he said, wrapping his arms around me.

I started a small growl in my throat, but there was no answering sound from Charlie, so I stopped. My arms remained stiffly by my sides because I wasn't expecting the hug.

"This is weird!"

We went into the kitchen first. He recognized the photo of himself as a baby next to the spreadsheet on the fridge. After I'd met Charlie for the second time, I'd turned it facing outward again, but I'd partially covered Ms. Katharine Hargreaves with a Sandhaven Council list of recyclable materials. "I'm wearing a *tiger* onesie! Still my favorite animal twenty years down the line." When I told him I'd found the photo in Father's wallet, he gulped and then he got something in his eye, which he had to remove with a piece of paper towel.

He followed me into the hall, his footsteps slowing. I opened the door of Father's study. "Fu…flipping heck! Bl… blimming hell!" Charlie stood stock-still. "I can smell him! His cigars." He reached out, hesitating, to touch one of Father's books, *Parachute Drop to Poitiers* by Major B. F. Gibson. It was a spy story, and I imagined it springing from the shelf at Charlie's touch and bursting open on the floor, spilling out a lie or something secret from between its pages.

I slapped myself on the wrist, something I'd seen Sylvia do. "Father spent a lot of time in here, reading and smoking and telephoning people," I told Charlie. When I used to play in the garden, I'd see him through the misted-up study window, leaning back in his chair, a hazy presence like one of Shelbie's *after* photos, the telephone to his ear. I frowned, realizing something. "He might have been telephoning your mother." A picture came of Ms. Katharine Hargreaves, in a fuzzy, pink, hand-knit cardigan and silver dancing shoes, smiling into the phone, a BBC4 program about Ancient Mesopotamia that she was pretending to understand on in the background.

"Yeah." Charlie tilted his head to read the book titles. "He did phone Mum a lot. Every Friday night for sure. I remember that. I always wanted to go to the cinema or out for a pizza, but she never would because we had to stay in for that phone call. Mind you, he *phoned* because she hardly ever saw him."

"He didn't only use the phone on Fridays," I said. I leaned against Father's desk, no longer quite so bothered about touching it, watching two magpies squawking and clattering at each other, fluttering their feathers and taking little jumps off the ground. One for sorrow, two for joy. There wasn't much joy in going over how Father had lied to me.

Charlie arched an eyebrow. "What was he up to? Who else was he phoning? You just never know with Dad, do you? Come on then, show me the rest of the house. You don't mind?"

I shook my head. "It makes his two separate lives more real."

I smoothed down my sweater. "In the end it's better to know things. Then you know where you are, and you're not telling lies to yourself."

"You're as wise as an orangutan, Ells." Charlie put his arm around my shoulders. He moved us toward the stairs, his face set. "I've psyched myself up for feeling bad," he said. "It's going to be weird seeing what Dad kept secret. After the weirdness we'll have to compare notes, get things straight in our heads. And feel *really* bad, probably."

Charlie was right. We did feel really bad. But that was later.

⎯⎯⎯

"No offense, Ells, but your house looks *so* different from ours. It's all vintage. Or, what do they call it? Shabby chic? Like being in a time warp! A museum!" We were back in the study and Charlie waved his hand at the bookshelves. "And this, it's like a *stage set*, somehow. Do people even have studies anymore? I've got some academic textbooks at home and Mum's got a few knitting books, but mostly we use our Kindles."

I knew what a Kindle was because Karen had one. She read it during her lunch break. I turned around. I was surrounded by books on all sides except for the windows.

"I like books." I pressed my lips together. "I like my Mills & Boons." They were in my bedroom. Three shelves of them in alphabetical order, because Mother hadn't allowed them in the study.

Charlie squeezed my shoulder. "It's what you're used to, I suppose. My mum's really modern, but then, well, she's quite a bit younger than your mum."

I raised my chin. "Mother had me late in life." I nearly added that *she* hadn't gone around sharing other women's husbands. I really wanted to say it, my hands clenched, but it wouldn't be *Polite* or *Diplomatic*.

"It's not that I don't like your house, Ells. It's just that it doesn't seem real. I feel as if I'm playing a part in a film here." He gestured toward the stairs. "And all that dark furniture, that massive wardrobe… Don't you feel it's kind of oppressive?"

"It's been handed down through generations. Mother was proud of it." I felt a rush of loyalty.

"They're beautiful things"—Charlie nodded—"but not what you'd expect in, well, quite an *ordinary* suburban house. A lot of your stuff looks like it's escaped from a stately home."

I frowned, thinking about the stately home. Mother had been brought up in a castle, Father said, which might or might not be true. I reached out to touch the back of the little carved chair. If all the furniture *was* modern, *I* might disappear. It was part of me. The wardrobe, Mother's cherub clock, all those things, weren't alive—I knew that—but they had their own personalities, a sort of *role*. When I wasn't there, I worried about them missing me.

Charlie went on. "I suppose what I expected was a mirror image of my house. That was a bit stupid, since our mothers were really different, by the sound of it."

"Mother didn't look in mirrors much. She said as long as you were clean and tidy and didn't have spinach sticking to your teeth, anything else was vanity."

Charlie laughed. "My mum's vain then. She's always doing her hair, trying on clothes."

"Charlie," I said, "talking about the wardrobe reminds me I want to show you something."

"It's not a skeleton, is it, or a mummified corpse, or a stuffed bat?"

"No." I stopped in the doorway, staring at him. "It's none of those things. Why would there be a dead body in Mother's wardrobe?"

Charlie put his head in his hands. "Sorry, sorry, sorry! It was just a joke."

"It wasn't very nice. It could give me nightmares." I shot Charlie a quick frowning glance. "I've always hated jokes," I added, going upstairs.

I returned with Father's black leather shoes. "Have a look at these. There's something strange about them."

Charlie laughed. "In this house, even shoes are mysterious." He felt them carefully. "Expensive leather. Very soft."

"Feel inside." I looked away, then screwed my eyes shut for a moment, remembering the night I'd come across them, the night in the wardrobe. And the time I'd hidden there from Roxanna. Sylvia had said afterward that Roxanna had been frightened I'd completely disappeared.

Charlie shook the shoe. "Hmm. The inside's built up."

"I thought there might be hidden compartments inside. Secret ones." I stared at the study carpet, a dark-red Persian design, and bent to pick up a paper clip. "Before I knew about you, I thought Father might have been Away on Secret Government Missions." I pulled the wire of the paper clip apart. "Spying."

Charlie didn't laugh. "I'm not surprised, Ells. When people *don't* tell you stuff, your imagination goes into overdrive. And you were right about what he was doing being secret." He held up the pair of shoes like a Show-and-Tell at school, only then it would have been a dead frog, or a foreign stamp, or a railway timetable, or Poppy's alphabetized list of characters from *Coronation Street*. "Know what? I think they're *ladies' man* shoes. The secret built-up bits were just to make him look taller. Nothing more sinister than that." Charlie shook his head, a faint smile on his lips. "They must have added about two inches to his height. To his charms."

So Father hadn't been as tall as he'd looked, or felt. I remembered him stooping down to kiss me. Wearing built-up shoes had been another kind of cheating.

"The old devil, eh?" Charlie stretched his arms above his head and yawned. "One mystery solved, anyway. He certainly was a devil for the ladies. I've never said, but I've sometimes wondered if Mum was the only one. Besides *your* mum, of course. I wouldn't have put it past him to have had a third family somewhere!"

I put a hand to my mouth. "No! He couldn't have!"

My heart began thumping. I turned to look out the study window again, thinking. Charlie had said they hardly ever saw him. We hadn't seen a great deal of Father either. My hands strayed to the hem of my sweater. There *could* be more relations out there. I was only just getting used to Charlie. Sharing Father…Dad…with him. Ms. Katharine Hargreaves had been one of Father's secretaries. Mother had said Father had gone through lots of them. There might be a whole chain of secretaries, all with small children looking like Father, typing, knitting, reading Kindles. Another thought came.

"Charlie, there were some postcards." I ran upstairs and brought them down. "This one particularly. From *D*. It's signed with a kiss."

"Hmm." Charlie took it, sitting down on Father's chair. "Let's think. Well, it's only from *one* person, whoever she is. No family mentioned. And there weren't any other bequests in your mum's will, were there?"

"No. And no other photos in his wallet." I was still holding on to the hem of my sweater.

"That's true." He sat for a moment, shaking his head.

"Tell you what, Ells." He reached for a pencil. "Let's compare dates and establish some sort of timeline for Dad…Father. We could rule a third family out altogether then. We'd know where we were. Where *he* was!" Charlie's laugh didn't crinkle his eyes. "Try to get his *affairs* in order, eh?"

Affairs. A familiar word. One I'd heard Mother use about Father. "Not all of me *wants* to know the truth," I said, rolling (not twisting) the sweater's hem between my fingers. "We might find out things we don't want to."

Charlie gave my shoulder a quick squeeze. "But, like you said, at least we'll know where we are. We don't want any more secrets, do we? And, well, if he *was* hiding something, we'll face it together."

I took my hand from my forehead. "That's what families say in *Coronation Street*."

"Yeah? Well, we *are* family now, aren't we?"

I stood in the doorway, half in and half out of the room, wanting to know exactly when Father had been Charlie's dad and when he'd just been my father and where he'd been in between. And dreading it at the same time. I thought about what Charlie had said might be in Mother's wardrobe. I leaned against the doorframe, the sand shifting beneath my feet, a sensation I hadn't felt for weeks.

RULE 6
It's better to be too Diplomatic than too Honest.

Reason behind rule:
Most people don't want to hear negative comments about themselves.

People don't always need to know *everything*.

Useful phrases:

"You don't look fat." (even if they do)

Hints and tips:

Don't make personal remarks.

Don't give an opinion unless it's asked for.

Don't ask personal questions.

Don't always just say what you think.

If you can't say anything nice, don't say anything at all.

Rule followed? ☐

39.

People always do find out in the end.
—Charlie Hargreaves (Carr),
half brother

W e'll try and check, shall we? Be scientific about it."
Scientific meant taping sheets of paper together to make a timeline for Father. It meant me fetching my "Japanese" notebook and some little diaries I'd kept over the years until it had gotten too boring to just keep putting *Went to the Library*.

"And his passports," shouted Charlie from downstairs. "You said they'd hardly been used."

He put on the kettle and brought in the cookie tin. I'd showed him where it was hidden. Inside were some Bourbons and Ginger Nuts, the remains of a packet of the Peek Freans Family Assortment. There was less to be scared of with a cookie in your hand.

I took a Ginger Nut—a solid, reliable cookie—and gave Charlie Father's date of birth and the dates of his National Service and when he'd met Mother. The photo of Father in his tropical hat, still lying facedown on my bedroom floor, had been taken then.

"You weren't born until 1988, so they were married a long time without having children," Charlie said, his pencil hovering over the timeline. The pencil was mine, from school, with an eraser on the end. It had a red spotted design because it had been a present from Poppy. We needed it to write about Father and erase mistakes, because of his identity shifting.

"They had me late in life," I reminded him. Mother had been forty-five, Father forty-eight. I crunched on the Ginger Nut. "I can't remember, but Father can't have been around much in the early 1990s, because Mother used to say how tiring it had been, on her own, as an older mother. He must have been Abroad on business trips."

Charlie turned around. "But you said his passports had hardly been used."

"Yes, yes I did. No, they hadn't. I keep forgetting the lies." I clutched the cookie.

We checked the passports just in case there was a Japanese stamp hiding somewhere, but they were as empty and unused-looking as before.

"Never been out of Europe, then," said Charlie. "Mum did say he'd taken her to Paris once."

"That must have been when that photo was taken." Katharine Hargreaves, a brazen harlot, in jeans, with windswept hair, holding Charlie, a serious-looking baby in a tiger onesie. I tried to swallow, but my throat constricted. Charlie had vacationed Abroad with Father, but Mother had never allowed *me* to go.

Charlie wrote down the passport dates, groaning. "It's hard finding out your dad's a cad."

The cookie crumbled in my fingers as I remembered how Mother used to get upset when Father went Away and then, when I was older, angry. *Your Father's not what you think he is, you know*, she'd say. *He's got feet of clay.* I'd thought she meant like a Terra-Cotta Warrior, noble and protective, but Sylvia had since put me right on what the expression really meant. All my life, I'd thought Father was what I thought he was. Smiling, trustworthy, never cross. How *could* he be anyone else? Now that he *was* someone different was being proved scientifically.

Charlie took a Bourbon. "Early 1990s, not with you, you said, and not abroad. So where was he? I wasn't born until 1994, but like I said, *we* hardly saw him. It was something Mum went on about. He definitely wasn't with us the Christmas before the millennium. We were going to go into London for the fireworks. I would have been six. He never came in the end, and I was heartbroken."

I screwed up my face, concentrating, "I was twelve then. No, that was when we went to Mother's friend Jane in Dunstable. Her house was really cold, and I wasn't allowed to open any presents until I'd helped wash up. Father wasn't with us either."

Charlie looked at me. "Both our mothers must have gotten fed up with him going away."

I didn't like him linking them together. Father had been *married* to Mother. I was the *senior* child.

"It's a pity they didn't get together to compare notes," Charlie added.

Mother's jar of dust and ashes was squatting watchfully on the living room mantel. *What a ridiculous suggestion!* I heard. I went and closed the door.

Charlie said that, although his mum had known about us, *Mother* hadn't found out about them until he'd been knocked down by a car. He'd been ten and in a coma, and his mum had phoned our house, something she wasn't supposed to do because of the disabled child thing. Charlie winced. "Sorry!"

My lips tightened. Women weren't *supposed* to contact other women's husbands at all. Ever!

A thought struck me. The reason Father hadn't left Mother was *because* I was disabled. I'd *helped* them stay together. Together, I thought. They hadn't been together very much. I remembered Mother, her suitcase packed and waiting in the hall, leaving practically as soon as Father had arrived back home. All the times between his visits, it had been Mother who'd stayed with me.

"When your mother answered the phone," Charlie continued, "she said, *My dear, you must have the wrong number. Either that, or you are not in your right mind.*" I nodded vigorously at Charlie's words. Good for Mother. "And then, Dad…Father came on, and the next thing I knew was waking up in the hospital and him being there. This must have been 2004. I'll put it down."

"2004," I echoed. "I was sixteen." Things were coming together. Mother had gone off to Dunstable then to stay with Jane, and Mrs. Carver, my old babysitter, had come to stay. She'd still opened a box of Milk Tray every Friday evening, but she'd given me the Vanilla Fudge as well. Nobody had explained anything to me. "So *that* was when Mother found out about you," I murmured.

"It's good to get these things clear." Charlie unfolded his long legs and rearranged them in a cross-legged position, like Father's Buddha that contemplated the study from the shelf of books on Eastern Religions. The Buddha had curly hair and an earring, like Charlie, but was shaped more like an orangutan. "We've still got gaps, though. We still don't know where he was when he wasn't with either of us."

I remembered something. Months ago, I'd found a letter from Father to Mother. Not one of the love letters she kept on the top shelf of her wardrobe, but a lone one, bookmarking a page in Mother's *Mozart: Master of Illusion*. It had toppled when I'd been dusting a shelf. The letter had looked old, I remembered, yellowed and brittle. I hadn't read it because it was private. I fetched the book for Charlie now.

He took the letter out, skimming it, eyebrows raised, "November 1990. Before I was born. 'Darlings Agnes and Vivi.'" My heart swelled, and I had to squash it back by remembering the only reason Charlie was looking at the letter was to find out if Father had had a third family somewhere. "Um…he seems to be asking for money here, and then he says, 'Only four more months until I'm home.'" Charlie looked up.

"Home from where? And then he goes on, 'P.S. Darling, if you possibly can, send me some cigars, would you? I can't buy them here, and a bottle of English Leather would give me such a boost. There's only Lynx or Brut available, and most of the men smell like animals. One shower a week is hardly adequate.' And that's it. 'Lots of love,' etc. So, wherever he was writing from in 1990, he was with a crowd of men." Charlie made a note on the timeline, added another question mark, and put the letter back.

I shifted my position on the Persian rug. "I'd have thought Father would have liked Lynx aftershave because of the wildcats."

Charlie's face was blank. I paused, feeling stupid.

"But, of course, that was just a story," I added, my face burning. "It didn't really happen."

"No," Charlie agreed. "Wouldn't it have been fantastic, though?" He put his cupped hands to his mouth and made a loud, howling meow. "Gregory of the Wildcats!"

I joined in his laughter, although I wasn't sure what it was about, and then I gazed out of the window, thinking. It couldn't have been long after 1990 when we'd moved from the big house.

I'd never understood why. Charlie wrote this down, his pencil hovering around 1993.

I glanced up at him. "There were other things I've never understood too. Mother used to say she'd been brought up in a castle. I don't think that was a lie. I don't think she made things up. I mean, apart from Japan, which was Father's fault."

"No, she sounds straightforward, your mum."

"And she had a Trust Fund. It's mine now. Mr. Watson, her lawyer, said it was to protect her inheritance."

"Interesting. The obvious person it needed protecting from was Dad." Charlie scribbled more notes. "It sounds like they had a financial setback. Perhaps Dad lost his job. Two long, unexplained absences—1990 and the next year, then 2000." Charlie chewed the end of his pencil. "Living just with men, and with only basic plumbing—sounds like he was back in the Army. Drastically downsizing their house... The mystery deepens."

He sat for a moment, staring at the timeline, then he checked his phone. "Half past four. I promised Mum I'd be back in Crawley for dinner. She's cooking lasagna. My favorite."

I made a cup of tea. I saw Charlie having dinner with his mother, Ms. Katharine Hargreaves. She'd be wearing a fluffy sweater she'd knit herself, her hair immaculate because of often checking it in mirrors. They'd be eating their lasagna in a kitchen diner, with no animal horns on the walls, and reading their Kindles. Ms. Katharine Hargreaves would be using a finger to help her follow *A History of the British Colonization of Africa*, and she'd have to keep stopping to ask Charlie what a word meant.

I looked at the menu schedule I'd recorded on the new

calendar Sylvia had given me for Christmas. It was a Primates of the World one, and January's picture was of a gorilla. I *could* swap Spaghetti Bolognese for lasagna in case Charlie ever stayed for a meal here. *My* lasagna would be made with Quorn and lots of vegetables. I sipped the tea, frowning. The past was moving, shifting. It wasn't a good time to change the menu schedule as well.

40.

Exercise is good for you.

     —Mrs. Sylvia Grylls, neighbor

I drew open the living room curtains and saw Sylvia coming down her drive. There was something different about her. She wasn't taking the teetering, clickety-click steps she normally did, but striding. She was wearing shiny gold trainers, and her hair was swept back with a leopard-skin headband. She waved.

"New regime! Doctor's orders. Got to do a walk, a *brisk* one, mind, every day." She moved her arms like pistons. "I could kill him! Put the kettle on, pet. We'll have that cuppa, shall we?"

Sylvia had been bad-tempered recently. I knew this because she'd told me. "I'm sorry, pet. I'd invite you in, but I've got a lot on my mind and it's making me snappy," she'd said when I'd called around with a punnet of Asda grapes. "Josh and Shelbie splitting up. It's taken it out of me." She'd patted her chest. "Sent the blood pressure up again."

"Sylv," Trevor had called from inside, "put your foot down."

I'd looked at Sylvia's leopard-skin shoes, tensing because of Trevor. Both her feet were already down, although they were not completely flat on the floor because of the heels.

"Thanks," she'd said, taking the grapes. "We'll have a cuppa soon."

―――――――

Now I prepared the tray for the cuppa with Sylvia. Would feeling *snappy* and your doctor making you do something you didn't want to lead you to kill him? My hand hovered over the tea caddy. It was unlikely because Sylvia was a kind person. Figure of Speech, I thought with a flash of irritation.

"Bless you, pet." Sylvia laughed, sitting down with an *oof!* of expelled air. Her cheeks were pink, and she smelled of laundry dried outside. "You're right. I didn't *really* want to kill him. Actually, he's right about exercise being good for you."

She nibbled her cookie, a Rich Tea from a package I kept for social occasions with Sylvia, so as not to offer her much temptation. Behind the serving dishes in the cupboard was a new tin of Family Assortment. I was keeping it for when Charlie came, so we could each choose our favorites.

―――――――

The cuppa didn't last very long because Sylvia wanted to get home to do some proper stretches and to have a shower and blow-dry her hair. As I went to pick up the tea tray from Father's carved wooden chest, I tripped. There was a crash, the plate of Rich Teas slid into Sylvia's half-empty mug, and tea splashed everywhere. I ran to get a dishcloth. Some tea might have gone inside. I hesitated. Mother had forbidden me to open the chest because it contained fragile items from Abroad. But they could be damaged and stained by the tea. I sat back and looked up at

Mother's jar. It was near the edge of the mantel. I got up and pushed it back, the squeak as I moved it sounding impossibly like *Not that way!*

I knelt with my back to the mantel and lifted the chest lid right up. The creak as it opened was like the creak of coffin lids in Classic Horror Films. I threw back the lid and felt a jolt of electricity like the one I got from standing on Sylvia's nylon dining room carpet.

Inside was an old brocade curtain, completely dry, and underneath that a rectangular shape. I drew the curtain back slowly, so as not to damage the fragile items. Would they be African figurines? Animal horns? Cut-glass decanters like I'd found in the attic? The rectangular shape was a large cardboard box labeled *Clarks Shoes*. It didn't look foreign. I took in a deep breath and opened the box. Oh! I slumped back. Inside were some folded, yellowing copies of the *Daily Telegraph*.

I sat back on my heels, disappointed. Why had Mother kept those? Why had she lied and said the items had come from Abroad when they were English? The newspapers *did* look fragile. Some of the pages were torn, and the print was worn away from where they'd been folded. I looked at the dates. They went back as far as 1984, more than thirty years ago! Why hadn't Mother recycled them or given them to Sylvia for her kitchen bin? Why had she *hidden* them?

I wiped the tray and ate a Rich Tea cookie that was too soggy to put back in the package. I chewed slowly, staring at the newspapers. Mother must have kept the *Telegraph*s for a reason. Once upon a time I'd have thought they contained articles about Father's Secret Government work. Missions he'd performed in "Japan." I swallowed the last of the cookie, the noise sounding unusually loud in the silent living room.

The *Telegraph*s must contain *something* secret for Mother to have hidden them. Something else I'd trusted in could turn out not to have happened. Or something surprising might have happened without me being aware of it. One of the *Telegraph*s was dated the same month—November 1990—as the letter in Mother's book, *Mozart: Master of Illusion*. I chewed my lip. Was I brave enough to search through them? When what I discovered might keep me under the duvet for days and make my hands red and raw from cleaning?

I shivered, thinking about coffin lids. In films, whatever lay beneath was something you wished you hadn't seen. Then I thought of the Lucky Dip at St. Anne's Christmas Fair, which had contained surprises too, nice ones, *quite* nice ones, under the sawdust. I took a deep breath and plunged my hand in. I lifted out the *Telegraph*s and piled them on the carpet. They looked shabby and smelled of attics. I wondered if they'd powder into dust now they were exposed to the light and the air.

I went into the kitchen to wash up the tea things and to think what to do. I let the water run and scrubbed at the tea stains on the bottom of the mugs.

Even if I put the *Telegraph*s back in the chest and covered them up, I'd still know they were there, rustling with secrets, waiting to ambush me. I'd never be able to rest the tray on the chest again without thinking about what lay beneath. I banged the pie dish down on the draining board. I ran upstairs to get the "Japanese" notebook and a sharp pencil, then, jaw clenched, eyes narrowed, I picked up the *Daily Telegraph* of July 19, 1984.

41.

Google never forgets.

—Charlie Hargreaves (Carr),
half brother

*C*harlie, his face contorted, pushed away a *Telegraph.* "Dad did all this, so what does that make *us*? Are *we* going to become criminals too?" He knelt on the living room floor, sorting through the yellowed newspapers. He was doing it so roughly that I thought they might tear, although that wouldn't matter. Accounts of your father's crimes weren't the kind of things you treasured.

Until this morning, when Charlie had driven down from Bath, I'd thought I'd been hallucinating. All my old mistaken thoughts about Father's identical twin brother and his spying career had rushed through my mind. But Charlie had an active brain. He understood what was true. He'd read all the *Telegraph* articles on Father's court cases so closely, making notes as he went through, marking the dates and background details with Post-it Notes, so there couldn't have been a mistake. I *had* gotten it right; Father *was* a criminal. The headlines called him *Corrupt Civil Engineer* and *The Fraudster with Film-Star Looks*. Underneath were blaring subheads: *Man Abused Position of Trust to Line Own Pockets!* and *Confidence Trickster Exploited Friends*.

Father had not been with a third family. (Charlie thought that the postcard from D—*Still remembering Brighton*—must just have been from a woman he'd had a fling with a long time ago. I flinched at the word *fling*.) He hadn't rejoined the Army. He'd been in prison, had written the letter that marked the page in Mother's *Mozart: Master of Illusion* from there. He'd been caught on five separate occasions, committing the same sorts of frauds and deceptions, and had served three sentences, the first before either Charlie or I was born.

I thought of *Coronation Street* episodes where I'd seen prisoners smoking rolled-up cigarettes, rather than cigars. They'd worn denim workwear and eaten their dinners from plastic trays with compartments, metal doors banging and jangling in the background. Poor Father, having to spend month after month in places like that. Then I remembered that he'd broken the law. He was being punished!

I stretched my sweater over my knees, staring at the carpet, my eyes glazed. "I don't want to be a criminal."

"Nor me." Charlie snorted. "It would make sense, though, wouldn't it? We're both children of, effectively, single-parent families, and our father's a liar, a thief, and a jailbird! We should be out robbing a bank now!"

My eyes stung. "I don't want to rob a bank."

Charlie turned toward me and ran a hand through his hair. "Nor me, Ellie. We're both far more decent than anyone would expect. You're the most moral and truthful person I know." He piled up the newspapers, thumping each one down. "Do you know I find this harder to take than him having two families?

This time I'm really ashamed! I mean, he was exploiting the vulnerable here. Taking advantage of people he was friends with."

I wiped my eyes. "I don't know if I can get any more ashamed."

"I phoned Mum as soon as I got your email. When I asked her outright if she knew about all this"—Charlie made a pushing-away gesture with his hand at the *Telegraph*s, lying forlorn and ashamed on the carpet—"she admitted it. She knew, although it had taken her a long time to find out. Thought Dad's schemes were standard business dealings, at first. Believed him, of course, like everyone did, like *we* did. That kind of optimistic way he had—'Of course I know what I'm doing, of course it's going to be successful…' Well, you just sort of got swept away."

Charlie shook his head with an expression that meant he was feeling sick. "Mum thought she could change him. But as soon as he came out of prison, he seemed to be starting some new scheme. One that was going to be a winner this time—yeah, right. And when it wasn't, when people lost money, he just washed his hands of it. Avoided people, didn't answer letters."

I thought about the shaven-headed men that Mother had been Not At Home to. They could have been people trying to get their money back. And there was Mother's briefcase, not filled with pencils and notebooks for her Opera research, but with cigars and chocolate and English Leather aftershave. Those must have been presents for Father in prison! That was what made it seem true, remembering those sharpened pencils I'd put in her briefcase.

Charlie threw the pile of *Telegraph*s back into the chest. A small cloud of dust drifted upward. I thought of Mother's jar of ashes and wondered if Father featuring in these dusty newspapers made *him* part of the Cosmic Swirl. I jumped as Charlie slammed the lid.

"I asked Mum why she'd stayed with him, once she knew. I mean, he'd been to prison, and he was married to someone else! She said, first time I'd heard of it, she'd been planning an escape route. Once I'd got into uni, got settled, she was going to leave. They'd had that dreadful row the night before Dad's heart attack. Mum had gone on about having no future with him and still being young enough to start again."

"She was right," I said, "about having no future, because he died the next day." It was annoying that Ms. Katharine Hargreaves had correctly predicted the future.

"She was looking into opening a wool shop, a knitting shop, in Spain," Charlie said, "for expats. It was going to be a fresh start. She'd already started learning Spanish at evening classes."

I saw Ms. Katharine Hargreaves, red-faced, frowning as she failed to remember the Spanish words for "Can I help you?" wearing a fluffy pink bolero and sweating in the heat. The window of her tiny shop would be plastered with red *Special Offer!* and *Half Price!* signs, because of no one wanting to buy her wool.

"She wasn't going to tell me about Dad's past until I was settled. And then he died before I even got to uni, the day after that row. I don't think she had the heart after. She said his saving grace was that he'd been a good father, and him going to prison hadn't changed that." Charlie, for some inexplicable reason, mimed playing a violin.

He sat down on the sofa. I shifted along it, shoulders hunched. I wasn't interested in Father's relationship with Ms. Katharine Hargreaves. Except for Charlie. It was still hard to share, even if Father was a criminal.

"Well, it's changed things for *me*! My whole life feels a tissue of lies," Charlie said.

I nodded, but Father's lies felt stronger and more hard-wearing than a tissue to me, more like a piece of canvas or leather.

"Mum started crying, because of having kept it all a secret from me"—Charlie put his head in his hands—"and *I* ended up feeling like shit for telling her off, when it's *him*"—he jabbed a finger at the chest, the *Un*lucky Dip, the *No*-Treasure chest—"it's Dad who should have felt like that. And didn't, obviously. Amoral bastard." He laughed without smiling. "No, sorry! Forgot. It's *me* who's the bastard."

There was another silence and then Charlie turned to me, frowning. "Why the hell did *your* mum keep taking him back?"

"They were married. He was her husband." Mother had been obeying Laws and Commandments, reliable, definite things.

"Not a very good one."

No. You were only supposed to have one wife at a time. I was silent.

"And it didn't even sound like a marriage anymore. Sorry, Ells, but you did say they had separate bedrooms. And that she went away practically as soon as your dad arrived."

Yes. It had been as if she didn't *want* to see him.

Mother had gone Away to teach Opera, or to stay with Jane and visit Ancient Buildings with her, if Jane's spine was up to it. Father had stayed to look after me. We'd done the shopping together in Asda and bought extra things like french fries and Jammie Dodgers, throwing away the packets before Mother got home, although I'd saved one for my collection. Father and I used to watch Lowbrow Television and Classic Horror Films together in the living room and eat chocolates even though it wasn't Christmas or anybody's birthday.

"You said your mother had to protect her own money," Charlie went on, pacing the living room now. "She must have come to her senses, after her fingers got burned."

I blinked at the burned fingers. They'd talked about money,

and stopped when I came into the room. I saw Father reaching out to put his arm around Mother's waist, and her, upright,
drawing back.

"But *why* stay with him? And why keep all…all this evidence? It's almost as if she wanted you to find it."

"You said"—I twisted one of the red sofa tassels—"people
always *do* find out in the end. Perhaps going over what Father
did helped her make sense of it. I have to do that with things."

"Maybe rereading the details of Dad's crimes inoculated your
mum against his charms." Charlie held up bent index fingers to
make quotation marks around *charms*. "Made him having my
mum as his bit on the side easier to bear. Perhaps, when you
weren't around, she whipped one out to remind herself why she
should keep him—Dad, Father—at arm's length."

I was silent. Whipped. "Mother…"

"I meant, *took* one out," Charlie said.

Oh. Yes, I nodded. "Perhaps she kept them as evidence, like
in a mystery novel, to show to anyone new who was taken in by
him. A new Bridge Club or Civic Society member. To make it
clear *she* wasn't responsible for any of it." I could imagine Jane
giving Mother that advice. "And then, after he died, well, maybe
she just forgot about them, forgot they were still in the chest."

"Mmm," Charlie agreed. His pacing came to a sudden halt.
"Tell you what, Ells, we'll give ourselves another little treat, shall
we? Inoculate *ourselves*. Find out the worst. We'll Google him."

"But"—I struggled to my feet—"I've done that already. I tried
it months ago. There wasn't anything about Father. It was all
about a *footballer* called Gregory Carr." I scurried after Charlie,
hope rising, "Does that mean all those things in the *Telegraph*s
might not be true?"

"I doubt it very much." Charlie tossed the tribal throw onto the floor. He typed in *Gregory Carr*, his fingers jabbing at the keys, and pressed Search.

The Irish professional footballer's varied career came up on-screen. Charlie scrolled down impatiently and aimed the mouse at page two.

"Oh." I bit my lip. "I didn't do that. Micky said it was a waste of time."

"Yeah? Google never forgets, though. Dad'll be hiding in there somewhere."

Dad…Father was hiding at the bottom of page two. I screwed up my eyes as his name appeared with links to the *Telegraph* stories: *Suave Fraudster, Shamed Civil Engineer, Corrupt Civil Engineer Faces Second Jail Sentence.* The computer, so often *my best mate*, was my enemy now, a hostile machine, spreading Father's crimes and misdeeds worldwide. My whole body trembled as the awful, increasingly familiar words about Father flashed on-screen.

Charlie scrolled through all the references to Father's crimes. It took a long time. Near the bottom of the third web page were articles from the *Sandhaven Courier*. I covered my face with my hands. Our local paper had written about him four times! Mother had managed to keep it a secret from me, but other people must have known! Sylvia sometimes bought the *Sandhaven Courier*, and there was always a copy at the Library, so Juliet Underwood would have read it. It was on sale in Asda, so Janice and Clive probably knew about Father too. My teeth chattered although I wasn't cold.

Charlie clicked on another link. He stopped to stare at the screen, squinting. "Oh no!" he groaned, banging his head down on his folded arms. "I don't believe it! Gregory wasn't even his real name!"

I heard a long, shuddering sigh and was surprised that it came from myself. Little snaps of electricity tingled up and down my arms. My whole body seemed to vibrate. I began to rock to and fro, and then I couldn't take any more. I ran upstairs.

42.

Things are better out than in.

          —Mrs. Sylvia Grylls, neighbor

*E*llie! Ellie, where are you?"

Charlie's voice was muffled by the duvet. I pulled it higher over my head and stuck my fingers in my ears.

"Ellie, are you there?" His voice came upstairs. I remembered Roxanna searching for me and opened my eyes a crack. But Charlie was a grown-up. I didn't have to look after him. I screwed my eyes tightly shut again. There was a knock on the door.

"Ellie! Are you in there? Are you all right? You just vanished!"

The door opened. I wished I'd hidden in Mother's wardrobe. Then he'd never have found me.

"Ellie," Charlie whispered. "It's dark in here. Are you feeling ill?"

I stayed still, my body rigid, fingers blocking him out, telling him silently: *Go away! Leave me alone!*

"Ellie," he whispered again.

I flinched. Was he going to shout up here too? In my bedroom? Where would I go then? Why had I ever contacted Charlie in the first place? I'd had nothing but shocks and unpleasantness since I'd met him.

"Ellie!" He was bending over me. "All this about Dad, Father... It's really upsetting. I can't get my head around it either." There was a soft, sweeping sound of him running his hand through his hair. "We both need time to take it all in." I heard him moving toward the door. "I'm going to give you some space, Ellie." He was speaking slowly. "I'll get off now. Back to Bath. I'll email you." He paused. "But first, I'm going to make you a cup of tea."

For a moment I wondered if Charlie had been to a Special School too, but, no—I swallowed a bitter taste at the back of my throat—that was unlikely. *His* brain was far too active.

I trembled under the duvet, my brain spinning. Father had accepted bribes from building firms to get them council work, and from foreign governments for engineering contracts. He'd defrauded members of the Cricket Club and the Bridge Club, which is why they didn't speak to Mother (*not* because she couldn't make conversation). Charlie had said he was *amoral*, which sounded even worse than *immoral*, but I had no intention of going downstairs to look it up in Father's dictionary.

In the future, I'd look all my words up online. Sylvia said I used too many long words anyway. Knowing lots of words and what they meant was one of the few things I was good at, but Sylvia had said people might see it as showing off. I'd had to add a note about it to the Rules spreadsheet, under Rule Two (If you Look or Sound Different, you won't Fit In): Using very long words and formal language can intimidate other people.

My brain felt as tangled as a plate of spaghetti before I'd found the end of a strand. Father had been a good person *At Home*. It was when he was *Away* that he broke Rules. If he'd had the spreadsheet, it might have stopped him. I opened my eyes to think about this. Would it have? Actually, Father had seemed to know the Rules really well. He *had* been diplomatic and charming, but definitely not honest. He'd never worried about his mistakes. He could get around anybody, adjust to any situation. And the reason he'd been so good at fitting in was because he'd lied all the time. What was the point of me trying to be *normal* when this was how a NeuroTypical behaved? Badly! Why follow Rules if they were designed to help me deceive people?

"Yes, I did know, pet." Sylvia held my hand. "Your mum told me when he went to prison the last time. She knew it would be all over the papers anyway." I stared at the carpet, listening to Sylvia explaining, again, the reasons behind things. "But your dad, you see"—she squeezed my hand—"he always looked so innocent. You'd either have to believe him or forgive him. You couldn't help yourself. Nobody so good looking, so smartly dressed, can be a wrong 'un, can they? But that was me, pet. Your mum, well, she had to face the consequences, didn't she?"

Sylvia leaned closer, her eyes on my face. "I think she was bewitched by him at first, you see. And in the beginning, he *did* make money out of what she'd inherited. Then he got into debt, had to remortgage your posh house, then bankruptcy, prison. *That's it. I'm not taking him back*, your mum would say, but then he'd turn up again, always so confident, and he only had to put his arm around her..." Sylvia trailed off. "Of course, in the end, what with the affairs…Charlie. She kept things civil for you, of course, protected you. Let your dad keep visiting." She looked at me, her eyes soft. "It's a shock, pet. Hard to take in."

My body was rigid and stiff, except for my lip, which was trembling. "I wish I'd never replied to Charlie's card. It hasn't been just one shock; it's been lots of them, one after another."

Sylvia patted my arm. "That's not poor Charlie's fault, though, is it, pet? Most of it's been a surprise for him too. Anyway, things are better out than in, I always say."

"Wow!" Shelbie's mouth hung so wide open I could see the wad of chewing gum on her tongue. She'd popped in for Sylvia to look after Roxanna, because of a last-minute salon appointment.

I'd told her about Father straightaway, before she'd even sat down. *Things are better out than in* (Sylvia), and *People always find out in the end* (Charlie).

"Was he inside for violence?" Shelbie asked. "No?" She closed her mouth. "Oh well, there's some men that've done a lot worse than that, and they've never even been to prison. Bankers and that. And a couple of the travelers I was brought up with." She chewed for a moment. "We look up to our dads, don't we? And, sometimes, they let us down. *My* dad stood in *my* way at the beginning, with the hairdressing."

"Karen." I twisted the corner of the sheet I was folding. "My father was in prison."

Karen didn't look up from her screen. "All right, all right, no need to boast."

"I'm not boasting." My throat tightened. "I wish he hadn't. He was in prison three times."

"Blimey." Karen whipped round. "What for?"

I stared at a row of orangutan photos. "Doing fraudulent things with money."

"Golly! He must have made a bit of a habit of it. Did you find that out from Charlie?" Karen pushed back her wayward crest of hair.

"We sort of found out together. Charlie's angry."

"I bet! He's probably in shock. Still, if your father didn't murder anyone…"

"No, he didn't. We'd have found that out. He'd have had a much longer prison sentence. It would have been on Google."

Karen blinked and turned back to the computer. "My dad's a bit of a dead loss too, in his own way. Drinks too much, always at the bookies, never takes the dog out." She yawned. "Nothing *he* did could surprise me."

"Wow!" said Paul. "*Three* times! What for?"

I told him. He picked up his Coke again. "That doesn't sound very bad." He wiped his mouth with the back of his hand. "*My* dad's a really good guy, but my *mum's* a bit flighty. Walked out on us four years ago. Lives with another bloke. Well"—he belched—"you know all that. I still see her but…" He swung back in his chair. "Dad says she won't ever win a Mum of the Year Award."

I sipped my tea. Mother had thought competitions were

tawdry. I'd looked up the word but, so far, hadn't used it in conversation. And, I sighed, if I took Sylvia's advice, I never would use it. Since Mother would never have gone *in* for a competition, *she* would never have won an award for Mother of the Year either.

———

Charlie and I sat next to each other on Ravel's gilded chairs. He looked around at the black-and-white photos of musicians and the starched white tablecloths and sparkling glassware. "So this is where Dad took your mum?"

I nodded, twisting a corner of the linen napkin Jean Christophe had unfurled, with his familiar flourish, onto my lap. Our greeting had gone as smoothly as before. Two things that hadn't changed. "For special occasions."

"*This* is a kind of special occasion. We've found out some really difficult stuff, Ells, haven't we? Stuff about Dad I'm still struggling to get my head around, quite frankly. I think we deserve a treat." He picked up the menu. I didn't need to read it because I already knew what I was going to have. Charlie sighed and put it down again. "*I* looked up to Dad, you know. Thought he was a cool guy. But, finding out he took *bribes*, conned people out of money, basically…well, that's the kind of behavior I despise."

He shook his head, staring down at the table. "Stuff about Dad I'm still struggling with quite frankly. Can't concentrate on finishing my thesis, can't seem to focus on anything except Dad. I had a word with my professor, told her everything, actually, and she's going to let me take a year off." He leaned toward me, shifting his long legs under the table. "That's another reason I wanted to bring you here, to tell you I'm off to India next month."

My stomach lurched. "To live?" I asked. Charlie was my family now. I'd only just found him.

"No." He took a slice of French bread. We were waiting for the Onion Soup to arrive. "Just for a few months. Karen, you know, your mate at Animal Arcadia, she's been sending me information about a big cat sanctuary out there."

I nodded. "She told me to email you about it."

"Yeah, that's the one. It returns ex-circus lions and tigers, like Vikram, back to their natural habitat. Not the wild exactly, but the next best thing. I'm going out there to volunteer in their education center. Help me get my head straight." He leaned toward me again. "How's *your* head, Ells?"

I felt my head. "It's OK, no headache or anything."

"Good," Charlie took a large bite of bread. He chewed in silence for a minute, then, "How are you feeling about Dad...Father?"

"I don't know." I twisted the napkin. "I can't manage secrets so I've told everyone about him going to prison three times. Some of them knew already, and none of them were very interested, not once they'd found out it wasn't for violence."

"No." Charlie sighed. "The same for me really." He poured two glasses of sparkling water from the chilled carafe on the table and took a long gulp. "My whole life, since I got your mum's bequest, seems to have gone off-kilter. I knew Dad had another family, but it wasn't *real*. Being in your house, *seeing* his other life, made me realize I didn't know him at all. And then discovering his criminal past..."

I nodded. I sipped my glass of water, the bubbles rough and salty on my tongue.

"There's another reason for me bringing you here...well, two reasons." Charlie turned the butter knife over in his hand. "One is to celebrate us finding each other, because meeting you has been the only good thing to come out of all this."

My face went hot, and I had to press my knees down to stop them from bouncing.

Charlie smiled at me. "Now that I've soft-soaped you, I'm going to ask you a favor. You'll need some time to think about it."

I braced myself, staring at the basket of freshly cut bread.

"You haven't met my dog, Akira, yet, 'cause Mum has him while I'm at uni, but if I'm away for months…" I felt his quick sidelong glance. "Well, I wondered if *you'd* look after him?"

"Oh!" I drew in my breath. I put both feet flat on the floor as the sand shifted. I thought about the responsibility and the barking. Then my toes bounced a little as I thought about the face-licking and the company and the fur.

"He's really friendly and well trained." Charlie's eyes were still on me. "I've put you on the spot a bit. Tell you what, next time I'm down, I'll bring him and then you can see how you get on."

I nodded. "I've always gotten on better with dogs than with people." And then reached out for another piece of bread.

43.

Animals do best in their natural habitats.
—Charlie Hargreaves (Carr),
half brother

*A*kira looked up at Charlie, his plumed tail waving. It wagged again when I was introduced to him.

"Here." Charlie unzipped a pocket of his backpack. "I've got a couple of his toys here and his poop bags. Try throwing this." He handed me a worn-looking rubber bone. I hurled it to the end of the garden and Akira raced after it, his short legs bunching into a gallop. After four throws, he disappeared inside the house with the bone.

"Looks like he's had enough," Charlie said, following him. "Now, where did he go?"

Akira lay curled up on Mother's chair, his bone abandoned on the floor.

"Akira, make yourself at home, why don't you? Sorry, Ells." Charlie moved to push him off.

I looked at Akira, snuggled on the chair, his nose tucked under his tail. I'd see him like that every day soon. My toes flexed in my trainers. "No, let him stay. It's nice he feels at home. It's strange, though, seeing Mother's chair with someone else in it."

"She'd have had a fit!" Charlie smiled.

I was just about to correct him when I noticed his smile. Epilepsy wasn't a thing you smiled about. "FOS?" I queried and Charlie nodded. He'd suggested that when he used a Figure of Speech—he found it hard not to, he said—he'd say *FOS* for short, so I'd know what he was talking about. It would be a private code. My face got pink each time I said *private code* to myself.

I scratched the top of Akira's wiry head. Mother had liked dogs, but she'd never have allowed one on her chair. *Down, Tosca, down!* I could hear her saying. *You may be a love rival, but you do not sit on my chair.* Tosca would jump down and gaze up at her, ears flattened, eyes wide and melting, as Mother unfolded her crossword. Sometimes Tosca would whimper and place a paw on Mother's knee. *But I know who you've learned that imploring expression from*, Mother would say, not looking at Tosca. *And it no longer has* any *effect on me.* Her words had been baffling, but she could have meant Father. I avoided looking at the jar.

"Charlie, before Tosca"—a dim memory floated up—"I think Mother's family had their own pack of beagles."

"Blimey!"

"I don't know if that was made up, though." I sighed, watching Akira's eyes close. "Or if she remembered it wrongly, or if I did, or if it was something Father said. Or something he made up."

"Sometimes everything feels like fiction." Charlie pulled another hand-knit sweater, a charcoal-gray one with a broad black stripe, over his head. "Especially Dad."

"Charlie," I said, taking a deep breath, "I've got something to show you."

"No!" he groaned, tossing the sweater on the sofa. "Not more revelations."

I chewed my lip. I'd kept this secret to myself for days. It was something Charlie needed to see. "We know the worst now, anyway," I reminded him.

Charlie sat down on the floor next to Akira, head back, eyes shut, as if he was expecting someone to hit him.

I returned with the wooden box I'd found in the attic. "It's like the missing bit of a jigsaw. I've only just realized where it fits." I showed Charlie the maker's name on the side: H. Gloucester. I'd worked out that the two other initials, which had been difficult to read, were M and P.

Charlie whistled, and Akira's head shot up from his paws. "Her Majesty's Prison, Gloucester. So that's where he was, well, at least once. What's in the box? A file, handcuffs, an illicit still?"

I shook my head. "Look." I got out the tiny pieces of furniture and arranged them on Father's carved chest. "He had these made for me when he was in prison. For Christmas." My eyes stung. "Aren't they beautiful?"

Charlie picked the little cupboard up and pulled its tiny drawer in and out.

I could play with them, I thought, *with Roxanna*.

"Ellie, Ellie!" Roxanna's voice called from outside, as if I'd conjured her up by thinking about her.

Akira's ears pricked up. I went to the door.

"Ellie! There was a dog in your garden," she shouted from behind the fence.

"Yes, there was. He's here." Akira had followed me outside, tail wagging.

"Can I stroke him?"

"You won't be able to reach."

"Ohh!"

Sylvia waved from her french doors. "Is that your Charlie's dog? Friendly, is he? Bring him over then, pet, and Charlie. Come and have a cuppa."

Charlie sat next to me with Akira, eyes half-closed, at my feet. Roxanna was on my other side, combing Akira's fur.

Shelbie hurried into the living room. "Are you ready, sweetheart?" She stopped. "I didn't know you were having a *party*, Sylv. Hi, everyone. Well, no, you're all right. It would be rude to just rush off…" Shelbie sat next to Charlie. "So, Sylv says you're a student. What are you studying?"

"Ecology." Charlie smiled. "Not very glamorous, I know."

Shelbie examined her nails and buffed them up against the skintight fabric of her jeans. She didn't ask what ecology was. Usually Charlie had to explain it. "What will all your studying lead to then?"

Charlie leaned forward, hands clasped. "Well, promoting green technology, advising the building trade…"

"Much money in that?" Shelbie asked, pushing down a cuticle.

"I hope so, eventually. Actually, I'm going to take some time off soon. Ellie's going to look after Akira while I go traveling."

"Traveling! Where to?" Shelbie gazed at Charlie, her eyelids fluttering.

"India," he said with a slight stammer I hadn't noticed before. "I'm going to volunteer at a sanctuary where they return ex-circus tigers to a natural environment."

"Yeah? I remember seeing tigers at the circus when I was

Roxie's age." Shelbie clapped a hand to her chest. "When they snarled, it didn't half give me a fright!"

"Well," Charlie hesitated, "you see, all animals do best in their natural habitats. That's where I come in."

"Circuses are cru…" I began.

"Yeah, taking tigers back to India sounds fun. I love traveling, me. I haven't been to India. Yet," she added with a laugh. "Of course, with the salon, and my marriage not working out… unfortunately. All very civilized, though. Isn't it, Sylv?"

Sylvia nodded, silent.

Charlie gulped down the last of his tea. "Well, I think we ought to be going, Sylvia. Got to give Akira a bit of a walk before I head back to Crawley." He stood up, suddenly tall.

"Of course!" Shelbie jabbed a purple-tipped finger at him, "You're related to Ellie, aren't you? Long-lost half brother, or something?"

"I am, yes." Akira got up, stretched out his front paws, and stood next to Charlie, tail wagging.

"So, it was *your* dad too that was the jailbird. Fancy!" Shelbie looked at him, chewing rapidly.

There was a moment's silence. "My dad made mistakes, that's for sure," Charlie said. He bent over Akira, fastening his leash.

"All a long time ago now, pet," said Sylvia, pushing herself up from the armchair. "All done and dusted and paid for."

———

"Look at the way he can cling although he's so tiny," I murmured to Paul. The new baby orangutan, Jinnga Bulu—"orange fur" in Indonesian—had just been born. He was a small wispy scrap half-hidden in the fur of his mother's chest.

In a corner of the enclosure, Rojo lay in his hammock, chewing a carrot. I could hear the crunching. One day tiny Jinnga would be as big as him, would father babies of his own. Orangutans didn't mind their males having babies with different mothers. There were no worries about sharing.

I let go of the fence. Akira would be arriving in a few weeks' time, as soon as Charlie's visa had come through. "I've been buying things for him already," I told Paul. "A big dog chew to help him settle in."

"Awesome! I could get him a ball! Can I? When he's settled, can I help you walk him?" Paul's eyes shone behind his glasses. "I'll bring the ball. My dad could take us to the beach again."

I nodded, feeling a wave of responsibility. I *had* looked after Mother, I reminded myself. But *she'd* still been in charge. It would be the other way around with Akira.

"Hello, dear," an elderly female voice greeted me on the phone.

"Hello." Jane from Dunstable. I twisted a corner of my apron, the one with Dog Breeds of the World on it. I'd been wearing it to get used to Akira coming, although he was an assortment, rather than a definite breed. I could feel my heart beating. Jane was Mother's deputy. She'd be phoning to check up on me. Mother's jar of ashes was still waiting on the mantel.

"How are you getting on, dear? I've been meaning to ring you for ages. I promised your Mother I'd keep an eye on you, but"—her voice faded—"I live such a long way away, and my spine, of course, is a constant restraint. So, dear, tell me what you've been doing. It's been months since your dear mother passed away. I expect you've been finding it a struggle without her. I know dear Agnes put a lot of…organization into your care. So dear, have you been able to…to, say, manage the shopping by yourself?"

I took a deep breath. "Yes. I've made a weekly meals rotation and a master shopping list. I don't need to go every day anymore."

"I hope you're still buying fresh vegetables, dear. Think of the vitamins. And how are you occupying your time? I expect it weighs heavily on your hands."

I was silent. I stretched out the hand that wasn't holding the phone. How could it weigh time? How could *anything* weigh time?

"What I meant was"—Jane's voice was louder—"how do you *occupy* your time?"

"Oh." A *FOS*. I made a mental note of it. "I research things on the computer. I learned to do it at the Library with Micky."

"You've got your own computer! And you *can* use it, can you, dear?"

"Yes." I paused, then straightened my shoulders, adding, "Actually, it's easy. And I still go to Bay View Lodge to help with the Pet Therapy Sessions once a fortnight."

"That's kind of them, dear."

"And I volunteer every Tuesday at Animal Arcadia. That's an animal sanctuary. I put newsletters into envelopes and sort out things people donate."

"Goodness! And you can *manage* all that, can you, dear? Not too much for you?"

"No. Karen, she's the girl I help there, says she can't do without me."

There was a moment's silence at the other end of the line. I heard Jane swallow. "Well, that was nice of her."

"Sometimes I babysit Roxanna next door as well. She's Sylvia's granddaughter. And, next month, I'm going to look after Charlie's dog while he's Abroad."

"And are you coping with all this, dear? It's not quite what I expected to hear." Jane gave a tinkling laugh. "I think dear Agnes would be rather surprised!" She stopped suddenly. "Charlie? Who is this Charlie with a dog?"

"Charlie Hargreaves. My half brother. He traced me after Mother died."

"Half brother! Did you say *half brother*?"

A secret was better out than in. I took a deep breath. "Father had another family. They live in Crawley." I breathed out all the air I had left, remembering Mother's flight to Dunstable. "You might know about them already."

"Indeed I do! Oh my goodness! Poor, poor Agnes. Your father treated her abominably."

"Abomina…abominably," I echoed, stammering over the second *b*. I'd have to look it up to get it right. Online. I hadn't used Father's dictionary in weeks. I remembered an Abominable Snowman, a Big Foot, that had been featured in a David Attenborough Documentary. It had been hairy and terrifying. Father had lied, been dishonest and unfaithful, but he had been neither of *those* things: in fact, he'd had very smooth skin.

When I was small, I'd watched him from the edge of the bath, enveloped in a cloud of steam, a towel around his neck, tilting his face against the razor. And his shoes, his built-up shoes, had been on the *small* side for a man, Charlie said. *Not* abominable. I didn't disagree with Jane openly because *It's better to be Diplomatic than too Honest* (Rule Six).

"I hope this young man, Charlie Hargreaves, isn't the gold digger his mother was."

"No, he's studying *ecology* at university."

Jane sniffed. "I'm surprised he's got the brains to study *any* subject at university. Agnes considered his mother to be decidedly lacking in intellect. A flibbertigibbet. She had absolutely nothing in common with your father." Jane sniffed again. "Of course he always pandered to his baser instincts."

I wanted to get *everything* out into the open. "We found out that Father went to prison three times." I twisted the hem of the Dog Breeds apron. The living room door was wide open. I thought I heard a faint muffled exclamation of *Apron!* from Mother's jar. There was a sharp intake of breath at the other end of the phone as well, as if someone had pricked Jane with a pin.

"Dreadful business. He was on the front page of the *Daily Telegraph* for days." She tutted. "Your mother tried to keep it from you. Said you'd always brought out the best in Gregory, or some such nonsense." My toes clenched at her words.

There was one last secret. I held the apron tighter. "Did you know Father's name wasn't Gregory? His real name was Gordon."

"Gordon!" There was another harsher laugh. "He even made up his own name, did he? Now why doesn't that surprise me?"

"I don't know," I said. I held the phone tightly to stop myself from slamming it down.

"I always suspected he was from a far-humbler background than he appeared. Appearances are deceptive as your poor Mother discovered. He was a liar, a bigamist, and a criminal. I'm sorry you've had to find all that out—ignorance is bliss in some cases—but it is the truth. The man had no redeeming features. He even tried to flirt with me. Me! With my spine! If I were you, dear, I'd forget all about him and concentrate on cherishing your dear mother's memory."

"Mmm," I said, my heart pounding.

"I must say, dear, you do sound very well, all things considered.

Quite a surprise!" Jane laughed her tinkling laugh again. "Well, I've been standing here for some time, dear, and, nice though it is to chat, my spine is beginning to protest. I'll have to say good-bye."

"Good-bye." I wanted to bang down the phone, but remembering *politeness* (Rule One), I made myself put it down carefully. Then I ran upstairs, picked up Father's photo from the bedroom carpet, dusted it off with my sleeve, and returned it, facing outward, to Mother's dressing table.

44.

Change can be good.

—Charlie Hargreaves (Carr),
half brother

Sylvia went for a brisk walk every morning now. She over-
took me one Friday as I came back from Asda and slowed
down for a *breather*.

"Ten points off my blood pressure," she said. She tried to
encircle her waist with both hands. "Tah-dah! Four inches off
my tummy! I'm a new woman."

"But you're…" I stopped. I was going to add, still quite an
old woman, but Rule Six (It's better to be too Diplomatic than
too Honest) sprang to mind just in time. Sylvia was a big fan
of this Rule, in spite of Father's *dis*honesty having caused so
much havoc.

She stopped walking altogether for a moment. "Shelbie and
that photographer, Lewis, *are* officially an item. I did have my
suspicions." She paused to get her breath back. "Josh and her
have never been right for each other, not really. She's too ambi-
tious for Josh. He needs a placid type, someone who'll take an
interest in his bike and let him make the decisions."

"Tell me more about Josh's Internet dating," I said. Josh had posted a photo of himself, astride his bike, on a dating website.

"Yes! He's quite in demand. Not met anyone serious yet, but that's only a matter of time. Trev's got some news too. I must say, it's all change in our house at the moment." Sylvia bent down to smooth a wrinkle from her leggings. "Yes, Trev's been going to an open mike night down at the club. He took Josh there once. I don't know if you remember?"

I nodded, my face flushing. *You learn by making Mistakes*, I reminded myself. "I thought they were going to watch a man called Mike open something. I couldn't see how that could be interesting."

"Bless you, pet. No, it's where people who think they're funny tell each other jokes, and the audience laughs or boos. Anyway..." Sylvia took off her leopard-print headband and shook her hair loose. I didn't know what the gesture meant, or if it meant anything at all. "It turns out," she went on, "Trev's been quite a hit there. They've asked him to come back. Even put his name on a poster." She prodded my arm. "It says: 'Think *your* dad's grumpy? Come and meet Trevor!'"

Trevor would be able to jut his beard at an audience, frown over his glasses at them, and make sharp comments. It sounded like they'd *enjoy* him behaving like that. Good. It might make him forget about me and Sheltered Accommodation.

Charlie and I took Akira to the park. The last dog I'd walked had been Tosca. I held Akira's leash tightly, feeling the weight of being in charge.

Akira trotted sedately by my side, looking up at me at

intervals, one ear drooping. "Nothing to worry about, boy," Charlie soothed him. "I'm leaving you in good hands." Akira waved his feathery tail, ears flat against his head. "He often puts his ears back like that. Makes him look apologetic. I think he's trying to make up for his short legs." He laughed. "Like Dad! With those shoes that were supposed to make him look taller."

I was glad I hadn't told Jane the secret about the shoes. She would have called Father another horrible name. I related our conversation to Charlie. "She said Father had no redeeming features. He was just a liar and a criminal. And a bigamist." I'd looked up the word earlier. I didn't have to *use* it all the time. I just wanted to know what it meant.

Charlie's pace slowed. He stared out over Sandhaven Park Lake. There was a faint honking from a Canada goose. Akira's ears pricked up, even the drooping one.

"He *was* all those things." Charlie snorted. "Well, not quite a bigamist because he never actually married Mum." Akira looked up at him. We hadn't done dogs' Facial Expressions at school, but Akira's looked like *Worry* or *Concern*.

I stopped to let him sniff a tree trunk. "Jane was only *partly* right about Father. She didn't say anything *good* about him."

Charlie looked down at me. "Remind me about the good things 'cause I'm struggling to remember any."

"Well…he brought Mother back flowers and chocolates, expensive, handmade ones and…"

"But"—Charlie stood stock-still in the middle of the footpath—"that was to soften the blow of where he was coming back *from*: prison or Mum's, *not* from some jaunt abroad! Shameless beyond belief!" Akira looked at him, his head on one side, and Charlie lowered his voice. "Most prisoners come home with a black bin bag of dirty laundry, don't they? I mean that's the *usual* thing!"

I'd never seen Father with a black bin bag. It had usually been me who put the bins out. I patted Akira. "Father *was* a cheerful person, though. He was always smiling."

"Huh." Charlie snorted. "Probably congratulating himself on how well he was deceiving us." He frowned. "*And*, if you remember, he mostly smiled at *women. Ladies' man* is the polite way of putting it."

"Mmm. He always smiled at *me*"—I guided Akira past two Yorkshire terriers with pink ribbons in their topknots—"and not everybody did. Or does," I added.

"OK." Charlie stuck his hands in his pockets. "Yeah, he was a cheery bloke. He could be a lot of fun. That was how he got around people, I suppose."

"He was always patient." Words were ordering themselves in my brain. "He never minded explaining things or waiting for me to understand."

"No." Charlie sighed. "We built a lot of Lego stuff together, bridges mostly, now that I come to think of it. Sometimes they took the whole morning."

"Another good thing about him was"—I tightened the leash as Akira pulled ahead, ears pricked, spotting a family of swans— "he was really affectionate. He used to call me Vivi." I swallowed. "*Darling* Vivi."

Charlie reached out to squeeze my shoulder. "That makes it all the worse somehow."

"Even in prison he had those tiny pieces of furniture made for me."

"Yeah." Charlie gazed out over the lake, suddenly silent. Then he turned to me and said, "*That* was why your mum stayed with him, wasn't it? The real reason? For *you*." He looked back at the water, at the swans gliding toward us. I remembered they were another species that mated for life. "Crook though he was, maybe that *was* his saving grace."

He was silent again except for a deep sigh. The father swan, in the lead, stared at us beadily, hoping for food. I crumbled up the four cookies from my backpack's Safety Kit and threw them to him. "Maybe Mum *was* right, maybe he wasn't a totally bad dad." Charlie stuck his hands deep into his pockets. "Perhaps he even loved us in his own slightly shop-soiled way."

Now it was my turn to stop, until I realized he'd used a *FOS*. Goose bumps rose on my arms as I thought about the rest of Charlie's words and Akira looked up at me anxiously. "Good boy," I murmured, and then my throat seemed to close up and I couldn't say anything else.

We walked around the rest of the lake in silence, until Akira, straining on the leash to greet a golden retriever, brought us back to the present.

"We've been through a lot together, Ells, haven't we, these last few months?" Charlie said, smiling down at me. "And even in the short time I've known you, you've changed, you know."

I stopped again. Akira fidgeted at the end of his leash and gave a short, polite bark. "Have I? I don't like change," I said. "It's things staying the *same* that make me feel safe."

"But things change all the time. And people. You can't stop change. It can be good!" He stretched his long arms wide. "Makes things less boring. It's how you grow." He looked at me. "You've had to cope with loads of it since your mum died, Ells. And you *have* coped."

We carried on walking. I stumbled; it was hard to keep my toes from bouncing with pleasure. "I still don't like it, though. I just get someone in a sort of box and think I know what they're like, and then they do something unexpected and I have to completely rethink things."

Mark's panted swear words as he forced me against the orangutans' fence came back to me, and I kicked at a stone. It went a surprisingly long way. Akira chased after it, as far as his leash would let him. "Father particularly, and Mother, but all NeuroTypicals really. It's exhausting."

Charlie put hands in his pockets. "Not so much of the NeuroTypicals, if you don't mind. I thought you wanted to get away from labels. I'm just me. And rethinking things... Well, that's one of your rules, *Rules change depending*—"

"*On the Situation and the Person you are speaking to,*" I finished. "I always have trouble with that one. I could add a note underneath: *Change* can *be good.*"

"Yeah! Make *people change* your new mantra. Hark at me, preaching, when I'm not sure of things myself! Don't follow those rules of yours slavishly, though, Ells. You can't reduce something as complex as human communication down to seven rules."

Couldn't you? But that was the whole point of them.

"You're fine as you are," he went on. "Your condition's *part* of what you are. The world would be a much duller place without people like you around."

My toes flexed, bounced again. *I* bounced, I couldn't stop myself, then—"Come on boy!" I called to Akira. I held on to his leash and ran, leaping and jumping, Charlie loping behind, until all three of us were out of breath.

RULE 7

Rules change depending on the Situation and the Person you are speaking to.

Reason behind rule:

No rule is absolute, unchanging, right for every occasion. Every rule has an exception.

Some rules are more important than others. For example, "you shouldn't physically harm someone" is more important than "you shouldn't smoke here."

Sometimes it's all right to break a rule. For example, "you should always tell the truth" may hurt someone's feelings.

People often hide their true feelings to avoid hurting another person or themselves.

People can feel one emotion but act out its opposite for the same reason.

Hints and tips:

This Rule takes practice and exposure to different situations; you have to apply rules differently and see them from other people's perspectives.

Change *can* be good!

Don't enforce other people's behavior and rule-keeping. You're not the police!

Rule followed? ☐

45.

"…only dust and memories now."

—Charlie Hargreaves (Carr),

half brother

I unclipped Akira's leash. "I'm trusting you not to chase anything except the ball and to come back when I call you," I
said in a pack leader's voice. Mother had been pack leader, I
thought suddenly. Each wolf team had a lead female wolf and a
lead male one. Mother had definitely been a lead female.

Father had probably been a lead male. I thought of the short-
haired men at his funeral—*henchmen*, Charlie said they must
have been—and the postcard from Tel about Father meeting up
with *the lads*. Akira's ears were flat against his head but whether
that was because of the wind or because he was listening to me,
I wasn't sure. Sand flew underneath his claws as he wriggled free.

"Here, Acky, Acky, Acky!" Paul hurled a tennis ball along the
shoreline. Nose pointing, short legs gathered under him, Akira
raced after it.

At home, Akira and I both kept to a routine. He had a different flavor of dog food for each day of the week, and we went out
for two walks a day, morning and afternoon.

Charlie sent us regular emails from India. I read them to Akira, who listened carefully at the beginning, one ear pricked, but got fidgety toward the end. The tigers had satnavs on their collars, like in his car, Charlie said, but smaller, and he recorded what they got up to. One had even had a swim in a river last week. He was enjoying the feeling of doing some good in the world, Charlie put at the end.

Charlie emailed Karen too, because she'd sent him the information about the Big Cat Sanctuary in the first place, but she didn't read out his messages. She did tell me she'd finished with Matt, her boyfriend, though.

"Yeah. Dumped him last month." Her sticking-up crest of hair quivered like a small angry animal on the top of her head. "I mean"—she turned to me—"there were three people in our relationship: me, him, and his bloody surfboard."

I wanted to explain that a surfboard wasn't a person, and had to dig my nails into my palms to stop myself. Karen would know this already; it was either an *FOS* or a joke. "Mmm," I commented, shaking out and refolding a striped sheet.

"Anyway"—Karen turned back to her screen—"he can spend *all* of his time with it, now that he's single."

"Does that mean you're single as well?" I asked, adding the sheet to the pile.

Karen tapped the side of her nose, where her stud had been until last week, in a gesture I now knew meant *I know something you don't know, but don't ask me what.* I was going to use it myself before I next gave someone an unusual Fact about cookie packaging. "Ellie, my little NCO," Karen said, "that is top secret information which I am not at liberty to disclose. But," she added, with a beaming smile and an upward flick of her crest of hair, "watch this space!"

Since I'd understood nothing of what she said, I had to rely on her facial expression which was *Happy*. I stretched my mouth upward. "That's good," I said. Then I took a deep breath and asked, "Karen, what *is* an NCO?"

———

Paul and Akira were far ahead, racing each other along the sand. Close behind me was Paul's dad, chatting and laughing on his cell phone.

"He's got a new girlfriend, well, *woman* friend," Paul had told me last week, taking off his glasses and polishing them. "He met her on an Internet dating site. Time to move on from Mum, he said." Paul looked at me, blinking. "Her name's Debbie. I'm not keen, actually. There's a lot of giggling. And worse. *And* she's brought a fruit bowl. But," he added, his eyes sparkling behind the newly clean glasses, "she *has* got a dog!"

Paul threw the ball again, and he and Akira tore after it. I gazed out to sea. Far beyond it was Charlie, tracking tigers; fifty miles down the coast was Lyme Regis, where Father, in a suit, tie, and cuff links, had rescued me from drowning. Brave, kind Father. With me, beside this part of the world's ocean, were my good friend Paul and his dad, and my foster dog, Akira. It was a moment where everything seemed to fit together into an orderly and satisfying pattern.

———

Akira and I went out with Paul and Paul's dad and Debbie, his new woman friend, and *her* dog, Trixie, a bossy sheepdog cross with a strong herding instinct.

I'd been told many times I wasn't a team player, but with Trixie, there was no choice. While Akira raced ahead, looking back for Trixie to follow, she nudged the back of my calves, pushing me forward to join the others, and if I got *too* far in front, she blocked my path, ears pricked, black-speckled nose on front paws.

"Been watching too much TV. *One Man and His Dog*," Debbie commented.

I asked about her favorite TV programs, my toes twitching when they included *Casualty* and *Coronation Street*. Her favorite food was pineapple. We had a six-minute, twenty-second conversation about vegetarian meals, and I only mentioned cookies once.

Akira and I joined Sylvia on her morning fitness walks. Sometimes she used a pair of sticks, Norwegian poles, to propel herself along as if she was skiing, and then even Akira struggled to keep up. She could get into sparkly low-necked tops now, like the ones she'd wanted me to wear.

Sylvia and Josh looked after Roxanna every Saturday. She stayed overnight while Shelbie went out with Lewis, the photographer and ladies' man. "She'll have trouble keeping hold of him," panted Sylvia, striding forward, "you mark my words." Afterward I wrote down her words and underlined them. I did wonder, though, if it had been an expression.

If she wasn't shopping with Sylvia, Roxanna came over

to play with Akira. They sat on the floor together watching Nature Documentaries. Roxanna knew quite a lot of Facts about animals now. Sometimes I tested her to check how much she'd remembered.

I took Akira to Asda with me on my twice-weekly shopping trips. He wasn't allowed in, even on a leash, so I had to tie him to a railing at the shopping cart collection point. He whimpered and wouldn't sit down, and people stared. I had a brief hot flashback to Mother at Bay View Lodge before the iPod. Clive parked a row of shopping carts and scratched his head. Then *Hang on*, he said, returning with four sausages from the cooked foods case, one day before their sell-by date. While I was inside with the list, Clive rounded up stray shopping carts and gave Akira a piece of sausage each time he returned. This was when I realized Clive was a true friend even though we did not see each other socially.

Karen invited Akira and I over for Sunday dinner. She'd cooked my regular Sunday meal of Stuffed Baked Potatoes with Leeks. Karen was a kind person, although she did not smile much. She'd told me her flat was a tip, but actually there was very little rubbish on the floor. I offered to draw her up a schedule for housework, but she said she'd take a rain check on that. A rainy day was quite a good day for doing housework, though.

After we'd washed up, Karen made a cup of tea and opened a Family Assortment Tin. We talked about Charlie and watched a

Documentary about blue whales (who weren't really blue). Akira and I left at eight o'clock, but I didn't mind going home in the dark because Akira was with me.

———

I pressed Send and went into the kitchen to keep busy. Akira, who'd been asleep under the computer, padded after me, his claws clicking on the linoleum. I emptied out the cutlery drawer and cleaned inside it. Yesterday, I'd Googled Poppy, my friend from school—who liked alphabetical order and red things, and who I hadn't seen for nine years—and found her email address. I'd just sent her a message. Heart thumping in my chest, I'd asked her if she would like to go to the cinema, or for a walk with me and the dog I shared. I'd signed off, *Tah-rah, chuck*, an expression from *Coronation Street*, because we both liked it.

I moved on to the fridge, taking all the food out, removing each shelf, and wiping it with a soapy cloth. I put everything back and shut the door. That had been an extra household task, not actually on the weekly schedule. I looked at the Seven Rules spreadsheet, a little faded and dog-eared, its explanatory notes smudged from my finger running down them. I only needed to consult them now when I was completely baffled and there was no friend or relation handy to ask or email.

I'd learned all the Rules, some (for example, Not Everyone who is Nice to me is my Friend) painfully. And had begun to understand them. Understand that they were imperfect, just a beginning, a framework, and that learning to fit in was going to be a lifelong process. Humans, and situations, were complicated; it was *not* believing they were absolute and unchanging that helped you to grow and change and make friends.

I took the soapy cloth into the living room, removed Mother's jar of ashes from the mantel, dusted its bronze plastic surface, and replaced it carefully in front of the large white envelope that had been there since Charlie left for India.

"This is an advance thank you," he'd said, handing me the envelope. "For looking after Akira."

I'd turned it over in my hands. "I don't want you to pay me." I'd looked, briefly, into his eyes.

"No, it's not money. I'm only a poor student, remember. Open it!"

I drew out two big pieces of card and held them up. "Tickets! Boat tickets!"

"Yes," Charlie said, his gaze on me. "It's only for a day trip to Cherbourg, I'm afraid, not exactly a cruise. I thought we could lay your mum to rest *and* get you abroad at the same time. We could go to a *hypermarché*, like Asda, only French and twice as big, and you could buy some French cookies. Kill two seagulls with one stone. *FOS*." Charlie leaned toward me, his eyebrows sloping downward. "What do you think?"

I sat down suddenly. "I don't know. I don't know if I could manage it."

"I'd be with you, remember. Although I'd go below deck for the actual ceremony. I don't think your mum would want *me* there at the end."

I chewed my lip. "I'm not sure Mother would want *me* there either. She wouldn't have expected it to be me doing the scattering."

"But who better?" Charlie asked gently. "You're her daughter. I think she would be pleased. Surprised, maybe, but pleased."

I looked at the tickets again. "The fourth of August. Mother's birthday."

"Yeah! That seemed rather fitting, don't you think?"

"I don't know what to think. Not yet. I'll need a passport. And there's got to be that special music she said. 'Remember Me.'"

"You've got her two iPods. I'll fix up the speakers."

I looked up at Mother's jar, waiting on the mantel, still flanked by her African tribal figures. It gleamed in the spring sunlight, like Mother's eyes behind her glasses. *Ashes to ashes, dust to dust.* I put down the tickets. "Once we've done the scattering, Mother will be completely gone."

"Yes," said Charlie, as gently as before. "It's not for months, though. That way you've got time to get used to it." He bent to squeeze my shoulder. "Remember, she's only dust and memories now."

I returned the tickets to their envelope and went over to the mantel. I reached up and lifted down Mother's jar and held it against my chest for a moment, and then I put it back in exactly the same position. I pushed the envelope behind it, *her*, and turned to look at Charlie.

"Not Mother's way of doing things, mine."

THE SEVEN RULES

Rule 1: Being Polite and Respectful is always a Good Idea.

Rule 2: If you Look or Sound Different, you won't Fit In.

Rule 3: Conversation doesn't just Exchange Facts—it Conveys how you're Feeling.

Rule 4: You learn by making Mistakes.

Rule 5: Not Everyone who is Nice to me is my Friend.

Rule 6: It's better to be too Diplomatic than too Honest.

Rule 7: Rules change depending on the Situation and the Person you are speaking to.

And, Rule 8: Use the Rules to help with difficulties, to make life easier, to understand what's acceptable, to enhance your strengths, but after that,

… do things your way.

READING GROUP GUIDE

1. Discuss Elvira's relationship with her mother. Do you think Elvira's mother cared for Elvira in the best possible way? What are the differences between the two characters?

2. Why do you think Elvira likes to stick to a routine? Describe your own daily routine. What are the benefits of having it? What are the drawbacks?

3. How does Sylvia help Elvira cope after Agnes's stroke? Discuss Sylvia and Elvira's relationship. Have you ever had a mentor in life? How did they help you?

4. Why does Elvira call Social Services? How do Sylvia and Elvira move on after the incident? What do you make of Sylvia's reaction? Of Josh's?

5. Elvira grew up believing that her father was a businessman who traveled "Away" often. However, she soon finds that that is not the case. Have you ever discovered something about a family member or friend that took you by surprise? How did that make you feel?

6. What are some of the challenges Elvira faces through-out the story? How does she overcome them? What skills does she use?

7. If you had to live life by seven rules, what would they be?

8. Imagine seeing the world from Elvira's perspective. What differences would you find? What would be the challenges? The strengths?

9. Elvira discovers some independence when she begins to learn how to access and use computers at the local library. When did you discover your own independence? What event triggered this?

10. How does Elvira's life change after volunteering at Animal Arcadia? Think back to your first job. What was it? What did you learn there?

11. How are Paul and Elvira similar? How are they different? What do you think of their friendship?

12. Describe how the different characters relate to Elvira and her "condition." How do they treat her? Who do you think understands Elvira the best? The worst?

13. Have you ever misread or misinterpreted a social situation before? How did it make you feel? How did you overcome this?

14. Why do you think Elvira decided to contact Charlie? If you were in Elvira's situation, would you do the same? Why or why not? Do you think having family around is beneficial to Elvira?

15. What is the significance of Rule Eight at the end of the book? What does this say about Elvira?

A CONVERSATION
WITH THE AUTHOR

What inspired you to write *The Seven Rules of Elvira Carr*?

It's hard to pin these things down! I work with adults with learning difficulties, my husband used to work in a monkey sanctuary, and my mother had a stroke. I think experiences mingle in your subconscious mind and emerge in a new form. And I wanted to give a voice to a marginalized character.

What do you think is Elvira's most admirable quality?

Her acceptance of others without criticizing or judging them (very much). Especially as she has often not been accepted herself.

If you had to choose seven rules to live by what would they be?

Be kind.

Don't blame—find the reason for the error/conflict and work to stop it happening again.

Don't let the past or the future color the present.

Don't let other people's expectations of you define your life. (Elvira has to learn this.)

Don't let your life be defined by your job. Life outside work is just as important.

Have the courage to tell people how much they mean to you before it's too late.

Don't look like prey—meaning, if you appear vulnerable, unfortunately, you may be taken advantage of.

Were there any challenges to writing from Elvira's unique perspective?

Yes, I had to keep reminding myself that Elvira wouldn't pick up on that comment or facial expression or body language. I had to remember that she wouldn't understand the nuances of a joke and would be likely to take things literally.

What would you like readers to take away from your novel?

I'd like to have shown that adults with learning difficulties face the same human trials as those without them. And that people with Asperger's are not cold and unfeeling but, often, eager to help and upset by the pain of others. They just need guidance and explanation of how best to express it and to show support. I hope that readers might be prompted to think that people with Asperger's have a lot to offer—a lack of guile, a childlike trustfulness, a creatively different attitude to solving problems—to those who don't have their difficulties.

What advice would you give to someone who doesn't feel like they fit in?

Your time will come. You haven't found the right place or the right social circle yet. And remember, outsiders are best placed for illuminating the inside of everything.

ACKNOWLEDGMENTS

For information and inspiration: *Autism and Asperger Syndrome* by Simon Baron-Cohen (Oxford: Oxford University Press, 2008); *Songs of the Gorilla Nation: My Journey Through Autism* by Dawn Prince-Hughes, PhD (New York: Three Rivers Press, 2004); *Unwritten Rules of Social Relationships: Decoding Social Mysteries Through the Unique Perspectives of Autism* by Dr. Temple Grandin and Sean Barron and edited by Veronica Zysk (Arlington, Texas: Future Horizons, 2005); *Planet Ape* by Desmond Morris with Steve Parker (London: Mitchell Beazley, 2009); and the National Autistic Society (www.autism.org.uk).

For indefatigability and wit: my agent, Juliet Mushens. For eagle eyes and encouragement: my editors, Sam Humphreys (Mantle) and Shana Drehs (Sourcebooks), and my copy editor, Silvia Crompton. All four helped this to be a much better book.

For opportunities: the first novel competitions run by *Good Housekeeping*/Orion, *Mslexia*, and Lucy Cavendish College.

For "cheerleading," support, facilitation, and kindness: Ed, Tam, Celia, Eileen, and Monique.

And, for opening the door: Jenny E.

To all, my heartfelt thanks.

ABOUT THE AUTHOR

Frances Maynard is a part-time teacher of adults with learning difficulties, including Asperger's and dyslexia. *The Seven Rules of Elvira Carr* was short-listed for the Lucy Cavendish Prize, and it was runner-up in both the 2014 *Good Housekeeping* First Novel Award and the 2015 *Mslexia* First Novel Award. Maynard is married with a grown daughter and lives in the UK. This is her first novel.